# False Step

*For Ellen & Kim —*
*Hope you like this book —*
*Jo C. Hiestand*

## Jo A. Hiestand
## and
## Paul Hornung

L & L Dreamspell
London, Texas

ISBN:        978-1-60318-499-1

Library of Congress Control Number:  2012949394

Visit us on the web at www.lldreamspell.com

Published by L & L Dreamspell
Printed in the United States of America

## Acknowledgements

This book came together through many persons' help. I'd like to thank Dr. Ruth Anker, for her medical information that helped me dispatch my victim. As always, my deepest gratitude and friendship to Detective-Sergeant Robert Church, Derbyshire Constabulary, and Detective-Superintendent David Doxey, Derbyshire Constabulary (ret.), for unlimited, untiring, expert help in detection, proper procedure and forensics. Accolades to Paul Hornung, St. Louis-area police officer, who took care of our arch villain, wrote and planned the Great Caper, and brought Scott back into the series with his fine sense of escapade. More thanks than I can voice to Liz and Paul Davenport for their details about Haddon Hall, and for dance information. A big hug to the members of the Maltby Phoenix Sword Dancers for their brilliant performance and creative character names.

Thanks, also, to my publisher, Lisa Smith, for letting the Derbyshire CID Team's latest adventure into the world.

Jo A. Hiestand
St. Louis, September 2012

~

### Dedication

*For the Maltby Phoenix Sword Dancers.*
*In appreciation of September 2011.*

Thanks to my family for continued support, my fellow coppers for their dedication, and Jo for her persistence. – Paul

Author's Note: The village of Nether Haddon did exist but is no more. It came into being to house the staff and laborers who worked at Haddon Hall. I have relocated it a few miles farther from the Hall than it actually was. Haddon Hall, outside Bakewell, Derbyshire, exists. It is a magnificent medieval stately home. I've used it as a stage for my drama. While the hunt is fictional, the object is not. Nor is the history connected to it. The historical question cannot be answered, but my fictional one is. I have also removed the restriction of the private living quarters of the Hall, thereby allowing my fictional public access of the entire Hall, courtyards and grounds. This was done so I could make the hunt more formidable in scope. Please take it all as I have intended it to be: great cerebral fun.

Map of Nether Haddon

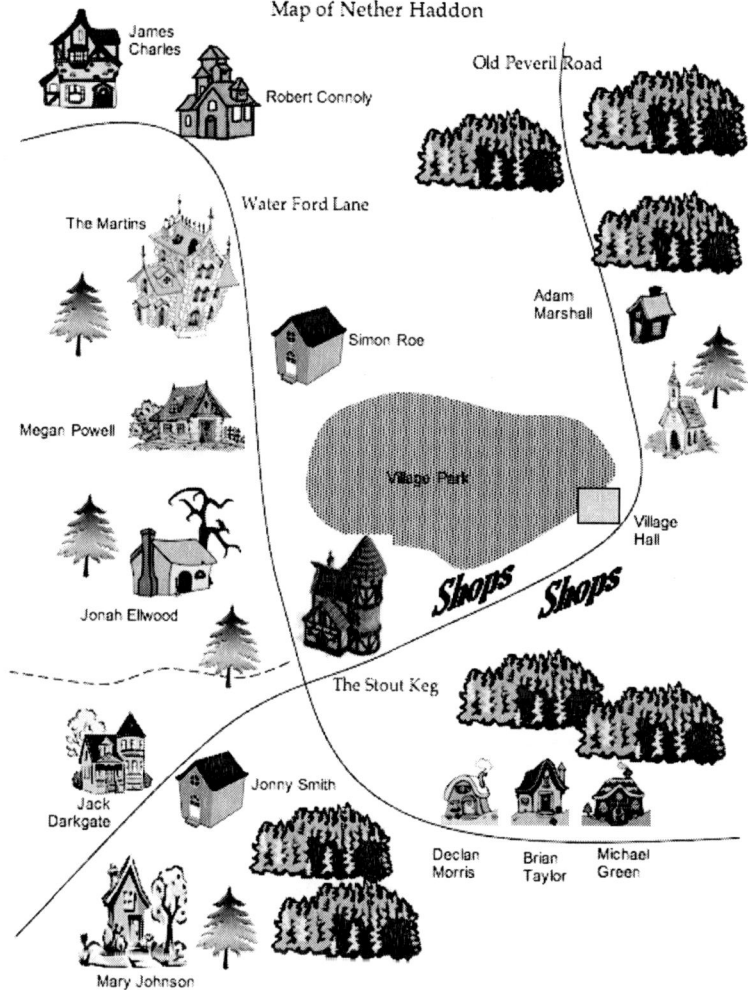

James Charles

Robert Connoly

Old Peveril Road

Water Ford Lane

The Martins

Simon Roe

Adam Marshall

Megan Powell

Village Park

Village Hall

Jonah Ellwood

*Shops* *Shops*

The Stout Keg

Jack Darkgate

Jonny Smith

Declan Morris

Brian Taylor

Michael Green

Mary Johnson

# Cast of Characters

**Locals:**
The Nether Haddon Rappers
  James Charles: owner of This Green Isle Nursery
  Robert Connoly: Haddon Hall's restaurant manager
  Jack Darkgate: fiddler, volunteer in Haddon Hall gift shop
  Michael Green: "The Betty," electronics shop owner
  Mary Johnson: cook at Haddon Hall's restaurant
  Alastair Marshall: cook at Haddon Hall's restaurant, Simon Roe's cousin
  Nicholas Martin: newspaper columnist
  Declan Morris: mortgage loan officer
  Megan Powell: jewelry designer
  Simon Roe: head gardener at Haddon Hall, Alastair Marshall's cousin
  Johnny Smith: "The Tommy," shoe shop owner
  Brian Fireman: under gardener at Haddon Hall
Wilton Burgess: vicar of St. Agnes Church
Fiona Doherty: day care helper, friend of Nicholas Martin
Jonah Ellwood: publican of The Stout Keg pub
Delmar Goodfellow: friend of Declan Morris
Alison Martin: bank clerk, wife of Nicholas Martin
King Roper: career criminal
Hugh Claxton: Senior Prison Officer
Dr. Robert Paladin: surgeon at Leeds General Hospital
Davis and Smith: members of the Dodders criminal gang
Cobb, Pennington, Middleton, and Conroy: members of King Roper's criminal gang
**The Police of the Derbyshire Constabulary:**
Detective-Sergeant Brenna Taylor
Detective-Chief Inspector Geoffrey Graham
Detective-Sergeant Mark Salt
Detective-Constable Margo Lynch
Constable Scott Coral
Sergeant Adam Fitzgerald
Jens Nielsen: Home Office forensic pathologist
Karol Mattox: police surgeon
Detective-Superintendent Simcock

## One

The screams echoed through the village. They erupted from the astonished spectators and lured the stay-at-homes outside. They shook the rooks from the church roof and the sparrows from the surrounding trees. They crescendoed as they funneled down the narrow lanes and slammed against buildings. They withered beneath the searing sun; they seeped into the breeze. Only when the intended victim fainted did the screams die.

At least everyone assumed that Simon Roe had escaped by the grace of God and an injured ankle. Simon's cousin, Alastair Marshall, hadn't lived long enough to debate the question. He touched the light switch and after several seconds fell to the ground, dead.

Some of the spectators ran to disengage Alastair from the electric current coursing through his body; some people yelled for water or beer and tried to revive Simon, who clutched his chest on sitting up and began yelling for his cousin. Some ran to get the vicar, first aid supplies, and ice. Some stood immobile with distress. Some slowly sank to the ground or clung to others, their legs unable to hold them just as their minds were unable to believe. One person thought to ring up the police.

Which is where I come in on this—Brenna Taylor, a detective sergeant in Derbyshire Constabulary's CID Team. Though, I'd got it second hand, at the briefing, by my boss, Detective-Chief Inspector Geoffrey Graham. I'd been late to arrive, requested back at work and, therefore, having missed the preliminary scene investigation. Karol Mattox, the police surgeon, had been called in and she suspected foul play. So she turned it over to the CID Team.

Alastair Marshall's body had been taken to the mortuary, his cousin Simon Roe had been tranquillized, and the Team gathered in the village hall. I didn't need to be included from the beginning to know they had already put in several hard hours of work by the time I arrived. If truth be told, I felt guilty joining them this late, but Graham had asked me to come, so I showed up.

It was just getting on to nine o'clock, a good six hours after Alastair Marshall's death. Though in a village and building I'd never visited, the inquiry room held the familiar feeling of countless others in which I'd worked with the Team. And here we were again: Detective-Sergeant Mark Salt, a thorn in my side since we'd met at initial police training school but had gradually drawn me to his side through his increasing maturity and kindness; Detective-Constable Margo Lynch, my confidant, best friend and frustrated life-coach; and of course Graham, the object of my affection in our early association, but now merely a mate and my boss. Other officers and civilian employees rounded out the group, but Mark, Margo, and Graham meant most to me.

"So, what have we got?" Graham asked us as we settled into our chairs in the hall. He loosened his tie, an emerald green silk that complemented his green and blue striped shirt and tan suit. His green eyes shone nearly black in the glare of the overhead florescent lighting. They opened up his soul and mirrored his mood. I knew that mood only too well: it spoke of untiring investigation and determination to find Alastair Marshall's killer, if it headed that way.

I watched his face as he waited expectantly for a response, a nice face that was male model handsome but held no sign of ego. He stood over six feet tall but at the moment he leaned against the edge of the table. For which I was glad, for I needn't stare up into the glaring lights to look at him.

Police Constable Byrd, who'd been the first of our team at

the scene, glanced at his notebook before saying, "Death by electrocution."

A general stir of incredulity wound through the room. I glanced at Mark, who sat beside me. He pulled his attention from Graham and looked unwaveringly at me without saying anything. He didn't need to; the seriousness of the event was etched in his unsmiling face.

"Why do you say that, Byrd?" Graham said, rolling the dry erase marker between his palms. "We've no postmortem results yet."

"Well, sir, I examined the light switch that Alastair Marshall had touched, and I discovered the exposed electrical wires. The insulation had been cut away."

"Sounds a bit suspicious, or am I hopelessly pessimistic?"

# Two

*Inside the walls of Wakefield*

Michaels and the other guards were busy staring down the chaos of yet another prisoner defecating and throwing it at the closest guard. It gave Roper all the time he needed for the handoff. It always amazed him how the slightest distraction could attract the undivided attention of so many 'experienced' prison officers. Somebody breaks wind, they all look. Somebody sneezes, they all look. Somebody gets a shank in the kidney, well, then they all look. And then go running. Comical.

Roper opened the sliver of paper. He read:

*9712£ 827+ 572-*

It was what Roper felt that surprised him. For a man who sensed nothing after killing or maiming eighteen people in his life, this slight, odd sensation puzzled him. What was it? A chill? No. As he quickly interpreted the code's meaning he felt very much alive. It was time. Could it mean a guard? A rival inside? Either way he continued mulling over the message. He smiled as he swallowed the paper.

*Watch Your Back*

Oh, I will. Even with one arm I will. A transfer to have surgery in two glorious days. Day after tomorrow. Time to give the signal. My return to Derbyshire will be quite eventful. Roper's thoughts could only focus on one thing: it wasn't his 'back' that needed watching; it was those whom his blade would find again and again. Like that scum Coral, whom he would have finished if it weren't for the ligaments he somehow snapped in his right arm. Oh, and his old friend Graham. Ahh, Detective-Inspector Graham. And that bitch Taylor...

He continued mopping the prison floor as the guards resumed their normal positions after tazing Mr. Shit Thrower. They called it maximum security at Wakefield, the worst of the worst. The Monster Mansion. That was okay. With the con he was putting on with 'good behavior,' he would get his surgery and full use of his right arm again soon enough. The media headlines of his escape would be framed in his house forever.

King Roper stopped, then dunked the mop into the dark and murky water once again. As he did so he inhaled deeply and closed his eyes. The rancid air of thirty men holed up in living hell in this section of Wakefield assaulted his nose. But the smell of flesh only made him smile more with the memory of his blade ripping through Coral's shoulder. He'd mentally relived the scene so often that it felt as if it'd happened yesterday instead of two months ago. He began to laugh as Graham collapsed and went unconscious. But he shuddered with almost orgasmic delight as he envisioned what would happen to the next person who got in his way. The warning he got today was the third in the last week. Something wasn't right. No matter. It was good to be alive and revenge was oh, so sweet.

As he licked his lips, Roper asked Michaels if the floor looked good enough for him. Michaels, as usual, nodded and said, "Good job, Roper. We wish we had more like you here."

# Three

I don't know if the heat of the July night or the sudden tension in the room was the more oppressive. Graham didn't create trouble. Or crave an eighty-hour workweek. He'd be happier if we got to spend the weekend at our homes. But that hung on the postmortem finding.

We shifted uneasily in our chairs, watching Graham's face, waiting for a nugget of information, but he remained mute, his eyes searching ours. His statement silenced what little noise there'd been among us. A bead of sweat trickled down my neck. My linen blouse had become unbearably heavy and damp, and I hooked my index finger over the edge of the scoop neckline, pulling the fabric away from my skin. Margo, seated on my other side, tugged at the ends of her long hair. Mark loosened his tie and fumbled with the collar button as though he were choking. Graham's gaze traveled around the group, perhaps waiting for our reaction. Byrd broke the quiet.

"That's what Karol Mattox thought, sir. It being suspicious, I mean." He colored suddenly, aware that he'd nearly portrayed our boss as pessimistic. "Those exposed wires were deliberately shoved through the screw hole in the switch socket plate and the wire ends were stripped of insulation. The screw is missing."

"As I said, suspicious."

"It's a metal box, rectangular, and screwed to a wooden post. It houses several four-socket outlets as well as rocker switches for the spotlights and indirect lighting lamps around the outdoor stage. The box is kept locked so people can't plug in their boom boxes and portable tellies and things. There are two keys. One remains with the publican of The Stout Keg and is never loaned out. The other key is signed out when people need to use the electrical outlets for any event they're holding. Only authorized groups who have permits to use the area are given the key. It's a safety precaution," Byrd added, his voice holding the irony of the situation.

"Who checked out the key in this instance?"

"Johnny Smith. He's the Tommy and leader of the dance group that was scheduled to perform today. The victim was a member."

Graham's head jerked backward ever so slightly and he blinked. "Sorry? The Tommy?"

"Yes, sir. The Tommy is a stock dance character in the rapper dance."

Laughter and amused comments rippled through the group.

Mark's left hand gripped the back of his metal chair as he angled his body around to look at Byrd. "You're joking. Rapper...like 'Yeah, okay, baby girl. We talkin' real bad.' That kind of rapper?"

Byrd waited for the laughter to fade. "Good try, Salt. No. Rapper sword dance. A traditional folk dance. A rapper is a flexible steel band one inch wide and 18 to 28 inches long. It's got handles fitted on both ends so two people can grasp one rapper sword. Each person has one. The dance is quite complicated, a lot of twists and knots made as the dancers move around. The Tommy's costume is normally a dinner-jacket, silk top hat and cane."

"Sounds quite Fred Astair-ish," Graham said.

"Yes, sir. Fixed personalities, like the Doctor is for mummer and morris dances, and the buffoon and Robin Hood are for the Abbots Bromley Horn dance. A lot of these traditional dances have their own characters that signify something. Johnny Smith—the Tommy—is a long time member of the Nether Haddon Rappers, the sword dance group based in this village. Our victim joined the rappers two years ago."

"A newcomer, no doubt, by the measurements of other members in the group."

Byrd shrugged and looked slightly uncomfortable, as though his tea didn't agree with him, or he wondered if he should've checked that out. "I wouldn't know, sir. I've not had time to talk to everyone yet. But I suspect so."

Graham nodded and looked out of the open window. Dusk was little more than a hint, it being just after nine o'clock at night. Sunset was ten minutes or so away, but already the land lay wrapped in gray light. The fragrance of honeysuckle and evening primrose streamed into the room, warm with the daytime heat and bringing the approach of night closer and more palatable. A night bird threw his song to the breeze and was answered by a far-off chirping of crickets. An oak branch bobbed in the wind and momentarily looked like the Tommy waving his cane. Or a sinewy arm brandishing a long sword. I closed my eyes and, on opening them again, was relieved to find the image gone. It was too early in the investigation to concoct phantoms.

Yet, Nether Haddon did have its phantoms, centuries of ancestral ties to the Great Hall on the opposite hill. And a long trail of shadowy historical episodes. But that was the past. Today the tiny village had shaken its ancient purpose of birth and now lived as any other independent community. It sprawled in a hollow on the west bank of the River Wye where it witnessed the setting sun's gilding of Haddon Hall, which perched like a crown high on the east-facing slopes. The river did more than physically separate the two communities; it emphasized the feudal system of lord and servant. Nether Haddon had been built to house the staff who provided care and comfort to the Titled residing within the Hall's crenellated walls. Though those days were over, I was glad that the village had survived, for I liked the setting and the quiet that I assumed usually prevailed in its lanes.

A dog barked somewhere down the road and broke the enchantment. Graham angled his head back toward us, rubbed his chin, and restated the facts for people such as I who hadn't seen the crime scene yet.

"Alastair Marshall died near the outdoor stage in this village. He was a member of the village sword dance group. They left this village at nine o'clock this morning, danced at Haddon Hall and villages around the area until two o'clock, which is when they returned here for their three o'clock performance.

"There's nothing unusual in this segment of their day; they do this every year for Haddon Hall's Heritage Day. More about that later." He paused to go to the whiteboard and write down events and times. "Today was incredibly hot, with little breeze anywhere—though I'm sure I don't have to tell any of you that. The group members were hot from dancing nearly all day. They have two large box fans that they use to give a bit of relief to the dancers on stage, so Alastair went to the light box to plug in the fans. He unlocked the box and flipped the light switch. When his hand came into contact with the exposed ends of the wires he received the full current of electricity and fell onto the ground.

"Despite attempts at reviving him, he died. Probably nearly instantly, but we'll know more after I get the postmortem results. The area where the light box is situated is to the right of the stage, as viewed from the audience. As Byrd stated, it's on a wooden pole and this pole is about ten feet from the stage. The ground around the light box is barren, as is the ground surrounding the stage. The stage is wooden and raised about three feet from the ground—we'll get the measurements in the morning when we can see properly. The height is so the audience can see better. I'm told that the stage is used just about monthly.

"Anyway, small landscaping lights ring the stage area and are connected to the main power supply. The village has a portable microphone, loud speaker and other pieces of audio equipment, but these are available for residents only—or organizations to which they belong."

"Like the dance group?" Margo asked.

"Yes. The group's members live in the village, but a few other persons of interest live nearby. A member of the organization requesting use of the stage or park has to apply for it and is responsible for the key to the light box, should that be required.

The Nether Haddon dancers arrived here around half past two. They were scheduled to dance at three o'clock. Alastair unlocked the box a few minutes to three as the fiddler tuned up and the rest of the group got ready to go on. PC Scott Coral got the call about the accident and arrived five minutes later. That's when he called PC Byrd." Graham paused, his right hand holding the dry marker resting at the end of the word he'd just written. He seemed frozen, perhaps staring at the whiteboard, perhaps seeing something entirely different in his mind's eye. He stood like that for probably half a minute. I looked at Mark, silently asking if he knew what was going on, it being so unlike Graham. We never saw anything other than tightly-controlled firework-like energy and laser beam-sharp mental focus, never knew him not to waste a minute of time. That's why this lull puzzled me.

Mark mouthed "Ask a question" and inclined his head toward Graham.

"Like, what?" I murmured.

He shrugged, his eyes on Graham's back. "Anything. Something about the victim."

"We don't know anything about the victim."

"That's why you need to ask a question."

I was about to jab my elbow into his ribs—his yelp being the disturbance we required—when Margo touched my arm. The confusion on her face spoke more than any words she might whisper. I grimaced and sank back in my chair. Though I had a good working relationship with Graham, I hadn't the courage to disturb him. Maybe one of the senior officers... I turned in my chair and looked around the room. Every man except Mark was a constable or a civilian. Mark was the only male of higher rank. I angled toward him and whispered, "You do it, Mark. Even if he's annoyed, he won't hold a grudge. He likes you."

Mark whispered back, "He likes you, too." He nudged my arm and nodded again toward Graham, as if telling me to get on with it.

I raised my arm, which was a daft thing to do, since Graham's back faced us, and cleared my throat. Graham didn't respond.

"Tell him how late it's getting, that we need to stop for the night awfully soon."

I glared at Mark. No one in her right mind would suggest that to a superior. But I did say aloud, "Speaking of keys, Mr. Graham, I assume the publican will leave the door unlocked so we can get to our rooms later."

The words must've been magic. Graham turned around, exhaled deeply, and said, "So, what do we have to ask ourselves right now, at the beginning of our investigation?" He paused again, but this time it was normal. He was back to form and it was as though the past minute had never happened. His gaze flitted to each of us as he waited for a response. He had the patience of the Old Testament Micah. Even though we were investigating a death, he took it as a time to teach, to hone our skills.

Mark shifted his weight and his metal chair squeaked, startlingly loud, drawing everyone's attention. He glanced at me, embarrassment and amusement mixed in his gray eyes. A hint of a blush crept upward from his neck as Graham asked if Mark had anything to contribute to the discussion.

"Well, sir," Mark said, changing his position again. He talked over the chair's squawk. "We need to find out who knows enough about electricity to rig up the wiring like that. Someone whose job or hobby gives him the ability to do that, probably."

Graham began writing a bulleted list. "Any ideas?" he asked, his back to us as he jotted down Mark's point.

"Perhaps an electrician. He could also be a cable jointer, electrical fitter or overhead line worker. Could be a maintenance mechanic, I suppose, or an electrical engineer. Might also be hobby-related, as I said."

"Such as?"

"Oh, a toy train enthusiast, a ham radio operator, a bloke who moonlights as a DJ for parties, even someone who set up his own stereo system."

"In other words," Margo said, leaning forward to talk around me, "nearly anyone."

"Yeah. 'Fraid so."

"I couldn't do it."

"Good," Graham said, turning around after he'd finished writing. "I won't add you to the suspect list, Miss Lynch. Anyone else have ideas?"

Margo said, "Our suspect will need to have an unbreakable alibi."

"But that's a problem." I glanced at Margo and then at Graham. "We don't know when our nameless suspect changed the wiring. He could've done all that early today or yesterday or last week. We have no idea of the time line so the alibi doesn't do us much good."

Margo screwed up her mouth and sank silently back into her chair.

"About our nameless suspect—no matter if it proves to be murder, we *still* have a suspicious death," Graham said, walking up to the table. "How did he change around the wiring?"

"Sorry?"

"I don't mean what tools did he have or the method he used. I mean how did he gain access to the box? Tell the group again, Byrd, about the box."

PC Byrd's voice rang into the room. "A metal box, kept locked, that houses four four-socket outlets and rocker switches. The box is mounted on a wooden pole and the key is available only if a group requests use of the electricity for their event."

Graham smiled, repeating Byrd's phrase. "The key is available *only* if a group requests use of the electricity."

"Yes, sir. Someone in the group needs to sign for it and return it after the event has ended."

"So, the question is, then, *when* did Johnny Smith get the key from…where does he get it, Byrd?"

Byrd said rather loudly, "From the vicar, the Reverend Wilton Burgess."

Graham drew a picture of a key on the whiteboard and wrote Burgess' name next to it.

"I don't suppose the publican used the key," Byrd said. "You know…least likely suspect because he doesn't loan out the key, just keeps the master for emergencies. Folks forget he's got it over time." He shrugged and cleared his throat, looking vaguely uncomfortable. "Perfect alibi."

"If he did, and he rigged up the electric wiring, you don't think he's going to say so, do you?"

Byrd mumbled that sometimes people made slips of the tongue.

"Then, talk to him, Byrd. He may not have anything dynamic to add to our information, but he might tell you that he gave the key to someone months ago and never got it back."

"Right."

"And while you're at it, find out from the vicar who had the key prior to Johnny Smith. Ask *that* person if the wiring was all right when they used it. I suppose it was, or they would've said something to the vicar. Or someone in that group would've suffered an electrical shock and we'd have a prior accident."

Mark cleared his voice and Graham asked if he'd though of something else.

"Yes, sir. I think we need to find out who had a grudge against the victim."

"Do you know if someone fought with Alastair?"

"No, sir. I don't know much about him. But if the wires were deliberately reworked, and I can't believe they weren't, then that speaks of anger and hate toward Alastair. So we need to find out who might've harbored that anger and hate enough to want him dead."

"I agree. Why don't you look into that, Salt? Talk to members of the dance group, his family, people in the village who knew him. The motive's there. We just need to uncover it."

"Doesn't sound like much," I whispered to Mark. "He's asking us, indirectly, to find the killer."

# Four

The night rushed up to greet us as we stepped onto the lane, leaving the village hall lights behind. We departed in small groups, each team assigned a job of work. The House-to-House Team was to canvas the entire village, asking if anyone saw or heard anything, create a list of everyone who resides in the village, their addresses and alibis. There was no spouse, so Mark and I were to talk to Alastair's dance teammates; Margo, PC Tom Oglethorpe and other constables were to interview the villagers who'd known him outside the dance group. All in all, I think we covered everything.

Including Margo inquiring about Alastair's dog, a brown and white Springer spaniel that she was already asking about adopting. I thought Simon might want it, him being Alastair's cousin, but didn't want to burst Margo's bubble. I also wasn't certain she'd find a neighbor to look after the dog, if she got it, when we were away on a case, as we were now. But who am I to stand between a woman and her dog?

We'd been given a photocopied sketch of the village, to help us find our persons of interest, as Graham put it. I glanced at Mark's copy. Nether Haddon lounged in a verdant dell and looked up at Haddon Hall on the opposite hill. Both lay within the borders of Derbyshire's Peak District, a five hundred fifty-five square mile area of moor, forest, mountains, valleys and rivers. It also lay at the southern end of the Pennines, a mountain range stretching into Scotland. Nether Haddon's buildings clustered along two roads that loosely formed the letter X. Water Ford Lane was a grade B or lesser road that ran parallel to the larger A6 a half mile away. Most of the residences sprawled along its length, their backs against a wooded hill and stony rock cliff. Old Peveril Road, the cross road, intersected Water Ford Lane at the pub. A ribbon of bare soil that constituted a walking trail started opposite the pub, on Water Ford Lane, angled straight between two houses, and twisted up this hill, where it lost itself from view behind the curtain of trees and massive boulders. The church, shops and a handful of other houses dotted the road, which wove in and out of the forest claiming most of the land opposite the River Wye. The smell of dust, heat and dry vegetation hung in the village air even at this late hour, but I thought the village would be lovely in the spring with the scents of honeysuckle and lilies of the valley.

The four of us paired off, Mark going with me. We'd obtained a list of the members of the dance troupe. Johnny Smith, the Tommy character, was the leader of the group. Mark rubbed his hands when I brought that to his attention.

"Let's talk to him first," Mark said, glancing at Johnny's address and then at the rough sketch of the village.

"Why? He's third on the list."

"Since when do we have to take them in any specific order?" He looked at his watch, then at the western horizon. "We've just time to talk to one person tonight, and I don't want Mr. Johnny Smith to get away."

"You think he'll do a runner? You know him?"

"I don't know him, but I know enough about his character, the Tommy, to imagine what Smith's like."

"Such as?"

"Extrovert."

"That makes him a killer? *You're* an extrovert, Mark."

"You interrupted. I'm not finished. Probably he's a bit of a showman—no doubt a prerequisite of the position."

"What's that mean?"

"Obvious, isn't it? Outgoing, glib talker, quick thinker, maybe a bit of a joker as well as an actor."

"You're describing yourself," I added.

Mark glared at me.

I smiled back at him. "The outgoing personality, easy talker and quick thinker I'll give you. You'd have to think quickly and talk easily if a problem occurs with the dancing. He's there to make light of any goofs as well as to explain to the audience what's going on during the dance. But being a joker? Are you serious, Mark? That's the Betty's part, isn't it? You know, the comic character that does funny bits during the dance."

"Mainly the Betty's part, sure. But this Tommy character is the announcer, the bloke who ad-libs and keeps the audience amused. Surely there's a bit of a joker in the bloke's personality if not in the job description." Mark stared at me, unblinking, his face impassive.

He had a nice face: tanned from work outdoors, a squarish chin that went with the rest of his solid physique, and collar-length, wavy brown hair that had grayed at his temples and curled slightly at the ends. I can admit now that he was handsome; I wouldn't have divulged my opinion to anyone back in Mark's and my police school days. He'd led the other males in the class in harassing me, the only female in our group. So naturally my estimation of Mark's good looks and charm was tainted. But he'd matured since those days, and his friendship and concern for me were genuine. Which also helped raise him to near-Adonis level.

Not that I should even admit this now, for I was engaged to be married to Adam Fitzgerald. Blue-eyed and blond, Adam worked out of an office at police headquarters. He had a romantic streak as long as he was tall, which is to say 'very.' Not that his marriage proposal had been terribly romantic, but he'd been persistent. Which was a good thing for both of us. We'd set the date for December, five months from now. But I shoved my mental images of Adam to the back of my mind and concentrated on the matter at hand.

"All right," I conceded, realizing the time. "We'll talk to Johnny Smith tonight. But don't come over all macho and know-it-all."

Mark's mouth dropped open. "When have I ever—"

"We've not enough time right now for me to jog your memory. Come on." I started walking toward Johnny's home, leaving Mark standing by the church lych gate.

The sun had set, plunging the western wood that surrounded the village into a mass of deep gray. Beyond the incident room and disappearing into the wood, the village spread out like a dark veil sequined with bright baubles. Most of the villagers had probably retired early, the horror of the afternoon's event impelling them to seek the safety and comfort of their homes, if not their beds. A few households were either immune to the emotional effects of the murder, or discussed the event over tea or something stronger, for some homes had a lamp or two lit. The ochre light cheered me as we walked the dark lane. Still, I grabbed Mark's arm when a fox yapped deep in the wood.

"It's not the killer," Mark said, his voice a blend of humor and information. He swung the torch around so that the beam of light illuminated a patch of the forest nearest us. The tree trunks popped out of the anonymous darkness, strangely three-dimensional against the flat backdrop. Clumps of ferns and creeping softgrass nodded in the light breeze and cast black shadows against the massive trunks. The shadows took on the distorted look of images reflected in a hall of mirrors, arcing across the curve of the trunks and tapering into pencil lead-thinness before they merged with the smoothness behind. Directing the light again onto the road, he added, "I think our killer won't announce himself so blatantly. He'll make us work to find him."

"I know," I said, rather irritably. I dropped his arm and plunged my hands into my trouser pockets. Unfortunately, sometimes his jesting was spot on.

"How many people are on this dance team?" He pushed a branch of honeysuckle out of my way, holding it until I had passed. The branch flung itself back into place when he released it.

"Twelve."

He let out a mild oath. "And we've got to talk to all of them?"

"We've interviewed more people than this, Mark. It won't take so long."

He seemed not to have heard. "Twelve. Christ. There are only eleven people on a cricket team, six on a volleyball team, and four on a polo team. "Mission: Impossible" had five members." When I looked blank, he said, "You know. That American television series in the late '60s."

"A bit before my time, Mark."

He seemed not to hear my reply, for he went on. "Even ballroom dance competitors are a team of two. Why so many dancers in this rapper group, Brenna? They only use seven in the actual dance."

"I guess they have extras when the first group wears out."

"You mean, like extra pairs of shoes?"

I shrugged, not really troubled about who relieved whom. We walked for about a minute in silence before Mark said, "If you ask me, that vicar-key lead won't go anywhere."

"Why?"

"Well, think about it. If you were going to kill someone using that exposed electrical wires set up, would you sign out for the key?"

"Of course not. I might as well sign a confession that I killed Alastair."

"Precisely. When this case is wrapped up, we'll see that someone sneaked the key. Or had a duplicate made."

"Yeah." The comings and going of the principle players welled in my mind. "I wish Scott was around to help."

"I didn't know Coral was back at work, not until Graham mentioned it just now. Did you know?"

"No." I refrained from saying I was slightly hurt that Scott hadn't told me; I assumed our friendship would've warranted that bit of good news. If not from a courtesy to a colleague, at least from my concern about his health. "I guess he was too busy to ring me up."

"Well, he'd not be allowed back if the doctor had any qualms about his fitness."

"I guess not. No."

"But…" Mark bent forward slightly to see my face.

"The doctor wouldn't take any chances, I know that."

"You don't sound convinced."

"You know Scott," I said, still determined not to reveal my true feelings. "He can finagle just about anyone into anything."

"Meaning, I suppose, he conned the doctor into letting him return to work before he should've."

"Well, yes."

"Not a chance. That sort of thing can't be faked. Coral's all right, Bren. Don't worry."

I nodded, and we passed the pub, still ablaze with light. The laughter and music spilled out onto the road. So did the fragrances of fried chips, grilled steaks and beer. Mark glanced at the open door. It was a mute invitation to enter the merriment and escape the heat. "Good idea, that. I could stand a beer. Damn, I'm hot." He pulled at the knot in his tie again and fanned his shirt.

"When we're finished, Mark."

"Yeah, well, this heat's finishing me off."

"It *is* hot for July, but I don't think it'll kill you."

Mark snorted. "Famous last words. You know, Bren, I'll bet you right now that Johnny Smith turns out to be Alastair's killer."

I was glad of the darkness so Mark couldn't see my astonishment. "Are you serious?"

"Doesn't have to be a big bet, Brenna."

"I mean about Johnny Smith. We've not talked to him yet."

"I've just got a feeling about him."

"I wish you didn't. You need an open mind, Mark. It's death to a copper if he approaches an investigation already thinking he knows who the guilty party is. You've got to be objective and then form your case."

"I'll get the information, don't worry. When have I ever got into trouble?"

"I'll pass on answering that, shall I?"

"So, what about it? Like to wager?"

"If for no other reason than to show you how moronic this is, yes. What's the bet?"

He must've had it already thought out because his response came quickly. "A kiss."

"I hope I don't get burned, but all right." We shook hands. His grip was particularly strong, as though he were emphasizing his imminent win.

"This is it." Mark flicked the beam of the torch onto the front door of a house we were approaching. It was the first on the lane after the cross street. Light from the front room painted the windowpane egg yolk yellow and fell into the front garden.

"I hope he's still up."

"He will be. One of their group died. He'll not be in bed so early. Come on." He unlatched the front gate, held it open for me, then followed me up the path. The door rattled slightly in its frame as Mark thumped the brass doorknocker. It produced a deep-toned, dense resonance, indicative of a solid wood sounding board. Mark released the brass ring after the third knock and winked at me, as though implying three times was the charm.

It must have been. A man of medium height and build opened the door almost immediately. He looked to be in his thirties and had thick, brown hair that he wore short. The left side of his face stood out in start relief against the darker background of the hallway. Light from a table lamp to his left showed his lowered, dark eyebrow and a small mole on his cheek. By contrast, I could barely discern the right half, though a speck of light danced when he shifted his gaze from Mark to me. His left hand gripped the doorjamb at shoulder height, barring our entry. "Reporters already, then?" Weariness, resolution and defiance permeated the question, and his shoulders sagged slightly, as though already overwhelmed with paparazzi and police interviews.

"We're from the police," Mark said as we displayed our warrant cards. "We'd like to ask you a few questions about Alastair, if it's not too late."

Johnny Smith stared past us, at the lane, as though expecting a crowd of photographers and news reporters aiming their cameras and microphones at him. Evidently seeing we were alone, he nodded, stepped aside to let us enter, and followed us into the front room.

"Can I get you something," he asked, standing beside an overstuffed chair. It fit the décor of the room: dull colors, worn furnishings, and a feeling of faded elegance that could not be restored, as if the money that had bought all this had run out long ago. Though new, bright fabric did array one chair, and a large flat screen television announced perhaps he'd come into better financial position. A photo of a group of people angled out from the lamp on a side table, and a seascape in oil paints claimed the space over the fireplace. A handful of books, their spines as dusty and ragged as the room, occupied the lowest shelf of the bookcase; souvenir plates and cups and framed postcards consumed the remainder of the space. I found it all rather sad and cheerless.

Mark and I sat on the sofa, having been herded away from a chair with a wobbly leg. We thanked him for the coffee offer but declined and waited until he'd settled into his chair before expressing our condolences.

"Thanks," Johnny said. The word came out dull and listless, barely audible. "It's a terrible thing to have happened, never mind what it'll do to our group."

"Alastair had an important part, then," I said. I opened my notebook and wrote as Johnny talked.

"Nothing like the Tommy or the Betty, but he was probably our best dancer. He was an amateur historian on sword and rapper dancing. He loved that type of thing, researching and learning how things came to be. He had a quick mind—not for maths or science, but more creative stuff, like cooking and puzzles and music. Did you know he devised some of our dance patterns?" He paused, expecting Mark or I to respond.

I said, "I can't imagine how anyone would set about doing that. He must have been very inventive."

"We had moves no other groups had. It helped us win competitions. Though not all competitions liked new moves. Tradition is the word in many of these dance events. Still, we weren't in it to win, though it was nice when that happened. We liked doing steps no one else did. It set us apart."

Mark leaned forward, resting his forearms on his thighs. "We're sorry to make you go over the day's events, but we'd like you to tell us what happened. It'll help our investigation."

Johnny glanced at the clock on the fireplace mantle, perhaps as a check on reality. He nodded and collapsed against the back of the chair. He briefly closed his eyes, as though he were focusing on the unfolding of the day's events. When he looked at me, it seemed like all the energy had evaporated from his body. "We started the day at nine o'clock at the Hall. Haddon Hall, that is. Today's Heritage Day. It's held every year on the first Saturday in July. I suppose there's a reason…most everything has a reason. I've forgot why they picked that date." He paused and glanced at us, perhaps waiting for us to supply the information. Nodding, he continued. "It's a strenuous day for the dance team. We dance at the Hall four times throughout the day, as well as a few of the villages nearby."

"Which is why you have more than seven dancers in your troupe," I said.

"Right. To spell each other. I don't think anyone would be very lively at the end of the day if we didn't take turns."

"So your first dance was at nine, then."

"Yes. We left Haddon Hall at nine thirty and got to Little Hill, where we danced around ten o'clock. Back to the Hall for lunch and danced there at noon and one thirty. Or close enough to it. We left at two, got back here to Nether Haddon a half hour later and were supposed to dance at three and again at five." He pulled in his bottom lip to keep it from quivering.

"Who usually gets the key to the light box?"

"I do. Always. We all have our bits to do. It doesn't vary much each year. I get the key from the vicar."

Mark made a noise and we looked at him. "Not from the publican?"

"No. Never. Unless it's some strange occurrence. He keeps the original key hidden some place. It's never loaned out. The vicar keeps the working key, we call it…the one that's let out to people. We learned a bit ago that keeping the keys separate like that proved to be a good safety precaution. If both keys were kept in the same place, folks tended to borrow both keys. And that did present problems. We never knew who had the key. They were lost frequently. So the key that's actually used stays with the vicar."

"If you get the key from the vicar, why don't you unlock the box, then?"

"Pardon?"

"If you trot up to the church for the key, why does someone else unlock the box? Why doesn't the vicar do it, for instance, if he has the key originally?"

"Well, he isn't always around to unlock the box. Being a Saturday, many times he has a wedding or funeral or something going on. We tried that at the beginning but discovered he wasn't a reliable source—nothing about his character. I mean because he may not always be available."

"Does he leave the key for you somewhere if he can't unlock the box himself?"

"No. He's had nothing to do with the electric box for ages. The key's kept hanging on a hook in the church porch."

Mark said, "Do you need a key to get into the porch?"

"Oh, the church is unlocked during the day. There's no problem getting the light box key."

"You have the key, then. So, as Detective Taylor said, why didn't you unlock the light box?"

"Would be simpler, wouldn't it? It's part of our show. As the Tommy, I'm the master of ceremonies for the whole thing. I start our dance by singing a welcome song. That brings the dancers on stage. Throughout the dance I make comments to the audience, explaining moves and making jokes about the Betty. You know all this, what the Betty is?"

I nodded but quickly added, "Although your group may be traditional, most dance troupes have their own variations on characters and moves. We'd like to hear about your group."

"Sure," Johnny said. "The Betty traditionally is played by a man dressed in women's clothes. Michael Green is our Betty. The costume varies slightly from dance troupe to dance troupe, but Michael wears a white dress. It's got ruffles on the hem and end of the sleeves, I think. He also wears a blonde wig and white gloves. That's usually a standard, as it helps disguise the fact that a man's playing the part. The Betty's role is to try to mess up the dance. Not really, of course, but to make it seem like it will happen. He weaves in and out of the dancers and does little bits like opening an umbrella or mopping the floor where they are... things like that. The Betty adds a comical element and keeps the audience guessing: will something really happen to cause a cock up. It's great fun."

"And all the time the dancers just carry on with their dance."

"Right. It takes incredible timing. There's this one bit when the five dancers are in a row facing the audience. They've formed a solid line by holding the end of their own rapper sword in one hand and their neighbor's sword in their other hand. Dancers two and four execute a backward somersault. The Betty walks from behind dancer four to in front of him, bending down and scuttling through the gap in the line as the dancer is flipping over. Like this," he said, grabbing a pen and piece of paper when Mark looked confused.

"Blimey!" Mark shook his head as he stared at the sketch.

"It's a crowd pleaser, for sure. Anyway, the Betty's timing has to be impeccable if he's not going to bump into the dancers and ruin the whole thing. The character just adds to the entire dance. We've augmented the show by playing up the key presentation. I get the key before we start and come back on stage. Just before we're ready to dance, I hold the key up in the air. Michael Green—the Betty—has a handkerchief tucked in his pocket or down the front of his dress. Michael withdraws the handkerchief in a flourish, holds it out, and I place the key on it. He then presents it to Simon, who unlocks the box. It's all a bit of foolishness, of course, but we realized that it added another element of amusement to our act. Sometimes Michael uses another dancer's handkerchief. He'll walk around the group, eyeing them in a lecherous way and making comments. Usually, though, if he uses another handkerchief he'll use Simon's. Michael's quite good at pulling the handkerchief out of Simon's waistcoat or hoggers—that's the knee-length trousers most dance groups wear. Sometimes Michael surprises everyone and hands me a beer mug or handbag or some such thing, so I put the key in that. It always gets a laugh from the crowd. One time he yanked the wig off his head, held it upside down, and I put the key in that! He wasn't supposed to break out of character, but it got a huge laugh."

"I want to be certain I have this right," Mark said, looking up from his notebook. "The key's in the church, hanging on a peg."

"Yes. The church is open during the day, so there's never a problem with getting the key."

"*You* get the key from the church. You put the key on or into whatever the Betty supplies for that."

"Right. I never know what it will be, so seeing my reaction is part of the fun for the audience."

"Then Michael presents the key to Simon, who opens the light box."

"It probably doesn't make much sense to you unless you see it, but it's all fairly straight forward and quite funny. Of course, most of the humor derives from my and Simon's reactions. So Michael tries to vary it quite often and obviously keeps it a secret from us."

"If Simon opens the box usually, why, then, did Alastair open the box today?"

Johnny laid the pencil down and briefly closed his eyes, as though shutting out the sight of Alastair on the ground. When he looked at me, his eyes seemed to hold all the guilt and pain of Alastair's death. "It should've been Simon, you're right. He usually opens the box. But Alastair bumped into Simon just before all this started. Simon took a nasty fall, sprained his ankle, scraped his palm. He tried to walk, but his ankle was hopeless. He let Alastair take his place and accept the key."

"How bad is Simon's ankle?" Mark asked, "Is it swollen?"

"Oh, yes. Puffed up like a rugby ball."

"You saw it?"

"Certainly."

"Did you administer first aid? Is that when you saw it?"

"I got the first aid box from the village hall. It's kept in one of the cupboards. But no, I didn't treat the injury. Megan Powell did. She's one of the dancers."

"What did she do," I asked.

"She got some ice from the pub. Luckily, it's next to the park, so she didn't have far to go. She kept the ice on the ankle for a bit, then wrapped it in an elastic bandage. Quite expertly."

"I assume Simon was taken home by someone, since he couldn't dance."

"Megan did, though Jack Darkgate, I believe, got Simon into Megan's car. John's our group musician. If it wasn't John, it could've been Michael Green. I'm not sure. It was rather confusing, what with people seeing to Alastair, the police coming. You know."

I said I did, then asked when Megan and Simon left.

"Not right then. Sometime later. Simon was extremely upset about Alastair—well, we all were—and wouldn't leave. Then the police came and questioned everyone. So it wasn't until much later that Megan drove Simon home. Sorry I don't know exactly when."

"We'll ask. And Simon's sprain occurred at the beginning of the dance set, right?"

"Yes. Just as the key exchange bit was happening."

"How did Alastair trip?"

Johnny blinked as though one of the stage lights blinded him. "How?"

Mark nodded. "Did you see it happen?"

"Afraid not. I saw him fall into Simon, but I didn't see the actual stumble."

I made some comment about Alastair's family.

"If there's any consolation in this whole tragedy, it's that Alastair wasn't married and didn't have any children. His parents aren't around—they predeceased him a few years ago. Simon's his only family. Some sort of cousin."

"How is he taking Alastair's death?"

"Quite bad. He blames himself. Well, he would do, wouldn't he?"

"But he wasn't to blame," I said quickly. "You said Alastair caused the initial accident that put Simon out of the dance."

"True. But all the same, Simon's the one who normally unlocks the box. Simon's the one who would've been dead if things had been normal."

"What did Alastair do for a living?"

Johnny rubbed his forehead. His whole face had gone deathly white. "He was a cook at the Hall's restaurant. Simon works there, too. At the Hall, I mean. He's head gardener. A bunch of us in the dance troupe work at the Hall. Robert Connoly, for one. He's the manager of the restaurant. Mary Johnson, another group member, is also a cook there."

"Do you work at the Hall, Mr. Smith?"

"Me?" Johnny dropped his hand from his forehead and frowned. "That's a bit more creative than I can muster up. No, I own a shoe shop in Bakewell. Alastair's death is a huge blow to us."

"Because he created some of the dance patterns, you mean?"

"Well, that, sure, but he was liked tremendously. We-we're

all shaken by this—Simon more than anyone. The doctor had to sedate him, he's taken it that bad."

"Losing a family member by such a tragedy would be hard to accept, yes."

"There's that, of course. I-I don't mean to sound crass about all this, but you'll hear it all eventually, our tiffs and schemes and jealousies." Johnny took a deep breath, evidently about to bare the group's soul. "Simon was dying to dance today. He'd talked about it for weeks. So you can imagine his disappointment when—"

"Why was today so special? He danced earlier, at the Hall, didn't he?"

"Sure. But it was at the village, here, that he really wanted to dance. A reporter and photographer were here from some newspaper. Simon saw this as his big chance to grab a bit of publicity, get his picture in the paper, maybe get quoted in the article. With him on the sidelines after he sprained his ankle, I know he felt like hell. Felt like he missed his chance. I could see it in his eyes, when we all convinced him to sit it out. Hell, he couldn't even walk after he took that tumble. How was he going to dance?"

"Were those people from the newspaper there when the accident happened?"

"They were close by, but I don't think they were at the stage yet. I knew those blokes were around, for we'd set up this media event a week ago. They were going to come over when the music started, if not earlier. I guess they got to talking to someone, for I didn't see them at the stage. And then, when all this happened with Simon spraining his ankle and Alastair getting...hurt... well, I forgot about them for a bit. I guess the police kept them away from the accident."

"Why did you label this as a tiff or jealousy, Mr. Smith?"

"'Cause that's all Simon talked about and lived for during these past few weeks. He was keen to get into the paper and he would've died rather than give up his big chance."

I told Mark as we left Johnny's house that maybe someone in the dance group had thought the same thing.

# Five

It was too late to talk to anyone else that night, so Mark and I walked back to the village hall. Graham was just finishing his statement to the press. Mark and I stood in the back of the room and listened while television cameras filmed his speech.

"Police are investigating the death of a thirty-year old man who died at three o'clock this afternoon in the village of Nether Haddon. The police are treating the death as suspicious at this stage. A postmortem examination will be carried out during the night, when it is hoped a cause of death will be established." He concluded the announcement by saying that this was all he was prepared to explain at the moment. A flurry of questions followed him as he left the room.

Mark and I left soon afterwards and walked to the pub, where the team had rooms. The Stout Keg was a relic in an equally ancient village. Modernized to include indoor plumbing and electricity, the pub held little else of modern merit. Except the ale, Mark informed me, as we sat in the main room. Few people were about, which I silently applauded. Fewer people to overhear us if our conversation turned to the case. Which it usually did at times like this, even if Mark and I were finished for the day. Margo and the other detectives were probably wrapping up their talks about now but would start again tomorrow. Graham had left after attending the postmortem exam and giving the press statement. I often wondered how many folks who saw the police appeals on the telly actually gave it any thought. I said as much to Mark.

"An unanswerable question, Brenna," he said, setting his glass down squarely on the beer mat. "We just do our job, like anyone else, and hope for the best."

"But ours is so public," I countered. I traced my initials in the condensation on the side of the glass. "Whatever we do we seem to get criticized."

"Is this about police work, or is it some cryptic inference I'm supposed to grab about your upcoming nuptial?"

"Why say that?"

"Because you wrote BS instead of BF on your glass. Even BT I could understand, you've a nice name, but not BS, unless it's an abbreviation for the stuff we put up with on this job." He smiled over the rim of his glass.

"Funny man." I wiped my finger over the initials, erasing them.

"Just observant. Of course, your subconscious could be saying something else."

"Like what?"

"Your name won't end up being Brenna Fitzgerald, but rather Brenna Salt."

I glared at him. "Bad joke, Mark. Try it on Margo."

"Worse things could happen, Bren. Why not marry me?"

"I'm marrying Adam. Adam Fitzgerald, sergeant in the Derbyshire Constabulary, as we are. I love him and will marry him. Besides, the wedding details are all set."

"Oh, yes? Last time I heard you were squabbling over where to have the wedding, how elaborate it would be, and other little facets of hardly any consequence."

"Yes, well, we're beyond that. Thanks for your concern, Mark, but it's not needed."

He shrugged and finished his drink in one long swallow.

"Besides, we've put the deposits down on everything."

"You trying to convince me or you?"

"Just stay out of it, Mark, and put your brain to use on this case."

"Pity, when I could easily do both. Oh, well. You want another?" He nodded toward my nearly empty glass of shandy.

"No. Thanks anyway. I may not shine every day, but Graham's got enough to contend with without puzzling over my dullness tomorrow."

"That'd give him something else to puzzle over, then."

"Besides the death, you mean?"

"Well, yes, but I meant the bit of poetry the lads found in Alastair's house. On a sheet of paper, on his desk. That was before you got here, I think."

My fingers wrapped around the glass. "Really? What poetry? Does it have a bearing on his death?"

"Too early to know yet but it's odd. We can't make head nor tail of it."

"What is it?"

Mark took his notebook from his trousers pocket, flipped through some pages, then handed the book to me. "I wrote it down. Graham's got the original, of course. What do you think?" He leaned over the table so he could see the page. His head nearly touched mine.

I read the words aloud, softly, hardly above a whisper. "'E is more worthy than I. 'E on the Rise though I on the Hill. 'E with his Ring and I with none. One step for Love? Aye, count it ten more. From depth to height and so to Heaven's Vault and the Eyes of the Stars. My love 'E covets like a Plume worn but ceded by six and one.'" I looked at Mark, the notebook limp in my hand. "What's it mean?"

"You've asked The Question, Bren. That's what we're all wondering."

"I suppose it couldn't be code. Do the capitals spell out anything?"

"The capitals?"

"Sure. Some words are capitalized and some aren't. Though it could be just the style, but it's not very consistent."

Mark angled the notebook toward him. "I see what you mean.

Love is capitalized when it first appears, but not the next time. Here." He grabbed an unused beer mat, turned it over and asked me to read off the capitals.

"E, I, E, R, I, H, E, R—"

"Enough!" Mark stopped writing and looked at me. The right corner of his mouth was skewed in a look of annoyance and skepticism. "It's sounds like 'Old MacDonald's Farm.' It's no code. Must be the era it was written. What do you guess... Shakespeare's time?"

"You suggest that because it's the only time period you can name off the top of your head."

"It sounds like something in *Romeo and Juliet*. Is it, do you think?"

"What? Some sort of quote?"

"Yeah. Why not?"

"Why would Alastair have it? Women do that sort of thing. Put quotes or sayings in calligraphy or needlepoint samplers so they're displayed on their walls. But men?" I gave the notebook back to Mark.

He turned the beer mat face up and tossed it toward the back of the table. "Well, it's got to mean something. Why else would he have it on his desk?"

"I suppose one of our lads checked it with a computer."

"Don't think so. Probably in the morning."

I stood up and grabbed my shoulder bag. "You want to earn points with Graham?"

Tossing several pound coins onto the table, Mark motioned for me to precede him. "I may need these points."

Five minutes later, in the incident room, Mark sat at one of the computers. I sat in a chair next to him and watched as he typed the first sentence into the computer's search bar. The first few offerings were lyrics to songs. "That's not it," Mark said as his eyes scanned the lyrics. "Too modern, for one thing."

"Subject matter's not the same." I leaned closer to the monitor. "What's another one from the search?"

Mark clicked back to the search results. "Here's an Islamic prayer or something. About reconciliation of your differences is more worthy than all prayers. Nope. That's not it." He scanned down the page. "What about..." He pointed to the subject line 'The complete concordance to Shakespeare' and grinned. "Romeo and Juliet, do you think?" He clicked on the link, and pages from a text popped onto the screen. The phrases 'more worthy' and 'more than I' and other combinations of our original sentence were highlighted in yellow down the columns. Phrases from Shakespeare's works, complete with play or sonnet and page reference, stared at us. I quickly eyed the list as Mark read them aloud. "Worthy his frowning...no. Leave not the worthy Lucius...no more of worthy lord...why, worthy father...worthy Othello...no more worthy heaven..." He clicked the back arrow and the page dissolved. "Sorry. I thought we were on to something, Bren." He looked disappointed, as though the hunt were something personal.

"It's only a few searches, Mark. Don't give up. What else is there?" I took the mouse and scrolled thru a few pages. Articles on the Boston Red Sox baseball team, another song, something on English law and the bible, and a book on nature popped onto the screen. I gave up after several pages of offerings. "Nothing that we want."

"Anyway, it would've been the first suggestion after I typed in the sentence. If it had matched something like a Shakespeare sonnet, it would've shown at the top of the list. We're headed in the wrong direction."

I turned my chair around so that I faced Mark. "What else could it be? Alastair could've written it, I suppose, but that language is archaic. Why write something so medieval sounding?"

"Could it be for a play? Or part of their dance troupe performance?"

"I don't think anyone speaks but the Tommy."

"Alastair could've written it for him. Remember Johnny said Alastair was very creative?"

"Yes. He made up steps and maneuvers for the dance group. Do you think he made up things for the Tommy to say?"

"Don't know, but Smith did say the Tommy comes on stage first and sings some sort of introduction song." Mark read the poetry aloud again. When he'd finished, he shook his head. "I don't think so, Brenna. This is by no stretch of the imagination a song. It doesn't even rhyme. Besides, the Tommy's part is humorous. Not like the Betty, granted, but he makes funny comments. This bit of verse isn't funny."

"Maybe it's a first draft of a song and he was going to polish it."

"Even so, wouldn't a poet at least make his first draft so it rhymed?"

The silence fell between us, bringing the darkness closer. We'd turned on one light switch in the room, not wishing to rouse the village or increase the electric bill. The bank of fluorescent lights above the serving counter in the kitchen gave enough illumination to the closest table, and the computer screen stared back at our gaze, never blinking. The rest of the large room slumbered in an indistinguishable blackness, the stacks of folding tables and metal chairs, the posters announcing tournaments or village events, the cupboards stuffed with sports equipment and crafts supplies and additional dinnerware. Outside, car tires crunched slowly, deliberately, on the gravel that littered the edge of the lane. I got up and went to the window, cupping my hands on both sides of my face. The car hesitated, then crept forward again until its taillights faded into the night.

"Almost had a visitor," I said, staring after the retreating vehicle.

"Yeah? Who?" Mark joined me at the window.

"I don't know. He didn't stop. Just slowed down and then drove on."

"Maybe he thought better of talking to us. You know how some folks think they'll tell the cops something, then get frightened and don't."

"What's he got to be frightened about? It's dark; no one can exactly see him."

"That's the point. He can rat on his neighbors or friends without anyone knowing. You ready to go?"

I glanced at my watch and said I was more than ready. But the puzzle wasn't ready to leave me alone. I dreamt about it that night.

Next morning, I got down to breakfast before Mark did. Margo sat alone at a table, so I joined her. Food digests better with friendship.

"Your partner in crime out and about already?" Margo said as I took the seat opposite her. She strained to see if Mark were behind me. "Or just being typical Mark? Late night?"

"I think the typical Mark you allude to is no more. You've seen how he's changed these past few months. A really sweet man. You know, considerate, warm, generous, patient."

"You're describing a Boy Scout, Brenna."

"He's quit gambling and he hasn't made advances to a woman in…oh, I don't know how long. He's really done an about turn on his life."

"I know, Bren. I've seen the change, and it's all for the better. He'd make some woman a super husband." She picked up her teacup and eyed me over the rim of it as she took a sip. "You look nice."

"Really?" I glanced at my navy blue trousers and blue print shirt. "Nothing new. You've seen it before."

"Maybe it's your hair. You put conditioner on it or use a new shampoo?"

My hand automatically went to my coppery locks. "No. Same old same old. But thanks."

Margo smiled. "Maybe it's love that's put the bloom on your cheeks."

I made a face. "What are you up to today?" I gave my order to the waitress and returned the menu to the end of the table.

"Probably more of yesterday."

"Is that good or bad?"

"Good! Can there be any doubt? Graham's finally pulled me off bank account snooping and I'm now talking to real people."

"You were before when you asked questions about the suspect's account."

"Don't be obtuse. You know what I mean. I'm directly involved in the investigation. Like yesterday." She set her cup on the saucer and leaned forward. "I asked around about Alastair."

"The victim? What about him?"

"Well, you know how we try to get a picture of what the person was like—personality, friends and family, arguments, appointments and movements during his last week…"

"Finances."

Margo glared at me but was kind enough not to reply directly. "So, I start asking the people in his dance troupe about some of this stuff."

"Logical move."

"I find out from Michael Green that Alastair owed Michael money."

"Not so strange, is it? They knew each other, danced together. If Alastair needed a few quid to tide him over until pay day, he might go to a friend to help him out."

Margo smiled and winked at me. "But it *is* strange when Alastair owed Michael Green nearly £600."

"You're joking."

"Cross my heart and hope to…well, take it as true."

"Did you corroborate this? Did you delve into his—" I stopped before Margo could scream.

"I'm not going near his bank account. But I don't know why Michael would lie about that. Besides, it seems to fit Alastair's personality, at least, from what I'm finding out so far."

"He borrow from others?"

"Seems to be one of his hobbies. He's run up a sizable tab here."

I glanced at the bar, as if expecting to see a stack of bills or used glasses as evidence. Jonah Ellwood, the publican, was drying beer mugs and putting them away. "It's common knowledge, then? Michael knows about the pub debt?"

"I think most of the people in the dance troupe know about it. Jonah declined to extend any more credit to Alastair. He had to pay his bill before Jonah would let him put anything on account again."

The waitress brought me my melon slice, scrambled egg and toast. Margo let me take a few bites before she continued. "And it doesn't stop there, Bren. Alastair tried to hit Nicholas Martin for a few quid."

"Nicholas Martin," I said slowly, trying to recall the name.

"Big name newspaper columnist."

I nodded. "Yeah. I knew the name was familiar."

"Nicholas dances with the troupe, but his wife stays on the sidelines. I don't think she dislikes dancing; after all, she attends most of the troupe's performance. It could be because she—"

"Margo."

"What?"

"Get on with Alastair and his borrowing saga."

"Oh, right. Anyway, Nicholas didn't lend Alastair as much as a pence."

"Do you know why? Aren't they particularly friendly? How'd you get the information?"

"Nicholas told me. I guess they're amicable enough. Nicholas didn't say he hated Alastair's guts, or anything. But he did say that Alastair's tried to borrow from him before."

"When was that?"

"Oh, nearly a year ago. Nicholas didn't give Alastair anything then and he didn't give him anything now. Nicholas is in debt, too, so why should he compound his trouble?"

"Bravo for him."

"Jack Darkgate's in nearly the same situation, but not quite."

"The group's fiddler?" I asked. "Why's he in debt?"

"Not in debt, Bren. One of Alastair's targets."

"Alastair asked Darkgate for a loan, too?" This was becoming more than a joke.

"Not recently. Two or three months ago."

"Still, he went with his hand out." I laid down my fork. The melon slice grinned back at me, the orange-colored fruit particularly vivid against the blue plate. I pushed the happy fruit to the edge of the plate. "I hope Alastair didn't make the rounds of the troupe. Or the village," I added, envisioning Margo's endless job of work. "What was that outcome?"

"His hand was still out when he left Darkgate's house."

"Darkgate refused to lend him money?"

"Yes. And I'm pleased he did."

"Why? Hadn't Alastair paid him back on a previous loan?"

"Darkgate's hardly in a position to lend money to anyone. He relies on his old age pension for most of his income. And there's precious little of that as it is. If he'd given a chunk of it to Alastair..." She shrugged and laid her napkin beside her plate. "Who knows when Alastair would've got around to repaying him?"

"If he's that desperate for money, it's likely that any reimbursement will be a while in the future." I swallowed the last of my eggs and melon while Margo touched up her cherry-red lipstick with another coat.

"I hope, Bren," Margo said as she dropped the lipstick into her handbag, "that you're going to let me do your makeup for your wedding."

"I learned how to put on lipstick when I was a teenager, Margo. Thanks all the same, but I think I'm sufficiently big enough to do that."

"And that's exactly what you'll do. *All* you'll do. Swipe a lipstick across your mouth, blot most of it off, and if Adam's lucky, you'll pinch your cheeks before heading out. It's your big day, Bren. You should look your best for him."

"If I'm too gorgeous, the shock might be too much for him. You want me to be Cinderella-at-the-ball for one day and have the poor man live with Cinderella-at-home for the rest of his life."

"He doesn't have to. You could wear lipstick, blush and mascara every day, you know. It wouldn't kill you, and it'd take you two minutes to apply in the morning."

"Adam knows he's not marrying Kate Middleton."

"Sure, but can't you let your beauty out now and then? You've got it, you know. You just keep it bottled up, for some reason."

"Practice your amateur psychology on someone else, Margo. I need to start my day. Now, if I could find Mark…" I turned in my chair to glance at the staircase behind me when Mark strolled up to our table.

"Morning, ladies. Lovely day when I'm greeted by two beautiful faces."

I glared at Margo. "You told him to say that."

"I did not!"

Mark sat down beside me and grabbed a menu. "What am I interrupting?"

"We were just talking about Brenna's wedding," Margo said, closing her handbag.

Mark grinned and tossed the menu onto the table. "My favorite subject."

~

Graham greeted us that morning with the postmortem report on Alastair Marshall. He didn't look thrilled. "Perhaps you will not be surprised to learn that the postmortem examination revealed that electrical current caused cardiac arrest. An entry wound is quite obvious on his hand, where he touched the wires, and there is an equally apparent exit wound between the toes of his right foot."

Margo leaned close to my ear and whispered, "Sounds terrible. You ever see a victim who was electrocuted?"

I shook my head, my gaze still on Graham.

He must have sensed Margo's concern, for he added, "Electrocution is nothing particularly gruesome. Just two small bright red spots indicating the two wounds. The skin isn't blackened; there's no smell. It's not really a burn. It's a shock." He paused, as though waiting for Margo to add some comment for everyone to hear. When the room remained quiet, he said, "Dr.

Nielsen confirmed that a surprisingly small electrical current *can* kill a person if it hits the heart at the wrong time in the heart beat, the peak that can be seen on an electrocardiogram reading. This could occur even if the person had a healthy heart.

"This electrical shock was exacerbated by the condition of Alastair's body. I don't know if you recall the temperature yesterday, but it was hot. Alastair, having danced nearly all day and right before they arrived at the village, was drenched with sweat. As were the other dancers, so don't go looking for something nefarious in that. He had a glass of beer in his hand and bumped into Simon, thus spilling some of the beer on himself."

"Wet from the sweat and wet from the beer," Mark said. "Nice conductor of electricity."

"I agree, Salt. But it may still be an accident."

"So," Margo finally said, "we're still investigating a suspicious death."

"Yes." He affixed a photocopy of the poem to the whiteboard. "This note was discovered at Alastair's house. While we have yet to determine if it has any bearing on his death, I've sent the original to the lab for fingerprint testing and for metal filings treatment."

A round of coughing, throat clearing, and whispering circled the room. I glanced at Mark and added my comment to the general undertone. "Graham's got to be leaning toward murder, Mark. He wouldn't go to all the expense and time to see if any imprints or erased writing is on that paper."

Before Mark could reply, Graham said, "I'm also having the handwriting analyzed to ascertain if it is Alastair's. The paper used for the poem appears to be off a small notepad that was found on the top of his desk, but that is also being confirmed. The notepad, by the way, is a standard variety carried by major chemists and stationer stores—thick, white sheets, sized six inches by eight and a half inches—so I doubt if we'll be able to trace that."

A constable behind us asked if any other papers were being analyzed like that.

"No. This poem, or whatever it is, is the only thing found that is a bit of a puzzle. It may be original with Alastair or it may be some stock quotation. If the later, I'd like to know what it is and what it means to Alastair." He dismissed us after handing out the day's assignments.

～

Mark and I got to Simon Roe's house around ten o'clock. The heat smacked me in my face as we stepped outside, pulling the air from my lungs. It promised to be another hot day, for already the ground felt like it simmered beneath a boiling sun. Clouds of dust rose from the bare patches of earth and coated my shoes and lower portions of my trousers. Mark stopped every minute or so to rid himself of the dust, then trot back to me. I waved away the floating dust or stopped to let it settle before I continued. My mouth felt like it was lined with sandpaper.

"It's too hot to jog, Mark," I said, already wishing I'd brought a bottle of water with me. I undid another button of my shirt, hoping the air would at least cool off my upper chest.

"I'd like to make it hotter." He flicked a fly from his sleeve. "For the killer."

"If there is one," I reminded him.

He ignored my comment. "It'd be nice to wrap this thing up quickly and get back to our offices." He looked as though he was already feeling the air conditioning.

"Graham might have something to say about rushing through this case."

"I'm only wishing out loud, Brenna. You know I wouldn't compromise a case. I want the killer caught as much as the next man."

"He will be. What do you think about the postmortem report?"

"Comforting and horrendous at the same time. Electrocution was a terrible way to go, even if it was fairly quick."

I nodded, my reply sticking in my throat.

"Graham didn't seem surprised by it."

"He hasn't seemed especially responsive to much lately. Did

you notice how absent minded he was yesterday at the briefing, Mark?"

"Staring out the window, you mean. He must've been thinking."

"He was thinking, all right. About something else. He didn't appear to be concentrating on the case. It's not like him. It's as if he were someone else. You know how he is, Mark. All focus and no room for jokes or relaxation. He's a lightning bolt targeting one spot and he never deviates from the bull's eye. Something's worrying him."

"It's the case. You know how he gets with some cases."

"Sure, I do," I said, "but that's usually when the victims are old age pensioners or children. Women, too, usually."

"And since the victim in our case is a 30 year old healthy male, he ought not to be feeling especially sorry for the bloke."

"Don't be so crass. You know that's not what I mean. You're doing Graham a huge injustice talking about him like that. I merely am saying that he's distracted by something colossally important. His mind and emotions are elsewhere. And that could spell disaster for the case and for his career if he takes a false step in the investigation."

"He did seem rather like a hound on a false scent yesterday."

I tried not to think of the consequences to Graham's career if he went off on that false scent and mucked up the investigation. When I could speak, I said, "Which house is Simon's?"

Mark held out the hand drawn map of the village and pointed to the house in question. "First on the right. Nice that it's so close to the pub, isn't it?"

I nodded, unable to swallow. I was already hot and the postmortem report talk made me feel a bit uneasy. "But it's on the far side of the park. We've still got a small hike."

"Maybe he'll give you a glass of water. Just coming to the publican's house on the left. Won't be too much longer."

It wasn't, actually. Another minute brought us to Simon Roe's house, a barn-like structure of stone and slate, and I soon had my glass of water. It looked like Simon had something stronger, for a bottle of scotch sat on the side table near him. A pair of crutches huddled next to the chair. His ankle was still swollen, with splotches of yellow and purple where the skin had bruised.

Simon's eyes held the look of a man haunted by nightmares. Red rimmed and sunken into his skull, the eyes peered dully from beneath his dark brows. The shadow in which he sat no doubt added to his gargoyle-like look, and I thought he usually was a nice looking man with a smooth, rosy complexion and dark eyes that might be capable of twinkling in a shared joke. Now, however, his skin sagged beneath his eyes and his hands jiggled in his lap.

"You want to know about yesterday," he said, eyeing Mark and me.

"If you would," I said. I was almost reluctant to speak. In some back room music played—a tape recording or CD of great male singers. Bryn Terfel, Aled Jones, Andrea Bocelli, the Three Tenors, Chanticleer… To speak would be to step on their golden tongues, to spray paint graffiti on the gate of heaven. I let Mr. Terfel finish singing "*Verdi prati, selve amene*" before I cleared my throat and spoke. "If the doctor has confirmed that it's all right to talk."

Simon laughed, short and bitter, and stared at me. "It'll never be all right again. Never. I blame myself for my cousin's death. Do you know what that feels like, knowing he'd be alive if he hadn't unlocked that light box?"

"No one's faulting you, I'm sure, Mr. Roe. I understand it was an accident."

"Him stumbling into me and knocking me down, yes. But his death…" He glanced at his hands. They shook and he pressed them together between his knees. "His death was obviously intentional. And meant for me."

"Yes, sir. Have you any idea who might have rigged up the wires in the light box for that? It's obvious that it was done on purpose, as you said. And since you usually open the box…"

"I should be lying dead and Alastair should be talking to you. Yes, you're quite right." He picked up a bottle of medication, shook out two pills, tossed them into his mouth and recapped the bottle. Then he grabbed the half filled glass on the side table and, taking a sip, downed the pills. The ice cubes clattered slightly as his hand shook. "Sorry. The doctor left these for me. They're supposed to calm me, help me sleep, but I don't think they're working too well. I-I still have the jitters and I still see that awful, damnable scene, him lying there." He took a deep breath, as if forcing himself not to cry. In the brief quiet Aled Jones began singing "Did You Not Hear My Lady." I would've given most anything I owned to be able to sit and listen to the complete song, but the job at hand nudged me. "I don't know what is most agonizing," Simon said, "my cousin's death or that I was the intended victim. The pain from my sprained ankle is nothing compared to what I feel about Alastair." He winced as he shifted his bandaged foot.

"Have you quarreled with someone, either recently or a long-running argument?"

"Lord, you make this sound like a film script."

"Someone had to rig those wires, Mr. Roe, and it's common knowledge in the village that you turned on the switch for the microphone and fans."

Simon set the glass on the coaster and rubbed his eyes. "I know. I just can't bear to think of it."

"Does anyone like that come to mind?"

"Well, I hate to accuse anyone without evidence."

"You're not." Mark's voice took on an edge of impatience. "You're giving us information. Someone you have a disagreement with, then?"

"It was in the heat of the moment, sergeant. You know how it is."

"The name, please."

"Two people, actually."

"Give them to me one at a time and explain the quarrel, if you would."

"Well, I had a bit of a dust up with Robert Connoly. He's a member of the dance group."

Mark glanced at me. "What was that about?"

"I'm embarrassed about it now."

"No need to be. We're all human, Mr. Roe. We all get mad at one time or another. What happened with Robert Connoly?"

"Connoly's the manager of the restaurant at Haddon Hall. And, being the manager, he was Alastair's boss." He took another sip of water and rested the glass on his thigh. The condensation trickled down the glass and pooled onto his trousers. He seemed not to notice or mind. "Alastair and I wanted to go on holiday together. I had my time arranged with my supervisor, but Connoly wouldn't let Alastair off. I was madder than hell and I let Connoly know about it."

"Did he give you a reason?"

"He said Mary already put in for that same week and he couldn't have two cooks gone from the restaurant at the same time."

"And Mary is…"

Simon reached for the pill bottle and turned it slowly so he could read the label. "Sorry. I just need to see when I can take another dose. I feel like hell. Mary Johnson. Happens also to be a member of the dance group." Simon pulled in his bottom lip, as though he were biting back tears or an uncomplimentary remark. "When I found out that Mary had requested the same dates that Alastair and I wanted, I talked to her, asked her to switch her week. She said no." Simon's free hand jerked suddenly and he set his glass down. "I asked quite politely, and she said no."

I said she might've had something she couldn't rearrange.

"Must've been important. And secretive. She wouldn't say."

"Probably not. It was her own affair. You couldn't have rescheduled your week to coincide with a time your cousin could get off?"

"Yes, but we were going to a conference. It had a set date."

Mark said, "When was this quarrel with Mary Johnson?"

"Last week."

Mark and I exchanged glances before he said, "Is there

someone else, Mr. Roe? You mentioned two people."

"You're going to think I can't get along with anyone."

"Not necessarily. Who else?"

"Brian Fireman. He's one of the under gardeners at the Hall."

"What was the problem between you two?"

"His work. He's been lazy for nearly a month. Doesn't get the work done that's assigned to him. I've had to go behind him and re-do some of it. Ordinarily I'd make him do it over, and I have done for most of it, but we had to get ready for the Hall's Heritage Days as well as another big event. The gardens needed to look their best. Brian was late to work some days and slow as treacle on others. I gave him two warnings to get his work done on time or I'd have to let him go."

Mark scribbled something into his notebook and glanced around the room. The modern décor contrasted sharply with some vintage family photos and a needlepoint coat of arms that hung over the fireplace. "Were you and your cousin close?"

"Like brothers. I've a sister in New Zealand but I don't see her but every few years. Alastair has no living immediate family so we did a lot of things together. Especially during the holidays."

"Were you or he keen on genealogy?"

"Genealogy? Are you serious?"

"Just wondered. Have you ever seen this before?" Mark took a folded piece of paper from his trousers pocket, unfolded it and handed it to Simon.

"What is it?" Simon read the words slowly, his eyes lingering on each line. When he finished, his eyes skated back to the top line. Without looking at us, he said, "Where'd you get this? Why show it to me?"

"We're hoping you know what it is."

"Know what it is?"

"The CID lads found it in Alastair's house, on his desk. We wondered if you'd seen it before."

"No. I don't even know what it is. Some Shakespeare quotation?"

"Your cousin never mentioned it, then. Never talked to you about it."

"No. Like I said, I don't know what it is."

"So you don't have any idea where it came from. It has nothing to do with your family."

"Why would you even think that?"

"No particular reason. I noticed you seem keen on family so I wondered if it was something from an ancestor."

"'Fraid not." Simon handed the paper back to Mark. "Strange little thing, isn't it?"

"Did Alastair go in for poetry or medieval activities?"

"Alastair was no writer, either of books or poetry. And the closest he came to medieval activities were the re-enactments held at the Hall. He liked to watch them and chat up the participants."

"He didn't have any other hobbies that this might tie in to, then?"

"The sword dance troupe took up most of his off work time. I introduced him to it."

"How'd you get involved with sword dancing?"

"I thought I'd give it a whirl. I did a bit of Irish step dancing until five or so years ago, and the sword dancing sounded interesting. Alastair likes that sort of thing, so after I'd been doing it for a while, I told him about it. He did like to read and play the guitar, too. But none of those would necessarily have anything to do with that paper."

"He couldn't have been writing it for you, could he?"

"For me?" Simon blinked and frowned. "Why would you think that?"

"Just trying to explain the writing's existence. He wasn't going to get it done up in calligraphy and framed for a birthday gift for you."

"He could've been planning on doing that, of course. But I don't see why. It's not something in his character. Or anything I'd particularly treasure."

"Sure. I understand. Just thinking out loud." Mark sounded

disappointed and put the paper back into his pocket. "And it wasn't something you'd given him, either copied from something existing or written yourself."

"No."

"I just thought maybe you gave it to him and he was going to pretty it up so he could frame it."

"Well, I didn't. I'm sorry to end this, but I can't take any more of this right now. I need to ring up my doctor for something stronger. This medication is not doing a thing for me." He stood up, the pill bottle in his hand, and looked at it. "If you will excuse me, I need to lie down. I'm-I feel like hell. All this talk about my cousin…" He grabbed the crutches and positioned them under his arms. "No, I need to get up," he said in response to my protest. "Short hobbles are fine. If I can't do anything else right, let me be the proper host." He shuffled to the door, opened it, and leaned against the doorframe as Mark and I stood up.

"I hope you feel better, Mr. Roe." I hesitated outside, waiting for Mark.

He handed Simon a small white card, told him to ring any hour if he thought of anything.

Simon stood in the doorway, his eyes deep caverns of black even in the morning sunlight. "Anything to catch my cousin's killer." "What Wondrous Love Is This" seeped out of the house while the door closed slowly and gave a final click as the lock slid into place.

# Six

"Now where to?" I asked as we paused outside Simon's front gate. A blast of hot wind, its temperature reinforced by the heat of the blacktopped lane, hit us full force. I turned toward the house in an attempt to shield myself from the breeze and bent over slightly. The heat settled in my throat and lungs and I tried to swallow.

"You okay?" Mark asked, patting me on the back.

"Just inhaled at the wrong time. Thanks." I cracked a smile and turned back to the road.

"Just take it easy, Brenna. We can't have you prostrate with heat exhaustion."

"I doubt it'll come to that. Who you want to talk to next?"

"I'm kind of curious about Robert Connoly."

"The manager of Haddon Hall's restaurant."

"And recipient of Simon Roe's anger at a foiled holiday."

"I wonder how they can live in the same village and work in such close proximity as Haddon Hall."

"I can beat that. I wonder how they can dance together without showing their anger."

"Maybe they couldn't," I said. "Maybe Connoly rigged up that shocking surprise for Simon."

"Seems kind of over the top, doesn't it? So you're angry with someone. Most people don't go around plotting murder."

"If Simon was particularly angry that he and Alastair couldn't take their holiday right then, he could've exploded in Mary's face. She could've rigged up the electrical surprise. Doesn't have to be Connoly."

Mark made a small coughing sound in his throat. "Do we know what their hobbies are? Barring electrical engineer, I'd settle for cable television installer."

"Probably nothing so obvious. Is this it?"

We'd walked up the incline to the crest of the hill, following the curve of Water Ford Lane. Robert Connoly's house was a multi-storey Victorian pile that sparkled with a new coat of paint and a patch of flowers spreading from the front door to the tarmac. I wondered how he had time to garden but as we approached the door I realized all the plants were native wildflowers. The patch took care of itself.

Which appeared to be the same for Robert Connoly. He presented himself at the front door scrubbed, polished and dressed like a prisoner trying to impress the judge. His coolness extended to his demeanor; he didn't seem surprised to find two police detectives on his doorstep. He took our questioning in stride, too, standing in front of his fireplace, his left arm draped across the mantle, his right hand toying with his cigarette. All he lacked was the cigarette holder and monocle.

"I can give you…five minutes," Connoly said, consulting the time on his watch. He gave me the impression of a corporate lawyer exasperated at an underling. "What is it you wish to know? I assume it's about yesterday's tragedy."

Mark opened his notebook and I told Connoly we had heard of the problem with Alastair's holiday time.

"Though you haven't labeled your source of information, I doubt if I'm wrong when I assume Simon Roe told you. Doesn't really matter who told you. It's true. You can verify it any number of ways."

"Why didn't you allow Alastair to take the week he wanted?"

"It wasn't a case of not allowing, miss. Mary Johnson had already requested that same week. Normally something might have been worked out, they could have easily switched days off, but Mary couldn't accommodate Alastair this time. Of course I was sorry he and Simon couldn't do what they had planned, but I really wasn't involved. It all rotated around Mary, and she wasn't going to disrupt her plans."

"May we know the reason?"

"I think Mary should tell you. I respect my employees' privacy. Anything else?"

"How many people do you manage in the restaurant, Mr. Connoly?"

He took a drag on his cigarette, flicked the ash into a hammered copper tray on the mantle, and looked at me. I thought he was refusing to answer the question, but he smiled slightly and said, "Fourteen. Five cooks, four dishwashers, and five bus boys. The restaurant is open seven days a week all year, except for Christmas and New Year's Day. Due to the large volume of visitors to the Hall and the extended hours of operation, we have two shifts of workers each day. They rotate days on and off work, of course."

"Five cooks."

"Yes. They normally work in a group of three. It's staggered so some people are off while some are on."

"The third person couldn't have covered for two cohorts being gone, I can see that."

"Not all week, no. It would've been physically draining. And the restaurant can't afford to skip on quality. We have a reputation to uphold."

"Did you and Alastair get into an argument over this?"

Connoly blew a smoke ring and watched it float to the ceiling. He said, rather haphazardly, "Heated words were exchanged, yes. He was keen on going and I couldn't let him. I explained that Mary had that week but it didn't make any difference with Alastair. He asked if I could hire another cook to take his shift that week. Of course, that was impossible."

"Another cook couldn't prepare the food listed on your menu?"

"Certainly. But my budget didn't allow for another person's

salary, even if it was one week. I was stretched to the limit already from problems that happened earlier in the year. I wasn't about to go into the red by hiring another cook, no matter how Alastair cajoled and threatened."

Mark held up his hand. "What did he threaten? When was this?"

Connoly shrugged and laid his cigarette on the edge of the tray. Evidently the curling smoke didn't bother his eyes. "Wednesday."

"Three days before his death. Did he say anything specific to you?"

"Just the generic phrases that you hear on the telly. I'll be sorry, I better think about this again. You know the sort."

"Seems to me he was taking a chance talking to you like that. You're his boss."

"I didn't take him seriously. I knew he was disappointed, that it wasn't his true nature to spout off like that."

"Takes an awfully mature person to view it that way. Most folks would be ringing up the police and reporting a death threat."

"Alastair's not got a vengeful bone in his body. As I said, it was the heat of the moment speaking."

"What about Mary? Alastair talked to her about switching holiday dates. Did he get angry with her?"

"I don't know. He may have talked to her outside the restaurant. I wasn't privy to the conversation. You'll have to ask Mary about that."

"And you didn't get angry over this?"

"Why should I? Alastair ranted. I didn't."

"He was disrespectful to you as his supervisor. He talked back to you in front of the other employees. Surely you must have been outraged by that. If nothing else, it might have belittled your standing with the others."

"Hardly. As I said, I knew Alastair wasn't usually like that. I thought it best not to harp on the subject. Besides, I showed greater strength of character by not responding in kind. Rather than putting me in a bad light, I bolstered my position as supervisor."

I walked over to an oil painting of a man dressed in a wide lace collar and fur-trimmed cloak. He wore an intricate piece of jewelry on the side of his black, rimmed hat, which merged with the dark, flat background. Though he gazed at the viewer, his eyes held no mirth; his lips pressed together, barely discernible between his moustache and beard. "Seventeenth century?"

"Yes. You like it?" Connoly came over to me. His eyes crackled with life as he looked at the portrait.

"Very much."

"One of my prizes. I got it at an auction last year in New York. Just me and another bidder at the last, and I'm proud to say I beat him."

"It's very nice."

"I made certain it was authentic before the sale was closed. I wasn't going to pay that amount of money on a rendition done by a student."

"Even if it was an apprentice of a famous artist, I shouldn't think that would detract from the beauty of the painting."

"Perhaps not, but it would lower its value in my estimation. I don't like imitations."

I glanced at the pewter bowl and spoon resting on top of the highboy, then asked if Alastair's death would encumber the dance troupe any.

"Lord, I hope not. Please don't take that the way it probably sounds. I'm stricken by Alastair's death. It's unimaginable that anyone would plan that! We've twelve in the group—well, nine if you don't count the Tommy, Betty and the fiddler. That's two dance teams. We spell each other in the all-day competitions and exhibitions. Like we did yesterday. So we're fine in that respect. But the man who dances in the second position can't just step in and dance in the fifth position, for example. Have you ever seen a rapper dance?"

I shook my head and Mark said he'd never even heard of them until yesterday.

"Well, they're quite involved. The dancers move to create interlacing knots and patterns with their rappers. It's not just follow the leader; each dancer has a specific path to move through in order to make the pattern work. Alastair's part can be danced by someone in the second team but we will eventually have to find someone else to replace him. That person will never get any rest when we do an all-day stint."

"I assume it takes a long time to learn the dance, where to go and such."

"There's a lot of stumbling around at the beginning, of course. But you soon fall into your position."

"Is there anyone who's shown interest in joining the troupe?"

"Some hanger-on whom we could recruit, you mean. Not to my knowledge. Although Declan Morris is matey with some bloke...can't think of this name. Declan's a troupe member. Mortgage loan officer. His mate shows up at many of the rehearsals and most of our performances. Maybe he's just waiting for Declan so they can get a beer or something."

"Have you someone in mind to take Alastair's place at the restaurant?"

Connoly's hand went to his left temple. His fingertips pressed against his skin and he held them there as he spoke. "I can not believe I never thought of that. God, I'll have to go through all that employment process again. Ads placed in the employment columns, hours spent on interviews and sifting through mountains of applications. And with the economy so bad right now, with unemployment figures up, there'll be hundreds of applicants. Perhaps I could employ a lottery at the offset to reduce the numbers." He shut his eyes and breathed deeply before looking at me again. The rosiness drained from his face, leaving it ashen and gaunt. "I'm so sorry, miss. Please don't misinterpret my true feelings for Alastair. I liked him; we all did. I'm shocked and sad to lose a friend. But I never thought what his death meant until you mentioned it. Finding a good cook isn't all that easy, and with the restaurant associated with the Hall...well, you see how important it is that I get the right person." He sighed, perhaps thinking of the long hours ahead of him. "And us in the middle of the summer. It's peak visitor season, as you can imagine. The one good thing is that Mary's holiday is in a fortnight. I can work around her absence if I've not found anyone by that time. I could hire a temporary cook if needs must, though I'd rather not."

"Perhaps you'll be fortunate and find someone straight off."

"Thank you. I do, too. Something always seems to ruffle Life's waters, doesn't it?"

Mark caught my eye. His shocked expression echoed my unspoken sentiment. "Well," Mark stood up, "I'm sure our five minutes are up. You must be getting ready to go to work."

"Yes. It's a short day, thankfully. That will help get us all through the hours. The restaurant has reduced opening hours on Sundays. Still, I have to be there." He stood in the open doorway, paused like a television game show hostess.

"You have a nice home, Mr. Connoly," I said. "Were your antiques in your family?"

"Gracious, no. We never had enough money for anything like that. I've acquired them over the years."

"Collecting them is a hobby of yours, then."

"Books, paintings and silver, mainly. I knew not a sausage about collectibles when I began, but I've managed to acquire a degree of knowledge about some areas."

"Restaurant manager, antiques collector and dancer. Must keep you busy. I wonder you have time for anything else."

Connoly allowed a faint smile to crease his impassive face. "I make time for what's important."

"More people should make that their motto."

Mark and I thanked him and stepped onto the porch as the door clicked shut behind us. When we were on the road, I pretended to consult the map of the village. "Wait a minute," I said, barely audible against the rooks cawing overhead.

"Why?" Mark stopped short and turned to see what I was doing. "You want to see where Mary Johnson lives?"

"Not right this minute. Did anything strike you odd about our little chat with Robert Connoly?" I kept my head down, my gaze on the paper.

"I'll probably give the wrong answer, so why don't you tell me."

"Starting with the monster of a house itself, then going on to the furnishings. How can Robert Connoly afford all that on a restaurant manager's salary?"

"Maybe he inherited money."

"He implied his folks weren't wealthy. And his little collection shouted Wealth. I know I'm no expert in this field, but the silver tea set, not to mention the salver and miniature portraits, must have set him back a hefty sum. How'd he pay for it all?"

"Wise investments, winnings at the dog track or casino, poker games. I don't know. But nothing smells illegal."

"Smells like three day-old fish, if you ask me."

"Come on." Mark yanked the map out of my hand. "Maybe your curiosity will be solved when we talk to Mary Johnson."

"Connoly didn't look like he was grieving over Alastair's early demise."

"As you've pointed out to me many times, Brenna, people express grief in many ways. He's probably a private person."

"Mourning the loss of his cook and fellow dancer is so personal, then."

"What do you want? Connoly to sob uncontrollably in public? Even then you wouldn't believe his emotion is real."

"I'm only saying that he didn't get all that on a restaurant manager's salary and that you need to keep an open mind about him."

"Open mind or eyes wide open?"

I grinned. "Little of both, to be certain."

Mark pointed to a rough-drawn square on the map. It represented Mary Johnson's house, the last one on Old Peveril Road and about as distant from where we were as you could get in the village. "We'll see if Mary Johnson can produce a distressed face for you—and maybe some relevant information about the killer."

I fell in step beside him, walking more quickly and easily now that Water Ford Lane led downhill. The village park was vacant at this hour but I didn't doubt that a few hardy souls would brave the heat in the afternoon, and picnic or play badminton, perhaps. Or gape at the crime scene.

An industrious police constable had enclosed the performing stage and electric light box within a rectangle of blue and white crime scene tape. The circle extended out several yards from the area involved. Graham was a stickler for giving the immediate scene breathing space; it protected the larger scene in case something significant was found nearby.

The tape hung absolutely still; no breeze fanned it or the tree boughs. A constable at the far end of the stage paced a small route the length of the wooden platform, turning leisurely and looking around as he meandered back. Though the stage sat in the shade, the constable's red face spoke of the heat saturating the air. Bare soil, packed hard as steel and throwing back the desert-like temperature, threw up swirls of dust with each step he took. The dust sparkled golden and white in the shafts of sunlight angling between the leafy boughs overhead. The constable coughed periodically, his fist over his mouth, and turned his head slightly to avoid directly inhaling when the wind whipped up the desiccated earth. He blotted his forehead and cheeks with a handkerchief, then stuffed it back into his pocket. Turning at the end of his beat, he clasped his hands behind his back. He paced with his shoulders squared and his head erect. The silver constabulary emblem on the front of his helmet caught the sunlight and threw it variously onto the ground and the white work tent encompassing the light box and marking the spot where Alastair had died.

The lads had sealed off the area yesterday, holding the Curious and Thrill-Seekers at bay and keeping the scene as intact as possible. Though, outdoors like this, it was fairly difficult. Still, it protected the body and scene, and kept those prying eyes of the press and public from viewing the body. It had been no time for Alastair to get lead story status on the nightly television news.

As we approached the pub, the bells from St. Agnes church

drifted down wind. I gazed up the hill to my left. The church's gray stone tower nudged through the nearly impenetrable screen of pines dotting the hill. It and the wooden lych gate were the only visual hints of the church's existence from this viewpoint. Trees and bushes crowded into the tiny churchyard to the north and farther up the hill, making the camouflage complete. It would be a dark, unnerving spot at night.

"Isn't that Scott?" Mark nudged my arm and I shifted my attention to a police cruiser idling at the curb outside the pub. Graham stood at the driver's side of the car, his back bent as he leaned forward and talked to the man behind the steering wheel.

"Could be," I said, trying to discern the face inside the car. A shadow filled the interior. "I wish Graham would move a bit. He's making it hard…yes, that's Scott." Although not part of the CID Team proper, Scott Coral had helped us on a number of cases. His skill in surveillance and trailing was top notch and I wondered how long Scott would remain a response driver. "Their talk seems serious."

"Why do you say that? Let's go over and welcome him—"

I grabbed Mark's arm, holding him back. "No. I don't think we should."

Mark stared at my fingers wrapped around his upper arm. "Why the hell not? He's one of your mates. He's been gone a long time on sick leave. We didn't know if he'd be back in the job, let alone live. Why wouldn't we want to greet him? He'll think we're rude."

"It's not a good time. Please, Mark. Don't go over there." My fingers tightened on his arm, not only to restrain him but because an inexplicable fear started to consume me. In May, Scott had been in hospital due to a knife wound in his shoulder. He'd been in a fight with King Roper, a career criminal, and no one had known how the stabbing would affect Scott's life or career. That Scott had given Roper an equal if not worse injury gave us little solace if Scott ended up on disability…or dead. But now, seeing Scott back on the job, the joy I thought I'd feel at seeing him again was absent. Instead, apprehension nearly paralyzed me.

"What's got into you, Brenna? You and Scott are best friends. Just because he's chatting with Graham—"

"It's not a chat," I said, watching Graham lean closer to the car. "It's something serious. See? He and Scott aren't smiling, and Graham's bending down so that his head's nearly touching Scott's. That's conspiratorial conversation, Mark."

"You're daft. You've still got residue in your brain from the MI-6 case."

I shook my head. "Something's going on, Mark. Something serious. Remember how distracted Graham was yesterday?"

Mark snorted. "So the man had a senior moment. Cut him some slack. He's only human."

"And now he and Scott look like stand-ins for the Sphinx. Where are the slaps on the back to greet an old chum?"

"Graham's not the slap-on-the-back type, Brenna."

"A figure of speech, Mark. Look at them."

By now, Graham's tall frame was nearly bent double, his forearms resting on the car door, his hands thrust through the open window. His head was half in, half out of the space, within inches of Scott's face.

"He could say welcome back without doubling up like a pocket knife," I said. "They're whispering. Or close to it."

"Graham's not doubled up."

"A figure of speech," I said again, a hint of exasperation in my tone. "What are they talking about?"

"They'd clam up for sure if we go over. But I agree, neither of them is too happy."

I don't know how long Mark and I stood there, watching Graham and Scott. I suppose I should have made a pretext of looking for something in my shoulder bag, or Mark could have pretended to make a mobile phone call. But I wasn't thinking like a police officer just then. I was all too conscious of the suspicion whispering from the depths of my soul. I trembled and Mark slid his arm around my shoulders.

"Hot on a day like this?" he joked, though his eyes betrayed his concern. "They're both big boys, Brenna. If something really serious was up, Graham would tell us. He knows how close you and Scott are. Not to mention I, and a great many others of our team, also like him. Don't worry. If it was something, we'd know."

"Just like we did in May with the Mahmood murder case."

"God, you're stubborn."

"Am not. I'm just concerned. Look, Scott's leaving."

Graham stepped back from the police car and gave one wave. Scott returned it, tapped on the car brakes, then swung the car onto Old Peveril Road and sped uphill. I watched until his car disappeared in the thickness of the forest.

"He didn't even say hi to us," Mark said, his tone conveying his disappointment and disbelief. "Us standing here, across the road, in full sight, and he didn't even wave." His grip on my shoulders relaxed and his voice trailed off, leaving him staring in the vicinity of the church, and his eyes dark in the sunlight. "Maybe you're right, Brenna. Something stronger than day-old fish smells."

"Not that I want to be right..."

Graham, too, had hurried away. The front door to the pub closed before I could consider going to talk to him. Which left Mark and me standing on the pavement, the sunshine beating down on us, and questions as thick as the flies buzzing around us finding voice in my throat.

"No," Mark said, his grip on my shoulders increasing and steering me down the hill. "It's not our place to ask Graham about that. He'll tell us if we need to know."

"Maybe if I phone Scott..." I started to search for my mobile phone when Mark's hand dropped onto mine. He squeezed it and shook his head.

"Same thing, Bren. If Scott wanted you to know, he'd ring you up. Let it lie. We've got our own riddles to solve with this case. Come on." His fingers wrapped around mine in a friendly handhold, simultaneously encouraging and prompting.

I nodded and smiled back, but relegating Scott and Graham to the back of my mind would be difficult.

The road suffered from early Sunday morning syndrome: front gardens were deserted, no cars traveled to or from anywhere, no dogs romped or barked. Either the residents were in bed, breakfasting, or already at church. The quiet was nearly unreal.

"This must be the place," Mark said minutes later, his voice nearly making me jump.

We had left the crossroad and walked farther down Old Peveril Road, submersed in the thickness of pines, oaks and firs. The air temperature dropped dramatically and the scent of pine needles, moss and stock wove around me. I paused at the iron gate that enclosed Mary Johnson's front garden. The metal beneath my hand already held the heat of the July morning. Mark leaned forward, his shoulder touching my back, and pushed the gate open. Our footsteps rose dully from the tan flagstone walkway.

Mark rang the doorbell and looked at the upper storey windows while we waited admittance. "Could be at work," he said as he punched the button again. "She's a cook, the restaurant is open."

"Looks rather shut up at that," I agreed, noting the closed curtains. I shielded my eyes from the glare of the sunlight on the pane of glass.

"Maybe she's just shutting out the heat."

"I think she's gone. It's too quiet. You want to try the restaurant?"

Mark shrugged in his easygoing manner. "Sure. It's nearly noon, anyway. We can grab lunch before we talk to her."

He closed the gate after us and twenty minutes later we were seated in Haddon Hall's restaurant.

The Hall Restaurant occupied the former hayloft of the old stables, a clever use of space that loaned a bit of history to the diners. Done up in shades of pale gray, white and cream, the room mixed ancient oak beams with modern laminated chairs. Glass cases and cabinets containing food and drinks formed a U along the back walls of the room. Mark went through the line, getting our food, and I claimed a table in a dim corner.

"Too much summer?" he asked when he brought our lunches.

I grabbed my salad and scone from the tray and spread my napkin across my lap. "Too much of something." I waited until he had taken a bite before I said, "Did you ask if Mary Johnson is working today?"

"I thought it best to take 'em by surprise. If she's guilty and she learns someone wants to speak to her..." He clapped his hands together and raised the left hand into the air, imitating a fleeing subject.

"Looks rather like Scott's departure at the pub."

"Scott's not a suspect."

"Neither is Mary Johnson."

"Not yet, at least." He swallowed a forkful of pasty before asking, "How are the wedding plans coming along?"

I bought some time by taking a sip of orange squash. What could I say? I didn't want to lie, but I didn't want to turn this into an Agony Aunt episode. So I took the middle road, shrugged, and said, "All right. There's so much to work out. I'm a bit over-whelmed with it all."

"I still say the marriage is more important than the wedding. If he really loved you, he'd let you have your simple wedding and forget all this church, organ, attendants and reception nonsense."

"If I didn't know you, I'd say the voice of experience spoke."

"I don't have to be married to see logic in this. I'd give in and let my fiancée have whatever she wanted. Why not start the marriage off on the right foot?"

"I love Adam," I said, finding I needed to defend my statement and him. "But—"

"But his parents are the stumbling block, right?"

"I'm wondering how they'll be as in-laws. Maybe it'll be fine once we're married. Maybe, as Adam said, they're just trying to help us avoid their own wedding mistake."

"So you don't look back fifty years from now and regret you didn't have the church and tiered cake and all?"

I nodded. Had something gone wrong with the restaurant's air conditioning unit? The room felt incredibly warm, like all the south-facing windows had opened and July poured through the openings. "It won't be so bad."

"You trying to convince me or yourself? Look, Brenna." Mark laid down his fork and grabbed my hand across the table. "If you can't talk about this to Adam now, what's going to happen later on, when you're wed, and the really big, crucial events happen?"

"Yeah, that's occurred to me."

"I'm not saying his parents will run your lives, and I'm not saying Adam will be dictatorial, but I wish it wasn't three against one. If it were just you and Adam, I'd not be concerned. I know you can hold your own one on one. But you've got the added pressure of trying to be nice and sweet and gentle in his parents' eyes."

"Pleasing everyone isn't my strong suit. Ask my own folks."

"Well," Mark said, taking a breath and picking up his fork, "December's a way off, yet. I think something will present itself."

"Always darkest before the dawn, right?"

"Something like that."

We finished our lunch in chitchat, cleared our table, and introduced ourselves to the cashier. I asked if we could speak to Mary Johnson.

"She's in there," the cashier said. She jerked her head toward the open door leading to the kitchen. "You won't be too long about it, will you? The lunch bunch is still struggling in." She eyed our warrant cards with obvious worry and curiosity, and perhaps wished the room design had placed the cash register and the kitchen door closer to each other. "Just through there. Yes, that's right. She's the one who's singing."

We thanked her and walked into the kitchen.

The room was an ocean of white, chrome and glass. Sunlight from the skylights seemed to have magnified and intensified as it hit the white tile and chrome. I found myself squinting and discretely waving air into my shirt. Even with a huge wall-mounted fan silently whirling away some of the hot air, it still seemed as hot as the inside of an oven.

The aromas of baking pastries, lemon and dishwasher detergent filled the air. I caught the scent of chlorine disinfectant from the chrome worktops, and warm chocolate as a cook stirred it into a batter—fragrances that resurrected memories of home even in this unfamiliar setting.

Mary Johnson closed the oven door on a tray of rock cakes and looked up as Mark spoke her name. The song she sang died on her lips, the third verse of 'The Swans' Courtships.' She looked surprised to find someone other than restaurant staff in the kitchen, and seemed confused as to what to do. But, not finding the cashier or manager running after us, she gave us a smile and came forward. Thirty-something, average height, slim and dark eyed, Mary looked more like an actress in a television sitcom than she did a cook. Weren't all cooks plump?

She set the timer on the oven, said she could give us ten minutes, and led us to a corner where we could talk. Her coworkers seemed annoyed by her decision. "I'm that upset by it all," she said, thrusting her hands into her apron pockets. Her eyes held the traces of crying. "Alastair was a fine dancer, an innovative choreographer, an excellent cook, and just a smashing person. Why anyone would want to harm him is beyond my understanding. And to die like that…" She blotted her wet cheeks with her apron. It, as well as her white shirt, was dusted with flour. The shirtsleeves, rolled up above her elbows, displayed reddened skin that matched the hue of her face. They were muscular arms, I thought, good for lifting heavy saucepans and kneading bread dough. Yet, her fingers were slim, smooth and shapely; they were also devoid of any rings. Perhaps she removed them when she worked.

"Did you notice anything odd yesterday, right before the key exchange?" Mark held his pen on a page of his open notebook, ready to write anything pertinent.

"Not really. We'd just assembled near the stage. Johnny got the key from the church. At least, I assumed he did. He wandered off that way. I couldn't see if he went inside. The wood comes down the hill farther north and practically envelopes the church. The stage in the park isn't in line with the church door."

"That's not important right now, Miss Johnson. We know Smith had the key. What else?"

"Well, Johnny makes his usual big deal about handing off the key to Michael, who's the Betty. The audience likes that because both Johnny and Michael are such clowns about it. I know that's why both men hold down those character roles—you need a feel for the audience and what gets a laugh. Did you know that Johnny wants to land a job as a host on a television game show? He's got that warm, outgoing personality. He can talk to anyone."

"Must be an asset as the Tommy," Mark agreed.

"It is. Anyroad, when Michael gets the key he usually presents it to Simon Roe. Only, yesterday before we went on Alastair stumbled, Simon fell and hurt his ankle, and so Alastair opened the light box." Her fingers played with the strands of her brunette hair, stroking them and tucking them back beneath her white cap. "I-I just can't believe he's gone. Not like that." Her gaze shifted to the oven, perhaps wanting this to be over so she could get back to something that didn't bring her such pain.

"So you don't hold any resentful feelings to Alastair, then."

Mary gaped at Mark and stammered, "No. Of course not."

"Neither Alastair nor Simon got upset with you about the holiday dates? They didn't come down hard on you, anger you, maybe frightened you? Two men confronting you, even singly, could be intimidating. Even if you weren't intimidated, perhaps one of them threatened you. Then, when you had time to mull it over, you got angry. You had the dates chosen first; it wasn't right that Simon should demand you change your plans. So you thought you'd teach Simon a lesson and you rigged up the electric. Except Fate stepped in yesterday and Alastair, not Simon, opened the box." He waited for Mary's response, watching her for some physical indication that she was lying.

"I-It's not like that. You've got the wrong end of the stick."

"Really? Then set me right. I'm trying to understand what happened."

"I was upset, sure, when Simon asked me to change my holiday. Demanded, actually. I got angry. Who wouldn't have done, the way he went about it? Like he and Alastair had a right to that week. Well, I did, too. And I requested it first. They had no right to come over like that. It was upsetting enough, me having to take that week, and Simon didn't make it any better."

"Where are you going? You've not taken it yet, from what your boss has told us."

Her thumb and index finger ran along the hem of her apron, perhaps giving her a physical anchor like worry beads. "No. In a fortnight. I-I'm going up to Inverness. For a memorial service for my gran. She died a month ago."

I agreed that Mary couldn't have changed her holiday dates. "Do you know anyone else—doesn't have to be associated with your dance troupe—who might have been upset with Alastair?"

"Upset enough to want to cause him harm, you're saying." Mary leaned against the tile wall and screwed up her mouth.

The sounds from the dining room floated back to us: the jangle of cutlery, the clink and thud of plates and cups, the whir of the cash register, the hum of dozens of conversations. I glanced at my watch. The rock cakes' time would be up soon. "You needn't have overheard a death threat," I said, trying to nudge her into speaking. "Perhaps you thought something was said in jest."

"Like, 'I could kill you for doing that'..."

"Precisely. A lot of truth turns up in a jest."

Mary shook her head and looked defeated. "Nothing. Sorry. We really didn't socialize outside the dance group."

"So you know no one who might have any motive to kill Simon?"

"Only Declan Morris."

# Seven

"Declan Morris is a member of your troupe?"

"Yes."

"Why do you think he had motive to kill Simon?"

"His girlfriend noticed Simon at a performance and after we finished dancing she talked to him. I think the attraction was instant and mutual, for she left Declan that week."

"Declan was upset, I assume."

"Not half. Pleaded with her to come back to him, flooded her letter box and door step with love poems, candy, flowers..."

"None of which worked, you're going to tell me."

"She stayed with Simon. Declan was like the stereotypical man possessed. He threatened Simon with physical harm if she didn't return to him."

Mark shook his head. "How can a person tell someone else to leave if they're in love?"

Mary sighed heavily and nodded. "That's the question, isn't it? It was ridiculous for Declan to say that, but when you're desperate and in pain you don't always think straight."

"When was this threat? How'd you learn about it?"

"I heard it. As did most everyone in the dance troupe. Declan shouted it out when we returned to the village after a performance two weeks ago. We'd just got off the van in the pub's car park and Declan strode up to Simon, pushed the girl friend away, grabs Simon by the collar, and screams at him. You'd have to be deaf not to have heard."

"What did the girl friend do? What's her name?"

"Jessica Arnold. She stood beside Simon, never gave Declan an inch of ground, and told Declan to get out of her life, that she'd left him. Declan yelled that sometimes accidents happen to folks when they least expect it, and then stomped off home. We were all so stunned at that outburst. I don't think anyone moved for a minute afterwards."

I made a notation of the girl friend's name and her address in my notebook. "All this happened a fortnight ago, correct?"

"To the day. It was like Declan had made good his threat that if he couldn't have Jessica back, Simon couldn't have her either. Scary, isn't it?"

"Do you happen to know if Declan has any electrical knowledge, either in his job or as a hobby?"

"No. We're not particularly friendly. You'll have to ask someone else."

"He was that angry about his girl friend leaving him that you believe he might have carried out his threat? It wasn't just anger talking?"

Mary shrugged. "It's hard to imagine anyone wanting to kill someone on purpose. I doubt if most folks would react so violently to being dumped by a girlfriend, but Declan's hard to know. Harder to love, I'd think. He wasn't outgoing or very personable. I know he hadn't many girl friends while he was growing up. I think that's why losing Jessica was so hurtful. He really thought they'd get married."

"Instead," Mark says, "she dumps him."

"Doubly hurtful for him, as he isn't much on good looks or personality, as I said. He'll find it hard to get another girlfriend, I'm thinking."

"How's Jessica taking all this?"

"She's under a doctor's care, from what I understand. She was at the performance yesterday at Haddon Hall, though not here in the village, thank God. That would've been too terrible if she'd seen the accident."

"Who broke the news to her?"

"Simon."

"Must've been difficult. So you don't know anyone else who might've had a grudge against Simon."

"No. He and Alastair were friendly, helpful men and I'm sorry Alastair's gone. Neither of them was too busy to do you a favor. When this blows over, I'm thinking of asking Simon to help me with a bit of genealogy I'm doing."

"Simon's interested in that, is he?"

"He and Alastair, yes. I've great hope that he can find out something for me. It's quite important, but after our altercation about the holiday dates…well, I hope he doesn't hold that against me and withdraw his offer to do the research. Perhaps I should've offered the date to him; then he'd not hesitate to return the favor." She gave a half-hearted smile and glanced at her watch.

"What genealogy research?"

Her eyebrows raised slightly, portraying the hope she felt, even in speaking about it to a third party. "About my family. I'd like to know if someone important is related to me."

"Like royalty?"

"Doesn't have to be. You see…" She grimaced, as though the subject were embarrassing. "I-I'm in love with Robert Connoly. I'm hoping we'll get married, even though he's not said a thing about that. He's very concerned with life style and bettering himself."

"I can't believe he thinks you're not—"

"Wife material? He's not said that in so many words, but it's just a feeling I have. I dress well enough, and I have nice pieces of jewelry, so he's not ashamed of me in that aspect. It's my job, I think. He's a manager at Haddon Hall and I'm a cook." Her voice had dropped during this last sentence, barely audible against the background noise. She lowered her gaze to the floor. I'm certain if the floor had opened up to swallow her, she would've jumped in.

"So, you're thinking that if you can increase your status through some ancestor, Connoly will propose marriage."

"Daft, isn't it?"

"Not at all. It's not a crime to want to share your life with someone."

Mark cleared his throat, bringing our attention to him. "Did everyone in your dance group arrive at the park yesterday at the same time?"

"From the Hall, you mean?"

"Yes. Did you travel together in two vans, for instance, or did you all take individual vehicles and arrive at various times?"

"Odd that you mention that. I'd not thought of it. Brian Fireman came late."

"He's...what? Under gardener here at the Hall, right?" Mark looked up from the paper listing all the dancers' information. "Why was he late, did he say?"

"No." She relinquished her hold on the apron hem. "Johnny was quite put out by Brian's late arrival."

"Late so they had to delay the key passing?"

"Oh, no. Brian showed up a few minutes before three o'clock. But he wasn't so late as to delay anything. Though Johnny was livid, of course. Told Brian he nearly gave him—Johnny—heart failure. An exaggeration, of course, because James could've danced Brian's part."

"James Charles, this is?"

"Yes. James is in the second team. I don't mean second as second best. With twelve members, we have two teams. It works out perfectly when we dance at these summer festivals. One team gets a bit of a break while the other team performs."

"So, James Charles could've danced Brian's part quite easily, without causing any mishap."

"I thought Johnny was over the top with his reaction to Brian's tardiness, but Johnny takes things so hard, him being the group's leader and such."

I asked Mary if Brian had left the Hall before the others in the group had.

"Like, you think he raced to the park, fixed the wires in the box, then sauntered in late to establish his alibi?"

"Yes."

"You're joking."

"Did he leave the Hall early?"

Mary hesitated, gazing off to her right. She appeared to be recalling the day, or perhaps considering the consequences of aiding and abetting. Somewhat later, she replied, though her voice had lost its previous chatty tone. "I don't recall. Ask someone else." Her voice grew instantly sharper, harder, almost daring me to find out about Brian.

"When the rest of you got to the park, were people there to watch you dance?"

She nodded and looked relieved. "Yes. Maybe thirty or so. I don't know exactly, but there were folks there. Milling about the stage area and elsewhere close to it. We were expected, you see. It's an annual thing we do, dance at Nether Haddon after we've finished at the Hall. The event was advertised for a month, folks look forward to it and turn up year after year to see us." The half-hearted smile hovered at the corners of her mouth. "People are always there when we go on."

Which shot down the idea of Brian tampering with the light box right before the group went on. Although why he would've done that, I didn't know, but it was early days yet, as Graham was found of saying.

"You're quite creative," Mark said, filling the silence. "Cooking, dancing. Any other things you like to do?"

"I play piano."

"Really? I often wish I'd stuck with my lessons. I regret it now." He glanced at me, silently daring me to blow his bluff. I merely smiled back.

"I find it a great stress reliever, of course. But I do love the music and just sitting at the keyboard and playing. You should get back to it."

"It's on my list of things to pick up when I retire. My folks had a baby grand. I was lucky."

"You were. I've got a little electric keyboard. Nothing wrong with it, but the sound's not quite right, is it? I miss the booming, supportive bass of a grand."

"Nothing like it. Well…" Mark shut his notebook and looked at his watch. "I think we've gone past the time you said you could spare us."

The timer on the oven went off and we thanked Mary for her help. She nodded and strode toward the oven, wiping her palms on the sides of her apron.

"Your ingenuity never ceases to amaze me," I said as we left the restaurant. "Piano lessons indeed."

"I had one once. I think. Anyway, we now know that Mary has an electronic keyboard in her house."

"How's that help? Alastair wasn't electrocuted by a piano."

"Don't you get it, Brenna? Electric light box, electric piano. Maybe Mary knows more about electricity than she'll admit."

"Maybe your brain's been fried, Mark. I bet there are thousands, millions, of electric keyboard players whose only electrical knowledge is how to plug in the power cord. Do my telly or hair dryer or computer make me a suspect in Alastair's murder? They're all electrical items."

"I just don't want to be caught on the hop if the case starts pointing toward Mary Johnson. Who next? Jack Darkgate works in the Hall's gift shop. You want to talk to him while we're here?"

"That would be logical, but I'd like to ask Simon about this genealogy request of Mary's. And talk to Declan Morris."

"If he's calmed down about Jessica leaving him."

~

Simon Roe made no effort to conceal his surprise or irritation at our return. He let us into his front room and, while he didn't slam the door closed, shut it firmly so that the doorknocker rattled. He hobbled over to his chair, leaned his crutches against one of the chair arms, and propped his bandaged foot on a footstool. He looked quite the gout-ridden squire, except that I knew he didn't suffer from that ailment.

"Why didn't you tell us that Jessica left Declan Morris and became your girlfriend?"

The question surprised Simon, for he coughed. "I didn't know my personal life had any bearing on what's happened to Alastair."

"It might if Declan did something about it and Alastair got killed by mistake."

Simon shrugged and tapped the liquid-filled glass on the side table with the end of his crutch. "Simple story, really. We liked each other instantly, she left Declan, he was mad as hell. That's life. Relationships come and go."

"Were you nervous that Declan would physically retaliate against you?"

"He'd be a right berk if he did. Most everyone in the village knows about his threat. He'd be the first person the police would suspect if anything happened to me."

"But something happened to Alastair," Mark countered.

"Unfortunately. I didn't really pay Declan any mind that day. I figured it was anger speaking and that he'd get over it. Most people do."

I asked Simon if he did any type of research for people.

He looked momentarily confused, then admitted that he sometimes did, but he hadn't been asked for any specific genealogy help. "I'd be glad to do that for Mary whenever she wants. Anything to give Cupid a chance."

"She mentioned that you and Alastair were keen on genealogy," Mark said. "Is that true?"

"I don't know if keen is the correct word, but I dabble in it."

"You didn't say that when we first talked to you."

"I don't believe you asked specifically. You talked about that poetry thing you found in Alastair's house. Genealogy never came up in the conversation."

"It's come up now. Do you know why it's so important to Mary?"

Simon's tone change from irritation to impatient and he

moved his leg so that his ankle hung over the end of the stool. "No. Why should I? Despite your insinuation, this is the first I've heard of it. As I said, I didn't know she was delving into her family tree. I don't know a thing about her ancestors, either. I don't go poking about in other people's lives without being asked. Anyway, genealogy concerns folks in the past. You need to speak to Declan Morris if you want to learn about motives for my cousin's death." Simon nearly bit the words in two.

Mark's eyebrow rose. "Bad blood between them?"

"I don't know specifics, but if you're looking for someone whose nose is in others' business, you've got your man."

"Why would you suspect him of murdering your cousin?"

"Ever hear of murder for hire?"

# Eight

"Who'd benefit from Alastair's death?" Mark asked, obviously stunned. "I'd think you would, Simon, being family."

Simon picked up his glass of amber colored beverage, held it up and stared at it. "I assume I will, too, but Alastair was as poor as a church mouse. Everyone in the dance group knew that. Alastair had no bank account worth mentioning, had no fancy house or car. You've seen those, so you know. He was a cook and lived on his cook's salary. Think about what that means and then tell me if I will get anything in his will."

"But you just mentioned murder for hire. If your cousin was struggling financially, it still makes no sense that Declan Morris or anyone else would kill your cousin."

Simon drained the beverage in one quick gulp and reached for the bottle of Scotch. "Not hired to kill Alastair. Hired to kill *me*. I should've been the person opening that light box, remember? Don't you have that down in your little book?"

"Why should *you* be a target?"

"It's obvious, isn't it? I know something." Simon shifted his gaze to the front door, as if making certain no one was about to barge through with a weapon. His fingers grabbed the armrests of his chair, blanching his knuckles. He lowered his voice. "About Declan Morris."

"What do you mean? Does he want the information kept from someone?"

Simon snorted and relaxed his grip. "He wants the titbit kept from *everyone*. It's a dirty little secret that's been buried for over seventy years, and he knows I can ruin his life and his family's life if I ever want to. Loose lips sink more than ships."

"What do you mean?" Mark sat quietly, leaning forward slightly in his interest.

"I'd think anyone is capable of just about anything if they perceive a threat or if they're emotionally upset. Not that Declan is right now, but you never know what sets some people off. Alastair's death has distressed all of us in the dance troupe, of course, and put us all on edge. If Declan feels I could be a threat due to his secret..." He grabbed the glass of scotch and downed a swallow.

I asked if he'd mind telling us the information. "If it has no bearing on Alastair's murder, we will forget it. But if Declan thinks there's potential that you'd shared the information with Alastair... Well, he could've rigged up the light box, hoping he'd get you, but when Alastair was killed by mistake Declan didn't mind."

"He'd still be able to come after me," Simon said, staring into the whisky. "That's what you're implying." As if resigning himself to the topic, Simon set the glass down and exhaled slowly. He pressed the tips of his fingers together, perhaps to still his shaking hands. Looking at me, he said, "Mary Johnson hired me to do some genealogy into Declan's family tree."

"*Mary* did? Why?"

"Declan had been talking about older family members, and the fact that he didn't know much about them or his family roots. He seemed interested in his family, so Mary thought it'd be a treat for his birthday if she could present him with information on his family tree."

"But it didn't happen that way," I said.

"No." He gave a sharp, bitter laugh and frowned. "I didn't want to cover it up. I have an obligation to tell folks the truth and present their ancestors to them as they are. Besides being unethical, it could do damage. You never know when you'll need the information or for what purpose."

"What did you discover that Declan considers a secret? Seventy years ago, you said." I did some quick mental subtraction. "World War Two?"

"Right. There are probably more secrets connected to wars than we realize. Anyway, through my research, I found out that Declan's grandfather had an important position in Germany during the war. The grandfather, being a perceptive man of directional wind shift and gradually turning into a lover of democracy, changed the family surname after the war and loaded up family, household and passports and landed in Britain. They took up residency in Derbyshire, thinking it sufficiently rural for their needs, blended into the wood if not the woodwork, and has used the new name ever since."

Mark looked up from his note taking. "What was the original German name?"

"Müller."

"There are a lot of German names in the country. Why so self-conscious?"

"Because Herr Grossvater was on the staff at a luft stalag," Simon said, sounding rather tired of the topic. He spoke slowly, breathing heavily between the sentences. "Besides being on the wrong side in the war and dishing out punishment for prisoners, he was suspected of taking bribes and thievery. The bribes and theft were never proven—I guess that got overlooked in the tumultuous ending days of the war—but the suspicion, plus having a hand in corporal punishment and having a nice job in a POW camp…" He finished the rest of his drink and sloshed more whisky into the glass. "*C'est la guerre,* right?"

"No one else but Mary and the Morris family know of the skeleton in the family closet."

"I wouldn't think so. Not something you'd like broadcast about. But it's not everyone in the family who knows, obviously. Declan didn't. His grandfather did a good job of keeping it all quiet."

"So, if Mary also knows about the name switch, why do you

suspect Declan might come after you in order to keep the secret safe? Wouldn't he also go after Mary?"

"He's not aware that Mary knows. She decided not to present him with the family history when she read about the Müllers."

Mark made no attempt to hide his surprise. His right eyebrow rose and his voice rose slightly. "Really? Then how did Declan learn that *you* knew about the Müller name change?"

"At the beginning, when Mary first hired me to delve into the past, she wanted to be sure Declan's wife wasn't going to do the same thing. Mary told Frances. Frances let slip part of the story, telling Declan just enough so he would infer that Frances had asked for the family history."

"Taking Mary out of the picture and leaving you in the spotlight."

"Yes. So you see, detectives, Declan thinks I'm the only person who knows about his grandfather's appalling past. As I said, if he gets the idea I'll blab when in my cups…" He held up the glass of whisky and saluted us with it. "He's getting scared, so he rigged up that light box to eliminate me as a potential information leak. Make it look like an accident, shift the scrutiny from himself. Only, it didn't work. Alastair, God rest his soul, was murdered by mistake. But I'll keep watching Declan. He's bound to make a mistake himself, and then I'll see he's up for murder." He slumped back in his chair and cried into his whisky.

～

Declan Morris might have known a great deal about Alastair, I thought as we parked the car in front of his house. Sharing an interest like dancing makes people chatty, and gossip sometimes galloped through a group. The most innocent remarks dropped in conversation often found themselves in the ears of others. And if those remarks hadn't been intended for general knowledge, the potential for trouble was real.

I'd been thinking over Simon's situation as Mark drove us to Declan's house. But not knowing Declan or how desperate he was to keep his family name and past a secret, I had no idea if he'd be a real threat to Simon. Even if I knew Declan, I might not know the depth of his distress. Some people excelled at keeping the stiff upper lip. So I let my thoughts on the subject die for the moment while Mark parked the car and I looked at the house.

The second one on Water Ford Lane, south of the junction and the pub, the house squatted between taller versions fabricated from the same color and type of gray stone and dark slate. Besides being only one storey as compared to his northern neighbor's and Brian Fireman's two storey homes, Declan's house differentiated itself by a bright blue door and window trim, and a basket of blue morning glories hanging from the lamp post's cross bar.

Declan looked up from his weeding as Mark opened the front gate. He got to his feet, dusted his gardening gloves against his jeans, and asked what we wanted. When I introduced us and stated that we were investigating Alastair's death, Declan visibly stiffened. He perched on top of the stack of mulch bags and indicated a wrought iron garden seat, which Mark and I accepted.

He looked to be in his late twenties. Whether he actually was, or whether his thick, blond hair and muscular build attributed to the illusion, wasn't important at the moment. Finding Alastair's killer was.

"I've no idea who might've wanted Alastair dead," Declan said in answer to my question. His voice had a twang that I couldn't place, and he clipped the end of his sentences, as though he were in a hurry to finish speaking. He loosened the knot in the blue scarf encircling his neck, pulled it off, and mopped his forehead with it. Sweat trickled down his cheek and onto his neck, giving his skin a golden glow in the sunlight. "That's part of the shock of this whole thing. He was a likable bloke. Before yesterday, I would've sworn he'd not an enemy in the world." He shooed a fly buzzing around his head. "You've really no idea who killed him, then."

"Timing seems to be important in all this," I said. "Who had time to rig the light box, what time and day it was done."

"Sounds rather hard to discover."

"*You* were mad at Simon, I understand. Jessica, your girl-friend, left you for him."

Declan eyed me warily. "What of it?"

"A rather casual reply considering the threat you made against Simon."

"That might be if Simon was dead, but he isn't. It's Alastair, or haven't you heard?"

"Other people have killed rivals in love," I said. "It's not so farfetched that your anger got the better of you."

"If you've got proof, charge me. Otherwise, you're just rab-biting on, hoping I'll say something you can use in court. Well, I didn't kill Alastair and that's all I'm going to say."

"People heard you threaten Simon."

Declan snorted and leaned forward. "If I wanted Alastair dead, I'd have chosen a method that would be sure to target him. You forget that Simon should've been the bloke opening that light box. Simon should've been dead. Why would I rig the light box and hope *Alastair* would switch on the lights when it was *Simon's* job? You need to focus on who wanted *him* dead."

"Do you know of anyone?"

"Not off hand. I don't normally spend my days creating lists of potential killers of people I know. I'll have to think about it."

"He's a man with no enemies, then."

"I didn't say that. We all have something to hide, something we're not proud of that affects us one way or the other. We all have people in our lives who wouldn't be that sorry to see us dead." He gazed at the trowel in his hand, perhaps figured I categorized it as a murder weapon, and dropped it beside him. "Before you go accusing me of murder, you'd best look more closely at Alastair and a motive for his death."

"Do you know of one?"

Declan glanced to his right, then to Mark's face and back to mine. "Alastair was a bit too interested in folks' pasts, if you ask me."

"Meaning...what?"

"All that history stuff he'd research. Ancestors, the history of the Hall, who lived in this area and when. That's what I mean."

"Did it bother people?" Mark asked. "Sounds like an innocent enough pastime to me. Unless, of course, he looked into the genealogy of the dance troupe and came up with some not-too-pleasant findings that he hung over folks' heads. Did that happen?"

"If it did, no one cried on my shoulder."

"You'd have heard?"

Declan sniffed and fished in his jeans pocket for a cigarette. "I get along with everyone in our group, but I'm not bosom pals with them all. I'd hear if Brian Fireman had been threatened with some nasty disclosure, for instance."

"Was Alastair like that? Would he have dug up dirt on people and then demand money to keep quiet?"

"I don't know. I'd like to think he wouldn't have done. Since I never heard of anything like that..." He lit his cigarette, took a drag, and rolled the smoke around on his tongue before exhaling. "And before you ask, no, I don't know if Simon shared the hobby. I'd tend to think not. Simon's more of a sports bloke. Sitting around with maps and charts and staring at a computer screen...that's not Simon's style."

"But Alastair might do it."

"Don't know, do I? Ask Simon."

"So Simon's the sociable fellow and Alastair's more of the loner."

Declan exhaled sharply and pointed toward the pub. "Simon goes in for team sports, it's true. He likes to dance with us, and he also plays rugby and cricket with some chaps he knows. He gets out occasionally with these same chaps on weekends to hike and fish. So, while Simon's more of an extrovert, I guess you'd call him, he wasn't immune to working a lot by himself at the Hall. More than would be likely as a head gardener who should be interacting with his staff. I always wondered what Simon did alone so much up there."

"You think his staff would know?"

"Don't know, do I? But it's worth a question or two, seems to me."

"When was this?" I tried to ignore my tightening throat, but it was hard to control my anticipation. This could be a major lead for us.

Declan pulled in the corners of his mouth and shrugged. "Not long ago."

"What constitutes not long ago in this instance?"

"Not more than a week. Several days, perhaps. I didn't ask."

"How do you know this? I could understand your knowing if you worked at the Hall, but you don't. So how come you're aware that Simon went off on his own?"

"Brian Fireman told me. We're mates. Brian mentioned it one evening when we were in the pub."

"He suspect Simon of something, or is he just angry at his boss for messing about on the job?"

"From what Brian said that night, he thinks something's going on at the Hall."

Mark snorted. "And that 'something' involves Simon."

"Like I said, we've all got events we wouldn't want in the limelight."

"What in your dim, dark past aren't you proud of, Mr. Morris?"

"Pardon?" Declan's voice took on a sharpness, and he spoke slowly, as if expecting a trap.

"You said not one minute ago that we all have something to hide. I assume you've included yourself in that statement."

Declan's throat muscles tightened. "I don't see what bearing this has on Alastair's death."

"It does if your embarrassment is connected to Alastair. Does it?"

"I'm not involved with his death. You'll discover this is true if you investigate a bit further. Now." He stood up, signally his irritation and impatience. "I've other things to do."

Mark thanked Declan for his time as he escorted us to the

gate. "If you think of anyone who might've had a grudge against Alastair or Simon—"

"Good day."

The closing of the gate still echoed in my ear as we got into the car. Mark drove up the lane and stopped just beyond Declan's house. I powered down the car window but no breeze offered respite from the climbing temperature. Mark inched the car forward, braking in the shade of a tree. It was better, but even here the heat rolled up from the dark pavement and poured into the car. I shut the window.

"Helpful, friendly bloke," Mark said. We sat in the idling car, the air conditioner blasting cool air at us, and considered our options.

"He either knows something or he's just naturally obstructive."

"Narrows it down beautifully."

"Wouldn't have done any good to ask about his alibi for the time of Alastair's death. We don't know when the wires were rigged."

"You fancy a drink or anything? We just happen to be quite close to the pub." Mark smiled and inclined his head toward the building in question.

"Odd how that happened."

"Life's filled with strange occurrences, Brenna."

"I think we better keep going on the case, don't you? If Graham sees us in there, I don't think it'll be good news for us."

"Coupled with his distraction last night and his chat with Scott this morning, right? Pity. We're so close to the oasis and it's so damned hot."

I ignored the pitiful look in his eyes. "Who next, Mark?"

"You'd kick sand in a thirsty man's face. Okay, you wouldn't. But I'm hot. Just so you'll know and you can tell the paramedics when I fall over."

"All right," I relented. "But nothing alcoholic and just a quick one. We ought to stop at a grocer's and get some bottled water."

"We can learn more at the pub," he said, driving the few

hundred feet to the pub. When he'd parked and got out of the car, he trotted around to my side of the car, opened the door for me, and followed me into his oasis.

The Stout Keg would see its main trade tonight, I thought as I glanced around the main room. A few people sat at the bar, a middle-aged couple occupied a table near the door, and a lone man threw darts at the dartboard. I waited at a table by the window while Mark got our drinks.

"You dying of thirst?" he said when he'd brought our drinks to the table.

"I thought you were."

"It can wait another minute. Guess who's playing darts over there."

I glanced at the solitary player, a rather tall figure. "I give. Who?"

"Brian Fireman. Fate, as they say, has intervened. I knew we needed a drink."

"How do you know it's Brian? You ask the publican?"

"Didn't have to. He was saying something to Brian when I came up to the bar."

"Opportunity is practically pounding on that door. Come on."

We left our drinks on the table and walked over to Brian Fireman.

He had the looks of a man who worked outdoors for a living: rough hands, sun-bleached sandy hair, and muscular arms and shoulders. I figured he was in his early twenties and probably had another decade before his back would start complaining of the heavy work. Mark called out Brian's name, and the man looked over his shoulder as we approached, his hand froze as he was about to launch the dart in his hand. He asked if we wanted to play. When we declined and introduced ourselves, he pulled the darts from the board, handed them to the publican, and joined us at our table. He sat opposite Mark, probably trying to make it as much man-to-man as possible, and set his glass on a beer mat. "What's this in aid of, then?" He forced a lightness into his voice that I suspected he didn't feel; his blue eyes appeared clouded with apprehension.

"We're investigating Alastair's death," I said, slightly annoyed with Brian's obvious good-ole-boys attitude. "We're talking to members of his dance troupe, as a matter of routine."

"You think I topped him?" He spoke to Mark. It'd been a long time since I received so obvious a brush off.

"We're speaking to everyone in the troupe." I was determined to control the situation. "You're in the troupe, we're talking to you."

"Take a lot of time, that will. You know how many there are of us?"

"Twelve." I slapped my hand down on the tabletop. "I'd appreciate it if you'd look at me when I speak to you."

He lifted his wine glass, took a leisurely sip, and said to Mark, "You're not concerned someone'll do a bunk? Awful lot of folks to keep your eye on."

Mark took the man's glass, set it down between us, and leaned over the table so that his face was within inches of Brian's. "Sergeant Taylor is asking you politely to speak to her. She's in charge of this interview. Now, before you really get up my nose, you can comply with her wishes or we'll trot you into Buxton and see how mannerly you are in a cell at the police station. Get my drift?"

Brian nodded, his glance shifting from Mark to me. He colored slightly, a reddish glow accenting his tanned skin and the tips of his ears. His dry lips cracked as he tried to smile away his agitation, but quickly faded when I merely stared at him.

"Fine." Mark patted Brian's hand, grinned and returned the wine glass. "Just so we understand each other from the start. You were saying, Detective Taylor?"

"You're an under gardener at Haddon Hall, is that correct?"

"Yes."

"Your immediate boss is Simon Roe, right?"

"Yes."

"How do you and he get along?"

He shrugged.

"How do you and he get along?" I repeated.

He sat there, perhaps considering his answer.

Mark slapped his hands together. The 'thwack' made Brian jump. "Sorry, Detective Taylor. Brian didn't hear your question. Would you please repeat it?"

I asked the question again, my voice noticeably quieter.

Brian gave that half-hearted smile again and nodded. "He oversees my work. We dance in the same sword dancin' group. I don't invite him over for tea but we're friendly enough."

"Your under gardener job must have you working long, hard hours."

"It does. But I enjoy it. I like bein' in the open. I'm aimin' to be head gardener one of these years, so I don't mind the extra time if I'm asked. I, uh, figure it's a good way for me to get experience, add to my education. You know…prove to the bloke who does the hirin' that I'm worthy, that I know my stuff. That's the way to land the job." Once he decided to cooperate, his tongue didn't know how to stop.

"And working such long hours at so hard a job, well, do you ever get resentful of Simon?"

"Resentful? What are you gettin' at?" Despite his effort to appear cooperative and female-friendly, his words sounded harsh. Fear or suspicion shone in his eyes and he pushed a lock of his hair back into place.

"We understand you've been sweating through the hours, day in and day out, while your boss Simon has been taking a bit of time off."

He smiled suddenly. "Oh, that. No, not that I've noticed. He's been at the Hall each day."

"That's as may be, but I'm referring to his time at the Hall when he's on the clock. Walking about the estate, keeping to himself." I watched Brian's face deflate from cockiness into confusion. "We understand he sneaks off on his own when he should be overseeing what the gardeners should be doing. You know anything about that?"

His fingers closed around the stem of the wine glass but he didn't pick up the glass. "If Simon's been sneakin' off, I wouldn't know of it. I've got all I can do keepin' track of my own work each day. Weedin', mulchin', prunin'. It's never endin'."

"You've not seen Simon wander off, then."

"Maybe he did stroll about. I may've seen him a few times. But I didn't think anythin' of it. Just thought he were overseein' our work, as he's supposed to. But if you want to know about Alastair—*him* I could tell you about."

"Oh, yes? What about Alastair?"

Brian slumped against the back of the settle, as though he expected to talk for a while and would need the physical support of the high, wooden back. "He'd come early to the Hall, way before his shift in the restaurant started."

"You knew when he worked?"

"Sure. When you see a bloke every weekday and you talk about work and dance competitions and the like on off hours, of course you know when he worked. He knew my work schedule, too. Nothin' so mysterious about that."

"So Alastair coming to work early was somewhat above and beyond his normal routine, I take it."

"Yeah. He liked his job and all that, don't get me wrong, but to get to the Hall an hour early… Man, he had to have been barmy! And he'd stay late, too. He'd still be there when I packed up my kit and left for the day."

"What was Alastair doing that demanded these extra hours? Not cooking, for he couldn't have been in the kitchen."

"He were walkin' around the gardens and down by the river."

"Each time you saw him before and after hours?"

"Yeah. Dressed in jeans and Wellingtons. Not his cook's apron and hat. Like he were expectin' to do some gardenin' or get dirty."

I glanced at Mark. I hadn't expected this.

Mark asked, "How long did this go on? Not hours—you said before and after his shift. How long did he roam about…a few days, a month?"

Brian took a sip of wine before replying. "Oh, a good while.

Must've been at least a fortnight. Could have been three weeks, but it's more likely a fortnight. Every day I were at work I'd see him trottin' about the estate grounds, sometimes before his shift, sometimes after."

"Did he always go the same route or go to the same place on the estate?"

"Naw. Kept at it diligent, though. He'd be roamin' around by the river one week, perhaps, then at the lower terrace the followin' week. Never knew where I'd see him."

"Did Alastair have anything with him while he was walking around?"

"Like, some other bloke?"

"That or any tools or papers that he'd refer to."

"I don't recall seein' any such thing. But he weren't within my sight range all the day, understand. I'd just see him walkin' to some spot. 'Course, every so often he'd be somewhere, like in the lower courtyard, and I'd come along to work there, and then Alastair'd take off real quick."

"He'd leave or start work at the restaurant, you mean?"

"No. Go to some other spot on the estate. I know that for a fact 'cause when I'd put my tools away or go get somethin', I'd see him elsewhere."

"Simon never did anything like this?" I said.

Brian rubbed his chin as he considered my question. Shaking his head, he said, "No. Not on that scale. I'd see Simon walkin' about, but I just put that down to him bein' needed at other parts of the estate. Simon's head gardener and he goes where he's needed a lot of times. Gives his advice, consults with the garden designer and estate manager, oversees the care of our tools, sees to repairs and such. I thought I saw more of him this past week, and I recall thinkin' he were takin' a lot of breaks, but it could've been just his work. I gave him my garden knife yesterday morning."

"The day your troupe danced at the Hall?"

"Yeah. The handle on my knife was loose, so I gave it to Simon to have it fixed. Blade had a nick, too, so I thought he could get 'em both done at the same time. Well, it's his job, keepin' our tools in good order. He took my knife and hurried off."

"I understood that your first dance set was at nine o'clock Saturday. Surely you didn't work before you performed."

"No. I got to the Hall early and remembered my knife needed fixin'. I got it and handed it to Simon. He said he'd get it taken care of."

"Did you arrive at the Hall early for that specific purpose, to give the tool to Simon?"

"I don't like to rush. Arrivin' just before we're to perform upsets me, makes me nervous. So I usually drive myself to our venues, if it's not too far away. I sit and relax and have a cuppa. That's what I did yesterday."

"Did Simon get there early, too?"

"Yeah. Him and Alastair."

"Did they wander off, like they did during a regular work day?"

The publican changed the television channel and the soundtrack from a music video blasted into the room.

Brian angled his head toward me, cupping his hand to his ear. "Pardon?"

The music's volume decreased quickly as the publican pointed the remote control at the telly. The room settled back to normality: conversations, glass mugs thudding onto table tops, voices coming from the kitchen. The computer near the dartboard chimed as a man played a round of poker.

I repeated my question.

"You mean, go off to the river or some spot in the gardens? Not that I saw. They hadn't the time, though Alastair was there before I arrived."

"When was that?"

"Oh, around eight o'clock."

"What was Alastair doing there so early? Did he tell you?"

"I didn't ask and he didn't tell me. Simon wandered about, too. Looked more like he were followin' Alastair, but I don't know for sure. Why would he be followin' Alastair?"

"That's my question."

"I thought he had to have a quick word with someone, like James Charles."

Mark said, "He's the owner of a nursery, isn't he?"

"Yeah. That's why I didn't think anythin' of Simon goin' off. I saw James there a few times before this, like maybe two or three last week. So it's obvious I assumed James and Simon were talkin' over a big job, isn't it? Or Simon might be consultin' James for some reason. Still, I think there were somethin' big in the works, some new landscapin' for the Hall grounds. They talked together quite a while. Then, once I saw James followin' Simon, or it looked like it. 'Course, James could've just been goin' the same way, but he weren't in a hurry to catch Simon up and walk with him. Maybe Simon grabbed a quick word with James before we had our first dance. Wanted to show him somethin' on the estate."

"Did James arrive late? Do you think he and Simon talked together before your troupe went on?"

"I didn't see." Brian drained the last of his wine, swallowed quickly, and asked if that was all.

"One more question. You were late getting to the village yesterday. So late that Johnny Smith got concerned you weren't going to make it and that James Charles would have to fill in for you. Why were you late?"

Brian tugged at the neck of his tee shirt and stared out of the window. "I-I had car trouble. A flat tire. Took a bit of time to get it changed." He flattened the fabric against his chest and held his hand there. It looked as though he were taking an oath.

Mark said, "Anything else, Detective Taylor?"

I thanked Brian and watched him escape to his game of darts.

Mark drank half of his lemon barley water before he said, "Alastair isn't the only late person connected to this case."

"Maybe we should call this the Case of the Late Suspects. What were they all doing, coming late to the village, spying on each other, roaming about the Hall grounds? Sounds like a French farce with people entering and exiting a hallway of doors."

"I'd be happier if it were more like that stateroom scene in *A Night at the Opera*. We'd have them all nicely corralled in one place." He tossed back the last of his drink and drew the list of names from his shirt pocket. "Now, then. On to James Charles," he said, consulting the list Graham had given us that morning.

"The owner of This Green Isle Nursery. Maybe he knows something about all this sneaking about at the Hall."

"It'd be nice, but don't hold your breath."

# Nine

Late afternoon painted the western horizon in egg-yolk yellow, ochre and gold, a prelude to sunset in several hours. A cluster of clouds, hunchbacked and tinted with sunlight, trailed off to the east. Behind them, the sky stretched taut and royal blue, with no other feature to mar its smoothness. No bird flew across its expanse; no jet trail smudged its pristine hue. It looked like something a watercolorist would create of an idyllic countryside scene, except somewhere beneath our sun and clouds a murderer lurked.

James Charles didn't look like a murderer, but there was no generic look. And we'd be rushing our fences to assume he was, this early in the investigation. I merely state this because sometimes the nicest days are turned upside down.

Although not a weekday, James was at the nursery. We'd tried his home, asked at the pub, and were steered to This Green Isle. The place was busy with people finalizing their plant purchases. We parked at the end of a long row of cars and snaked through the maze of container plants, mounds of mulch and fertilizer, stacks of decorative plant pots, and displays of garden ornaments. The packed chert paths were damp from the earlier plant waterings, and our shoes left squishy impressions where we walked. The moisture contributed to the already humid air, and the sun drew it from the earth and plants like a greedy, parch-throated man. I drew in deep breaths, reveling in the scents of wet soil, roses, mulch and steamy air. Swifts circled, reeled and dove high above our heads, perhaps feasting on insects drawn to the acres of plants. I watched the birds, then lost sight of them as we walked into the low roofed garden center.

We sat in James' office, a cozy clutter of computer, fax machine, phone, plant catalogues, sample merchandise and tea items. He seemed an antithesis of the interior: neatly dressed and groomed, his silk handkerchief tucked precisely into his shirt pocket, the lenses of his glasses spotless. I wondered how he could work in such a muddled environment, but then remembered that my brother hadn't the neatest studio. And he was a concert pianist. Or had been, I mentally corrected myself, until last month when he was convicted of smuggling and landed in prison.

I shook off my uneasy feeling and asked James about trailing Alastair or Simon at the Hall.

He looked at me as if I'd called a rose a weed, realized his reaction and recovered his dignity with a faked cough. Leaning back in his high-backed desk chair, he denied he'd done any such thing.

"Someone at the Hall saw you talking to Simon several times last week."

"He's head gardener of the Haddon Hall estate. I own a nursery. What better reason is there to work together? He consulted me about a new garden they were considering putting in. It was nothing mysterious." He said it as though he were ordering plants.

"We ask because we're conducting an inquiry into Alastair's death. All details need to be checked. I'm sure you understand."

James nodded, not unlike a judge acknowledging counsel's remarks. "Simon's talking to the three nurseries who are being considered. I make no secret that I'm keen to get the contract. Putting in the Garden of the Senses will increase my and my company's prestige in the community. A landscaping project of the size Haddon Hall is considering is probably most nursery owners' dream."

"You just mentioned a Garden of the Senses. I've never heard of that."

"It's laid out in sections, one each for four of the senses: sight, hearing, touch, and smell. For the section that focuses on hearing, for example, I'd employ wind chimes, a waterfall, reeds that would rustle in the breeze…things like that. Smell, of course, would feature plants that are not only very fragrant, like honeysuckle and evening primrose, but also plants that release an aroma when crushed. I always thought it a pity that sightless people are denied the joy of experiencing a garden. With this garden that deals with the senses, everyone will get something out of it, whatever their handicap."

"So, all your wandering about, with Simon or on your own—"

"Purely professional. Why? I could understand the interest in my roaming about, as you put it, but Alastair wasn't killed at the Hall."

"Did you get on with Alastair?"

"Certainly. Very few people didn't, I expect. I'm still coming to grips that Alastair's dead. Things like that don't happen to people you know, people you see most every day. A heart attack or stroke, even a car accident, are more common and somewhat easier to accept. While still tragic, don't deal us the blow that murder does. It's unthinkable that someone would carry through such a scheme. The person must be mad."

"How long have you been with the dance group, Mr. Charles?"

James visibly relaxed, perhaps preferring to talk of himself or glad the spotlight had shifted. "Ten years, I'd guess. I've not kept count."

"You like it, I assume."

"Yes. I need the physical activity after a day behind the desk. Although a lot of days I probably do more walking with clients, looking at project sites, than I think. Still, it's great fun and it's made us all friends."

"You weren't friendly with Alastair before he joined the troupe? He was your neighbor, lived next door but one."

"Of course I knew him, miss. But when you share a hobby as intense and personal as dancing, you become closer. Like teammates. You also tend to share more of your life, tell things to them. You know, as you do to your barber."

"Was there anything Alastair told you that seems pertinent in light of his death?"

"You mean, like a death threat?"

"If you know of one, certainly. But maybe something that concerned or bothered him, something he might've been working on, either through his job or some hobby, that seems more important now."

James leaned back in his swivel chair. The chair squeaked as he rocked slowly, his focus on something outside, for he stared through the window as though mesmerized. Mark looked at me, tapped his watch, and I nodded. I was about to repeat my statement when James spoke.

"He didn't bare his soul to me, nor reveal anything secreted in his sock drawer, and we weren't drinking buddies. We had no habit of talking over problems or sharing aspirations. About the only thing I know he was working on lately was something to do with his ancestry, but I don't know what it entailed. He didn't do much else but that, dance and work."

"Have you a hobby, Mr. Charles?"

"Me?" He blinked, then flashed a smile. "I collect movie memorabilia."

"Like, original posters, props and costumes?"

"Yes. Sometimes the competition for an item is incredibly fierce. The bidding can drive it way over its expected selling price. But having a jacket that Clark Gable wore in *Gone With the Wind*, or a prompt book, or anything else associated with a film gives you a kick unlike anything else."

I thought it also gave him a bit of an ego boost, too. Prestige seemed to be important to him.

"Sounds like an interesting hobby," Mark said. "Requires a bit of research, if nothing else."

"I do spend a lot of time on the Internet and at the library, yes. But I enjoy it. That's why the dance group is so important to me: I get off my backside and move about." He brought the chair seat forward and leaned over his desk. "Jack Darkgate's involved with ham radio. Now *that* is incredibly interesting, I think."

"Certainly has the opportunity to make a lot of friends via the air waves."

"He told me once how many QSL cards he has, but I've forgot. Some astronomical number. I believe he has some of them displayed on the walls of his radio shack. The more interesting QSLs."

"QSL cards?"

"Like fancy postal cards. Amateur radio operators mail them to each other to confirm their contact. Collecting those cards is a hobby in itself. A lot of hams in America are anxious to talk to someone in all fifty states. There's some type of award they get for that. Worked All States, or something. Jack wanted me to talk to a particular mate of his on the air one night but I preferred just to listen to their conversation. As I said, it's interesting."

"Although Alastair was killed yesterday," I said, "we realize it might have been a mistake. Simon usually opened that electrical box, we understand."

"Yes, poor old trout."

"I'll ask you the same questions about Simon: had he any enemy or was he working on something that might've lead to his death?"

"Motives are sometimes hard to see, aren't they? And that's what's wanted here with Simon. I heard about his dust-up with Robert Connoly and Mary Johnson over the dates for Alastair's holiday. But I can't for one second believe that had any bearing on Simon's death. People don't kill people over disputed holiday dates."

"Nothing else comes to mind regarding Simon, then."

"'Fraid not. Just a hard working chap, strapped for cash as so many of us are in this damned economy, and struggling to make ends meet. I doubt if he was going to be killed for his inheritance. Anything else?"

Mark glanced at me and, receiving no response other than a tilt of my head toward the office door, stood up and thanked James for his time. "If you think of something later that might help us, we'd appreciate hearing from you. We're working out of the village hall."

"I'd heard something about that," James said, rising. "I'll be certain to look you up."

He was making a phone call almost before we'd closed his office door.

~

We joined the rest of the CID team in the village hall later that afternoon. Graham liked to bring everyone up to speed, find out what we'd learned, and get us all thinking on the same wavelength.

"So, what do you think?" Graham asked when he'd written the bulleted items on the whiteboard. "Do we still have a suspicious death or is it taking off in another direction?" He stepped back from the board and glanced at it again before turning to us.

I said, "Even though most everyone seems fairly consistent on what a smashing fellow Alastair was, I think we're uncovering motives that point to murder." I felt my face flush and I hoped I hadn't set myself up for ridicule if Graham had evidence that definitely indicated accidental death.

He stood in front of the board, rolling the dry erase marker between his palms, and asked why I thought it could be murder.

I related what Mark and I had learned from Simon, Mary, Brian, Johnny and Declan. "There's enough anger among these folks for any of them to have killed Alastair. It's too coincidental that they all had recent run-ins with him for someone not to have acted."

"So you're focusing on Alastair as the intended victim instead of Simon, then." A slight smile played at the corners of Graham's mouth.

"Maybe we'll find out differently tomorrow from the others we talk to, sir. Someone had to have a tiff with Simon."

"You don't believe Simon was the intended victim," Graham said, testing my reasoning. "Remember, Alastair was a last minute substitute."

"Yes, sir. I'm just trying to think through all the ill feelings those people have for Alastair."

Mark eased forward in his chair and said, "I'd suspect Simon of setting this up, but *Alastair* stumbled and bumped into *Simon*, thereby taking Simon's place at the light box."

Graham nodded. "That false step cost Alastair his life."

"The only way it would've been an intentional trip is because Alastair wanted to grab the spotlight. Who told us about the media blokes being there?" Mark turned in his chair and looked around the room, as if one of the officers present would raise his hand.

"That's one reason Simon was so upset about the whole affair," Graham reminded us. "He wanted his photo and name in the newspaper, wanted it because he hoped it would boost his career. But he was knocked out of that, no pun intended, when Alastair bumped into him and caused him to fall and hurt his ankle. I'd suspect a bit of stage acting but Simon's ankle is swollen."

I said that we'd seen the ankle this morning and the injury looked to be genuine.

"So," Graham went on, guiding us through the case considerations, "if we consider Simon as the victim, however foiled that little plan went for the murderer, what does that get us? Anyone especially anxious to show Simon the door to the next world?"

"We learned that Declan Morris harbored a great deal of anger and possibly hatred for Simon." I explained about Jessica leaving Declan.

"And this hatred manifested itself in the light box."

"Only trouble with that is that Simon didn't know he'd be sitting out the dance. He'd planned on star billing in the newspaper."

I exhaled and sank back in my chair. "I'd like Brian as prime suspect, since he wandered in late and alone to the village, but he couldn't have got here fast enough to set up the wires. And people were already here. He would've been seen."

Mark frowned, his voice startlingly loud next to me. "Seems like nearly everyone we've spoken to is concerned with status, prestige and money. Johnny Smith wants to host a television show;

Brian Fireman wants to become head gardener; James Charles wants a jaw-dropping garden contract. Alastair may or may not have been working overtime."

Graham sat down on the table in front of us. "Not too uncommon. What's your point, Salt?"

"We saw Connoly's house, the interior. He has some nice things. Antiques, collections. How's he afford that on a restaurant manager's salary?"

Graham shrugged. "Inheritance?"

"Mary Johnson, who's obviously set her cap for Connoly, is concerned about her family connections and wants Simon to unearth someone so worthy that she can approach Connoly with the idea of marriage. The others are straightforward enough, Johnny wanting to snag a television show. But we know Alastair was keen on delving into genealogy."

Graham's eyebrow rose. "What are you getting at?"

"We're forgetting that little poem or whatever it is that the lads found at Alastair's house."

I nodded. "It read like something out of Shakespeare."

"What if it came down through Alastair's and Simon's family?" Mark began speaking more quickly, but he held his voice low. "What if Alastair and Simon were searching for something?"

Graham put the marker down beside him. "Like what?"

"Look." Mark held up his left hand and ticked off the items on his fingers as he spoke. "Even though Simon denied it at first, we learned that both cousins were delving into genealogy. Mary confirmed Simon's interest in the subject when she told us she would ask Simon to help her with her own research."

"So you told us."

"That bit of poetry found at Alastair's house sounds ancient, like 1700s or something. That ties in with ancestral research, if that's what Alastair and Simon were doing. Why else would he have it?"

"Could that be one of those love poems that Declan send his girl friend?"

Margo said the poem on Alastair's desk didn't sound at all like a love poem. "Anyway, why would Alastair have it if it was sent to Jessica?"

"Good point, Miss Lynch." Graham leaned forward, his forearms on his thighs. "What about Alastair's writing prowess? Do we know if he could write?"

"Sir?"

"I'm just thinking back to Cyrano deBergerac. He wrote love letters for his friend. Maybe Simon was trying to counter Declan's love poems with one of his own, but Simon didn't have the knack, so he asks Alastair to write one for him."

I frowned and Graham asked me what was the matter. "I'd believe it, sir, if Alastair's poem was sugary, but that thing is so cryptic. I don't think Jessica and Simon were together long enough to warrant such an obscure message. Anyway, a man wouldn't write his love like that these days, would he? Why not just say 'I love you forever' and put it with a dozen roses? I think that's a non starter, if you'll forgive me."

"Don't apologize for thinking, Taylor."

Mark said he still thought Alastair's poem was connected to the genealogy they did.

"Seems more plausible in the light of what Miss Lynch said. Go on, Salt."

"Simon admitted he's strapped for cash. What if this poetry thing is referring to a treasure and he's trying to find it?"

Graham leaned back, obviously startled. "You've nothing to base that on, Salt, have you? Nothing concrete. You're just giving voice to a scenario you've invented to explain a few things. What treasure? Who hid it? Why would Alastair and Simon have information about it, if it does exist? They're not related to royalty. If they were, they'd make the most of that tie." Graham picked up the marker. "But why don't you and Taylor do a bit of research on that? You might turn up something interesting. Anything else? No?" He got up and walked up to the front row. "I think we're looking at a murder. Simcock agrees and has given authorization to set up an incident room here. The lads will be moving in the computers and equipment tonight. I'll see you at the usual time in the morning."

From the village hall Mark drove straight to The Stout Keg, as if sensing my mind and emotional mood. The small, cozy atmosphere of the pub hugged me as we entered, and Mark chose a table in the corner. Away from noise and nosy ears, was what he said. But I knew the choice of table also was from habit: not many police officers willingly abandoned the protection and vantage point of a corner table. You could see everyone entering and didn't have to worry about your back.

We'd finished our meal and now talked over our drinks. The earlier diners had left, leaving a few dozen people eating or playing darts or drinking at the bar. Conversations were subdued, though an occasional groan or yell erupted from the telly watchers. No one would bother about eavesdropping on a sedate-looking couple.

He pushed the handle of his beer mug so that the glass rotated slowly in a circle. It left sodden rings on the beer mat. "You heard Graham," he said without any preamble. "I guess we better work on that puzzle tonight."

"I don't think he meant right away, Mark. Haven't you ever heard of sleep?"

"You know you're dying to solve that thing. You love mysteries."

"Not when I can't find a murderer."

"This could lead us to the murderer," Mark said, watching my expression. "You're always talking about getting points with Graham. This'll do it if we decipher the poem's meaning. Come on. What about it?"

I must've looked as though I were weakening in my resolve for he said quickly, "Fine." He swallowed the last of his beer and stood up. The determination in his eye squashed any rebuttal I considered. Handing me my shoulder bag, he said, "Your room or mine?"

Getting to my feet, I said, "Doesn't much matter. You're ruining my reputation whichever room we go to."

"Super." He rubbed his hands together, then had the grace to look embarrassed. "I didn't mean I don't care about your," he swallowed and grimaced, "I mean, if you're worried—"

I grabbed my bag and looped my arm through his. "We may as well go down in flames together."

"And me without my asbestos suit on."

"To the barricades, then, and damn the torpedoes!"

He tightened his grip around my arm and we strode toward the staircase that led up to the bedrooms.

Of course, it was then that we met Margo coming downstairs. She smiled at Mark and winked at me. "Working together?"

"As a matter of fact," Mark said, "we are."

"This sounds awfully mysterious."

I stepped closer to her. "Don't let him fool you, Margo. We're going to work a bit on Alastair's poem."

"Oh, right. Graham told you two to tackle it." Her eyes lit up. "I'm not doing anything right now, Bren. Do you want me to help you?"

Taking a quick breath, I said, "Ordinarily, we'd welcome your help, Margo. But we don't know what we're doing, much less able to give you something to sink your teeth into. I hope you understand."

"Sure. Speaking of teeth...remember Alastair's dog?"

"The spaniel?"

"I'm having second thoughts about adopting it."

"Why?" I said. "Is he vicious? Did he bite you?"

"Not me, but he certainly likes to gnaw. I'm leery about leaving him when I'm away from home. Who knows what my shoes and table legs and magazines will look like when I'm not there?"

"Doesn't surprise me, Margo. Many dog breeds, mainly

hunters, such as golden and Labrador retrievers, spaniels, and hounds are all genetically wired that way. They've been bred as gun dogs, and since they use their mouth to retrieve prey and things, they have a predisposition to chew and mouth things. It's only natural. You can't fault the dog for it."

"I'm glad I know that now, before I take him on. I don't think Alastair did, poor man. The dog must've had a field day chewing his way through the man's shoes and leather chair. Still, I guess a dog trainer can overcome that habit."

"Usually anything can be overcome with enough money."

Margo sighed, as though mentally calculating her bank account, household items and clothing against the puppy.

"You don't have to decide right now, do you?" I asked. "Has Simon made any noises about wanting the dog?"

"If he has, I don't know about it."

"Well, Graham will know. We're not about to leave the village, so you've got time to think about it. Here's your chance to buy stock in a rawhide bone manufacturing company." I tried to make it sound light hearted, but Margo frowned.

"If I hadn't seen the puppy, I wouldn't be in such a dilemma. He's so cute, Bren. Long ears, curly hair, brown eyes."

"Sounds like a former boyfriend of mine. Just joking." I squeezed her arm. "You'll figure it out."

"Speaking of which," Mark said, "we've got our little project to figure out. Night, Margo."

She wished us luck, clumped down the stairs and walked into the bar.

"Well," I said as we walked up to the landing, "my reputation can't be tarnished more than it is now. Of all the rotten timing."

"Margo won't say anything. Besides, she's on my side."

I looked at him, nervous that the two of them were planning something. "What's that mean?"

"Nothing. Just a figure of speech, Bren."

"I bet. Well, we might as well camp out in my room." I fished in my bag for my key. "The poetry is out and on the nightstand."

"Good. I don't know where my copy is."

We dropped arms and walked single file down the hall. It held the odors of lemon-scented furniture polish, tobacco smoke and perfume. It also held wisps of conversations and fragments of music that drifted up from downstairs. In keeping with the ground floor, the upper floor must have felt its age as well as shown it. The floor sagged and sloped slightly in spots, groaning and protesting as we tread on the wooden boards. Oriental style carpets, thin as a criminal's lie, did little to muffle the sound of our footsteps. Anyone listening could track our route. Wainscoting divided the walls into white plaster and strips of oak paneling. Small watercolor paintings punctuated the whiteness at regular intervals. Overhead light fixtures in keeping with the medieval style had been added some time during the 20th century but didn't intrude upon the atmosphere of the past. Mobile phones, iPods, MP3s, portable DVD players, and televisions did that.

I unlocked my room door and tossed my shoulder bag onto the bed as Mark grabbed the poetry and sat down in the chair by the window. I filled the electric kettle with water, turned it on, and asked if he wanted tea or coffee.

"What?" He stared at the paper.

"Tea or coffee? I've put the kettle on."

"Why doesn't whoever wrote this use the word 'he'? It sounds like a Jacobean cockney piece. Were cockneys around in the 1700s?"

Deciding for him, I dropped a tea bag into Mark's cup and went over to him. "What are you talking about?"

"See?" He tapped on the page and I read it over his shoulder.

"'E is more worthy than I. 'E on the Rise though I on the Hill. 'E with his Ring and I with none. One step for Love? Aye, count it ten more. From depth to height and so to Heaven's Vault and the Eyes of the Stars. My love 'E covets like a Plume worn but ceded by six and one.'" I shook my head and walked back to the kettle. Pouring boiling water into our cups, I said, "Makes as much sense to me now as it did last night. But I agree with your

Cockney assessment. Does rather sound like some dialect." I brought over our cups and handed him his before I sat down on the window seat. "Funny thing, too, Mark…I see what you mean about it sounding like some sort of treasure hunt. Last night I was caught up on the language and putting it into a historical slot. But reading it again…I think you're right."

He looked up from the page and grinned at me. His gray eyes crackled with thanks and excitement. "I'd like to know what this E and I business is. At first I thought it was something connected to E starting off three sentences, but the capital E comes three words in the seventh sentence, so I give up that idea." He took a sip of tea without taking his eyes from the paper. "You know more about history than I do. Does this suggest anything to you?"

"I don't know whether to focus on solving the E and I thing or the directions. It's got to be directions, Mark. 'One step… count ten more.' Do you think that depth to height is a direction, like going from a dungeon to a rampart, or the ground floor to a second storey? Or just some flowery language describing the poet's lost love?"

"All that about heaven's vault and the eyes of the stars sound flowery enough, but what's that plume thing? What bird has plumes? You're a bird watcher."

"Off hand I'd say an ostrich. Those plumes were highly prized for centuries. There are probably portraits of Queen Elizabeth I wearing plumes in her hair. Victorian ladies did on their hats, I believe."

"Well, this is no Victorian writing. You're closer with Good Queen Bess."

I took a sip of tea and read the piece again. It may have been clues to a secreted treasure, but it also sounded like a love poem, though not rhyming. And not current enough to be connected to Jessica and Declan. Still, it seemed ardent enough to be written to a lady. Did the unidentified woman, if it were a declaration of love, hold the solution to the puzzle? But that, in my opinion, would be nearly impossible. We didn't know who'd written it.

And if it were Alastair, as some type of exercise or piece for the Tommy to say, it was even less of a solution: Alastair had no girl friend or wife. There'd be no Shakespearean Dark Lady to contemplate. When I'd finished re-reading it, I said, "Maybe we can unravel it if we identify what's meant by the hill and rise."

"That 'E on the Rise though I on the Hill phrase." Mark angled the paper toward me, his tea forgotten. "It's got to be a place if we go by the assumption that the thing's directions for a treasure hunt."

"But isn't a rise the same thing as a hill? Or are we dealing with flowery language again?"

"You're the language expert."

I was tired of being the expert. "We're in big trouble, then. But I think a rise really means a slope or incline. Like the higher bank extending up from a river."

"A rise is just elevated, sloping ground from a flat meadow, for instance."

"That's what I always thought the word meant."

"So, the hill is higher than a rise."

"It'd seem so. The I of the poetry appears to be lamenting his status, perhaps. I says 'though.' Substituting another word, that sentence could mean E is on an elevation despite the fact that I is on a hill."

"I being elevated or higher up. Maybe exalted?"

"Like nobility?"

Mark shrugged and said he had no idea. "Just trying out different meanings for the word."

"Does that get us any closer to a flash of inspiration?"

Mark handed me the paper and downed half of his tea. I doubt if he even tasted it, which was probably a good thing, for it was probably lukewarm by now. "Not unless we walk around the entire country looking for rises and hills connected or not with nobility. Got any biscuits or sweets to go with this?" He got up and looked through the assorted packets on the tea tray. He grabbed a small package of cello-wrapped chocolate biscuits.

Opening it, he said, "It'd be nice if it was something from Good Queen Bess." He tossed the wrapper into the wastepaper basket, took a bite of the biscuit, and reclaimed his chair. "You know, her nicknames for her favorites. Like she called Christopher Hatton 'Lids' and Robert Dudley 'Eyes.'"

I nodded, remembering Elizabeth's long line of suitors. "And Francis, Duke of Anjou, was her 'frog.' Somehow, E and I don't have the same grandeur as Lord Burghley's 'Spirit.'" I read the piece again, this time more slowly. "Mark, should we be concerned that this poetry isn't completely in Elizabethan dialect? It seems rather modern in some aspects."

"It was probably translated somewhere along the line. You know how authors do for books: they change the spelling so modern readers can understand it."

"I suppose so. The ring that's mentioned could be a ring of some office or a wedding ring."

"Did they have rings of office back then?"

I shrugged, putting down the paper. "I have no idea."

"Badges and chains of office, I've seen. Maybe we can get Margo to do some research on the ring."

"Margo's busy on the case with another line of inquiry. As are the others in our team. Anyway, Graham told us to work on this." I tilted my head back and looked at the ceiling. "God, this seems impossible."

"Graham wouldn't have asked us to work on it if he thought we couldn't crack it," Mark reminded me. "Or thought it was a waste of time."

"I just hope solving this puzzle gets us closer to identifying Alastair's killer."

Mark leaned forward and gazed at me intently. "Look, Bren. This obviously means something. Forget Graham's faith in us for a moment. Alastair thought enough of it to have it sitting on his desk. It smacks of ancestry, which is what interested him and Mary and Simon. It's got to have some bearing on the case."

My mobile phone rang at that moment, delaying my reply.

Glancing at the caller ID display, I said, "It's Adam" and flipped open the phone.

"You busy?" His voice came across like a glass of wine and a cozy fire on a winter's day.

"Just finishing up my day. Perfect timing."

"Glad to hear it. What are you working on?"

"A case of murder by electrocution."

"Hardly the preface I would've chosen to tell you how much I love you."

"Any time is good for that." I felt my cheeks grow hot. Glancing at Mark, I lowered my voice and brought the phone closer to my lips. I turned slightly, trying to get a bit of privacy without insulting Mark. "Right. Go on."

Mark stood up, muttered that he could take a hint, and left the room. The door remained slightly ajar, I noticed. He'd be back.

He was. Several minutes later. Adam and I were talking about the pros and cons of various honeymoon destinations when Mark opened the door and looked at me. His raised eyebrows questioned his timing. I waved him into the room and indicated his chair. "I'm sorry to cut this short, Adam," I said, raising my voice slightly, "but it's getting late and we've got a full day tomorrow."

Adam apologized for keeping me up. "Catch those bad guys tomorrow." He rang off, leaving my blood tingling and my mind on other things than an ancient bit of poetry.

Mark hesitated by his chair and looked at me as I closed my mobile. "I didn't mean to break up the conversation."

"You didn't. We were just about finished." I patted the seat cushion of his chair and he sat down. "Come up with any revelation while you were listening outside my door?"

"Yeah, but not about the case." He finished the last of his tea, which must've been stone cold. "I looked up some of the people we talked about. On my smartphone."

"Who? Like Johnny Smith and Simon Roe?"

"No. Elizabeth I's favorites."

"Yes? Why?"

"I just got to thinking about their nicknames and this E and I business in this poetry scrap. The more I thought of it, the more it sounded like some kind of abbreviation or code or nickname."

"Find out anything?"

"Yes, but I don't know if it helps or not."

"We're gathering facts, Mark. Like any good investigation. We assemble all our data and then go through it all to see if anything leads us to a solution. What've you got?"

"I found out that Hatton signed his personal letters to Elizabeth with two small triangles."

"Instead of his signature, you mean?"

"Odd, isn't it, when you think of people back then as being so staid and courtly. The triangles symbolized eyelids."

"Hatton's nickname, Lids," I said, feeling a rush of excitement.

"That's not all. Sometimes Hatton resorted to a drawing of a hat on top of which he'd write the letter X." He waited, watching me, to see if I made the mental leap.

"His surname," I said quietly as the realization hit me. "A pun on his last name. Hat-Ten."

Mark smiled and kissed the back of my hand. "Worthy of a place in Francis Walsingham's clutch of spies. Good going."

"So, what's this get us, knowing about Christopher Hatton's little play on words and coded signature?"

"Just that it obviously was done in Elizabeth's time. So why wouldn't it be done whenever this poetry thing was written? E and I have to stand for something, no matter when the author penned the piece. It's important enough to have survived all these centuries and to have been noted in the first place." He picked up my teacup, stacked it with his, and took them to the tea tray. He remained by the table, his eyes dark in the lamplight, and leaned against the wall. "I think we're close to figuring this out, Brenna. Alastair's death may have been an accident, but I don't think it was an accident that he had this paper in his possession."

## Ten

"Mary said she was about to ask Simon to help her with family research," I said, picking up Mark's thought. "What if she asked *Alastair* first? What if he found out something?"

"Connected to Mary's family? Could have done, I suppose."

"That would explain him wandering about the Hall grounds."

"A discovery pertaining to his own family would also explain him wandering about the Hall grounds," Mark added. "Seems more likely, if he and Simon have this interest. Anyway, why wouldn't Mary have said she asked Alastair first, but he died before he could tell her anything, so she asked Simon? No crime in that."

"No," I said, reluctant to give up a promising lead. "No crime. So, we're practically back where we started."

"We've made some progress. It's not as dismal as you think." I mustn't have looked very hopeful, for he came over to me and hugged me. "It'll all be better in the morning. Thanks for the nightcap."

"I feel more in need of a dunce cap, if truth be known. That poetry thing gets to you, doesn't it?"

"It'll be a feather in whatever cap you wear if you solve it. Night."

He left so silently I barely heard the door close.

The room took on the emptiness so often felt at the end of a pleasant evening or at the departure of a loved person. I sat on the window seat, the room lightless, and looked outside. A bank of clouds masked the moon, throwing the landscape into a vague, two-dimensional black shape. Dots of light accented the blackness at irregular intervals, but for the most part, the village lay dark, silent and sleeping. I should have been sleeping, for tomorrow promised to be as long and energetic as today, but the historical puzzle's intrigue held me. I couldn't shut down my brain.

Taking a clue from Mark, I grabbed my mobile. I found what I was looking for immediately and spent the next hour reading and jotting down notes. When I couldn't think anymore, I shut off my phone, made another cuppa, and sipped it slowly as I watched the moon shake off the clouds and spill its silvery light over the world.

~

Late Monday morning the CID Team gathered in the incident room, which had indeed been put up overnight, to discuss the case and bring everyone up to speed. Nodding to Margo, who signaled to me to join her in the second row, and mumbling that I'd talk to her later, I grabbed a chair next to Mark.

Graham was talking on the phone, and from the look of his frown and the stiff, forward angle of his body as he looked at the computer screen I figured we had a few minutes before he started the meeting. I turned and grabbed Mark's upper arm, shortening the distance between us.

His head jerked back slightly and his right eyebrow cocked. "What? You ill?"

Which, considering my action and shallow breathing, wasn't such an outlandish question. I shook my head and practically whispered in his ear. "I'm fine. Just excited."

"Still feel the thrill of the daily briefing, then." His voice was low and steady but the joke shone in his eye.

"After you left last night I did a bit more research on Sir Christopher Hatton."

"You must've discovered something that pertains to our historical puzzle, from the way you're acting. What is it?"

"You'll hear in a minute. Graham'll want to hear, too. Shared

information, Mark," I said when he groaned. "A good team shares
its findings, remember?"

Reluctantly I relinquished Mark's arm and faced the whiteboard. Graham laid his notes on the table, picked up the dry
marker, and turned toward us. He stood there, not speaking, not
moving except for the rising and fall of his chest as he breathed
and the nearly imperceptible throbbing of his neck muscle. His
jaw seemed cast in concrete, so firm and angular it looked, and
his green eyes appeared black, with crackles of fire sizzling in
their depths. My hand sought Mark's, for fear suddenly gripped
me. I'd never seen Graham like this.

He remained like that long enough to cause multiple, si-
multaneous ripples of murmured speculation to dart through
the room. I wondered if Mark should get up and go to him, see
if Graham were all right. But that would embarrass him. And
Graham wouldn't thank us for the energetic rumors created by
our do-good effort. He'd endured enough gossip his first year in
the job, speculation of why he left the clergy to become a police
officer a tantalizing topic of conjecture.

"Is this going to happen every time we meet?" Mark whispered, glancing at me.

"I told you yesterday when we saw him and Scott together
that something was wrong. Now do you believe me?"

"Yeah. I wonder if it's a health issue."

"Can't be for Scott. He's back to work." The alternative possibility shouted in my mind. I could barely speak. "You don't think
something's wrong with Graham, do you?"

"No, I don't. If it were anything like that, anything serious,
Graham wouldn't be working. Someone else would take charge.
So put that idea out of your mind."

As if hearing me, Graham picked up a sheet of paper and
convened the briefing.

"Mr. Graham, sir," I said, raising my hand to get his attention.

"Miss Taylor. You seem uncharacteristically anxious to relay
something this morning. I assume it's for our general knowledge."

"Yes, sir." I shared the information Mark and I had found out last night before adding, "Sir Christopher Hatton was a particular favorite of Queen Elizabeth I. He had a history of crying and sulking away from court when he was not overtly in Elizabeth's close circle at the moment. Their relationship consisted of a long sequence of repartees, spats and reunions. Evidently, this cycle occurred so frequently that Hatton bestowed gifts on Elizabeth, a sort of bribe, to ease him back into her welcome and approval. One such gift was a jewel shaped like a true lover's knot."

"Fascinating. I assume this is leading somewhere pertinent to our case?"

"I believe so, yes. Gifts had been the norm in those days, they could appease Elizabeth's wrath if the gift was unique or costly enough. Maybe Hatton's whole life at court could be marked through the procession of presents from him to her. So, perhaps, could the others close to her." I hesitated, unsure if I should relate my speculation.

"These are facts, as far as we know from history," Graham said.

"Yes, sir. But I think it's given me part of the puzzle's solution."

"Don't keep us in suspense, Taylor."

I leaned against the chair back, the images and words whirling in my mind. Forcing a strength into my voice that I didn't feel, I said, "To Hatton, it was all about himself: his love for Elizabeth, his rising star in court, his hope of marriage to the monarch. It boiled down to I. His whole life was focused on his success, his happiness. I wonder if Hatton could he be the I of that poetry. And, if so, if Elizabeth could be the E."

You would've thought I'd uncovered a lifetime filled with espionage, double identities and treason from the team's reactions. Murmurs and applause filled the room and Graham said, "Could be what we're after, Taylor. Your E and I inference makes sense. Keep at it."

I murmured my thanks and grinned.

"Now, I'd like you, Miss Lynch, to relate what you found out about the previous group who used the light box in the park."

Margo uncrossed her leg and sat up straighter, as though Graham would reprimand her for sitting at ease. She glanced at her notes before she took a deep breath. "It was signed out to the Voyles family. They were having a family reunion last weekend. William Voyles made the arrangements, got the key on Friday morning from the peg in the church and returned it personally to the vicar Sunday afternoon. They used the electricity on Friday night, nearly all day Saturday, and on Sunday morning. They were a large group, around one hundred, so they needed the microphone."

"Large group, all right. Sounds more like a small army," Mark muttered. "Must've swamped the village."

"Everything must've been copacetic because no one in the Voyles group was injured when they unlocked the electricity box."

Mark turned slightly to address Margo. "Not necessarily. Whoever fixed up those exposed wires had to have opened the box to do that. And locked the box again."

"But if it'd been tampered with in the ensuing week, the unsuspecting party most likely would've suffered Alastair's fate," Margo countered. "Not knowing about the wires, the person would've touched them, as Alastair did. Can't help but do. They were exposed so it was impossible not to come into contact with them."

Mark conceded this could be possible.

"So it's still a very strong probability that when Voyles closed up this past Sunday the wires were all right. Someone had to have tampered with them in the ensuing week."

Graham acknowledged it might not have been so hard to do, since the whole village appears to know where the key is kept. "Anyone in the Voyles family know Alastair or Simon?"

"The Voyles are Welsh. Not that that means anything. They come from Pembrokeshire originally but now as many of them live in England as in Wales."

"Why'd they have their family gathering here and not in Wales?"

"The patriarch lives here. Being ninety-seven years old and rather frail, the family comes to him."

"A lot of people bee lining it to Nether Haddon."

"Yes, sir. No one in the Voyles family was hurt by the wires, so it was fixed up after they left." She moved her head, perhaps to see Graham's expression. Even if Margo didn't glance at me, I knew what ran through her mind. Ramifications. Months ago she and I had been given a dressing down by Graham when I'd left my police notebook somewhere. Unpleasant wasn't the exact word that I'd use to describe the incident. Explosion fits. So does Anger. As well as chastisement. I looked at Graham, too, trying to read his thoughts. His face was impassive, and in this instance that was good. Neither of us wanted to encounter that volcanic moment again.

Margo added, somewhat softly, that she hadn't assumed Graham would've wanted her to see if all one hundred people knew the cousins. Or, as she put it, use precious police time on a project that offered no obvious reason to stretch resources in an obscure direction. I admired her ability to form an excuse in officialese.

Graham, lucky to say, appeared satisfied for the moment. "It's early days, yet. If we find the investigation going in that direction, I'm certain Miss Lynch will enthusiastically throw herself into the fray. Anything else you'd like to share with your colleagues?"

"I talked to the publican of The Stout Keg."

"Had Jonah anything pertinent to add?"

"I believe so. Since most of the dance troupe members reside in this village, he knows them fairly well."

One of the constables in the back of the room made some remark about dancing being a thirsty hobby and got some guffaws for his effort.

"*Anyway*," Margo said, raising her voice slightly, "he certainly knows Simon. He's no idea if Simon is an alcoholic, but he said that Simon's drinking is notorious in the village. Probably elsewhere in the vicinity too. Simon likes his drink and likes them frequent and unceasing."

I glanced at Mark. Had the bottle we'd seen on Simon's table Saturday morning been whiskey? I couldn't remember.

"Jonah, the publican, served Simon as long as he behaved himself, but never served him when he was drunk. This led to some strained relations between Jonah and members of the dance troupe."

Graham asked why.

"Because Jonah doesn't want a reputation that drunks will be harbored at his pub. He doesn't want to risk anyone's life by allowing them to get back on the road. Jonah's very diligent about watching his customers to see if anyone's getting intoxicated."

"And Simon gets that way," Graham suggested.

"Quite frequently, to hear Jonah talk. If Simon doesn't dig up his drinks at Jonah's place, he'll have them elsewhere."

"Bravo to Jonah Ellwood."

"Simon's one of those funny drunkards. Loves all the world, becomes your best friend. Everyone who's been with him when he's in this state will tell you that he'll do most anything for you but he won't loan money."

"This happens often enough that folks know?"

"Yes, sir. Alastair, especially, tried nearly every time Simon was drunk to get money from Simon. Alastair wanted to buy a few rounds for the lads and Simon wouldn't lend him the money."

"I can't see Alastair being very happy about that. Why hadn't he money for this? Simon that strapped for cash?"

"That I don't know, sir. It could've been a case of Alastair merely trying to wheedle money out of someone whom he hoped wouldn't remember the next day, or Alastair might've been in financial difficulty. But he tried often enough to get Simon's money that it became expected that he'd try for a few quid."

"And Simon never gave in to his cousin's pleading?"

"Those whom I've talked to don't remember it ever happening. And this has been going on for over a year."

"Long time if the two of them frequent the pub every weekend."

"Yes, sir. It's a bit of a joke in the village, people wondering if Simon will ever be so drunk that he'll dig into his pocket and hand Alastair some money. But he never has."

"Even if you don't know Alastair's financial status, do you know if he had made big purchases recently? Had he outstanding bills, for example, or home repair or mortgage payments?"

"No one's said, but I'll check on that, sir."

"Getting back to the publican, did he have ongoing problems like this with any of the other dance troupe members?"

"No. Simon's name was the only one mentioned, which will help Jonah realize his dream faster, I think."

"What dream is that?"

"Jonah's a very goal-driven individual. He has several aspirations, which he's working hard to accomplish. Some are more pressing than others."

"For instance?"

"Jonah's in his mid-forties. Not all that old, but he's never been married and he's no children. He wants both. He also wants to increase his pub business."

"Surprise, surprise," Mark said. "Most people in business want to increase their profit."

"But Jonah counts on the dance troupe to bring in tourists who will patronize his pub. He's hoping that if enough tourists come he can open a second pub. Not necessarily in the village, but close by. So you see why he's in a bit of a tiff with Simon and Alastair and many of the other dancers. If Simon is habitually drunk in Jonah's pub, word eventually gets out that the place is rowdy and drunks may descend on it and spoil the atmosphere. Too many drunks, a potential for drunken brawls..." Margo shrugged, as though we should see the outcome.

Mark did. "Bye-bye tourists and their money."

"Precisely. It's a touchy subject with Jonah and some of the dancers. They're a top-notch troupe, having won the coveted

DERT award, as well as others. That gets around and is good for the entire area, drawing in folks who want to see them perform."

"As exemplified by this past Saturday."

"Yes. Tourists would do a lot of good for the area, so Jonah doesn't want to create a problem with Simon. Scaring away the tourists will hurt the village as well as destroy his dream."

"I wonder." Graham turned to the whiteboard and drew the now-familiar columns of Suspects and Motive on it. "I wonder if someone got so fed up with Simon's drunken bouts that he set about to end the problem permanently."

"Rigging up the light box to kill Simon, you mean."

"Who does that bring to mind, off hand?"

"Jonah Ellwood."

Graham added Jonah's name to the Suspect column on the whiteboard.

"I've a few others, sir." I reeled off the names of Mary Johnson, Brian Fireman and James Charles. "I'll probably add a few others to the list today, but those are the three right now."

"Why do they warrant our attention, Taylor?"

"Well, sir, Mary has a nice job but she's almost desperate to be someone of note so she can attract Robert Connoly."

"She wants to marry him?"

"Yes, sir."

"Why does she kill Alastair? Or Simon, if you're going with the idea that Simon should've opened the light box?"

"Simon could've discovered something in her family's past that he was going to use against her," and I explained that Mary might have asked Alastair or Simon for genealogy help. "Blackmail's an eternal crime for the victim. The usual way out is to kill the blackmailer."

Graham said it was a bit shaky right now, but he left it on the board. "And Brian Fireman and James Charles?"

"Brian is an under gardener who's yearning to have Simon's job. Killing off your rival isn't only for spurned lovers. Business people can be cutthroat competition."

"But Alastair got in the way and Simon's still around. Bad luck for Brian. Who else?"

"James Charles."

"What's his motive?"

I said that Alastair and Simon might have been looking for a family treasure. "We think James and Brian knew about it and were spying on Simon, following him about the estate in hope of seeing if he found the treasure. I know it sounds daft," I rushed on, not giving Graham time to scoff, "but this topic has come up several times during our investigation. James could've come upon Simon when he found the treasure, maybe saw where Simon stashed it. James was going to kill Simon so he could get the treasure."

"Why kill Simon if this is true? Why not just steal the treasure?"

"I don't know that yet."

"So Alastair's death was a tragic mistake and it should've been Simon."

"Yes, sir. I'd also like to add Declan Morris' name to the list."

"And your reason is…"

"Revenge for his girlfriend leaving him for Simon. I know Alastair was a last minute substitution," I said, "but I've been thinking about that. What if Alastair didn't stumble into Simon? What if Simon tripped Alastair? If the action was quick enough, people might not see. And if Simon fell and sprained his ankle, Alastair could substitute for Simon at the light box."

"Why not kill Alastair outright, then? Why the elaborate staging of the sprained ankle?"

"Because it would look like an accident, for one thing. We couldn't possibly suspect Simon of deliberately killing Alastair."

"And," Mark chimed in, "because Simon'd have witnesses that would give an alibi. I kill Alastair? I should've been the victim!"

"Simon might have hired Declan to kill Alastair," I said. "Probably to inherit from Alastair. Simon finally admitted that he dabbled in genealogy research, so what if he was competing with Alastair to solve the whereabouts of the treasure?"

"Did he?" Graham said.

"I don't know. He didn't admit anything to us about the poetry or even mention a treasure. But it's not so far fetched, sir. He's strapped for cash and Alastair's money would come in handy."

"Not to mention the cash from the sale of the treasure," Mark said. "If he found it."

"Well," Graham said, "that's all conjecture at the moment. Still, it bears keeping in mind." He jotted down the main points on the whiteboard. "What's the status on hobbies or careers that require electrical knowledge?"

Mark reiterated what we'd found out

"Thank you, Salt. Anyone have anything to add? No? Right. Everyone has his or her assignment..."

Which was his way of telling us to get on with our day.

Margo came up to me as the meeting broke up. "How are we going to pinpoint one person who can't account for every single minute last week? Is Graham kidding?"

Grabbing my shoulder as support, Mark leaned forward and past me, and practically whispered in her ear. "That's why you get paid the big bucks, Margo."

"I could say something unbecoming a lady, but I won't. Brenna, are you serious about this treasure thing?"

I told her some of the details of Mark's and my research. She lost her defensive look and stared at us. "That's why," I said, trying to ignore her open mouth, "I thought it a motive for either man's death. But proving it will be difficult."

"Unless one of them left a diary stating his daily progress."

"Big help. If you've no sane suggestion—"

Margo held up her hands. "You need more sleep. Or caffeine." She checked the time on her watch. "You two off to talk to more dance troupe members, then?"

"Only five more to go. But these will lead to other people, so don't think Mark and I have it easy."

"I've never thought that. You've come in contact with some awful people. King Roper comes to mind."

I shuddered, surprised the mere mention of his name could elicit such a response from me. And I doubted it had to do with Scott's hospitalization or my brother's involvement, however marginally or minimally, in Roper's gang. Or that my brother sat in prison at this very moment, fearful even behind cell bars of Roper's reprisals. Roper personified Evil, as far as I was concerned. I'd felt dirty just talking to him.

Margo and Oglethorpe left the village hall with the majority of the team. They stopped this side of the lych gate and consulted a piece of paper. Oglethorpe pointed to their left, Margo shook her head, Oglethorpe tapped on the paper and then to their left, Margo turned the paper around, pointed to their right and nodded, pushed her shoulder bag behind her, and they walked down the hill, toward the pub.

"Great comedy team, don't you think?" Mark's voice startled me.

"Along with Eric and Ernie, if not Hope and Crosby. You ready?"

I grabbed my shoulder bag and we walked outside. Mark drew the ever-present list of dance troupe members from his pocket and scanned down the list. Checkmarks dotted the column where we'd questioned those persons. "We left off with James Charles yesterday."

"Right. He mentioned Jack Darkgate is an amateur radio enthusiast."

"Anything to throw suspicion on others," I said.

"Open mind, remember? Darkgate might know a lot about electricity. More so if he's one of those blokes who's built his own rig. You know," he added when I looked puzzled. "Some blokes like to assemble their own transreceiver, usually from kits, rather than buy the equipment."

"Sounds like a lot of work."

"Probably like anything else, if you have a passion for it, it's not work."

We had passed the pub. Darkgate's house was farther down the road, on the right, around the curve. I slowed my gait. Mark had taken a half dozen steps before he realized I lagged behind. He turned, walked back to me, and asked if something was wrong.

"You're going to tell me I'm barmy."

"You giving me permission or just forecasting the future?"

"I can't shake the feeling that something serious involving Scott or Graham is going on."

"You on that again, are you? What set you off...Graham's dramatic pause this morning?"

"Once I could overlook, Mark, but it also happened last Saturday night and Sunday morning. You said yourself yesterday that he and Scott didn't look exactly like cohorts reveling in Scott's return. Margo mentioned King Roper a few minutes ago."

The name was like a bell to Pavlov's dog...or a not guilty judgment to a criminal. Mark's hands gripped my upper arms and he stood facing me, the light in his eyes white-hot. "What about Roper? Why would she mention him? Did she talk to Scott or Graham? He hasn't escaped, has he?"

# Eleven

*From the desk of Scott Coral*

"I'm fine…really. No, not a single pain. No discomfort of any kind. No, I don't know why Alexa told you that. I have full movement of my shoulder. Really. Lilly, I wouldn't lie to you. No, I'm not being macho or stoic. Really. I don't know what else I can say to convince you. I'm fine." Scott Coral took a deep breath and glanced at his wife. Genes didn't confine themselves to replicating physical qualities. He listened for another few seconds to the examination coming over the phone. "Lilly, I—if you don't stop this inquisition, I'll have to fly back to America to deal with you myself." The bark of anxiety exploded in his ear. "Relax, I'm joking. No…no, I'm ready for full time work again, and your daughter is more than ready to have me go, I can assure you. I started yesterday morning and, in fact, there are rumors of a promotion. I don't know, but maybe getting filleted was my ticket. Yes, it would be more money. Yes, I will. I love you, too. Ta." He hung up the phone and sighed heavily.

The match between Manchester City and Tottenham, which Scott had on the telly that morning and which had been so all-important moments prior to the phone call, now seemed insignificant. He clicked it off and moved slightly, disturbing his position on his favorite sofa, and called out to his wife.

"Alexa. Now I see where you get if from! Your mum is driving me crazy from 4000 miles away!"

Alexa Coral looked up from the magazine she'd been pretending to read during the conversation between her husband and her mother. From Scott's responses, she had a fair idea what her mother had said, but she couldn't understand why he was so bothered by it all. "Scott, really, she just cares about you. She's concerned, as we all are. You know, dear, she only hopes for your best health and if you're ready for full time work again." She looked at him, her eyes smiling with hope. "*I* think you'll be fine and *you* obviously think you're ready, so things'll work out for the best. Besides, the doctor wouldn't send you back if he weren't sure of it. No need to be so furious at us, teddy bear."

Scott felt the heat of embarrassment and frustration flood his face. He'd endured, none too silently and patiently, a month of lying around the house; now he had to listen to this. "TEDDY BEAR! That's it! Blathering on to your mum about my every movement in my own home is bad enough, but now nicknames?"

"Darling, what's wrong? Is your shoulder acting up?"

"No, my shoulder is not bloody hell acting up."

"You want another cuppa, or some eggs? You didn't have much breakfast." She glanced at her watch. "Nearly two hours ago. Toast doesn't stay with you that long. You're probably hungry."

"I'm not hungry. My stomach's fine."

"Then, what's the problem, muffin?"

Scott exhaled in a loud snort. He glanced at the clock. Getting back to work couldn't happen soon enough today. The nicknames echoed inside his head, bringing on nausea. "Chatting up your mum and using her as your diary is the problem. There are some things that I'd prefer stay between us two."

"I'll put the kettle on. I know that mood: you're grumpy."

"Just because I don't want every aspect of my life ending up in America you accuse me of being grumpy?"

"You out of pain pills?"

"I do not need another damned pill."

"Well, *something's* bothering you, dear. Did Mom say something that upset you?"

Scott momentarily closed his eyes and counted mentally to fifty before looking again at his wife. "I'd appreciate keeping my physical health reports within these four walls, if that could be arranged."

Alexa grimaced and she uncrossed her legs. "Bothers you that much, then. Sorry. Forgive me?"

"Yes, but on one condition—that you make some orange scones."

The magazine fell unheeded to the floor as Alexa got to her feet. Padding softly over to Scott, she frowned and pursed her lips. "Really? That's the *only* way you'll forgive me?" Bending down, she purred against his ear. As she wrapped her arms around his shoulder, her kisses trailed down his neck.

*Leeds General Hospital*

Dr. Robert Paladin had never operated on so notorious a criminal as King Roper. At least not that he knew. He had been with Leeds General Hospital his entire career, since leaving his residency at Manchester Royal Infirmary twenty years prior. Yet that Monday morning, for the first time in his twenty-four years as a surgeon, he found it necessary to remind himself that he'd taken an oath all those years ago, an oath to assist *everyone* who needed medical attention, regardless of the patient's social status. Still, the fact that he was about to operate on a known murderer made Paladin somewhat uneasy. He nudged the edge of Roper's file folder, squaring up the bottom with the edge of his desk. The handwritten sticky note on the file cover stated the man's condition in layman's terms.

"Roper: Extensive ligament damage caused during an assault on a Derbyshire police officer last month. Additional rotator cuff tearing with progressive fatty atrophy, all resulting in only thirty percent usage of right arm."

Dr. Paladin stared past his desk. It was a large cherry wood affair that matched the other furniture in the room, his first substantial purchase when he'd joined Leeds General, a notch on his mental yardstick that he'd 'made it.' He ran his fingers tips over the polished wood, recalling the financial sacrifices he'd endured to obtain it. But this morning he got no pleasure from the smooth surface; his office felt unexplainably claustrophobic. He blinked, concentrating on the cluster of photographs on the far wall. Although the morning sunlight slanted through the window blinds, the space seemed dismal and cramped, the photos barely discernable, as though farther away. As though he were gazing at them through a length of gauze. Or a cloud of gun smoke.

He picked up the manila folder, angling it in the sunlight so he could read the pages more easily. He was surprised at the thickness of the file; it must be several dozen sheets of paper, compiled over many years. He leafed idly through them. Typewritten pages gave way to computer printouts, officials' names varied, police departments and prisons changed, but the constant of King Roper's career remained unvarying. Unless severity in his crimes constituted a shift. Paladin glanced at the top page. The images of Roper's past swirled in his mind as the words on the paper came into focus. Smuggling, trafficking, kidnapping, murder. An assault on at least three in law enforcement.

Paladin lowered the folder slowly to his desktop. This was not going to be easy, surgery on the arm of someone so vile, so repulsive to his own morals. He gazed at the window, not really seeing it, but instead picturing what Roper might look like, what his personality might be. The face never did come into sharp focus, but no matter the presumed height, weight, or body type, Roper's image always ended up with dark hair and eyes. Perhaps it was a throwback to good versus evil, light versus dark. He most likely was muscular, Paladin thought, and perhaps his body carried physical remnants of fights he'd had. Perhaps he was unscathed, his fingernails manicured and his face clean-shaven, signs that his underlings did the actual dirty work. Or perhaps he stuck his manicured hand into it every so often, the taste for blood or the thrill of wielding the knife too strong to cede.

Whatever Roper turned out to be, both visions repulsed Paladin, and he found himself stiffening. *Am I patching him up so he can continue inflicting harm, perhaps murdering again? Is that why I'm a surgeon?* The minutes slipped away as the sunlight slowly slid across his desk. As his focus shifted to photos of his family on holiday in Barcelona, a chill seemed to emanate from his soul. His Hippocratic oath guaranteed he'd do his best during Roper's operation. But his family and faceless, nameless others whispered to him, silently asking for a surgical accident. *Things routinely go wrong on the table; could he rid the world of this monster? Would it honestly matter to Society if he did?* He glanced at the brass-cased clock on his desk. 0610 hours. Surgery on King Roper wasn't until 1100. He had five hours to struggle with his conscience.

*HM Prison Wakefield, West Yorkshire, England*

Most healthcare issues regarding prisoners were handled exclusively within the walls of Wakefield Prison. Due to the fact that most of the inmates were considered Category A prisoners, or 'The Worst of the Worst,' the idea of moving any of them out of the confines of the impenetrable walls made little sense. Most were never going to see the other side of those walls, anyway. King Roper had been an anomaly since arriving, however. He was one of the few not classified as Category A, and if you had asked the newer guards, he was a model prisoner.

Senior Prison Officer Hugh Claxton was in his eighteenth year at Wakefield, during which time he'd seen and dealt with the very worst of humanity. Long prior to his arrival, Wakefield was known as 'The Monster Mansion' due to its famous—or infamous—personnel inside. The very worst criminals were there: serial killers, sexual predators, and those uncontrollable in a traditional prison setting. Some current 'residents' even had movies such as *Silence of the Lambs* made based on their horrific acts.

Unlike most of the prison guards, Hugh Claxton was very

aware of King Roper and of what he was capable of doing. As the Senior Prison Officer within Wakefield, his highly skilled intel team kept him up to speed on the gang set communications discovered and decrypted on a daily basis. Claxton knew Roper was connected both on the inside and outside by small time traffickers in drugs, jewelry, and ivory. Never one to underestimate anyone who had made it all the way to Wakefield, Claxton knew 'small time' still conferred more than a sufficient number of days to order a kill at any time, from inside or out.

Claxton also knew Roper had enemies of the highest order in the Dodders, the most organized of all sets within Wakefield. Roper's henchmen had unknowingly crossed the Dodders, and to make matters worse, later testified against some mid level Doddington henchmen, resulting in a lengthy prison sentence. The fact that the Doddington leadership all personally held King Roper responsible was a well-kept secret known only to Claxton, his intel group, and the higher levels of the Doddington group. Those factors, along with the fact that Claxton had a personal hatred for Roper—a feeling unmatched in his career—set the stage for the coming day.

As it was 0700, and the transfer of Roper to Leeds General Hospital was scheduled for 0830, Claxton buried his head in his hands and said a silent prayer for today's events, a plan that he had set in motion some weeks ago.

～

King Roper could not sit still in his cell. He paced, hoping to use up the adrenalin that seemed to consume him, simultaneously burning and freezing him. But the cell area was too small for his frantic, swift paces—five steps, turn, five steps, turn, five steps, turn…

Cursing the enclosure that kept him caged, he dropped to the urine-stained concrete floor to do as many push-ups as he could. He winced at the first tightening of his muscles. The pain in his shoulder was intense. With a torn ligament and torn rotator cuff in the same arm, courtesy of that damned swine Scott Coral, the push-ups were difficult, if not impossible, to press out. But he did. Years of staying in incredible physical condition would not be altered due to half a functioning arm. Like his physique, Roper's will was quite formidable.

Roper retained a mental list, the one that kept him so full of hate and revenge, and what he termed Reasons For Living. Day in and day out within the confining walls he thought of the list and those on it. Constable Scott Coral, Detective-Sergeant Brenna Taylor, DCI Geoffrey Graham, and last but certainly not least Sam Taylor. His plans for each were different.

Different in the way he would gut them.

Sam Taylor had been all but gutted already during his current prison stay, but somehow that bitch copper Taylor had Sam moved the day prior to the hit. Brother and sister. A perfect pair of middens. No matter, both would soon feel his knife. Once free from Wakefield, nothing would stop Roper from finding Sam Taylor. And this time he'd finish him off.

Roper had performed the role of model prisoner since day one at Wakefield, with only occasional messages to his closest allies. Two with him on the inside, under his control, with seven more on the outside waiting for this historic day. He was aware of the Aryans, the Dodders, and the Shiekans, the groups and gangs inside Wakefield, all of which he despised. But he could think of nothing that would provoke them in any way. They respect me, Roper thought, smiling. They look up to me, know quality when they see it. And if they don't keep out of my way, they know I'll take care of business the old fashioned way.

He was wrong in that assumption.

~

At 0800, the team of security transport personnel arrived at Roper's cell. One team outside secured the ambulance. The paramedics were instructed to wait with the vehicle and to not have any contact with the patient or security team that would accompany him. Hugh Claxton did not want to involve an ambulance, but instead wanted their own transport of Roper both to and from

Leeds for his surgery. But protocol prevailed, and the fact that Roper had indeed been of little trouble for anyone at Wakefield made the governor's decision easier to follow.

The two-man team assigned to this detail knew Roper and assumed nothing would happen. Likewise, Roper knew the drill expected of him when they arrived. He would get up from his bed, walk backwards to his cell door and they would handcuff him. Then, as they opened the door, he would kneel down, and ankle cuffs would be secured around his ankles. Then a belt would be fastened around his waist—both his hand and ankle cuffs would be tied in to this, making it difficult, but not impossible, to walk. Running would not be an option, nor would punching or kicking.

As Roper was escorted out to the ambulance, Hugh Claxton stopped the security team. He eyed Roper, his gaze steady and serious, and came up to the man.

Despite his desire to remain cool and dispassionate, Roper's interest and confusion showed in his face. Claxton, Roper knew from their brief encounters inside, didn't say much and was a man of considerable status within the prison system. But now his words struck Roper as odd. "I understand this surgery is quite necessary, Mr. Roper. I hope you realize that all people get what they deserve eventually. I hope you deserve this."

*Leeds General Hospital*

Two security vehicles were assigned to the ambulance escort from Wakefield Prison to Leeds General Hospital. One driver in each vehicle, the two-man team with Roper in the ambulance. The drive was uneventful save for Roper's constant smile.

At the hospital, Dr. Paladin and his surgical crew were notified of Roper's arrival and they made the final preparations. Roper's move through the employee cafeteria doors and onto the service lift went smoothly; no hint of trouble, no false step made. When Claxton heard of it later he doubted if the public even knew Roper had been in the building. The security team joked and laughed with Roper all the way to the operating theatre, comparing notes on the reasons knives were so much better than guns for personal security. All were relaxed.

At 1100, just as scheduled, King Roper arrived at the theatre. Paladin noted a serious-looking security man outside the theatre door, but thought nothing of it. The sooner he'd get on with the surgery, the sooner Roper would be out of his life. The man was already leaving a nasty taste in his mouth.

The prep was done, the theatre sisters top of the tree, and the surgery went as scheduled. Recovery, however, would be quite painful and tedious. Both ligaments had been reattached to the bone in Roper's arm. That Roper had any use of it quite amazed Paladin, but Roper wasn't the standard patient.

*HM Prison Wakefield, West Yorkshire, England*

As Roper was wheeled to the postoperative area, Hugh Claxton received an anonymous text message at the prison. After reading it, he sent his own text message, equally anonymous and brief. That finished, he closed the door to his office and sat down at his desk. He grabbed his pen, hesitated, then wrote himself a note: Evil exists only because seemingly good people allow it.

# Twelve

I let Mark hold on to me, his fingers feeling like they were burrowing into my muscles. The pain kept me aware of my surroundings, told me this moment was real.

"Why do you suggest he's escaped? Roper's in Wakefield." I said it emphatically, reassuring myself of the truth, or convincing myself of a lie. "You know the reputation of that prison, Mark. No one's escaped from Wakefield. Ever. Thirteen feet thick walls has something to do with that, I assume."

A slant of sunlight fell across his face, revealing the strain of his neck muscles. His breath blew warm and quickly against my hair as his chest heaved. His grip did not lessen, however, and I could feel my pulse beneath his fingers and the restricted blood flow building in pressure across my shoulders.

"Do you know anything?" I asked, throwing the question again at him.

"No. How could I? I've been with you all the time."

"Well, something's going on. Maybe Margo isn't privy to information about Roper, but we can't discount Graham's behavior and Scott zooming off like he did. You've heard nothing on Roper's gang, I assume. You'd tell me if you did." My statement came out more as a plea, between friends. Mark knew my brother, Sam, could be in danger even in prison. Roper had long arms and never forgot a wrong.

Mark's grip relaxed and turned into a hug. He held me close against his chest for perhaps a minute before releasing me. Reluctantly, I thought.

"Don't conjure up dragons where none exist, Bren. Graham told you before when Sam was in danger, and he'll do it again if that ever happens. You've got to trust him. He'll speak if there's anything to tell you." He brushed my cheek with the backs of his fingers. "But you could be right about Sam. Wasn't he moved a few weeks ago from Wakefield?"

I nodded and started walking. "For Sam's protection. There was some threat. The governor took it seriously enough to transfer Sam."

"Well, that's it, then. Maybe they're going to move him again."

"Then why hasn't Graham told me? Last time he did. He wouldn't keep anything bad from me."

"Can't be too bad if he hasn't mentioned it." Mark's voice sounded artificially cheerful. He pulled slightly on the body of his pale yellow shirt, peeling it away from his sweaty body. He held it like that, probably hoping some air would dry him off. "If anything had happened or might happen to Sam, Graham'd let you know. Scott would, too. Now, don't worry about nothing. My gran used to say that there was enough to occupy our emotions without seeing the *Gean-canach* everywhere."

"Pardon?"

"The Irish faery. You know…he personifies love and idleness."

"Strange combination."

"Must be something to it, if he's the bloke to do it, Bren."

"So, what's wrong with seeing this faery?"

Mark smiled and patted my hand. "My dear, innocent girl. It is *very* unlucky to meet him. We're here, I think."

Jack Darkgate's house appeared liked a magician's rabbit, popping out from behind a dense cluster of hemlock and fir as we rounded the bend in the road. Two-storeyed, bulky and gabled, the house might have stood guard for the others on the road. Or lodged any number of Mark's faeries.

"What do you think?" I asked as we paused at the foot of his drive. It curved up the slope on which his house sat, with massive clusters of hostas, iris, and rhododendron nearly camouflaging its path. Mulched beds of enthusiastic roses hugged the house foundation, giving the appearance of Sleeping Beauty's fortress.

"I think he needs to lay off the bone meal," Mark said. He shook his leg to dislodge an iris stem. "And us without our machete."

"Think we can find the door?"

"We'll requisition a sniffer dog." He grabbed my hand and we walked up the pathway.

A woman walking her Dalmatian paused slightly as they passed on the road. "He's at his job."

"Sorry?" I said as Mark banged the violin-shaped doorknocker against the door.

"Jack Darkgate. You're wanting to call on him, are you not?"

"Yes."

"He's at his job. Mondays until five o'clock." She urged the dog onward.

"Where might that be?" I called after her.

She turned slightly, speaking to the dog first, then shouted, "Haddon Hall. The gift shop." The dog fell into a trot beside her as she continued her jog.

"She appeared and disappeared like a black dog," I said, not sure I liked bringing up the reference to the ghostly being. I'd had enough association with it last month. "Where'd she go? Was she real?"

"Who cares," Mark said, heading down the front drive. The iris leaves nodded in his wake. "If the info's good, it makes no difference to me if it comes from King Roper or Mother Teresa. You coming?" He withdrew his handkerchief and pressed it against his forehead.

I nodded and hurried down the walk, catching him up near the junction of the two roads. "You want to work on the puzzle tonight?"

"It won't interfere with a phone conversation with Adam?"

"We don't chat for hours, Mark. A few minutes. Besides, he might not phone."

"What's he doing that's more important?"

I jogged alongside Mark, trying to see his face to discern if he were joking. He stared straight ahead, his lips pressed together and nearly white. I turned to face him and jogged backwards to keep up. "I don't know. He didn't say. Why?"

"He doesn't work on the murder squad, so he's not knee deep in that sort of investigation. He's not with the drug squad, so he's not on surveillance. Why can't he get two minutes to ring you up?"

"This is important to you, isn't it?"

He walked faster and I abandoned my backward jog. Running alongside him, I said, "It's not Adam, is it? Something's bothering you. Do you know something about Roper?"

He stopped, and I took several steps past him before I could recover my composure.

"Mark, what's wrong? It's not about my brother, is it?"

Mark exhaled heavily. "I don't know why I bother. People have to live their own lives."

"Bother? What are you on about?"

"Obviously nothing important. I thought that if a guy was deeply in love, about to be married, he'd talk to his bride-to-be every day. None of us knows how much time we have on this earth, and wasting a day without telling your intended that you love her…" He snorted and started walking.

"I know Adam loves me."

"Wouldn't it be nice to hear it?"

"Why does this bother you so much, Mark?"

"Oh, never mind. Come on. Jack Darkgate won't be there all day." He strode up the hill, and I hurried after him, wondering what I had done wrong.

～

Haddon Hall's car park was half filled when we arrived late morning. Being summer and peak tourists season, this was not surprising. Jack Darkgate, however, was. I hadn't expected a 60-year old, white bearded man.

He stood behind the cash register at the gift shop's check-out counter, fairly surrounded by brochures, booklets, maps of the estate, and picture post cards. Haddon Hall merchandise of a more souvenir nature, such as china mugs, tea towels, CDs, books and boxed biscuits, filled the aisles, and gave the shop a snug, comfortable feel. Darkgate finished with a customer, looked at us in anticipation of a sale, and blinked when I introduced us.

"I must say," Darkgate said, leaning forward slightly, as though sharing a confidence, "I expected the police."

"Why is that, sir?"

"Don't you question everyone present at the time of the crime?" He cocked his head to one side, the light from the overhead fixture momentarily masking his eyes behind the lenses of his glasses.

"Did you travel from the Hall to the village with the dancers?"

"No. I drove myself."

"Anyone else with you?"

"No."

"When did you arrive in the village?"

"I didn't consult my watch. But it was just ahead of the van. I traveled ahead of them the entire way. Well, that makes it sound like we drove from Land's End to John o' Groats. You know the distance between the Hall and the village."

I nodded. We'd now driven it twice and it couldn't be more than a ten-minute drive. I asked if he'd seen anyone standing near the light box, or tampering with it.

"'Fraid not. Neither Saturday afternoon nor any time that week. Not that I'm constantly at the stage area in the park, but I do most of my shopping in the village. I never saw anyone. But, then, it would've been done at night, wouldn't it?"

"How did you and Alastair get on together?"

"Well enough. I didn't see much of him outside of our dance rehearsals and performances. Oh, of course I'd run into him in the village, but just to nod to. We didn't really socialize."

"So, you've no grudge against him."

"Why ever would I? He was pleasant enough, never did any wrong to me." He squared up the knot in his tie and smoothed the tie against his shirtfront.

"What about you and Simon Roe," I asked, then explained that perhaps Simon had been the original target. "Any animosity between you two?"

"Certainly not. I get along with everyone. Which doesn't mean I like everyone. Those whom I don't particularly like, I avoid as much as possible. It saves my blood pressure." He smiled, and I thought his statement genuine. "But Simon and I have no history of anger. I realize he was probably the target. He's done that unlocking the light box bit for years. Anyone who's seen the troupe more than once realizes that. So, yes, I appreciate how Simon must be feeling, must be blaming himself for Alastair's demise, but I honestly can't think of anyone who'd hold a grudge for either man, and certainly not so intense as to want to kill him."

"You're the group's fiddler, is that right?" Mark picked up a CD from the counter and looked at the cover. "You're listed on this." The amazement seeped through his words. "I'm impressed. You must be good."

"It's last year's Heritage Days highlights. Or lowlights, if you'd call it, since I'm on a track." He winked and tapped the CD in Mark's hand. "Everyone in the troupe thinks I'm a fiddler. So, don't let a real violinist hear it. She'd blow my cover and then how could I maintain my wealthy life style?"

Mark returned the CD to the display and picked up a map of the Hall. "Amazing amount of history between these walls. I'm blown away by it all."

"Know something? I am, too. And I've worked here for five years. The hall dates to the 11th Century. Yes, quite old. It originally belonged to the Peverel family, coming to them via William Peverel, the illegitimate son of William the Conqueror. Peverel is probably more famous in Derbyshire for Peveril Castle, in Castleton. Do you know it?"

I said I did, but didn't confess that the climb was just about beyond my physical endurance. The climb several years ago still lingered in my mind: not so much the village and land spread out below me but the impression I'd never get my breath back.

Darkgate folded his arms over his chest. The corners of his

mouth turned upward as he sighed. His eyes clouded somewhat, giving him a dreamy expression. "Quite romantic, I've always thought. Sitting on top of that incredibly steep hill. But it's
worth the walk up to see the ruined keep and the views of the
countryside. Anyway, the Peverels evidently thought the location suitable, on the rise above the River Wye and in the midst
of magnificent wooded land. The Hall passed to William Avenal
through forfeiture to the Crown in 1153. Richard Vernon acquired
the Hall nearly twenty years later by marrying Avenal's daughter. Generations later, Dorothy Vernon married John Manners
in 1558, thereby bringing the Hall into the Manners family, who
have held it ever since."

Mark whistled. "Incredibly long time."

"Yes. So nice that their line is unbroken for so long." He smiled
and pointed to a picture postcard of the hall. "The Hall has never
been bought or sold." He waited for our reactions. Mark's head
jerked backwards slightly and I exclaimed appropriately. "Yes.
Nine and a half centuries and it's been transferred from owner
to owner without money."

"Is the Hall original from the Vernons' ownership?"

"Nearly. Most of the buildings on the estate are the results of
the Vernons. Though Peverel Tower and a section of the Chapel
existed before the Vernons took over. It's really quite remarkable,
not only the continuous ownership of the place but also its condition. The Hall's undoubtedly one of the finest medieval houses
existing today." He shook his head and gently pushed away Mark's
hand. "You're interested in it, I can tell. Take the map with my
compliments. No, I shan't hear a word about it." Smiling, he dug
into his trousers pocket, pulled out his wallet, and placed the map
money into the cash register's till. "There. My little treat to you."

Mark thanked him and said he'd make good use of the map.

"The Hall has guides and is well marked, but there's nothing
like a good map to get you about."

"It's not really complete," I said, "without the guidebook. We
need to know the history if we're to wander about."

Darkgate said we were obviously serious about learning the story of the place, rang up the sale, and thanked me. "The guides can answer most questions, but a good book is an invaluable source. Especially if you're like me, who thinks of questions I should've asked when I get home."

"You seem quite keen on the subject," Mark said. "Are you as passionate about all your hobbies?"

Darkgate pointed to a table that held stacks of books. The display signs advertised Derbyshire customs and legends, folk music and dance, history, dialect, and a dictionary of English place names. "See that? Books on just about anything pertaining to the area. The sword dance is given a half dozen pages in that one book." He pointed to a large volume featuring a photo of a well dressing on the jacket cover. "A half dozen! The custom's older than a lot written about in the book, and those other traditions are given more space." He snorted and wrinkled up his nose, as though the tome gave off an offensive aroma. "Well, I'm going to correct that oversight. I've begun writing a book on the history of the sword dance—long sword *and* rapper. It's high time that folks know about it."

"That's quite an undertaking."

"Wouldn't have started it if I didn't want to. I don't do anything I don't want to." He smiled and crossed his arms over his chest, as though his statement were a challenge.

"James Charles mentioned you also are an avid amateur radio operator."

"Oh, I am that." His chest swelled and his eyes smiled behind his glasses lenses.

"You build your own rig?"

"Along the lines of a Heathkit?"

"They've gone out of business, haven't they?"

"I believe so." He removed his glasses and polished the lenses with his handkerchief. He seemed to concentrate on his task, as though it were the most important thing he could do. "I've a QSL contact in America who used to have an old Heathkit of his dad's. He sometimes talks about remembering his dad assembling it. But no, I don't build my equipment. Besides being all thumbs, I'd probably wire something wrong and then electrocute myself when I went to use it. I bought it. Too long ago to have the sales slip. Does that matter?"

Mark shrugged and screwed up his mouth. "Just curious."

"If it's important, perhaps Michael Green would have a record, though I doubt it."

"Did he sell the radio equipment to you?"

"Back a few decades ago. He owns an electronics store. Stereos, mobile phones, cameras. That sort of thing."

"Audio-visual cables, component parts and wires?"

"I believe so. Most everything anyone would need. He prides himself on the stock he carries."

"Do you participate in any of those field days a lot of amateur radio clubs have?"

Darkgate sighed, obviously regretful. "Occasionally. Many times they're on dates on which the troupe dances. But I have been to a few. Just seeing what other hams have in the way of equipment makes the day worthwhile."

I said he was probably busier than men half his age.

"Of course, I didn't do all this when I had a job. Since I'm retired, I can do what I wish and how much I wish."

"Oh, I thought you worked here."

"I do, but I'm a volunteer. It's nearly as good as a pay packet being able to work in the Hall. Have you taken a tour? No? You really shouldn't miss it. It's part of our history, it's who we are, even if we don't own it."

Mark waved the map. "We'll have a look around before we leave. The gardens should be nice."

"The roses might just be at their best, but the other areas are worth viewing, too. If you're a history buff, you may like to know that the gardens are Elizabethan in design and date."

"Impressive."

"Yes. Did you know the Manners were Protestants and the Vernons were Catholics?"

"Cause any friction during the civil war, with the two families married?"

Darkgate shrugged and glanced at a family who entered the gift shop. "I've no idea. But I'd like to think not. There's too much strife in the world in general without bringing it into families. May I help you?" He directed the family to the woolen clothing and Mark and I left the shop.

"Informative bloke," Mark said as we walked outside and started for the Hall. We had about a two-minute walk, crossing a brook, before we entered through the formidable wooden door into the courtyard. "I'm on information overload. I don't recall half of what he said about the place."

"I noticed your note taking lagged a bit behind his narrative." I felt incredibly small as we walked across the paved square. The Hall rose, massive and yet decorative, beside me. I wondered what the view from the tower was like. Especially with the dark clouds rolling in from the west. The scent of rain rushed to us as a gust of wind raced through the courtyard. "If I knew a rain dance, I'd do it. We sure do need a good, soaking shower."

"If nothing else but to cool us off for a bit. Did you notice that family? Looking at woolen scarves and hats in weather like this. Barmy."

"Probably from America or Canada and they want some authentic British woolens to take home."

"More power to them. Just the thought of those mittens…" Mark trembled and grimaced.

"Smell that air, Mark. If we don't get a downpour, I'll be surprised." I glanced at the gargoyles ornamenting the top of the drainpipes. "Too bad they don't make things like that anymore. There's probably some history in those, too."

Mark folded the map and jammed it into his trousers pocket. "For all Darkgate's tales, he did say something quite telling. Remember when I asked about Darkgate's radio equipment?"

"What of it?"

"He joked that he'd probably wire something wrong if he made his rig himself, might electrocute himself. He said he was all thumbs." Mark looked at me to see if I was on the same wavelength.

"He can't be all thumbs. He's a fiddler. He needs manual dexterity."

"Plenty. Have you ever heard the tempos they play some of those jigs at, Brenna?"

"It doesn't match his all thumbs statement."

"It may not be damning, but it waves a red flag. Although, I *will* ease off slightly with the Heathkit."

Thunder rumbled overhead. I watched a bird dive and snatch an insect in flight before I said, "Why? Radio equipment uses electricity. We're looking for someone with that knowledge."

"Sure, but a Heathkit required no knowledge of electronics, Brenna. I bet thousands of hams assembled their Heathkits without knowing a thing about electricity except which end of the electrical cord plugs into the wall socket. It's all laid out in the directions what Tab A fits into Slot B, as it were. If you can read and think, you can assemble a Heathkit. That was one of the beauties about them. Guys had the fun of making their own equipment, saving money, and getting a really decent set."

I shook my head, trying to sort through the implications. "Did he actually say he uses a Heathkit? Or was that just that guy in America?"

"He bought his gear from Michael Green. And if that's true, and he's not lying to us for some reason, perhaps we need to talk to Green."

I smiled and rubbed my hands together. "Right after we do a little sleuthing here at the Hall."

"What are we going to look for?" For the first time that morning Mark jogged to keep up with me as I headed for the main door to the Hall.

"What could be nicer than strolling through an historical house and gazing at portraits on a rainy day. Coming?"

We stepped inside the Hall as the clouds opened up in a downpour worthy of Noah.

# Thirteen

Haddon Hall is probably most people's idea of a medieval great house. It is mine. Oak paneled rooms, ornate plaster ceilings, leaded windows and tapestries appeared to be waiting for the next arrival of 17th century guests. I thought it a pity they would never come.

The Hall also spoke its age and ancestry through the heraldic devices of the Manners and Vernon families. Topiaries shaped into a peacock and a boar's head stood proudly outside the gardener's cottage; the same emblematic animals decorated the lead drainpipes clustered around the courtyard. These were just one example I felt of the Hall's history. The families appeared to be everywhere.

The feeling and their presence extended to the portraits scattered throughout the rooms. Charles I, James VI and I, and Henry VII gazed down from their frames, seeming to silently inquire of my presence. I stopped before James' painting, transfixed on his hat.

"What are you looking at?" Mark asked, coming up to me.

I flipped through the guidebook and stopped at the explanation of the James portrait. Pointing to the hat, I said, "Look at that jewel, Mark."

"That big thing he's wearing in his hat? What of it?"

"I don't know why I didn't think of it before. It's famous. It shows up in several paintings."

"It's nice, but what's it got to do with the case?"

"Read the description in the guidebook."

He took the book and read the section aloud. "Described as 'one fayre jewell, like a feather of gould, conteyning a fayre table-diamond in the middest, and five-and-twenty diamonds of divers forms made of sondrous other jewels,' the piece was rumored to be part of the batch of royal jewels and plate Charles I sold in 1625." Mark glanced at the portrait, and then at me. His eyes seemed to bore into mine in his excitement. "Are you thinking of that plume mentioned in the bit of poetry? I know a plume is a feather, and James' jewel is referred to as a gold feather, but isn't this a bit of a long shot? We don't know when the poetry was written. It could refer to something a century or two prior or after James."

"Of course, but it's worth researching, isn't it? Alastair and Simon both spent a lot of time here. Couldn't they have seen this portrait, connected it to the poetry, and come up with the location of the treasure?"

"Just about anything's possible, Bren. But didn't they spend their time outdoors wandering about? What would lead them to stare at an old painting, anyway? It's not exactly in a cook's or gardener's patch."

"It might be if they figured out part of the directions to the treasure and needed to verify that with the portrait." I took the guidebook, my patience wearing a bit thin at Mark's stubbornness. "Think back to your school days."

"That's ancient history, right there."

I didn't smile. This was too serious; I felt we were too near a solution. "Remember Charles the first?"

"Vaguely. A Stuart. Second son of James VI and I and his wife Anne of Denmark. He became next in line for the English throne when his older brother died. Why?"

"He sold the jewel, along with the other pieces of jewelry, to pay for the Thirty Years War."

"Fascinating."

"But it's never surfaced."

Mark's eyebrows lowered. "What do you mean?"

"The other pieces were accounted for, either in sales details or having been bought back years later, but the gold feather appears to have vanished into thin air." I paused dramatically, letting the information sink in. "Or into a hidey hole."

"You're subtly suggesting it's the treasure Alastair and Simon were after."

"Yes. It fits."

"So could a lot of other things. Look, Brenna, you've not only got the cart before the horse, you've still got the horse in the stable. There's nothing that points specifically to James' jewel."

"Of course not. The author of the poetry wouldn't have said 'Hey, I buried it in Haddon Hall in the kitchen fireplace.' Anyone coming across that poetry, as Alastair, Simon and we have, would know exactly where the jewel was. It would've been unearthed centuries before now."

"Well…" Mark gazed at the portrait again, then at the map of the Hall. "We'll figure this out tonight, after tea."

I smiled and kissed him on the cheek. "I knew you had a pirate somewhere in your ancestry."

"I didn't say I wanted the loot. I'm just intrigued by the puzzle, that's all."

"You can believe what you like, Mark. Thanks for going along with me on this."

"Now, if the rain's stopped…" He walked to the window and gazed outside. I stood on tiptoe and peered over his shoulder. Although dark clouds blanketed the sky, the deluge had stopped. A few raindrops splattered the paving stones in the main courtyard or dropped into puddles that collected at the lower ends of the stones or on the edge of the green areas. The wind rocked the tree boughs, shaking the water onto the earth where it ran off the grass and formed rivulets that flowed like blood coursing through veins. "Brave enough to chance it?" he asked, stepping back abruptly as he turned. His chest brushed mine and for a moment we stiffened, aware of our coursing blood and beating hearts. He apologized but made no effort to move. The tingle traversed my body, like electrical shocks or fingers of fire, yet I, too, remained rooted where I stood.

A crack of lightning threw our shadows onto the floor and gave us the look of one solid object. His hand slowly grabbed my arm as I finally stepped away. He pulled me toward him and kissed me, long and hard. Thunder rolled across the sky, mimicking my thudding heartbeat, and when I broke away I turned without saying anything and hurried outside.

Mark caught me up outside the door. He called my name, his voice breathless and urgent. I kept walking toward the car.

"Brenna, wait." He brushed past a group of tourists and squeezed past a large man at the nail-studded entrance. As I got to the car park, he grabbed my arm, spinning me around to face him. "Bren, wait a minute. What's wrong?"

"Why should you think something's wrong?" I didn't look at him, certain my face was flushed.

"You don't normally take off like that. Are you offended by the kiss? If so, I apologize. It-it just happened. I'm sorry. It won't happen again."

Unable to trust my voice, I nodded. My heart was still beating overtime as we walked to the car, and while he unlocked the doors, I looked up at the Hall. Did it hold the clue to the treasure's location, assuming the poetry hinted at a treasure? Had Alastair or Simon already unearthed the treasure and, if so, had that led to Alastair's death? It seemed almost preposterous to think any of this, but maybe Mark and I could figure it out tonight. I'd not get much sleep wondering about the jewel and the family, if they'd been involved in the civil war or with Charles I.

I voiced my thought to Mark and said I'd like to look around Alastair's house.

"For what?" Mark asked, the skepticism unmistakable in his tone.

"For anything pertaining to the jewel or the puzzle. Or ties to his family."

"Look, Brenna, if you want to partner up with someone else,

say so. I apologize for what happened just now. It-it won't happen again. You don't have to lie to me in order to distance yourself."

"I'm not, Mark. What we talked about with the portrait and the jewel has me wondering about Alastair. I want to see if he's got some notes on it. It-it'll make our hunt easier." It was the truth, and I wanted Mark to believe it.

He mumbled that he'd be in the incident room typing up his notes and that I could trot down from Alastair's house when I was ready to tackle Michael Green.

I nodded and we lapsed into silence, Mark probably still thinking I'd lied to him and I still tingling from our closeness at the Hall. His silence lasted the entire trip back to the village, so maybe he was wondering how to get us back together. I believed his explanation, that it had just happened, but it didn't make it easier for me. The possibility that it would happen again lurked in the back of my mind, and that wasn't the most comforting thing to live with as an engaged woman.

He let me off at Alastair's house with a silent nod. I watched him drive the short distance to the incident room and park in the car park, then walked up to the house. The crime scene tape still encircled the building, hanging limp in the lifeless air. Sunlight glanced off the white portions of the tape, as good a visual marker of police presence as any. I ducked under the tape, walked to the door, and nodded to the constable standing guard duty. He opened the front door for me and I slipped inside.

The crime scene techs had finished with the formal search of the house but Graham still retained it under security. Which came in handy for times like this, when an officer needed to see something or obtain something from the house. Though not the crime scene, the house, like any other residence of any other murder victim, often yielded clues and hints to the character of the deceased. I'd be lucky if I found anything pertaining to the puzzle.

The décor reflected Alastair's interests, I thought. Family photos, replicas of historical documents and antique maps, and culinary awards were sprinkled throughout the house. The furniture might have been family heirlooms and hand-me-downs, the warm patina of old wood and wax filled the air.

I started with the desk but found nothing out of the ordinary. The filing cabinets and bookcases also remained uncooperative. But I did find the papers I wanted in a box on top of his bedroom dresser.

I took the box to the dining room table and leafed through the contents. The quiet felt heavier as I quickly read bits of the photocopied articles and handwritten notes. It was as if I invaded Alastair's soul to glean his secrets. Outside, a motorcycle zoomed by, on its way to Bakewell, perhaps; a chatty couple walked their dog; a lawnmower revved. Yet within Alastair's house nothing stirred but the faint flutter of paper as I pulled each sheet from the box and laid them in stacks on the table. The mantle clock had run down and needed winding before its gentle ticks would fill the house. Margo's puppy, as she had me referring to it, had been removed to the care of the RSPCA while it awaited a new home. The house remained suspended in time, a silent relic of the past while its future had yet to be decided.

The papers fell into three categories: history of Haddon Hall, information about Charles I's royal jewels, and the Marshall family. But near the bottom of the box I pulled out several sheets of common, white computer paper that were paper-clipped together. I read them slowly, more anxious with each page.

They were threatening letters, arranged chronologically, from least to most recent. Each letter stated, in specific terms and with increasing pressure as the letters grew closer to Saturday's date, that something dire would happen to Alastair or his dog if he didn't cease his hunt for the royal jewel. They also hinted that the Marshall family had no claim on it, as it rightfully belonged to the Crown.

I studied the letters. Nothing physical gave away the writer; they were typed and printed on a computer. Police techs could discern if the printer was an ink jet or laser, but that was about it. However, common sense dictated that it could be only a few possible writers: people who knew about Alastair's search for the jewel.

That might possibly be Delmar Goodfellow, Simon Roe, or Alastair's co-workers at the Hall. I couldn't see him purposely talking about this to anyone, so the writer had to have special knowledge of the treasure hunt, either from personal involvement—Goodfellow or Simon—or observation when he wandered about the estate—his co-workers.

I rolled up the letters and put them into my shoulder bag, then tackled the stacks of paper.

James' gold feather had been a specifically commissioned piece. Queen Elizabeth I, obviously unknowingly, supplied the jewels for the feather when her jewelry was taken apart. James declared the royal jewels heirlooms 'to be individually and inseparably for ever hereafter annexed to the Kingdome of this Realme.' Specifically, he meant the gold Feather, the Mirror of Great Britain, and the Three Brothers, all pieces of magnificent size and wealth. But items from Henry VIII's reign were also lost. A gold cup called the Dreame of Paris, a gold looking glass, a large covered bowl of gold, and a salt seller decorated in diamond- and ruby-studded morris dancers and musician.

I glanced out of the window, trying to imagine these fantastic pieces. What a tragedy that they were lost.

There were other mentions about lost objects, but a small article on Charles' wife, Henrietta Maria, the former princess of France, induced me to read the entire thing. In 1642 Henrietta escorted her daughter to Holland for her wedding. The queen brought the ragtag remains of the royal jewels along, needing to sell them in order to finance Charles' upcoming war with Parliament.

So, what, if anything, did this add to our present case? Nothing more than speculation, I thought, gathering them up and putting them back into the box. But it did show that Alastair had been on one of the lost jewels' trail. And he had been serious about tracing down its location.

As I reached for the box lid I knocked it off the table with my elbow. I bent over. The lid had fallen top side down, revealing the interior. I picked it up and stared at it. Inside the lid, someone—Alastair?—had taped a sheet of paper that sported a handwritten list of places. The writing appeared to be contemporary and recent, for the ink was crisp and dark against the paper. I went into Alastair's office, gathered up several specimens of his handwriting, and went back to the dining room. I held the examples alongside the list. I admit I'm no handwriting expert, but it looked as though Alastair had compiled the list.

I returned the papers to his desk. Picking up the lid as I sat down at the dining room table I looked again at the list. It was fairly short, a mere seven places:

Apethorpe Hall, Apethorpe, Northamptonshire
Brooksby Hall, Brooksby, Leicestershire
Dunfermline Palace, Fife
Banquetting Hall, Palace of Whitehall, London
Hampton Court, London
Belvoir Castle, Leicestershire
Haddon Hall, Derbyshire

The places were associated with the Manners family; Henry VIII; Charles I; and his favorite, George Villiers, first Duke of Buckingham—royal residences and family homes. England and Scotland. A far-reaching hunt. Any place that had a link to Charles I and the lost royal jewels. The top six sites had an X to the left of the name; Haddon Hall was unmarked. Was this because Alastair hadn't explored the Hall enough to eliminate or establish it as the depository for the jewel? Or had he been killed before he could mark it?

I replaced the papers and the lid, and put the box back. As I left the house, the constable nodded to me and asked if I'd found what I'd been after. I told him yes, and left him to his hot, lonely vigil.

Traffic flowed easily on the A6 into Buxton, where Michael

Green's shop was located. Mark and I knew the store's location, passing it nearly every day, for the town housed the police station where we normally worked out of. Mark found a place to park on the High Street and we walked the few dozen yards to the shop. The pavement held remnants of the earlier rain, the concrete darker in color where it had soaked up the moisture, puddles formed where the slabs tilted. Rain had splashed onto the lower section of the shop fronts and mixed with the dust that coated nearly everything, creating streaks of mud that edged down the buildings' facades and bled into the puddles along the foundation. Scents of wet geranium leaves, wood and car exhaust, magnified from the wetting, hovered in the air. As I stepped over a large puddle I grabbed Mark's arm to steady me, then dropped it when I realized I was still holding it as we came to the shop. He seemed not to notice, for he said something about hoping Green was working now that we were here. We didn't wait long to find out. Music from the shop's CD player or radio welcomed us as we opened the door and walked in. Michael Green ambled over to us, all smiles, enthusiasm and rapid-fire talk.

Most of that vanished when Mark introduced us and explained the purpose of our visit. The smile, most likely permanently plastered on his face, remained through our talk. I found it disconcerting to be greeted with the same expression, no matter the severity of our conversation.

No, Green had no idea who might want to harm either Alastair or Simon, and frankly he'd been bothered about that. Especially since it now was considered a murder. "Do you know what that does to a person?" he asked, his smiling dimming only slightly beneath the overhead lights. "I could hardly sleep Saturday night. I didn't know but that the mad man was after me. Or planned to murder everyone in the dance troupe. You hear about that sort of thing on the television, don't you...lunatics going on sprees, people getting out of prison and seeking revenge. Even competitors eliminating their rivals. Those two women ice skaters in America...Nancy Kerrigan and Tonya Harding. The assault that broke Kerrigan's kneecap. People become fixated on winning and they'll stop at nothing. It's terrifying."

"Do you know someone like that, Mr. Green?" I asked, surprised the man took such a view.

"Certainly not. All I'm saying is that Alastair's death has the look of a madman. And the sooner he's caught, the sooner we all will be able to breathe easier."

I agreed, then complimented him about his shop.

"You like it?" Short, blond and thin, Green beamed and relaxed. He looked at the shelves, racks and display cases housing stereo systems, mobile phones, digital cameras, GPS systems, radios, headsets, tapes and miscellaneous items. His voice nearly purred when he spoke. "I'm about to open another shop. This one will be in Ashbourne. If that does well, I'm thinking of opening a third shop in Matlock."

"You've ambitions beyond this shop, then."

"Yes. Well, one has to, doesn't one, if one's to get ahead in life." He tightened the knot on his tie and pulled at the edge of his suit coat. I had the feeling he was preparing for the newspaper to snap his photograph.

"I'm surprised you find the time to dance. Opening a new shop must take an inordinate amount of time."

"It does, but of course I rely on others. I've sought the advice of James Charles and Robert Connoly, since they both manage or own businesses. And Jack Darkgate has been incredibly helpful designing the displays and advising me on what to order. Not that most of this isn't standard." He turned, silently indicating his stock. "But there are always new products, and some current products might not warrant the shelf space. So I seek others' advice."

"Even with help, how you find time to rehearse and perform with the dance group is truly remarkable."

"You make time for things you like, don't you? I realize that you must think this is all a lot of nonsense. I'm in my thirties, divorced, no children, so why am I working so hard when I've no one to pass the shops on to? Well, I'll tell you why: because

I'm an incurable electronics bore and because I want to leave as much money as I can to charity."

"Nothing wrong with that."

"I should hope not. If there is, all of the world's wealthy people would be in prison."

Mark asked if Green knew anyone who had wanted to hurt Alastair or Simon.

"No. That's why I think Alastair's death is a ghastly mistake. Or the work of a madman. No one in their right mind would harm those two. They'd go out of their way to help folks. I mean, look at Simon: he's a mate of Delmar Goodfellow, isn't he? He introduced Goodfellow to Declan and now those two are mates."

"Is there something remarkable about that?"

"There is when one of them is an ex-convict."

# Fourteen

"Who might that be?" Mark's voice hardened slightly, a sign his defenses were up.

"Goodfellow. You mustn't worry, though. He's not been in trouble since he's been out of prison. I truly believe he's turned his life around."

"Glad to hear it."

"That's what having the right friends will do," Green said, smiling broadly. "When Simon realized that Goodfellow was having a rough go of transitioning back into the real world, he befriended Goodfellow, and that's made all the difference in Goodfellow's life."

"Is he part of your dance troupe?"

"No. Though Simon did invite him. But Goodfellow said he was too clumsy."

"What's Goodfellow doing since he's out?"

"Working for James."

"At the nursery?"

"Yes. Unless that's changed in the past week."

Mark jotted the information into his notebook. "Do you know what Goodfellow does there?"

"Last I heard he was a lorry driver and laborer. He delivers and unloads purchases to residences or businesses, and plants the merchandise if the buyer paid for that. According to James, Goodfellow's doing quite well. He'd no prior experience as a stockman, nor did he know a daffodil from a cactus, but in one short year his knowledge has blossomed, if you'll excuse the pun." He paused and eyed Mark, who flashed a smile. "I do believe Goodfellow will eventually work his way up at the nursery. He's ambitious and he's shown himself a good worker as well as a fast learner."

"Well, I wish Goodfellow luck. So many ex-cons back slide into their former way of life."

"Don't worry about Goodfellow. He's content with life right now. I doubt he'd do anything foolish and land back in prison."

I asked Green when he left Haddon Hall and arrived at the village Saturday.

"Oh, I should think the same time as most everyone else. I left my car at my house—I live on Water Ford Lane, next to Brian Fireman—and walked to the pub. We met there at eight o'clock and it was already ridiculously hot at that early hour. I wondered what I'd feel like at the end of the day. Anyway, those of us who traveled together in the van left a few minutes later. We weren't due to go on until nine o'clock at the Hall, but we needed to warm up. After our performance, we made our usual round of the other places and finally returned to Nether Haddon. I don't know what was worse, crowded together in the van or dancing all day in this damned heat."

"Did all twelve of you ride in the van?"

"No. Brian Fireman drove himself, as did Simon. Oh, and Megan Powell did, too."

"Anyone else?"

Green pursed his lips and rolled his eyes heavenward, as though consulting with an oracle. "No. That's the lot. Those three drove separately."

"Did they all arrive at the village at the same time?"

"I didn't keep score, but I believe so...except for Brian. We were waiting for him, because he was so late. When he finally showed up, he said he had a flat tire. That's as may be but he nearly disrupted the performance. Johnny was about to break a blood vessel, he was so furious at Brian's tardiness. He was about to ask

James to fill in for Brian, but Brian got there in time, huffing and puffing like he ran all the way."

"No one else was late, then."

"Well, Megan nearly had to find her own way to the Hall that morning."

"Why is that?"

"She'd said she wanted to go in the van, but it was eight o'clock and she still hadn't shown up at the pub. Johnny was about to leave without her when she comes running up to us, apologizing like crazy."

"Did she say why she got there late?"

"I overheard her tell Johnny that she'd overslept. I've no reason to doubt her."

"Just the nine of you, then, in the van. No spouses, no friends."

"There wasn't room, for one thing. And for another, Johnny has this rule that restricts the van to members of the troupe. We bought it with prize money, donations and from what we earned. It wouldn't be right to deny seating to one of us and force him to find his own transportation."

"Where does the van sit when the troupe's not using it?"

"In the pub's car park. Jonah offered. He's keen to promote us, so he lets us keep the van there. It's got the name of the group painted on the sides, so it advertises us even when sitting at the pub."

"That's very decent of him to allocate you space."

"I should say so. But it's typical. Anything to help anyone."

"Does Delmar Goodfellow live in Nether Haddon? I don't have an address for him." I looked up from the map of the village and smiled expectantly.

"No. His place is in Bakewell." He wrote down Goodfellow's address on my list of names. "Close enough to Nether Haddon so he, Declan and Simon can get together for a game of darts or whatever. Will that be all?" Green clasped his hands and rubbed his thumbs together.

I thanked him for being so cooperative and wished him well with his new shop opening.

Outside, walking to our car, Mark said, "What do you think about Megan Powell's late arrival Saturday?"

"As good as any time to rig the light box for a surprise jolt."

~

We asked Megan about her late arrival Saturday at the pub. Megan worked out of her house back at Nether Haddon. A low roofed cottage of stone and slate, it nestled among a clump of fir and pine, cattycorner from the pub. And opposite the park. Quick enough to get to the light box near the stage and then over to the pub. But if anyone saw Megan coming from the park, no one had said. If I'd been the killer and I'd rigged the light box that morning, I would've made sure to double back and approach the pub from a non-incriminating angle.

Megan talked to us in her workshop, a bedroom she'd converted for her jewelry design business. She apologized for the unorthodox surrounding but said she was on a deadline. "I lost a day with this piece Saturday," she said, sitting at her workbench and picking up her shaping hammer. "It's for a wedding this coming Saturday. The groom's gift to the bride. You know. Something borrowed, something blue."

"And this is the something new," Mark said, standing to her left and watching her bend the half-inch wide piece of silver.

"I wasn't told but it could do. Anyway, I've never let a client down and I don't intend to start now. Besides, weddings are a once in a lifetime thing...or they should be. I don't want to become the dark cloud covering their sunshine."

"Is your jewelry in shops? I'd like to keep an eye out for your pieces, if they are. You have a company name?"

"Yes. It's Silver Wear." She handed us business cards, then picked up her hammer. "I specialize in silversmith work. Pieces to wear, not tea sets and the like. I've some pieces in Buxton, Ashbourne and Bakewell. My goal is to have my own shop, but right now these other places are all right. I have to start somewhere, don't I?"

"How long have you been doing this, designing jewelry and selling it?" I said.

"A few years. I started in my early twenties and now, at the ripe old age of twenty-six, I've branched out from selling in my home or via the internet to those shops. I'll make it." She said it with the confidence of a lawyer.

I thought her awfully young to be so successful an artist. Petite, blonde and green-eyed, Megan barely looked old enough to be out of school, let alone be on her own. But she spoke and moved with an air of self-assurance that was not egotistical; she was just sure of her path in life. I said, "Michael Green mentioned that you nearly were left behind Saturday morning."

"Burning the candle at both ends, I'm afraid. I overslept."

"Good thing you live near the pub."

Megan grabbed a stick of solder and her soldering gun, presenting her back to Mark.

"Living so close to the park, did you happen to see or hear anything odd in the few days before last Saturday?"

"What do you mean odd?"

"Oh, someone you've never seen before in the village, perhaps spending time near the light box. A light at night in the park. Anything like that?"

"No. Sorry. I've been working pretty steadily the past two weeks. I have a lot of orders I have to finish. There's no direct view of the stage or light box from my front room, and, as you see, my studio's in the back of my house. When I'm back here I don't see or hear much of anything. The house muffles out the sounds on the lane. I think a herd of Highland cattle could go bellowing down the lane and I'd not be the wiser."

Mark picked up a silver and coral brooch and turned it over slowly in his hands. He said rather off-handedly, "Being in the same dance group with Alastair and Simon...I suspect you knew them rather well. Did either of them show any odd behavior prior to Saturday?"

Megan took several seconds to reply. She bent over her work, working the melted solder around the seam. Her words were muffled and slow, as if she needed all her concentration for the silver work. "Uh, no. I saw them at dance rehearsal Tuesday, of course, and both of them acted as usual. Nothing to indicate either was having personal problems or expected trouble. In fact, now that you've brought this to mind, Simon did ring me up two days earlier."

"On Sunday?"

"Yes. Though not unusual, I thought it somewhat odd."

"Why?" I said. "You don't talk to each other outside of dance practice or performances?"

Megan shook her head and waved her hand, as though warning me away from something dangerous. "No, I don't mean that. Simon had been talking to me, either on the phone or in person, for about three weeks prior to Sunday, off and on."

"The same topic?"

Still holding her tools, Megan faced us. "Always. Like he was obsessed. And always different questions, or had I considered such and such before answering him."

"What did he talk about?"

Megan glanced at Mark, then back to me. Her brows had lowered and her mouth sagged at the corners. Her words were so quiet that I doubted I'd heard her correctly. "Peacock feathers."

For all of Mark's professionalism and years of 'hearing it all,' his head jerked backward slightly and his right eyebrow rose. "Pardon?"

"Daft, isn't it? Peacock feathers."

"Why ask you about that? Had you owned a peacock?"

"Never. But his questions had to do with jewelry design, so I suppose I'm a logical person to ask."

"What did Simon want to know? Were you able to help him?"

"I thought at first he wanted me to design him a piece in the shape of a peacock feather, a pendant or brooch. But he wanted to know about old jewelry like that, did I know of any expensive pieces that might have an historical significance? I saw how important it was to him, but art and jewelry history aren't my expertise. I suggested he contact someone at a museum. They're a wealth of information."

Mark tapped his pen on his notebook. I knew he was

considering Megan's statement. He asked slowly, "Did Simon mention why he wanted this information?"

"No. I just assumed it had something to do with his genealogical research. He looks up family trees for people, did you know? He's made quite a hobby of it. I suggested he make it pay...you know, charge folks for all the time he puts into digging around, but he says he couldn't ask for much. It's too much fun for him. Still, there are professional genealogists, so why shouldn't Simon get paid something? He works just as hard as those professionals, I'm sure. And he always seems to come up with a lot of family history."

"So other than Simon's search for feather info, neither he nor Alastair acted strange preceding Saturday, didn't mention any problems."

"Not that I ever knew."

"Did Simon ever find what he wanted?"

"You'll have to ask him. If he did, he hasn't told me."

"What about people who might have been angry at Alastair or Simon? Know of any personal problems?"

Megan glanced at Mark as she turned off the soldering gun and laid it down. "That's why this is such a shock. I thought the dance troupe was one big, happy family. No one's angry with anyone, at least not that I know of. It's pretty evident when you don't get on with a person, isn't it? Especially when you have to be so close together as dancing requires. You can tell by a facial expression or a casual remark or how close together people stand." She referred to the drawing of the piece, then grabbed a polishing cloth. "I can't fathom who would've wanted to kill either man. Murder seems so...I don't know, so drastic."

"Living so near to the park as you are," I said, "does that bother you? Are you fearful about the murder?"

"I'm uneasy. I won't deny that. I mean, I'm how many hundred yards from the stage? My timing must be off."

"Why do you say that?"

"I like to walk. Usually I'll hike the cliff path behind my house, or I'll stroll through the park. I didn't see anyone near the light box any of the times I walked. I feel bad about that. But if Alastair or Simon were targeted, I think that makes it worse. None of us knows for certain that we aren't also targeted."

"You live alone, then? Do you have a dog or house alarm system?"

"I've got a cat, and even if he thinks he's tough, he's no match for a killer if he's after me. Perhaps I can persuade my boyfriend to stay over a few nights until this blows over. Or I could bunk out at his place. Won't be for long, will it?" She looked at me, hope in her eyes and voice, wanting reassurance that we'd have the killer in jail by a specific time.

"If you feel unsafe, that may be a good solution. Would your boyfriend do that for you?"

"Yes. I'm not sure I'll do that, but it's a possibility."

"Your boyfriend's someone in the dance troupe?"

"No." Megan took a deep breath, as though she were about to launch into a long explanation, or a painful one. "Delmar Goodfellow. He works for James Charles' nursery. This Green Isle. Do you know it?"

"We're acquainted with it, yes."

"I always thought Michael Green should own it to make use of the name. But life doesn't always work out that way, does it?" She paused, perhaps waiting for some comment from Mark or me. When nothing came, she went on. "Delmar would look on his stay here as a prelude to marriage, though. That's why I'm hesitant to ask."

"You're engaged?"

"No. Delmar's been pressuring me to move in with him and have a kid with him, but that's not for me. At least not at this stage of my life. I need to concentrate on my craft, get a shop for it. I can't divide my attention between that and him. Besides, I don't know if I feel that way about him. I mean, I like him. Quite a lot. But whether it's love or not…" She scrunched up her mouth and shrugged. "I don't know what love is, or what it feels like. Maybe it's obvious when it hits you. But I do know that I don't want to be caught in the same predicament my friend Fiona is in."

"And what's that?"

Megan paused, and in those brief seconds of quiet I heard a motorcycle roar up Water Ford Lane. So much for Megan's statement of quiet at the back of her house. A magpie squawked loudly by the back door before Megan said, "Her name's Fiona Doherty. She had an affair with a married man. It was awful." Megan's face crumpled, as though she were going to cry. "I saw the trap she got into and I vowed that wouldn't happen to me. Of course sometimes you can't think straight, you're caught up in the emotions and the whispered words of love. But she's had a raw deal and didn't deserve how he treated her. That's not going to happen to me. I'm not about to let Delmar love me and leave me."

~

"Megan's a single-minded young woman," Mark said as we sat in his car outside the pub. "I wish her luck with her shop and keeping her eyes on the prize."

"I wish she'd seen someone tampering with the electrical light box."

"Unless she did, and she's not saying." We'd stopped on the road, the motor idling, as we considered our next move. On leaving Megan's house, Mark and I had checked out the line of sight from her front room to the park, noting if we could see the stage or the light box. It would weigh on Megan's statement if either could be seen, and raise the question why she didn't admit she had such a view. Which she did. So what or who was she hiding?

Lunchtime had passed but we decided to work straight through until tea and then attack the poetry puzzle. Mark checked Megan's name on our list and studied the village map. "I'd like to talk to Delmar Goodfellow next. He's becoming more and more interesting as his name crops up."

"He's looking a bit shady, if you ask me. What was he serving time for?"

"Burglary. He was an alarm installer in his former life."

# Fifteen

Mark and I shoved Delmar Goodfellow's talk a bit farther down our list. We needed to see where the light box key was kept at the church. A lot in this case came down to opportunity. If the church could be entered surreptitiously, the entrance hidden behind trees or the lych gate, for instance just about anyone could have lifted the key from its peg. It needed to be checked on.

St. Agnes Church stood like a bulwark between good and evil, a physical gateway between this world and the next. Not that it was a large building, for it wasn't—a village the size of Nether Haddon didn't warrant a cathedral-sized structure. But it was large enough. It squatted among ancient evergreens and moss-backed tombstones, its stone tower nearly as tall as the church proper. Its age and serenity suggested it had occupied this spot on the hill since the dawn of time, and that within its walls it held the answers to the mysteries of life and death.

"Pretty, isn't it?" I said as Mark and I got out of his car. He'd parked in the car park on the south side of the building. Though a gravel-strewn flat area devoid of grass, the lot would no doubt hold the worshippers' cars with ease. I sensed it'd been made in the high church-attendance days of the 1950s, when multiple Sunday services were the norm. I glanced at the green patina of the copper weathervane topping the tower. "I like its sense of age."

"I thought you weren't much of a churchgoer."

"I'm not, but I can admire the architecture, can't I?"

"Admire all you want, but let's get this done first." He strode up the gravel path, the heels of his shoes dimpling the damp surface. I sprinted after him, barely leaving a trace of my passage.

The change in temperature was startling. Even in the porch, with its two sides of leaded windows, the heat had diminished. I ran my fingertips over the back of the wooden bench, shiny in the sunlight and warm. Heat rose from the flagstone flooring and I thought how cold it would be in the winter. Mark opened the door to the nave and we entered a noticeably cooler space.

After the brightness of outdoors, I found it difficult to see. We stood near the south door, gazing up into the wooden rafters and into the gloomy interior. Everything seemed to be shades of gray with little distinction in the shapes. Yet, slowly the forms took shape; the grayness subsided, and light and color crept into the area.

"Beautiful window." I nodded toward the tracery at the end of the chancel. "It must be gorgeous in the morning with the sunlight pouring through it." I could imagine the jewel-like blues, reds and yellows of the stained glass tinting the choir stalls and altar during early service. The colors would probably match those in the embroidered altar cloths.

"Nice time for a wedding, I'd think." He stared at me, straight-faced, his eyes barely perceivable as he stood against the shaft of sunlight coming in through the south window. "Or in the evening, lit by candles." His voice had lowered and I thought I detected a note of disapproval in it. "You still have your heart set on an outdoor wedding? Have you and Adam finalized things? A shame to waste something like this, don't you think?"

I had no answer for him; he'd never shown any interest in my wedding before this, except to help Adam and me over some disagreements. I probably stared open-mouthed.

"Would you really object to being married in some place like this? It's so…I don't know…peaceful. There's a link with the past here that I've not felt in many other places. Makes me feel the future will be all right, if this church has been here all this time." He jammed his fists into his trousers pockets. "Do you feel that way?"

I finally found my voice and mumbled that I did like the atmosphere of the place. "It *is* reassuring, isn't it? I sense my place in time, here, you're right. It seems to be filled with that cloud of witnesses, people who have lived before but who are still here, watching and helping." I stopped, feeling my cheeks flood with heat. "Sorry. Daft thing to say."

"No, Bren. It's quite all right. I wouldn't have brought up the subject if I didn't feel that, too. Just seems like someone needs to be married here, share some love with it. It's, well, it needs to spring back to life again."

"I wonder if you have to be a church member to be married here. Do you know anything about the rules?"

Mark seemed not to hear. He had wandered into the center of the nave and looked at the chantry chapel. "Reverend Burgess?" His voice echoed against the stone walls and wooden pews, returning to us cold and empty. He listened for an answer. The only sound I heard was a faint drip of water.

In fact, the place held the aroma of damp stone and mold. A sense of unused, lifeless space, thick with musty air, compounded the impression the church was little used. And that the vicar was elsewhere.

Mark called again, walking over to the bell tower and standing in the open doorway. He angled his head back, gazing up the ladder that led to the ringers' floor overhead. Again, no one answered. "Reverend Burgess, this is Mark Salt. I'm with the Derbyshire Constabulary. I'd like to ask you some questions concerning Alastair Marshall's death." Pigeons cooing on the windowsill replied.

"Do you think he's in the rectory?" I said.

"Might be. Could be visiting a parishioner. Why don't we try later."

The south porch door squeaked open, letting in a slant of light and a blast of afternoon heat. A tall man entered, saw us, and stopped abruptly. He wore a short-sleeved tan and blue striped shirt, faded jeans and a battered baseball cap. He removed the cap, folded it in half and stuffed it into his back jeans pocket and came over to us. "Good afternoon. I'm Wilton Burgess, vicar of St. Agnes. You just looking around or is there something I can help with?" His voice, low and rich, resonated in the small space, bouncing off the stone columns and walls.

Mark repeated his introduction of us. "Would you have some time now to answer some questions?"

"Certainly. I always say there's no time like the present, whatever it is." Wilton nodded and gestured toward the end pew. "Is this all right, or would you prefer to talk in my office?" He moved toward the pew, hesitated to see if we followed, and smiled. A shaft of sunlight angling in from the windows dotting the clerestory illuminated Wilton's head. He appeared to be in his fifties, with a thick crop of salt-and-pepper tinted hair.

I said the pew was fine, and Mark and I joined him in the wooden seat.

"No," Wilton said after thinking for some seconds to Mark's question, "I didn't see anything Saturday afternoon. But, then, I wasn't standing outside and watching, either. I was in the tower, collecting the bell mats for washing and replacing a stay on one of the tower bells. It broke Tuesday during bell practice and this was my first opportunity to fix it. Saturday afternoons I'm rather busy getting ready for Sunday morning worship."

"I can imagine you do have a lot to do. Does anyone help you?"

"Flowers for the altar are on a rotation basis. People are responsible for supplying them and then setting them on the altar. I have two men who come in to help with the heavier work: mopping the floor, washing the windows, waxing the wood."

"They sound like a great help. Would you mind giving me their names?" Mark pulled out his notebook and pen.

"Delmar Goodfellow and Simon Roe. Yes, I see by your expression that you know Delmar's history: a former gang member of some tough named King Roper."

The corner of Mark's mouth scrunched up and I opened my mouth to speak, but he punched me in the ribs—hopefully not noticeable—and said, "Still former, do you know?"

"One can't know for certain, I daresay, but I'm willing to bet the vicarage on it."

I glanced at Mark, trying to catch his attention. Was Delmar or Roper the person Graham appeared to be worried about? Mark was listening to the vicar, so I shelved my question until later.

"Delmar's been a model for the reformed life as long as he's been here," Wilton said. "He's worked very hard at turning his life around. Unfortunately, the church job doesn't pay much, but it keeps him in groceries, and it was the first job he had on his release from prison. I don't say that to boast. I state it as a fact. When no one else would give Delmar a hand up, he came to me and I offered him the work. He's not actually a church sexton—more of a janitor. He's made himself helpful in the short while he's been here. I really don't know how I managed before he came along. He worked Saturday morning early, trimming the grass around the tombstones in the churchyard, weeding, generally sprucing up the area. Delmar particularly likes the outdoors work, so he does it exclusively. Consequently, he does less inside work than Simon. Still, they both do their share."

"Do Delmar and Simon work together or separately?" Mark said, looking up from his notebook.

"Oh, I can afford only one man working at a time. Though there are some instances when I do have to have both in together, such as setting up for the parish picnic or getting ready for our well dressing display. But that's not the norm. Most of the times Simon or Delmar work alone. We don't have that large a congregation." He grimaced and ran his fingers through his hair, making it stand on end. "I-I hate to mention this, but since we're on the subject…and you being a police officer might be able to offer some advice. Well, I know St. Agnes is a small congregation, but most Sundays we have a fair amount of our membership in the pews. I'm nonplused that the offering totals differ as much as they do."

"What do you mean?"

"It's nothing I can mark on the calendar and say 'Oh, it's the full moon this Sunday; the offering will be down by twenty-five percent.' It's just that the collections vary periodically, sometimes wildly. I can't put it down to some people giving their tithe monthly while others give weekly. Even the monthly collection totals fluctuate."

"Are you suggesting that someone's taking money out of the collection plate as it's passed?"

"This is so distasteful to say, but if I'm to solve this conundrum…" Wilton clasped and unclasped his fingers, and his eyes darted from us to the bell tower. "I suspect that money is taken after service has ended, when the collection is counted."

Mark sighed. "Who counts it? Does that suggest your suspected thief?"

"That's part of the trouble. Only two people count it: Delmar and Simon. But both men have proven themselves responsible. I'd not trust them with the collection if I thought otherwise."

"You have no proof, though, of any of this—either that money's gone missing from the collection plates or that either man is stuffing a few pounds into his pocket."

"No. It's just a feeling I have. You must remember, officer, that I've been a vicar for thirty years. I've had several congregations, all small, but one gets a sense not only of human nature but also of a rhythm to church life and services. This is the only congregation in which I've had the upsetting suspicion that part of the collection is being pocketed."

"Could you have two people count the collection?" I asked. "It'd be more difficult to take money if another person is present."

"It's set up that way now, but many weeks one person forgets or is busy or is out of town. Delmar and Simon usually count the money together, but Nicholas fills in quite often if Simon has to work at the Hall, for example. I can only believe, if my assumption is correct about the missing money, that one of them palms a note and sticks it into his trousers pocket. It wouldn't take much to do that: a small diversion, slip a note from one of the plates when you pick it up…that sort of thing." Wilton clenched his fingers into a fist and squeezed them until the knuckles turned white. "I do hope I'm wrong about this, but I don't know how to prove anything. And my suspicions of missing money don't always coincide when Simon, for example, is counting up the collection. That's why it's hard to suspect a certain individual. And it's so sporadic. Every few months, usually when we have a larger collection, as for Harvest Home or Easter or a disaster relief collection."

"Aside from the collection duties, do Simon and Delmar have strict times to work on Saturdays?"

"Yes. I have them on a schedule of alternate weeks. It's not set in stone, however. If Simon has a dance performance on a Saturday when he's down to work, he might change with Delmar. I'm not a strict taskmaster; just as long as one of them shows up Saturday afternoon to set the church right for the next morning, I'm happy."

"I know Simon wasn't here this past Saturday, so I assume Delmar was."

"Yes, miss. It worked out rather well, as it was his week to work."

"Did he mention anything to you, later that day or perhaps on Sunday, of seeing anyone earlier in the day, lingering around the light box in the park?"

Wilton's right thumb and forefinger stroked the corners of his mouth and he glanced in the direction of the bell tower. After what seemed like minutes, he shook his head. "No, sorry. Though perhaps he did see someone but thought nothing of it. Alastair's death hadn't yet happened, so a person lingering near the box had no significance. You'll have to ask him. Or have you?"

Mark butted in. "Do you know of any problems Alastair or Simon may have had, either personal or business related?"

"You're working from the perspective that either man may have been the target. I didn't know Alastair that well, he being Chapel and of course St. Agnes is C of E. I'd see him now and again, more than you might imagine, due to his house being close to the church. Just up the road a way, but you'd know that, I assume. When I'm outside I'll see him pottering about his own garden."

"Did you see him Saturday before he left to dance at Haddon Hall?"

"No. Simon was there early. I saw him drive up and park on the far side of the house. He was there perhaps a quarter of an hour, though he went to the boot of his car about five minutes after he arrived. Took what might have been a pair of shoes into Alastair's house, then maybe five or ten minutes later they both left in their own cars. I assume they went to the Hall for the performance. I never thought a thing about it until your question just now. But they left together, so that doesn't really have any bearing on Alastair's death."

"You said Simon got to Alastair's early. What time was that?"

Wilton scratched his chin and glanced in the direction of Alastair's house. "I can't say. I didn't think anything of it. They are cousins and often do things together. I had no reason to believe last Saturday might be something different."

"Is Simon gregarious? Does he socialize with you or others in the village?"

"You'll have to ask others that. Even though Simon worked here I didn't know much about his personal life. He kept to himself. Oh, not that he was a hermit or unfriendly. Just that work time was work time, and we didn't get a chance to chat. There are only a few hours to get everything ready for Sunday."

"Have you heard anything around the village, from anyone else, that suggested either man might be in danger?"

"I know gossip runs riot in villages, detective, but I've never heard anything like that. If I had, I'd have taken it as my duty to talk to the person mentioned. Sorry I can't help. I guess I spend too much time looking heavenward when I should be looking into people's hearts."

Wilton excused himself after that, stating he had to meet with a couple for wedding counseling. The key to the park's light box, he said, hung from a hook in the church porch. Not obvious to the visitor, but known to the villagers. He said we were free to look around and asked us to make sure the porch door closed firmly behind us, then left in a flurry of papers and schedules.

"You in a hurry?" I asked Mark when the dust had settled after Wilton's departure.

"Not particularly. What do you want?"

"If you wouldn't mind, I'd like to take about ten minutes to poke around in the church registrars."

"Want to look up someone?"

"I wouldn't know who. I'm curious about the church, that's all. I'd like to learn a bit about it. You can stretch out on a pew, if you want. Won't take me long."

"Would you object if I hunted with you?"

"Uh, no."

"Are you sure? You don't sound overjoyed."

"I— You surprised me, that's all. I didn't think musty tomes were one of your loves."

"They aren't, but I'm game for anything you'd like to do. Where do we go?"

No church office existed in the church proper. Medieval builders hadn't foreseen volumes of record keeping and the need for storage of candles, hymnals, paraments, cleaning supplies and tower bell equipment. The basement would be our best bet.

It was. Shelves of oversized, leather-bound books nearly wallpapered one section of the crypt. Despite their large number, Mark and I nearly missed seeing them, for the area was gloomy, illuminated by one small window at ground level and a low-wattage bulb. The space smelled of wet concrete, dried wax and dusty books. Discarded furniture, stacks of worn bell rope, outdated hymnals and signs advertising church picnics and roof repair funds littered the floor and slouched against the walls. Mark moved a cardboard box of moth-eaten pew cushions, creating a cloud of dust, and we picked our way over and around the debris to the registers.

Mark pulled a book off the shelf, disturbing more dust and breaking a cobweb attached to the upper edge of its binding. He drew the handkerchief from his trousers pocket, flapped it over the cover, and blew off any remaining dust from the top of the closed tome. "I offer no guarantee you won't sneeze."

"I hate to think of what we're breathing."

"Then don't. You'll sleep better tonight. Make your mind a complete blank on the subject. Follow my lead." He winked at me, then opened a book and slowly leafed through it. "Anything particular you want to know?"

"Not really. I'm just intrigued by the place, by its age."

He nodded and began skimming the text.

The reading was more difficult than I had thought. Handwriting changed with vicars and with era. Chancery, copperplate, cursive humanistic, secretary hand. The Reverend Hampson, the Very Reverend Bowyer, the Reverend Liggins, Dean Dykins.

"This is interesting." Mark stepped over the pew cushions, banged his shin into a wooden chair, and angled the open book toward me. His right index finger tapped on the pertinent entry.

"What am I looking at?" I asked. The light in the crypt had dimmed during our time there; I strained to read the faint, brown writing.

"A bit about the village during the civil wars."

"You're joking. No, you're not," I added as I looked at his face. It held no trace of a smile. "Astounding that someone would keep entries on that. It's what…how long ago…soon be four hundred years, right? What's it say? You've been deciphering it. I can't make it out. Awful handwriting, whoever's it is."

"The Reverend Crook wouldn't like to hear that." He repositioned himself next to me. "It's kind of a diary about how the war affects the villagers. Written about two centuries later, if my deciphering is any good. Evidently the original 1650 account was so ragged and brittle that our Crook painstakingly copied the more important bits. The original chronicler sites several examples of the devastation of the wars but he's very interested in the harm it does to the families whose loyalties are divided between Parliamentarians and Royalists. Whole families broke apart because son opposed son, or father opposed son in their points of view."

"Awful. I've heard the same thing happened during the American Civil War."

"Must be more common than we know."

"It still doesn't make it easier to live with if it's your family who's split." I didn't have to give my own family as an example. Mark knew of my parents, who had never approved of my career, who doted on my concert pianist brother and my operatic singer sister, who overlooked my achievements and me because my job didn't produce a scrapbook of three-dimensional accomplishments that could be framed and bragged about. The hurt had lessened through the years, but the wound opened at each family gathering.

"You'll be interested in the family whom the vicar documents."

"Really? I didn't think I knew anyone in Nether Haddon."

"No childhood chum, if that's what you're thinking. Have a look." Again he pointed to the page. His fingertip rested beneath the surname.

I stared at Mark. He grinned like a rookie nabbing his first bad guy. "Marshall," I whispered. The ramifications rushed at me.

"I did a bit of research last night when I left you. I've been digging into a few families in the village. Glad I looked up Marshall because now this all has significance."

"In what way?"

Mark stepped back and leaned against the wall. It was probably best that he didn't trust one of the discarded chairs. "Like many surnames—Miller, Fletcher, Baker, Farmer—Marshall originally denoted an occupation. The Marshall family was just that: marshals or keepers of the peace. As such, they all seemed to be loyal to the crown during the civil wars."

"If they weren't, they were biting the hand that fed them. Go over to Cromwell and they'd probably lose their royalist-supported job."

"I didn't do any family research on them per se, but if you like, we could do that tonight, see how involved they were with the wars and how many of them held office of marshal."

"Would the information be in these books?" The rows and stacks of aged volumes suddenly appeared mountainous. "How on earth would we ever find out anything in all that?"

"Do we have to?" He looked overwhelmed at the suggestion. "I just mentioned it because I know how much you value research."

"I haven't really thought of it. It's not vital to the case."

Mark knew me too well. He noticed the disappointment in my tone. "But you think it's important to something else."

"Well, I don't know, of course, but I hate to give up on a thread, even if I've not figured out where it will lead."

"And the Marshalls will lead us somewhere."

"Could do. The civil wars loosely fit the time frame of our puzzling poetry."

"If we had a definite time frame for that, it might help. Still..." He dusted his hands on his trousers and tapped his watch face. "Do you realize our ten minute excursion somehow mutated into a little over an hour? Graham'll have our guts for garters if we don't have something for tomorrow's briefing." He took my hand to steady my progress around the boxes. "I'm surprised the vicar isn't back yet."

"He might be. We'd never know down here."

We walked back upstairs and had just approached the west tower when Mark snapped his fingers.

"What?" I asked, seeing the excitement in his eyes. "You want to borrow that book for tonight?"

Mark held up his hand. "What you just said."

"About borrowing the book?"

"No. About never knowing if someone was around."

"Don't let it shock you too much, Mark, but that's usually the way it is."

"Wilton said he was in the bell tower Saturday afternoon, right?"

"To the best of my memory. I suppose this is leading some place."

"He said he couldn't see the park. From the church floor he

couldn't. But what if he was up in the bell tower and looked out of the window? I bet you my pay packet he could see the stage from up there."

I entered the tower and stood just within the door. Looking up at the ladder that reached at least to the ringing chamber overhead, I said, "I never claimed to be the sharpest needle in the pin cushion, but what's that get us? So what," I lowered my voice to a whisper and glanced around, "if Wilton could see the park? Besides lying to us, what crime is that?"

"Besides protecting the person he *did* see, you mean?"

"Why would he do that? I thought it was a sort of job description that they would be honest and helpful."

"Same with cops, but that doesn't stop some from going bad. But I think before we put too much brainpower into this, we need to know if he can see the park from the tower. You game?"

Ever gallant, Mark let me go first. Heights, as a rule, don't bother me. Normal heights, like treehouse high or fairground rides high or castle turret high. But crawling fly-like up a wall-mounted ladder, without the physical and emotional backup of stairs or a safety net behind you, took all my nerve. Mark must have sensed my apprehension, for he said, "Don't worry. I'm right behind you. Fall on me if you have to."

"Fine. What's going to hold you up if I come hurtling down?"

"Faith. Come on."

I wiped my palms on the sides of my trousers and muttered a prayer as I looked up at the ceiling. Mark watched me get halfway up the wall before he followed.

We came into a square room measuring, perhaps, forty square feet. The interior walls were composed of the same gray stone as the building but the floor was wooden and warped from age, squeaking occasionally when we put our weight on it. Arched, louvered windows claimed the top half of each wall, their white paint flaked or cracked. Peeled paint littered the floor beneath each window and mixed with the dust that continually drifted in through the wooden slats. The odor of warm straw and bird droppings hung in the hot, closed air. On looking up, I saw an obliging corner, near the rafters, harboring a bird's nest. I abandoned my gaze at the spidered bell ropes overhead and strolled over to the west window. Mark shooed a pigeon from the exterior sill and joined me.

The view from the belfry window was more spectacular than I had thought. Mark pressed against me, his chest touching my back and his chin nestled on top of my head as he maneuvered to see. Treetops masked the road at the church tower's base, then fell away to the clearing that housed the park, shops and the pub's car park. The land lay flat; flower gardens, an ornamental fountain, small statue, pond and wooden benches dotted the manicured lawn. Yet, human endeavor faded into the forest as the land reclaimed its own. The rock face backing up to the houses to the west had changed from early morning ash white to afternoon lead gray. With the sun behind it, the cliff threw indigo-hued shadows onto the houses sprawled along Water Ford Lane and pushed the sunny patches of light ever eastward.

"Well, what do you know?" Mark's voice, though hardly above a whisper, filled my ears. "Wilton can see the park from up here."

"Maybe he could, but if he were busy with the bell mats and other chores he might not have looked outside. Don't know why he would, especially. He's probably seen the view hundreds of time."

"Granted, but he said he didn't see anything because he wasn't standing outside."

"If he were in the tower, as he said, and we know he can see the park from there, why specify he wasn't *outside*?"

"To throw us dumb coppers off the trail?" Mark stepped back and I moved from the window. He went over to the mats positioned in a circle beneath the bell ropes hanging from the ceiling. Bending, he said, "Well, these look freshly cleaned. Maybe this part of his story is true."

"And maybe we're making too much of this. I still don't understand the importance of whether he could or couldn't see the park. He didn't kill Alastair."

Mark dropped the edge of the mat and stood up. "Do we know that?"

# Sixteen

On leaving the church, we stopped at the door and looked toward the west. Mark and I took different positions, noting what we could see of the village park from each vantage point. Neither Mark nor I could see the stage, which was nearer the opposite end, nor could we see the light box. From ground level it seemed to be a confusion of trees and a few rooftops.

"Not that I'm against nature," Mark said as we walked toward the car, "but a little pruning might be in order around here." He nodded toward the large hemlocks and yews embracing the church. "Maybe we could suggest to Wilton that he get those clipped. The topiaries of the peacock and boar's head at Haddon Hall were classy, don't you think?"

"Wilton had opportunity, I suppose," I said, mulling over Mark's statement. "Though why he wanted to kill Alastair or Simon, I don't know."

"As we said earlier, he may have lied to protect the killer. That he is the killer makes no difference."

"Wilton doesn't need a hobby like collecting keys, or have to worry about being seen coming and going at the church. The church is his realm; it's not strange to see him there. And if he wanted to fix the light box wires, the key's right here for him to take."

"But, as you said, Brenna, we have yet to discover motive."

"Where is the key kept again? He said, but I'd like to see so I know how advantageous it is."

"We just passed it. In the interior corner of the porch.

Shouldn't be hard to find; there are just the two inside corners."

It wasn't hard to find. Even in the thickening afternoon light we spotted the key moments after entering the south porch. The top third of the west window glowed golden from the sunlight that angled upward, leaving the majority of the leaded glass in gray shadow. Among the wooden rafters the air had turned ochre-hued, illuminating the specks of dust drifting above us. The rest of the air wallowed in the gloom that would eventually claim the west window and the entire building.

"It's here now," Mark said unnecessarily. "I wonder if there's a sign-out sheet for it. I forgot to ask."

"There'd almost have to be. What if two groups wanted to use the stage area and the electricity? Not that the village is that large, but that family from Wales had their reunion here."

"Not the best way to build neighborly love. Imagine that family coming from all over the country and finding that another group was using the area. Almost motive enough to kill someone, I'd think."

I couldn't tell in the waning light if he were joking or serious, but I opened the door to the church proper. "Let me check just inside the church. The paper or a book might be on a table with the visitor cards." I closed the door on Mark's comment and looked around the south aisle. A table to the left of the door held some prayer cards, a mug stuffed with pencils, and a tri-panel brochure on the church. A larger table in the north aisle offered more church-related items but I could find nothing about reserving the stage or electricity. Out of ideas where else to look, I called to Mark.

"Don't yell in church," he said, remaining in the porch and sticking his head through the doorway. His right hand gripped the edge of the door, holding it slightly open. "If it's not obvious, I don't know where to tell you to look. Did you check in the bell tower?"

"We were upstairs and I didn't see anything like that. Besides, why would people climb into the tower just to reserve the stage?"

"How about in a drawer? Does that main table have a drawer?" He walked across the nave and we looked at the table. It held no drawer. "We can check the porch again, but if it's not there we'll ask Wilton later. We've wasted enough time on this."

As we crossed the main floor, I heard the outside door of the porch open. A voice muffled by distance and the closed church door called, "Wilton? It's Delmar Goodfellow. Wilton? I need to talk to you. It's about Alastair. It's praying heavy—"

The voice stopped as Mark opened the sanctuary door. Perhaps the caller was uncertain of Mark's identity, for the murkiness of early dusk filled the space. Mark moved slightly as he held the door for me, and I appeared in the opening, another indiscernible figure shielded from the light by the door standing ajar. The man hesitated for the space of a heartbeat, then—perhaps realizing Mark wasn't Wilton—turned, jerked the outside door open, and ran.

"Bloody hell," Mark swore, fumbling for the door handle. I was close behind him as he dashed outside. Mark stopped abruptly beside his car and looked around. "Now where the hell…"

I pointed to a figure racing down the lane, into the village. "There! You want to drive?"

"Foot's faster. He'll dodge around the shops, trying to lose me, if he's smart."

As he spoke, I could see Goodfellow glance behind him and disappear between two shops. Mark swore and took off down the hill like a man possessed. I ran after him, my heart already pounding from the adrenalin of the chase.

Goodfellow had slipped between two shops but Mark and I weren't far behind. We thundered down the narrow passageway, our shoes slapping noisily on the cobblestones. My foot slipped and I thought momentarily I would fall and sprain my ankle, but I righted myself and dashed after Mark.

We emerged from the alleyway and onto the southern edge of the park. A scattering of evergreens screened the park from the shops, providing privacy and noise reduction. It also helped screen Goodfellow. Mark and I pulled up short, taking in deep breaths and looking around.

"Where the hell is he?" Mark took a few steps forward and scanned the area.

"Could've ducked into the back of any of these places," I said, wondering if we could just enter a shop from the back. "And the pub's down a bit to our left. He might've run in there." It seemed a near impossible task to find Goodfellow. While Mark and I were looking around in shops, Goodfellow could have doubled back up the road to the church or run across Water Ford Lane to disappear into the wood. Or seek refuge in one of the houses, like Michael Green's. "You want to try one of the shops and I'll try another one?"

Mark swore again, his frustration mounting as we wasted time standing there. Suddenly, he grabbed my arm and pointed to his left. "Over there. That's him, isn't it?" He began running in the direction of the pub.

I sprinted after him. My words were bouncy as I tried to talk. "Looks like. I'll go to the left, you stay to the right."

Mark nodded and I bolted ahead, angling between two shops and coming out on Old Peveril Road. I was a couple shops east of the pub but as I glanced through the passageway Mark passed the opening. I picked up my speed and rounded the corner of the pub as Mark came up from the other side. A shake of my head told him I hadn't seen Goodfellow. We jerked open the door and rushed inside.

A few patrons were seated at tables or at the bar, but as Mark and I scanned at their startled faces we knew Goodfellow wouldn't be there. It was too obvious. Goodfellow would run to ground somewhere unusual.

"Trouble is," I said, trying to breathe, "he knows the village and the area. He could be holed up anywhere right now, in a spot we don't know exists. I don't see how we'll ever find him."

"We need to talk to Goodfellow, Bren. I don't want to let him get away. If he's so innocent, why'd he run?"

"Ask him when we nab him. We know where he works, where he lives. We'll get him."

"Not if he stays away from his job and holes up with someone. Damn."

Mark bent over, silently cursing. No other police officer could be seen and I didn't want to stop the shoppers to ask if they'd seen Delmar Goodfellow running for his life. I was about to suggest we go back to the car when I saw a person walk away from the corner of Jack Darkgate's house. Tapping Mark's arm, I nodded in the direction of the movement. Goodfellow raced along the path leading up the hill, but we weren't far behind.

The trail plowed straight through the patch of grassland between Jonah and Jack's houses, from the lane to the base of the hill. From there it snaked uphill, alternately hiding and showing itself through the curtain of trees and boulders. As we came to the hill, I hesitated and glanced up. Late afternoon already wrapped the side facing us in indigo shadow; violet-tinted shapes that could be trees or stones stretched onto the path. A flock of jackdaws rose from the cliff face, screeching against the sky and wheeling over the hilltop. I called to Mark to stop. He turned, the look on his face betraying his annoyance at losing even one second.

"What?" His breathing was loud and deep.

"It'll be dusk soon, Mark. It'll be hard to see in the wood."

Despite his desire to rush on ahead, he glanced to his left. The wood held the last vestiges of daylight but farther to the west the trees lost themselves to the anonymity of approaching twilight. He exhaled loudly and shook off my hand. "I'm going ahead. You don't have to. I need to catch him." Before I could reply, he raced on.

I ran as best as I could, but the rocky path slowed my speed, and the nettles and twigs grabbed at my trousers. Mark evidently took no notice of this, for he was at least twenty yards ahead of me.

As the path angled upward, it leveled slightly and I made better time. The soil was less rocky here, although closer to the cliff face, and I slowed slightly so I wouldn't fall in the dusky light.

Several yards farther on, the trail veered to the left, leaving the cliff, and I plunged ahead as fast as I dared go. Mark was in front of me, and though I could see him, it was the sound of breaking twigs and his shoes pounding the trail that guided me.

Which gave me an idea.

A dozen yards ahead the wood thinned to a small clearing. The light here was brighter and I could see Mark pause on the other side of a dead oak. He stood where the path branched and looked at the ground. I jogged to him, careful not to step on the twigs and pinecones littering the area. Holding my right index finger before my lips, I turned my head to my left, listening for Goodfellow's mad crash through the trees.

At first, I could distinguish nothing but bird song. Then, as I became more attuned with the wood, I heard the whisper of wind and the echo of a woodpecker's drumming against a tree. I looked at Mark; he had taken a few steps down the right hand path but stood near a large stone, listening intently.

I was about to join him when several birds frantically rose into the air. Their fluttering wings showed black against the lighter patch of sky. I signaled to Mark and pointed to the place where the birds had been. A group of large ferns nodded in testimony to the perpetrator of the disturbance. Mark tiptoed to me. "Goodfellow?" he mouthed.

Whispering "Probably," I motioned for him to take the left path. I headed for the ferns.

It usually works in films—the partners splitting up and boxing in the bad guy. Either I hadn't seen the right film or Goodfellow had. I tried to move as silently as I could through the undergrowth, but snapping twigs announced my location. Of course Goodfellow knew Mark and I were following him, but my idea was to drive him toward Mark. Goodfellow had another idea.

I heard him, rather than saw him, at first—a sharp 'crack' as he stepped on a dry tree branch, a muffled moan as he slid into a boulder. Recovering, he moved suddenly, swiftly, a somber shape among the trees. I ran for him, ignoring the prickles and stabs of weeds and bushes, focusing my sight and energy on him. As a consequence, I didn't see a tree root. The toe of my shoe caught in it and I fell heavily. My shoulder hit a stone and for a moment I lay there, the breath crushed from my lungs, my shoulder on fire.

Mark and Goodfellow crashed through the wood, heading toward the northern edge of the village and wilder sections of the peak district. I doubted Goodfellow was making for Bakewell, even if he lived there. It was miles away and I couldn't imagine him spending the night in the forest, let alone going all that way on foot.

I got to my knees and took a deep breath. The sounds of the hunted and the hunter had faded. I could only imagine where they were and what was happening. Slowly getting to my feet, I brushed the pine needles, bits of dry leaves and soil from my trousers and my palms. The wood had returned to its normal quiet, punctuated by the occasional birdcall.

The light was fast failing, turning plants and boulders into fairy tale creatures. They'd be a convenient place for Goodfellow to hide, but I assumed he and Mark were not in the vicinity. I got my small torch from my shoulder bag, turned it on, and picked my way back to the trail.

I paused at the clearing, where the path branched. Trying to find Mark would be a waste of time as well as stupid; crashing through the forest at night was dangerous. Plus, I didn't know in which direction he'd gone. I considered sitting here a while but quickly discarded the notion. How long should I wait? What if Mark came down the hill farther north and walked back to the pub via Water Ford Lane? Should I wait fifteen minutes and ring his mobile phone?

It was a senseless exercise in guessing. No practical answer presented itself, so I walked back down the hill, hoping I wasn't leaving Mark hurt somewhere in the forest.

At the bottom of the hill I paused and looked back at the darkening shape so close to me. It had turned to hues of purple, dark gray and black, nearly one solid mass against the western sky.

A few trees that fringed the hill stood out in stark relief against the gray background, like two-dimensional cutouts against a backdrop. No light showed itself among the trees; no call floated downwind to me. I turned the beam of my torch onto the trail and walked toward the pub.

I had not yet come to Jack Darkgate's house, the closest residence to the cliff face, when I heard my name yelled behind me. On turning, I saw Mark limping toward me. I walked up to him, calling to find out if he needed help.

He bent over, hands on his knees, breathing deeply. "God, I hurt."

"What happened? Are you all right?" I played the beam of my torch on the ground at his feet. "I can go fetch someone. Who knows first aid?"

"I'll be fine, Brenna. I'm just winded and I tripped over something up there. Took a headfirst dive into a massive tree trunk. Luckily, my shoulder took the impact. So it's just a matter of rest. You could ply me with a beer or two if you feel sorry for me." He straightened up and grinned.

"I've got my own cure to see to, thanks anyway for the invitation to be Florence Nightingale."

"What happened to you?"

"We've been working together too long. We're picking up each other's habits."

"Whatever are you on about?"

"You tripped. I tripped." I stared at the hill, feeling as though it had conquered us.

"Is yours bad?"

I shook my head. "It's my shoulder, but it'll be fine. Probably have a beauty of a bruise tomorrow."

"We make a pitiful pair, don't we? I wonder if Goodfellow got off unscathed."

"You lost him, I assume, since he's not handcuffed and trailing behind."

"Brilliant deduction, Bren."

I looked past the spot where the torchlight ended, trying to see into the blackness. "We need to get Graham. Goodfellow's just put himself in the main frame of suspects. Remember what he said in the church?"

Mark nodded between gasps. "Sure. 'I need to talk to you. It's about Alastair. It's praying heavy...' Sounds pretty damning, however his sentence would've ended."

"Graham needs to know about that. Maybe he can get officers to search addresses where Goodfellow might be. I hate to think he'll get away. We almost had him."

"Yeah. But we don't. Come on. Let's find Graham, shall we?"

Focusing the light of my torch at our feet, I said, "Wonder why he took off like that."

Mark shrugged and fell in beside me. "Probably an occupational hazard. You know...a former con, leery of cops."

"Probably lives by the motto 'Avoidance at all costs.' Or something similar."

"Well, wherever he is right now, he's probably fumbling around in the dark. He never did turn on a torch, and I can't believe he had one in his pocket. In his car glove compartment or boot, sure, but he wouldn't have come with a torch in his hand just to chat up Wilton."

I grabbed Mark's arm, pulling at him. "You're brilliant."

"You being sarcastic or honest?"

"I bet you a drink in the pub that his car's still at the church." I flicked the beam of my torch in the direction of the building. "Even if he did elude us, there's no way he could've doubled around, got down the hill, across the village and up to the church in the time that we met up."

"You want to stake out his car after we inform Graham?"

"No. We know where he lives and works. I was just thinking there might be something in his car that would give us a lead."

"We can't break into his car, Bren. Goodfellow's not done a thing, as far as we know."

"How about a concerned citizen checking to see if the windows are up and the car's locked? Crime prevention, removing temptation and keeping the local kids on the right path?"

"No. If Graham got wind of any irregularity we might do, he'd have us up on discipline. I like my rank and pay packet, meager as it is, just the way they are. Besides, he'll probably get a warrant to get into and search Goodfellow's car. "

"But that'll take a while. Goodfellow could come back and drive off by the time Graham gets the warrant."

Mark shrugged and hurried me along. "What can I say? We abide by the law. Goodfellow doesn't."

I bit my bottom lip, forcing myself to keep quiet. Not for the first time I wished I were a private detective. Or an ex-copper who looked into cold cases, like that bloke Michael McLaren who'd solved the murder case of Marta Hughes last month. I didn't know him but that didn't stop my admiration of him. He'd not been stymied by police procedure and he got results.

"Drop the idea, Brenna." Mark grabbed my torch, essentially putting me out of business. "You don't want to get busted for doing something stupid."

I mumbled something about wasting a good idea.

"It's a better idea to keep on the right side of the law." We stopped outside the pub. Mark nodded toward the door. "I'll find Graham and tell him about Goodfellow. Then I'll go get my car—it's at the church. You order the drinks, take them up to your room. I'll be right back and join you."

"We won't be needed for the search?"

"I doubt it. He'll call out the special team for that. Besides, we're walking wounded. He'll let us mend."

I grumbled that all the excitement had gone from the evening.

"You're forgetting the puzzle, Bren." He pushed me gently through the pub's door. "We're going to solve that thing tonight, no matter how long it takes." He strode toward the stairs and I shuffled up to the bar, revising my opinion. Tonight might very well solve some things.

## Seventeen

*Leeds General Hospital*

Both Davis and Smith had been doing odd jobs for the Dodders for about a year. They had worked together before, and were over the moon at this opportunity. It was a step up for them, both in assignment importance and prestige. Something to gloat over, certainly, but the money made it even better.

They arrived an hour earlier than needed, feeling the enormity of the assignment. Advancing dusk helped a bit with their nerves, as though twilight's anonymity made their approaching job of work easier. Prying eyes, and all that. They sat in Smith's car at their designated place in the Leeds Hospital car park. Even though they'd handled big jobs before, both men were anxious. Davis picked at his nail cuticles; Smith ran his thumb over the irregular edge of his keys, as though he were saying his beads. Both men sweated. Their anxiety shifted up a notch when Davis received the call from one of the bosses. It was time.

The bag in the car's boot, which they had been told repeatedly not to open until being notified, contained two Wakefield Security uniforms. It amazed them, both at the power and seemingly unlimited access their superiors in the gang had—almost as if they had infiltrated every possible sector of society. The note with the exact location of Roper's room and the exact moment the Wakefield security team would leave their post was secured inside Smith's trousers pocket. Now they just had to get ready and wait.

Waiting was the hard part. Smith didn't mind admitting that to anyone. Waiting knotted up your stomach, thudded inside your heart, stretched your nerves to the breaking point. Nothing either man could do would relieve the monotony or the stress.

Davis reached for the power knob on the car's radio.

"What are you doing?" Smith asked, his voice sharp, betraying his nervousness.

"I thought a little music—" Davis didn't have time to finish his sentence. Smith's hand slapped down onto him.

"Think again, mate. We're supposed to sit quiet till it's time."

"Okay, okay." Davis shook his hand slightly and crossed his arms over his chest. "Don't get so bloody awful minded. Not the end of the world."

"It will be if we do a cock-up. We sit. In *quiet*." Smith shifted his tall frame in the driver's seat, trying to ease the stiffness out of his back.

They had dressed in the car, not an easy task for tall men, but they had no choice. If they used the loo in the hospital, someone'd see them walking in with bundles. So they struggled with the clothes in silence and in the cramped quarters. When they'd finished, they pulled out the remainder of the bag's contents. The two large knives…military issue…had a note attached to them: "Use these on the man who loves knives so much—and have some fun while doing so."

Smith nodded, grunted almost inaudibly, and folded up the note. He just wanted to get this done and grab a pint. He needed the money and wanted it now.

~

As King Roper woke from his post-operative sleep, he looked around. He'd been wheeled into a large, pale-painted room full of others also recuperating from surgery. Despite his grogginess, he focused on his upcoming freedom. Only a few more hours. The image of him roaming around Derbyshire again made him smile. As did his move to his private room, which no doubt would be soon. He threw back the sheet covering him, suddenly feeling trapped and impatient, and tried to rethink the plan. He needed to correct any weaknesses now, while he still had time, while he could contact everyone, but he nodded off once again.

~

Davis and Smith weren't the only people in the hospital car park. Roper's crew was also waiting rather impatiently. Cobb, Pennington, Middleton, and Conroy were all very seasoned and very loyal henchmen to Roper, proving their responsibility through the years. Oddly, no one but Conroy really liked Roper. Yet, even he didn't let on his feelings to anyone. He was merely a well-paid employee, he'd tell the other thugs in the gang. Just a dog's body to do the dirty work. Conroy, however, displayed an almost bizarre reverence for Roper—probably due to their shared interest in inflicting pain and their love for the various uses for knives. It and his extensive collection were topics Conroy could speak on endlessly. He'd been known to rabbit on whenever any-one was around, whenever he could, whenever there was a spare minute. Even now, while they waited. It was hell listening to him yammer in the confines of the car. More than once the others had told him angrily to belt up about it.

Cobb said something derogatory about the man's ancestry and turned in his car seat to look out the window. The darkness surprised him. He'd had his eyes closed earlier, trying to grab a kip while they waited.

The night was perfectly clear. Though unseasonably hot, the weather had been sunny and unusually calm for several days. Calm before the storm, Cobb thought.

As the four of them anxiously sat in the car and reviewed their roles for the last time, Middleton stopped his cross-exami-nation in mid-sentence. His face drained of color. He pointed to-ward the front of the car. It was uncanny that in a car park with hundreds of vehicles Middleton saw Smith and another hench-men of the Dodders. And not two rows in front of them, sitting in a blue Aston Martin.

As Conroy punched Middleton hard in the shoulder, yelling,

"Snap out of it!" Middleton broke the news to the other three. He sat, his gaze fixed on the other car, and debated temporarily canceling Roper's escape. Why were members of the Dodders here? Their unexpected presence made him jumpy. He was about to say something, but Conroy and Pennington were already out of the car and running full speed toward the blue car.

The lighting from the overhead lamps lay faint and spotty, not designed for surveillance. More helpful for the criminal, Middleton thought as Conroy and Pennington moved up to the blue car. They blended well with the night and made no noise. As if they floated up to their prey.

By the time Davis heard an odd noise outside his driver's side door, it was too late. Both Pennington and Conroy used the solid steel butt end of their knives to break in both car windows. As their arms went in, both had the experience and dexterity to twist both their wrists and blades back in a slashing motion. As they did so, layers of flesh were sliced open on Smith's ear and down into his neck. While he reached for his own knife, Smith's hair was grabbed from outside, and as his head was pulled through the window, the final slash across the throat was made. Davis fared no better. He had heard the noise outside his window and shifted his gaze. It was a deadly mistake: he looked directly into the oncoming shattered glass, which flew into his eyes. Davis had no time to think or react, for Conroy jammed the butt end of his knife into Davis' mouth, breaking several teeth. The knife was yanked out and jabbed into the neck, twisting back in a slashing motion so that Davis' throat was cut to the point of decapitation.

Middleton and Cobb followed at a more leisurely rate. Even so, the blood was still squirting when they came up to the car.

Cobb surveyed the car park but saw no one. Maybe Roper had been right; they were 'the chosen ones' in their exclusive 'club'. The fact no one noticed the massacre until hours later would be analyzed for years to come.

Conroy took charge and decided the plan must move forward now. Middleton reached into the car, through the broken window, and grabbed the slip of paper lying on the lap of the dead passenger. He read the time and room number; it confirmed the Dodders' intentions of what they'd been about to do. Good thing they'd been spotted. Maybe it would all work out well after all.

The moon slid behind a bank of clouds and the car park plunged into a deeper darkness. Conroy grinned, feeling more confident than he had in hours. He barked at the others and herded them toward the hospital. They might've been four mates wandering into a pub for a game of darts, from the way they chatted light-heartedly. But the two bodies in the blue car mutely spoke of something terribly different.

The other three strolled into Leeds Hospital as Cobb went back to move their car to its assigned point. He crossed the car park, noting the feeble pools of light from the overhead lamps. Thankfully the lamps were sporadic, dotting the vast black tarmac in a half-hearted attempt to keep the night at bay. The darkness held, thick and off-putting in that area of the lot where the Aston Martin sat. So, unless their luck turned and someone parked right next to the blood-soaked car, the coppers should not find the bodies until Roper and they were long gone.

The boldness of the plan, to walk right up to the Wakefield guards and butcher them before taking Roper out, had not been well thought out. None of the four had considered that other patients might possibly be in the area. Nurses could be walking by, or an entire platoon of guards might be milling around Roper's room. But, luck—or fate—seemed to be smiling on them that night; the private room where Roper was recovering was at the end of a hall. And no one was around.

Conroy and Middleton turned the room's doorknob and looked inside.

The guard was sitting in a chair angled toward the corner of the bed. He had a full view of Roper but only a partial view of the door. As Conroy entered the room, the guard turned and started to get up. "Yes? No one's allowed in here. This is a restricted area—" The rest of his sentence died with him.

Conroy wiped his knife blade on the blanket on Roper's bed.

"It's about time," was all Roper could say before sitting up and grinning.

~

Hugh Claxton could hardly contain his heavy breathing. The meeting with his security team had been little more than mind-numbing small talk, a source of great agitation. He glanced at his watch. How quickly could the Dodders be in and out of Roper's room? They hadn't much time to take care of things.

The Wakefield security team had been informed that Roper would be sedated for thirty minutes in his room. This would accommodate further tests the medical staff needed to run.

As H hour arrived, Claxton phoned his team and ordered them all to meet with him in the common waiting room on Roper's floor. They needed a briefing, he told them.

Keeping the guards and nurses occupied would be no trouble for a man of Claxton's experiences. Orders were orders, and the doctor seemed confident that Roper wouldn't wake for a while.

A half hour of freedom, the guards thought, and looked forward to stretching their legs and grabbing a smoke. But wasn't it a bit odd, Claxton calling them *all* to a meeting? Normally he briefed the men in shifts, leaving someone always on guard with the prisoner. The guards conferred among themselves and agreed Claxton must've cracked under the strain. He wasn't thinking straight. Not to worry; they'd cover his back and leave one guard behind to watch over Roper. They admired Claxton that much to correct his mistake.

The men flipped a coin for it, the loser staying in the hospital room. Good-natured moaning from the losing guard prompted his cohorts to promise they'd bring him a coffee and sandwich on their return.

"Throw in some biscuits or cake," the guard shouted after them. "Chocolate."

"You think we're the bleeding waitress?" one of them joked back.

"Just bring me something for my damned pudding. You owe it to me."

"That'll be a quid extra, mate."

"Not bloody likely," he said, rolling his magazine into a cylinder and waving it at the man.

"Plain or dark, then?" The door slowly closed as the guard gave them the thumbs up and settled into his chair with his magazine.

⁓

Hugh Claxton watched the staff and guards chatting and sipping coffee. They seemed relaxed, not at all what he would've expected from people in contact with a murderer. But not many criminals, members of Roper's gang or not, could just waltz into Roper's room, Claxton concluded. No one would have the effrontery to try it.

Of course, the meeting was a ruse, a window for Dodder members Davis and Smith to do their job on Roper. Claxton sipped his tea, tasteless and lukewarm, and glanced at the guards in the far corner of the room. He considered his career would probably be over after Davis and Smith's work was discovered—a security breach this major wouldn't be tolerated, never mind if it resulted in Roper's death—and privately cheered many in Wakefield and law enforcement. Claxton downed the remainder of his tea and gave his career a forty percent chance of survival. Either way, it would be worth it.

Claxton just didn't know his scheme at that moment was not going according to plan. Not at all.

# Eighteen

By the time Mark got back from getting his car at the church, it was nearly dark outside. I'd a good head start on him, having downed my glass of shandy and on to my first cup of tea. Mark grabbed his beer from the top of the dresser and eased into the chair he'd occupied the previous night. He drank one third of the beer before I asked if he'd seen Graham.

"He's taking care of it," Mark said. "He called in a bunch of lads and was printing out addresses where Goodfellow might be when I left. Oh, and he commiserates with us about our shoulders and hopes we'll be recuperated by morning."

"And the car?"

"He'll have the Automobile Association get into the car. Maybe they'll find something that'll give us a break on the case. Yes, I know that'll take a while to get the warrant," he added, forestalling my concern, "but he'll put a guard on the car until it's done. Don't worry. Now, where are we with the puzzle?"

I sat on the foot of my bed and spread out the papers so Mark could see. "Refreshing our minds, we saw that portrait of James VI and I at Haddon Hall today. What was he wearing that suggested a clue?"

"That piece of jewelry in his hat."

"Bravo. What does the Hall's guidebook say about it?"

Mark slumped back into this chair and stretched out his legs. He propped them on the edge of the bed and leaned his head back. "If I'd known this would be Twenty Questions—"

"Come on, Mark. I'm trying to get you to think."

He sighed heavily and glared at me before downing another third of his beer. "Something about being a fair jewel in the shape of a gold feather. Why ask me? You've got the bleeding book. Look it up."

"Your shoulder's hurting."

"Brilliant deduction."

I got up, went into the bathroom, and came back with some paracetamol and a glass of water.

"What's this?"

"I thought it was obvious. Take them." I held them out to him. "Come on, Mark. We haven't got all night."

He picked up the caplets, tossed them into his mouth, and swallowed them with his beer. "Marvelous."

I set the glass on top of the dresser and reclaimed the bed. "The guidebook tells a bit about the painting. The hat jewel is famous. It appears in several paintings. You're right about the description. 'One fayre jewell, like a feather of gould, conteyning a fayre table-diamond in the middest, and five-and-twenty diamonds of divers forms made of sondrous other jewels.'"

"What's that get us? I remember talking about it being in an allotment of royal jewels and plate Charles I sold to some bloke in Amsterdam."

"It was never accounted for, remember?"

Mark sat up, the boredom gone from his face. "Right. It's a possibility it's the treasure Alastair and Simon hunted for."

"It works out. Oh, another thing might fit, too, but this seems most logical. Why are they so obsessive about genealogy?"

"I won't believe it if you say they're illegitimate cousins of James, or some such nonsense."

"Not of James, but they're related to the ancestor who had a position in Charles I's court. He was a Marshall, remember?" I let the significance of the surname sink in. "Yes," I said as Mark nodded, "the keeper of the peace, the man in a position to guard valuables. Probably in the jewel house or perhaps some other position of trust. He could've been in charge of guarding or handing over the jewels to the Amsterdam merchant, only he hid James's feather jewel, saving it from sale."

"You're saying *could* have, *might* have done. Don't we know? Aren't there any bills of sale? What good is conjecture in this? We could say anything and we'd never be able to prove it."

"The officers looking through Alastair's house found this." I pulled a sheet of paper from the pile on the bed and handed it to Mark. "Now does my theory sound a bit more solid?"

Mark let out a low, slow whistle. "Alastair traced his family back to that chap, the one who worked in Charles' household." He let the paper sag onto his lap and looked at me. "Things are falling into place. Did this have anything to do with the civil wars? Was this Marshall ancestor in Charles' court a Protestant?"

"That might have been the reason for the jewel's disappearance after the initial theft. The wars pitted Protestant against Catholic, parliamentarians against royalists."

"When was all this?" Mark said. "I know blocks of history but dates always troubled me. Mid seventeenth century is all I know."

"The civil war ran from 1642-1651."

"When did Charles I sell the jewels? Do they match up?"

I read from my notes. "Charles I was desperate for money to finance the Thirty Years War—1618-1648. He sold the plate and jewels in 1625."

"And England became involved because…why?"

"Charles tried to negotiate peace, having intervened in the fight against Spain and France."

"Risky."

"But the financial problem of not enough funds, coupled with the defeat and assassination of the Duke of Buckingham, forced Charles to abandon taking a hand in European affairs."

"Which didn't sit very easy with the Protestant armies in Europe, I don't imagine."

"So, the Thirty Years War actually forced him to sell some of the royal jewels. Charles got a loan of £92,400 from the Dutch merchant, far less than the contemporary value of £200,000."

"Ouch."

"And though some pieces were bought back, some were melted down or taken apart."

"But there's no record of the gold feather being dismantled or bought," Mark finished.

"That's why I think Alastair's ancestor hid it. He wasn't supposed to have it—it was technically the property of the crown."

"Where does the connection to Haddon Hall come in?" Mark sat up and grabbed the paper. "It's not exactly near London, so how did the jewel get here, which is what you're implying."

"I can only suppose Marshall was related to someone at the Hall, or knew someone at the Hall. I don't know why it landed here; the civil wars hadn't begun, so there was no need to keep the jewel safe from parliamentarians."

Mark stared at the sheet of paper, then at the poetry and the portrait. When he looked at me, his eyes crackled with energy. "The feather jewel belonged to James VI of Scotland."

"Right."

"On ascending to the English throne, he became James I of England."

I nodded, my heart thudding.

"Which is why he's referred to as James VI and I."

"Does this remind you of something?"

Mark read from the poetry the CSI officers had taken from Alastair's house. "'My love 'E covets like a plume worn but ceded by six and one.'" His right eyebrow rose slowly. "Plume is another name for a feather. Six and one refers to James VI and I."

"And ceded? What's that?"

"To cede something is to relinquish or give up something. James' royal jewels went to his son, Charles I, on James' death. Ceded through inheritance and family." Mark spoke the last sentence very slowly, so soft that I barely heard it. "My God, Brenna, I think you've solved it."

"We solved it," I corrected, "but not quite all of it. There's this strange business about the E and I and whatever the directions mean."

"I forgot about the damned initials." Mark leaned forward and pointed to the first few lines of the poetry. "'E is more worthy than I. 'E on the rise though I on the hill. 'E with his Ring and I with none.' What the hell does this mean?"

"I wish I knew." I got up and poured some water into the electric kettle. "You need another beer?"

"I need something to make my brain work. Make me a cuppa, too, will you?"

Grabbing the kettle, I nodded. After adding more water, I set the kettle back on the little table and flipped on the electric switch. I set a tea bag in a mug and walked to Mark. "If we could crack that second or third sentence, we might decipher the thing. Look." I leaned over his shoulder as I pointed to the sheet of paper. "We said last night that a rise is a slope or incline."

"Right. Not tall enough to be a hill. Just an elevated section of land that, well, rises from the major part of the flat land."

"But the second sentence emphatically states that whoever E and I are, I is on a hill. Whether living or standing or whatever, I is on a hill."

"The hill normally thought of to be taller than a rise."

"That word 'though' says a lot, Mark. Though means despite the fact, or however."

"Thereby implying superiority of some kind."

The electric kettle whistled and I hurriedly filled the mugs. I gave Mark his tea and took a sip of mine while I thought through the inference. "Okay. We've got the narrator stating that E is more worthy than this person I. More worthy in what aspect, we don't know, but that sentence is underscored by the narrator saying in the second sentence that this is true *despite the fact* that I lives or works on a hill."

"Fine. I can understand that. It's a question of superiority, as I said. E may be living or born lower—on an incline or sloping section of land—than I, who's living or born high. On the hill."

I nodded, not wanting to lose the thread of my thought. "And *despite the fact* that I lives or was born on a hill, E has a ring and I has none."

"That's evidently important. Why else would you put it in the poetry?"

I took another sip of tea, willing my brain to work. "What's the first thing you associate with a ring?"

"Marriage. But I could be answering this from a twenty-first century viewpoint. Is there a ring of state or royal jewelry? We've been talking about James' feather jewel."

"Wonder how we could find out." I set down my mug and stretched. My muscles were beginning to ache and, though I wouldn't admit it to Mark, my shoulder was tender. I got some paracetamol from the bathroom and downed them with Mark's untouched glass of water.

"You have a headache?"

"I guess I'm thinking too hard."

"Cut the crap. You're doing fine. We've almost got this licked." He moved to the end of the bed and patted the space beside him. "Come on."

Picking up the sheet containing the poetry, I read it again. "That ring's got to mean marriage, Mark. The rest of the piece bears it out. 'One step for *love*? Aye, count it ten more. From depth to height and so to heaven's vault and the eyes of the stars. My *love* 'E covets like a plume worn but ceded by six and one.' See? The whole thing's about love."

"Okay. I'll grant you marriage. So E is married and I isn't. We still don't know who E and I are."

"And we don't know about heaven's vault and the eyes of the stars. Is that part of a quotation?"

"What? Like a famous poem?"

"It'd have to be well known so that whoever ends up with this poetry, as Alastair and Simon did, would be able to under-stand what that means."

"And be either contemporary with the writer of this puzzle

or famous in the years prior to the puzzle. Like 'How do I love thee? Let me count the ways.' You know…something recognizable so the meaning is clear."

"Well," I said, grabbing my laptop, "if you don't know—"

"There's the Internet, which does." Mark rubbed his hands, grinning with enthusiasm. "We're almost there, Bren. We're nearly at the treasure. I can smell that diamond and see ole James grinning at us."

I googled the phrases in question and soon found pertinent information. "Listen to this, Mark."

"What's it about, the vault or the eyes?"

"Kind of both."

"Our lucky day. Read on, Macduff."

"This is incredible, Mark. Peacock feathers—actually, the *eyes* in the peacock feathers—symbolize the vault of heaven." I paused, letting him react. He did: he swore. "They also stand for the 'eyes' of the stars." I looked up from the computer screen. Mark was rubbing his forehead. "What do you think?"

"Anything else that might relate to the poetry?"

I read through the list displayed by the computer search. "Nothing else remotely connected to it. This is our best shot."

"So, we've got a strong reference to a peacock, through this line in the poem and through James VI and I's hat jewel. Where do we find the peacock?"

I fell backwards onto the bed and stared at the ceiling. Were we really on the right track? How did James' hat jewel, peacocks, marriage and a hill come together to lead us to a treasure? I said as much to Mark, who finished his tea, got up, and walked to the window. "There are a lot of stars out tonight," he said. There was no humor in his voice. Rather, it sounded tired and close to defeat. "I don't suppose there's a constellation about a peacock. You know…vault of heaven, eyes of the stars, peacock feathers, standing beneath the constellation and digging for the treasure…" He glanced at me, looking hopeful.

"Let's find out." I typed in peacock constellation in the

computer search bar. A second later I said, "*Pavo* is a *constellation* appearing in the southern sky. Its name is Latin for *peacock*.*" Looking at Mark, I said, "I refuse to believe the treasure is buried somewhere in New Zealand or the Outback. This thing was written with references to James VI and Charles I. They had no connection with the southern hemisphere, as far as I know. And I don't believe someone in the 1600s would expect the treasure hunter to get on a ship for that part of the world, either. No, I think the peacock constellation is a non-starter. The peacock has to mean something else."

"To tell you the truth, I'm kind of disappointed. I'd like to travel with you to New Zealand. Or even along Old Peveril Road tonight. It's all silvery under the moonlight."

"Well, you'll have to be content with a local trip if we can figure out where this thing is hidden. Peveril Road is fine, actually. But maybe tomorrow night. I'm kind of achy from our hilly adventure." I was about to pour myself another cup of tea when I stared at Mark.

"What? Something wrong?"

I shook my head. "On the contrary. I think you solved the peacock conundrum."

"I did?" Mark came over to the bed and looked over my shoulder as I leafed through the Haddon Hall guidebook. Turning to the page I sought, I said, "Yes! You've solved it."

"I'm glad, but refresh my mind on how I solved it. I'm not remembering as well as I used to five minutes ago."

"Read it." I angled the page toward him.

"At the gardener's cottage are fine examples of topiary work. A Peacock and a Boar's head, respectively the arms of the Manners and Vernon families..." He left off reading and grinned at me. "I *am* rather brilliant. All right, we've linked the peacock to the Manners family. Does that automatically mean the royal jewel, or whatever we're seeking, is at the Hall?"

"If I were a betting person, I'd say so. Look at this." I turned a page, held up the book and he read it.

"The illegitimate son of William the Conqueror, William Peverel is perhaps more famous in Derbyshire for Peveril Castle, situated on a steep hill in the village of Castleton. Haddon Hall, once under Peverel's ownership, passed in marriage to Richard Vernon and then to his daughter, Dorothy. It, in turn, came into the Manners family on the marriage of Dorothy to John Manners in 1558. The Hall is situated on the rise above the River Wye…" He cupped my face in his hands, tilted my head upwards, and kissed me on the mouth. Then, releasing me suddenly, he danced across the floor. "So, where are we?"

"You talked about Peveril Road in the moonlight just a minute ago."

"You want to go for that stroll?"

"Not right now, thanks. I thought about the hill where we were earlier tonight, and the puzzle of the hill and the rise, and the E and I, and, well, it just came together. Have you noticed that usually when William Peverel is written, his surname is spelled with all E's? But when it's written in conjunction with the castle, it's written as Peveril, with an I?"

"So, the reference in the verse refers to the man Peverel, the E of our poem: 'E with his Ring and I with none.' A ring to denote William Peverel as the man and therefore able to be married, and I with none meaning the castle. Was William Peverel married? Was his father? Everyone knows William Peverel was a bastard, a product of a non-married union. Does that throw off our solution to the poetry?"

"You do keep me busy." I did another search on the computer. "You're safe. It says William married Adelina of Lancaster."

Mark frowned. "Dare we hope that we've identified the E and I of our poetry, then?"

"As I said, I normally don't bet, but in this instance…" I stood up and he hugged me, whirling me around the room.

When we finally separated, he said, "But we still don't know where at Haddon Hall the jewel is. Have we overlooked something in the rest of the verse?"

"There has to be. I've forgotten exactly, but when we first read it, we commented on how the last part sounded like directions, remember?"

He picked up the paper, by now getting a bit dog-eared and wrinkled, and read the last few sentences. 'One step for love? Aye, count it ten more. From depth to height and so to heaven's vault and the eyes of the stars. My love 'E covets like a plume worn but ceded by six and one.' We've identified the vault and stars to refer to the peacock."

"Which refers us to Haddon Hall."

"That depth to height, if taken with the one step and ten more do sound like directions. Depth to height could mean a climb, perhaps a hill or steps."

"But it's a short climb, eleven steps. Wouldn't that be more like stairs?"

Mark grabbed me again and, holding me close, whispered, "Let's find out tomorrow."

# Nineteen

Mark and I walked around the village that night. "It's a shame to waste the moonlight," was Mark's invitation to our midnight ramble. I agreed and, although I wanted to get some sleep, I was too excited to get into bed, much less close my eyes. We strolled up Water Ford Lane and passed Simon's house. Even at this late hour, a patch of yellow light slanted out of the front room window. The light abruptly disappeared as Simon evidently turned off the lamp. Night wrapped around the house in that instant, dragging it into flat darkness, featureless but for a smaller light toward the back of the house. It winked sporadically, slowly, defining the man's agitated pacing.

"What's with him?" Mark asked as we stopped to watch the odd lighthouse-type effect. "Can't he sleep?"

"We can't either."

"That's different. We've been working on a murder case."

"He's probably still bothered by Alastair's death. It's not been all that long ago."

Mark grunted and we meandered up Old Peveril Road.

We strolled as far north as St. Agnes Church, talking about the puzzle and the treasure, and speculated if Alastair or Simon had found the jewel first...if either had. We also ventured a guess as to where the jewel might be hidden.

"The Hall's got a hell of a lot of staircases," Mark said as we stopped opposite the church. "How are we ever going to figure out which one is ours?"

"I believe the Hall was pretty much built by the time Dorothy Vernon married John Manners. But I vaguely remember they built on the Long Gallery, I think, toward the end of the 1600s. Still, as with the rest of the verse, the stairs must be obvious to the recipient. Something that is significant to the family or generally known about the Hall."

"Anything come to mind?"

"No, but I'm not really up on Haddon Hall architecture. Should we ask Jack Darkgate?"

"Let's see what we can find before we call in the cavalry. I know he's a walking encyclopedia of Haddon Hall, but we've got this far with our brains and the computer. I'd like to finish it up, keep it our accomplishment."

"Sure, Mark." I nodded to the constable standing guard over Goodfellow's car as we passed.

Mark rubbed his chin and glanced around the area. "Where the hell is Goodfellow? It's nearly half past twelve."

"You don't think he's hurt, do you? Maybe he fell in the wood or took a spill down the hill." I glanced at the black lump on the western horizon, bigger and more menacing at night. Not a light shown on it, though if I expected Goodfellow to be sauntering through the wood or down the trail with a torch I should check in to the nearest psychiatric ward. If he'd run from us, he wouldn't announce his reappearance with torchlight.

"Unless he assumes we're asleep," Mark suggested. "As most sane people would be. Especially those working a murder case."

"I hope he's at a friend's house for the night. I know it's still warm, but spending the night in the forest... Ugh."

"The closest houses to that hill are Jack Darkgate's, Jonah Ellwood's, Megan Powell's and the Martins. He could be at any of them, I suppose."

"Is Goodfellow so close to the Martins that he'd hide there? I don't recall any mention of a great friendship."

"Hard to say. Goodfellow's friends with Declan Morris. I don't know about the others, especially. Anyway, it's odd that his car's still here. He ought to know we would put surveillance on it. Perhaps that's what scares him away."

"He might very well over react. Remember, he's an ex-con, and he's probably allergic to cops."

"Yeah, well, he better get used to it. The world's filled with us. Sweet dreams."

⁓

I didn't have them. In fact, I had a difficult time falling asleep. My words to Mark earlier in the day came back to haunt me that night, revolving and magnifying in my mind like an accusation. I'd put up a brave front before Mark, but alone in my room my facade dissolved. I felt alone, deserted, unloved. Mark had been right; I heard his words as I cried into my pillow. "I thought that if a guy was deeply in love, about to be married, he'd talk to his bride-to-be every day. None of us knows how much time we have on this earth, and wasting a day without telling your intended that you love her..."

I rolled onto my side and grabbed a facial tissue. I didn't know where Adam was, that was true. But Mark had also spoken the truth when he implied there was no job-related reason for Adam not to have two minutes to phone me.

The moonlight silently slid across the room as I lay there, trying to fathom why Adam hadn't called. I could've rung him up earlier in the evening, but I knew he wouldn't be available to talk. He hadn't said why. But busy all evening?

I blotted my cheeks with the back of my hand. I didn't understand it. Nor did I understand what had happened between Mark and me at Haddon Hall. Our brushing together had been accidental, yet neither one of us had moved. Nor had made any attempt to move. Even now I felt the tingles of fire racing through my blood, the intense sensation of being alive. Every sound, every color, every scent and touch had been magnified in those short seconds. Had I never existed before that moment? Now that I had been awakened, would I sink back into oblivion?

The light waned and I sat up. A bank of clouds obscured the moon, plunging my room into the physical darkness I felt.

Inexplicable sadness or apprehension gushed over me. Icy prickles crawled across my skin in waves, each one more intense, and I trembled and pulled the sheet over me. Was I really in love with Adam? What was love, anyway? Had I ever truly felt it or just grabbed at him from fear of being alone in my old years? Did Adam honestly love me?

I sank against the headboard and gave way to the sadness and fear. Tears streamed down my cheeks, and as I clutched the edge of the sheet Mark's voice again hovered in my ear. "Wouldn't it be nice to hear it?"

~

When I came down to breakfast in the pub Tuesday morning, Graham was seated at a small table in the far corner of the main room. It looked to be more than the usual cop-privacy-security measure—he had a sheet of paper on the table in front of him, a pen, and he was talking very quietly on his mobile. Almost as though he didn't want to draw attention to himself, for he barely moved except to write things down. I said as much to Mark when he came down a minute later.

"Probably getting an update from someone," Mark said. "You'll see. At this morning's briefing he'll tell us about the A.A. report or the warrant to search the car or the PM report. Did you sleep well?"

"We already know about the PM report."

"What do you want to eat?" He busied himself with ordering for us and I watched Graham.

When he'd finished with his phone call, he made a note on the paper, looked up something on his mobile, and soon made another call. I watched him as he talked; he leaned over the page as though to keep it from prying eyes, occasionally looked out of the window, and sporadically wrote.

"He doesn't look well," I said to Mark after our food arrived.

"What do you mean?" Mark turned slightly in his chair and glanced at Graham. "Looks all right to me. He's just preoccupied with something. That warrant."

"He's been preoccupied with something since Saturday

evening. He stared out of the window during our briefing, looked like he was in LaLa Land, conferred with Scott, and now this."

"Now this," Mark repeated. A hint of exasperation showed in his tone. "What do you mean? He's a chief inspector. He's in charge of this case. Of course he's preoccupied. You want a boss who sits around on his bum all day and leaves us to flounder on our own?"

I shook my head and mumbled that it would be ridiculous.

"So, let the man direct the show, Brenna. We've got at least a dozen people whom we're looking at for possible motive and opportunity. We've got a nasty method of murder. And Simcock's probably breathing down his neck. Cut Vic some slack."

Normally I would have asked Mark not to call Graham by that nickname, the Vic having come into being when he first joined the Force after giving up his position as a Methodist minister. But I let it go this time; I was too upset about the situation.

By the time the CID team assembled in the incident room, Graham appeared to have put whatever bothered him on a back burner. He was as sharp as ever during the briefing.

Mark, I, and the other officers related the main points of yesterday's interviews, and Graham jotted down names and key words on the whiteboard. Margo added to the list with information about Fiona Doherty.

"She's a day care helper," Margo said, an unmistakable tone of pride in her voice. She'd not been asked to check anyone's finances on this case, and her eyes and voice reflected her contentment. "But the thing I find interesting about her is that she's Nicholas Martin's mistress."

On the board, Graham drew a doubled ended arrow connecting Fiona's and Nicholas' names. "Did she tell you, or did you find out from Nicholas?"

"I've not spoken to Nicholas. Fiona admitted it readily enough."

"Does Mrs. Martin know about Fiona?"

"I don't know. Fiona seemed to think she and Nicholas had

kept the affair a secret. It didn't last all that long, anyway. One month."

"Who called it off, and why? Sounds like Nicholas got an ultimatum from his wife."

"Fiona ended the affair. She didn't mention anything about Nicholas or his wife demanding that she end it. It came down to finally accepting the fact that Nicholas was married and wouldn't leave his wife. Fiona started the fling, thinking she'd get marriage and a child by Nicholas."

"Is that significant...the child?"

"Yes, sir. I think it is. The Martins have no children. Fiona thought that if she could give Nicholas a child, he'd be so happy that he'd divorce Alison—that's his wife—and marry Fiona."

"Except it didn't work like that," Graham finished. "Does Fiona know why? Did Nicholas want children? That could be the reason he and his wife have none."

"I don't know why they have no children. Maybe Fiona never knew, either. But her idea to snag Nicholas didn't work, and she realized that a month into the affair. She admitted her mistake with Nicholas, and when she realized he wasn't leaving hearth and home for her, she gravitated to Jonah Ellwood."

"The publican?"

"Yes, sir." Margo glanced at her notebook before adding, "He's not married, so perhaps she'll have better luck with him."

"Better luck meaning...what?"

"Marriage. A home and children. That's all she's ever wanted. Stability in life."

"But she strayed to the wrong pasture at first."

"Yes, sir. I don't know why she thinks she can't find someone. She's a petite, attractive brunette. Very smartly dressed. I can't afford the labels she wears. But maybe she's had low self-esteem all her life, and she latched on to Nicholas Martin because he fed her the first smooth line she believed. She's awfully young, probably nineteen. She might just lack life experience and think every bloke who comes along is trustworthy."

"Or," I said, "maybe she was just ready to fall in love and Nicholas was convenient."

Graham said, "Did you confirm any of the details of the affair with Jonah?"

"All of it. Jonah was jealous of Nicholas when Fiona was with him. Jonah fancied Fiona even then, but he'd never approached her. They had one night together when Fiona had just started seeing Nicholas. That was a week into Fiona's and Nicholas' affair. Fiona became pregnant with Jonah's child. I think that tipped the scales in Jonah's favor and helped Fiona dump Nicholas."

"When was this relinquishing of Nicholas for Jonah?"

"Three weeks ago. But neither Fiona nor Jonah has said a thing to anyone about her pregnancy."

"And, presumably, Nicholas knows nothing about it."

"I doubt it. It really doesn't concern him."

"Except that Fiona was cheating on him with Jonah."

"While Nicholas was cheating on his wife. Yes, sir."

Graham exhaled slowly and scratched his forehead. "Oh, what a tangled web we weave."

"Yes, sir."

"Anything else? Anyone?"

PC Byrd stated that, on the same subject, he'd talked to Alison Martin. "She's a bank clerk in Bakewell. Says she knew about Fiona and her husband but she didn't confront him because she thought the infatuation would pass."

"Stoic woman."

"Yes, sir. She impressed me as being that way. Strong, serious, very single-minded. I guess she'd have to be, seeing as how she's a bank clerk. Anyway, you can imagine her relief when Nicholas comes trotting home and has stayed home."

"Has he shown any signs of straying again?"

"Alison says no. Home every night or else accounted for, as with sword dancing practice."

"But that doesn't automatically preclude his dalliance during the day."

"I realize that, sir. And no doubt Alison does, too. But she seems to think Nicholas has learned his lesson, as she put it."

"What lesson would that be?" Graham looked slightly puzzled. He stood on the far side of the table, his right eyebrow raised, rolling the dry marker in between his palms. "Seems as though Fiona's the person who learned her lesson about leaving married men alone."

"I didn't ask her. It probably doesn't mean anything specific. I did learn, however, that she knows Fiona is pregnant. And she believes Nicholas is the father."

"She's not bothered by that?"

"No, sir. She seemed to think it a joke. She remarked that perhaps she should remind Jonah of Fiona's tendency to wander."

"Did you get the impression, Byrd, that Alison was hiding her hurt?"

"I took her statement as she gave it: matter of fact, straight forward, and glad to put Fiona behind them."

"Do Alastair or Simon come into this anywhere, Byrd? How about your impression, Lynch?"

Margo said Fiona talked only of Nicholas and Jonah and that the cousins had nothing to do with Fiona's affair. Byrd confirmed that Alison's irritation focused on Nicholas and that it concerned just the three of them.

Graham reclaimed his seat on the table. "Yes, Taylor? You have something to tell us?"

I opened my shoulder bag and drew out the letters I'd found yesterday at Alastair's. They were still sandwiched between two sheets of unused computer paper. Handing them to Graham, I told him where I'd found them and that they might be crucial to the investigation.

He carefully arranged them on the table, taking care not to touch the papers, and read them silently. When he'd finished, he said, "If someone had planned to carry out the threat stated in those notes, Taylor, why was the light box rigged? As we know, Simon should've been electrocuted, not Alastair."

"Maybe the letter writer had something in the works for Alastair, but he mistakenly died."

"So the letter writer breathes a sigh of relief at not having to worry about alibi and police hot on his trail. I don't know..." Using the tip of his pen, he scooted the papers into a stack and sat down. "Kind of a thin thread, but we'll see if we need them. Anyone else have any bright ideas about this, or something else to contribute. No? Well, I've a bit from Jens Nielsen."

Mark grinned and whispered, "See, Bren? I told you Graham was getting a PM report this morning."

I reminded Mark that Jens already gave us the report, but Mark seemed to ignore it.

"You have something to tell us, Taylor?" Graham said, looking at me. "Or perhaps Mr. Salt would like to contribute something constructive."

Mark cleared his throat, glanced at me, and said he had nothing to say.

I apologized for interrupting and eased down a bit in my chair.

Graham thanked us for our undivided attention. "The shoes Alastair was wearing for the dance performances Saturday were not what he normally wore."

Murmurs and suggestions swept through the group. Graham paused while the speculative chatter rose and fell. When it was quiet again, he continued.

"Alastair wore an old pair of Irish step dancing shoes, the bottoms of the toes and heels of which, as you may or may not know, are covered in round-headed nails. These provide the 'tap' sound for the faster dances such as jigs. These nails, being metal, proved to be an excellent conductor of electricity. You may remember that Alastair was sweaty and had spilt a beer on himself."

Mark asked why Alastair had worn different shoes that day.

"I presume they were his, but that's something you can find out."

"Maybe something had happened to his usual pair of rapper shoes."

"As I said, Salt, you can ask about that. I don't like to leave anything to chance, no matter how small or insignificant it seems. Which brings me to the disappearance of Delmar Goodfellow." Graham briefed the team at length on what had happened last night, the application for the warrant to search the car, and how the search for Goodfellow was progressing. "The team is questioning everyone we know who has a connection to Goodfellow. He's not turned up at work today, which signifies he's either hiding out or something's happened to him. But we're bound to find him soon. Right, then. Everyone know what she or he has to do today?" He paused, looking at us, waiting for someone to ask a question. We remained silent, ready to get on with the job. "Fine. I hope to hear good things later."

Mark and I walked outside, discussing our schedule for the day. I interrupted and pointed to the car. It still sat in front of the church and it shone painfully bright in the sunlight. We walked to the car and I peered inside. The constable on guard nodded to me and claimed the shade of a nearby tree. "You know, Mark, I don't think this is Goodfellow's car."

"That's absurd. We saw it last night. A white Volkswagen Beetle. This is a white Volkswagen Beetle."

"But I don't think it's the same car, Mark."

"Why not? What's different about it?"

"Granted, we saw it at night and the light's different at night. But Goodfellow's car...or the one he drove here in...had a sticker from a garage in Bakewell pasted to the front window. This car doesn't have one."

Mark walked around to the front of the car and looked. "Are you sure? You said yourself the light's different at night."

"Different in that you can mistake certain colors, but I couldn't mistake that decal. There isn't one here now. Besides, the number plate frame advertises the name of a car rental company."

"Why would someone else park a similar car here, and when?"

I shrugged and picked up my shoulder bag. "To confound us poor, dumb coppers?"

Mark swore and kicked at a stone. "That fish odor just got stronger. How'd he get home if his car is here? Okay, *someone's* car is here? Cars still had to be traded."

"Someone gave him a lift and the cars switched before Graham put the guard on the car."

"I wish Coral was here. I think we're going to need him." That said, we walked back to the incident room and waited while Graham ran a police computer check on the car's registration number. It wasn't Goodfellow's.

～

Delmar Goodfellow wasn't at home. We made certain. No one answered Mark's doorbell ringing and door knocking. We walked around the house, peering into windows and pounding on the back door. The place held the air of desertion.

"The house has no furniture," Mark said, his face against a window. The curtains had been pulled aside, exposing the room's interior. "You can't tell me he lives like that."

"Let me see." I shielded my eyes from the light and stared into the bedroom. "No bed, no dresser, no chair. Not even a stray sock on the floor. Are we sure we have the correct address?"

Mark read off the information on our list.

"That's this place, all right. This is weird, Mark."

"Let's see if there's a neighbor or someone... Oh, sir!" Mark called to a white-haired man who was gradually making his way to the back of his house as he watered his perennial border. "Sir, could we have a moment of your time?" We introduced ourselves, showed the man our warrant cards, and asked if he knew Delmar Goodfellow. "He lives here, doesn't he? I ask," Mark said, "because the house looks like he's moved out."

"You've just missed him. He moved away yesterday. Why? What's he done?"

"Why do you ask that?"

"He's an ex-con. I figure if you cops want him, he must've done something."

I said we just wanted to ask him a few questions about a person he may have known.

"Well," the man said, pouring water on a clump of daylilies, "looks he might have, since he left."

"Do you know when he moved? Do you know which removal company he used or where he went?"

"I didn't see him. Just two blokes I took to be mates of his. Don't know what they looked like on account of it being night, but one was tall and skinny, and the other was medium height and build. Didn't have overalls on…you know, like a company uniform. Just dressed in split jeans and tee shirts. They came to the house and moved out his stuff. Used both their cars and a small trailer. Goodfellow didn't have much, being as he just got out of the nick. But he had enough for the two cars and the trailer."

"Did you get a good look at the vehicles? Could you identify them?"

"Not license number, if that's what you're after. One was an old Volkswagen bus, dark color. The other just seemed like a regular car. You know…four doors, hardtop. A newer model. Maybe a Ford Fiesta or Focus. Black or dark blue, I'd guess."

"What time was this?"

The man straightened up from his watering and scratched his chin. His eyes were a washed out hazel color, barely discernable against his tanned skin. "I know pretty much down to the minute. I'd just finished watching a show on the telly. I got up to make myself a cuppa and listen to a book on tape before turning in. I heard the two cars and the men talking outside. They weren't loud, but it was different voices from what I've heard, so I looked. They had a key; there's no question of burglary so I didn't ring up the cops. But as to time, well it was just after ten o'clock."

"Close to when we were having our bit of hilly exercise and before Graham formed the search team," I murmured to Mark.

He nodded and asked the man, "Did you speak to the two men? Did they say where Goodfellow was or did you get his new address?"

"Young man, I got to my age by minding my own business and not making waves. I watched for a bit to make sure they weren't stealing stuff, but they locked the door when they finished, so that satisfied me that they were helping Goodfellow. His car wasn't here; I figured he was at his new residence, getting that ready. And I didn't ask his address. We weren't particularly chummy when he was here; I saw no reason to continue the non-existent friendship over the miles."

"Did the men say anything among themselves about Goodfellow?"

"Just something about hoping that his new quarters would last longer and that he'd rest in peace. That help you at all?"

Mark thanked the man and we slowly got into his car.

## Twenty

"So, who do you think those two guys were at Goodfellow's?" I asked Mark as he drove us back to Nether Haddon later Tuesday morning.

"I've got a better question. Where was Goodfellow when all this was going on—loping along the hill in front of me or hiding somewhere and perhaps talking on his mobile to these blokes?"

"And why the secrecy? In the dead of night two guys move a tenant out of his house? Every stick of goods? And where's his car?" I sank back into the car seat and exhaled deeply, gazing out of the window. "Your three day old fish has suddenly become a week old."

"You know what, Bren? I've got a bad feeling about this whole thing."

"Because Goodfellow's mates moved him out of his house?"

"That, plus that parting shot they said."

"Yes. That's bothers me, too. Rest in peace is usually reserved for…" I couldn't complete the sentence. Mark's bad feeling was catching.

We tried to alleviate the bad feeling first by updating Graham on the incident, then by asking Goodfellow's girl friend, Megan, if she'd seen him recently. But the feeling only intensified when she said she hadn't seen him for two days. Though she had seen someone new in the village last evening. When she described the person my heart rate kicked into overdrive.

"Sure. I remember him. I doubt if I'll ever forget. Tall, thin, muscular shoulders, neck and arms. Dark eyes...maybe black. Black hair that was graying."

Minutes later, in Mark's car, I said, "Did Megan's description of the stranger sound familiar?"

Mark's hand gripped the car's steering wheel, forcing the blood from his knuckles. "She left out the Maori tattoos."

I nodded, afraid my voice would break or I'd start crying. "King Roper," I managed to whisper.

"How the hell could that be, though? The bastard's in Wakefield. He hasn't a twin, has he?"

"I hope not." I trembled at the suggestion.

We sat for several minutes, busy with our thoughts. I'd had enough of King Roper in May. And certainly more than enough in March. And I'd not been as directly involved with him as Graham and Scott had been. If anyone had reason for concern about Roper and his possible escape from prison, it would be them. Roper had tried to kill each of them but, luckily, had failed. He might succeed the next time, however. His anger would goad him into retaliation.

"But it *can't* be Roper," I said finally. "Graham would've informed us of Roper's escape. He'd not keep that information to himself. He's aware of how dangerous Roper is. We need to know if he's at large."

"What if Graham doesn't know? I'm not aware of any man hunts."

Which was true. If Roper had escaped, each Force in the areas where Roper had lived or had committed a crime would be notified; countywide searches would be instigated.

We ducked into the incident room and told Graham about the stranger, figuring it might be important. Though he didn't say anything about Roper, he blanched slightly on hearing the description. I put it down to his run-in with Roper in March. When Graham repeated that he didn't need us on the Goodfellow inquiry, we went to talk to Nicholas Martin.

Nicholas sat at his desk in the newspaper office, a bustling, large room in a once-modern building off Bakewell's main road. High, plaster ceilings, tall windows and a scuffed linoleum floor delegated the space to an earlier century; computers, mobile phones, faxes and copiers gave it a contemporary look.

As did Nicholas. Around thirty years old, Nicholas looked every inch the man of *GQ*, Yves Saint Laurent and Paris runways. His suit jacket hung over the back of his chair and his tie was loosened, yet his casual shoes shone from a recent polishing and his fingernails were clipped. Every item on his desk was filed, stacked, contained or dusted, down to the regimental row of sticky notes along the edge of his computer monitor.

"I admit I let the affair begin," Nicholas said, nudging the phone on his desk back a few inches to line up with his desk lamp. He glanced at the adjacent desks; neither writer was in the room. Nicholas's neck muscles relaxed and his shoulders eased. "But after the initial infatuation wore off, I realized what an idiotic thing I was doing to Fiona. And my wife. I love Alison. I didn't want to lose her. I-she would've divorced me. I couldn't have lived with that."

The corners of Mark's mouth contracted slightly and he looked at Nicholas for several seconds. His eyebrows lowered in a slight frown as he leaned forward. "Did she say she would divorce you?"

"No. She never said a thing about the whole damned business. But I believe she would have if the affair had dragged on."

"You implied you were also hurting Fiona by the affair. What do you mean?"

Nicholas grabbed a pen from the pencil holder and clicked the button in and out. "Fiona deserved marriage, a husband and a family. That's what she wanted. I couldn't give that to her. The longer she stayed with me, the less chance she'd have of obtaining that. I told her I was breaking off the affair, that she should focus her energy on finding someone whom she could spend her life with. A proper marriage and her own home. Of course she was crushed when I told her we were through, but she soon realized the truth of what I said."

"How long were you two involved with each other?"

Nicholas glanced at the wall clock, as though that could help him calculate days. "I didn't mark when it started, but I'd think about a month. Certainly not much more. I think we both realized fairly soon that the fire would die quickly. We needed love and friendship for the affair to develop. It never did."

"Speaking of friendship…were you friends with either Alastair or Simon?"

"We were in the same dance group. Of course we were friends."

"I don't mean just friendly. Friends whom you'd have a pint with or spend time with outside of performances. Close enough so you'd know if someone wanted to kill one of them."

"I'd like to think so. We weren't best mates, which is what I assume you'd really like to hear. But we did have the occasional pint together and talk about our jobs and such. Complain about bosses and the economy and the local football club. But neither of them mentioned someone was mad enough to try murder. That's rather slim, isn't it? Knowing someone is after you?"

"Depends on the person and the circumstance. Threats are made more often than you'd think, verbally and in writing." I wanted to mention the stack of threatening notes I'd found at Alastair's but didn't. "Not all of them are acted upon, of course, but some people do follow through and actually attack, if not kill."

"Sounds like a novel."

"You mentioned that Fiona wanted a family. She informed us that she is expecting. Is that—"

"No. It isn't my child."

"You know for certain? If you two were sleeping together, isn't it likely that you fathered it?"

"I paid for a paternity test, if you must know." Nicholas sat up, his back poker stiff. "And my wife doesn't know about it. Not that I'm trying to hide anything from her, but it would've been upsetting for her. I dealt with the situation and it's taken care of."

"Do you know the father's identify?"

"No. I didn't wish to know. My only concern was whether the child was mine or not. It isn't, so Fiona has no claim on me. As I said, we've seen the last of each other."

I let a few moments of silence fall between us before saying, "Alastair was wearing the wrong shoes Saturday when he was murdered. Do you know anything about that?"

"Wrong shoes?"

"Yes. Irish step shoes. The hard soled, old kind with nails in the soles, used for jigs. Did he wear those on occasion?"

"No. If he did, it would've given a different sound to our clogging."

"What shoes do you usually wear? Everyone wears the same style, then?"

Nicholas nodded and, for the first time, his serene façade cracked. His eyebrows lowered minimally and his bottom lip flattened. "Yes, the same style. The shoes are black leather oxfords. A second, hard sole is attached to the shoe's original hard sole. This extra sole adds weight to the shoe, which produces the tap or clog sound when we dance. This is standard fare for sword dancers, either the long sword or rapper groups. So, I'm astonished Alastair was wearing the Irish jig shoes. Completely unheard of for sword dancing."

"I know the Irish shoes have nails covering the bottoms of the shoes—"

"That's not entirely correct, miss. The older style does, but the newer version uses fiberglass on the toe tips and heels. But if you're talking about the older model, on the Irish jig shoes the areas from approximately the ball of the foot to the toe, and then the entire heel, are built up with another layer of sole. It's a little trickier with the toe area, since the shoe's sole curves up slightly, the second sole in that spot is quite thin at the ball and thickens to about three-eighths of an inch at the front of the toe. The nails cover only the front half of the ball/toe area and sit in a two-row crescent at the heel." He took a swallow of coffee. "I didn't mean to give you a lecture on soles of shoes. You should have stopped me."

"So, you've no idea why Alastair wore the Irish jig shoes that day."

"Haven't the faintest. I don't know who he might have borrowed them from, either. Maybe they were his father's, or a friend's."

"Could be, of course, but that doesn't explain how he got them or why he wore them. Did he also do that type of dancing? Were the shoes his, perhaps?"

"He never mentioned it to me. Besides, I wouldn't know when he'd have the time to go to a *feis*. The Irish dance competitions are usually held on weekends so people can attend. Same with most of our sword dancing performances. If Alastair were doing both styles of dancing, I'd think the dates would collide and he'd have to miss one of our gigs."

"And he's never missed a performance with your group."

"Never. Anything else? I've got to finish my column."

I thanked him for his help, and Mark and I left the building, discussing Irish jig shoes and why Alastair had worn them.

## Twenty-One

After lunch we went back to my room. Mark claimed his chair at the foot of the bed, propped his long legs on the bedspread, and sipped his tea while we talked. This was becoming a normal activity for us; his presence here was slipping into a permanent fixture. And it wasn't displeasing.

"The only thing left," Mark said, leaning back and stretching, "is to identify which staircase the puzzle is talking about. We could spend our life at Haddon Hall, counting steps in every staircase, but there's got to be a shorter method. I want to grow old gracefully, not spend my best years counting from one to eleven. I'll have nightmares."

I picked up the guidebook to the Hall. "If we follow our reasoning from the other things—"

"We're sunk already."

"Right. It would be a pretty good bet that Peveril or Peverel would be involved."

"Unless it's that Dorothy Vernon stairway. That's almost a no-brainer feature. Probably the most famous element of Haddon Hall."

I thumbed through the guidebook, found the information on the stairway and read it aloud. "Legend relates that Dorothy Vernon left her sister's wedding party, sneaking out of the Long Gallery and down some stone steps to elope with John Manners. The fabled eleven-step staircase known as Dorothy Vernon's Steps, are situated at the room's east end. Romantics will be sorry to hear there is very little evidence for the story, as the stairs were most likely installed at the Hall while John Vernon's grandson oversaw it." I closed the book. "Not what we wanted to hear."

"But there are eleven steps, Brenna. And aren't we looking for eleven steps? That bit in the poem states 'One step for love? Aye, count it ten more.' Last time I looked, one and ten equaled eleven. You don't know of any other staircase at the Hall that has eleven steps, do you?"

"No. And it doesn't have to be a staircase of just eleven steps, Mark. It could be the eleventh stair from the bottom." I looked at him, wanting to see a smile or excitement. "Do you think we should have a look?"

"Wouldn't hurt. We can't go excavating, though. Pity."

"I wouldn't think Alastair or Simon did, either. The jewel had to have been fairly easy to get to, never mind it being hidden for these hundreds of years. No one we've talked to has said a word about either man digging up anything. Besides," I said, grabbing my shoulder bag, "that would be a dead giveaway. Someone would ask questions. Any treasure retrieving would have to look like it was part of the gardener's normal work."

"You're voting for Simon as the finder, then."

"I'm not voting for anyone. I'm simply saying that it couldn't have been a major process. If wheelbarrows and ropes and pick axes and the like were employed, that would call attention to the treasure hunt. And these men didn't want attention."

"Alastair, as a cook, walked around the grounds a lot," Mark closed and locked the room's door. "You're right. He'd need to make sure his sniffing about and treasure recovery looked ordinary. It's an instant neon sign over his head if he strolls about with shovel, gardening gloves and crowbar. Do we ask permission of someone at the Hall?"

"Let's check out our theory, first. If we find the hollow step or loose brick, it's time enough to talk to the estate manager."

~

Dorothy Vernon's Steps did, indeed, number eleven, but

despite Mark's and my shoving and pounding and prodding and trying to shift the pacers and risers, nothing moved. I answered Mark's question by saying no, I didn't think Alastair or Simon had cemented the hidey-hole in place. "For one thing, that would require all that equipment that would call attention to the hunt. And for another, this cement looks old." I bent over and surveyed the edges. "I doubt if it's been replaced in years."

Mark sagged against stone handrail. "Any bright ideas of what we do now?"

"There's got to be another staircase. This place is riddled with them."

"But, as you said, it has to have some connection to Peverel—either spelling—or the peacock. Maybe that heaven's vault just meant it was above ground level. Is there a staircase—what?"

I punched Mark and read from the guidebook. "Two courtyards comprise the foundation for Haddon Hall's layout. The upper courtyard houses the spectacular Long Gallery, famous for its Elizabethan architecture, and the Peverel Tower, also known as the Eagle Tower." I smiled and looked at Mark. "Peverel is spelled E-L."

Standing up, Mark gazed across the courtyard to the Tower. He slowly recited the last half of the poetry and I came over to him, standing beside him and looking at the answer that had been so plainly in sight but so cleverly obscure. "One step for love? Aye, count it ten more. From depth to height and so to heaven's vault and the eyes of the stars. My love 'E covets like a plume worn but ceded by six and one." He looked at me, fear and excitement in his eyes. "The covetous person is an E, Bren. E as in Peverel or Eagle Tower."

"Dare we hope?"

"The bloody hell we do."

We stood there, holding hands, needing each other as an emotional anchor. Were we about to uncover James VI's gold feather jewel?

"From depth to height and so to heaven's vault and the eyes

of the stars," I murmured as we walked toward the tower. "Eyes of the stars, peacocks, the Manners family…"

"Peverel," Mark added. We stopped at the foot of the tower stairs.

"There are more than eleven," I said, my gaze sweeping the length of the tower. "But the verse says from depth to height. I think the hiding place will be the eleventh step from courtyard level. What do you think?"

"I think you're a genius." He counted the steps as we climbed. When we reached the eleventh step, he asked me to mark it.

I looked around. "I don't want to get hauled off to the nick for defacing private property, Mark."

"Okay. Put something on the step. Your bag will do." He grabbed it and set it down. "Right. We won't mistake it. The tread has to shift slightly, or maybe there's a loose stone in the wall adjacent to it. As you said, it can't require major surgery to recover the jewel."

We stepped down and bent over the step. Mark pushed and pulled the tread, muttering and swearing and gritting his teeth. Half a minute or so into his exertion, the tread shifted. He grinned and pulled harder. The stone moved enough so that we could peer into the hollow cavity.

Mark's grin faded fast. "Nothing. Not a damned, bloody thing. Hell."

I angled the beam of my small torch into the space and bent over it. Nothing presented itself. Not trusting my eyes, I stuck my hand into the cavity and felt around. Still nothing. "I bet it was here," I said as I withdrew my hand and snapped off the torch. "It had to have been. Everything fits. The name, the directions, the number of steps."

"I agree. I doubt if any other step has a movable tread." To underscore his statement and perhaps contribute to that night's sleep, Mark pushed and pulled on several other treads in the stairway. None of them budged a millimeter. "What do you want to do now?"

"Sit and think."

"The restaurant okay for that?"

"I'd rather not. I need quiet. Maybe my room. Or a walk."

"Awfully hot for a walk. Nice, cool pub is what you want."

"Too noisy. Really, Mark, I need to think about this where I can concentrate. I'll meet you for tea, if you like, but right now I need the quiet of my room."

He shrugged, said we all had our own methods, and drove us back to Nether Haddon in silence.

When I left my room some time later, Mark was at the bar, a drink in his hand and a frown on his face. I waved to him and he followed me to a table in the corner. Pulling out my chair for me, he said he was glad to see me.

"You want a drink?" he said before I had time to reply. "Shandy?"

"Fine. You want money?" I started to reach for my shoulder bag but he put his hand on mine and squeezed it.

"You can get the next round. Or toast me at your wedding. Be right back." He set his beer on the table and walked over to the bar. He returned in little more than a minute with my drink.

"Why the frown?" I said when I'd thanked him and taken a sip of the beer-lemonade drink.

"Pardon?" He sat opposite me and reached for the menu.

"At the bar. Just as I came in. You were frowning."

"Probably because you weren't here."

"Did something happen? You have a bad afternoon?"

"Other than us getting to the treasure site too late and not nabbing Alastair's killer yet?"

"I know who the killer is, Mark. Does that brighten your day?"

"Second only to being with you." He put down the menu and leaned forward. "Who is it?"

Lowering my voice, I said, "Simon."

Mark's upper body jerked backward. "You're joking."

"Never more serious."

"But we assume he was the real target of the electrocution.

Alastair knocked him out of his role of electric light box opener. Simon couldn't have foreseen that."

"That's the beauty of it. Simon planned the whole thing. No, hear me out before I tell Graham."

Mark downed a long swallow of beer but held on to the mug. "Okay. What's your reasoning?"

I tried to be as succinct as possible, for it was a fairly involved plot. Once or twice I hesitated, but Mark's expression urged me on. "It all comes down to control," I said, keeping my voice low. "Simon controlled everything. It may have started months ago, even years. We may never know, but that's not important. One day, Simon got the treasure-hunting bug, perhaps from Alastair. That verse about James VI's and I's jewel had been handed down in their family for generations. Maybe Alastair solved it or maybe he didn't, but I think it very likely that he and Simon were trying to find the treasure independently of each other. Remember how Simon denied seeing the poetry when we showed it to him?"

"Yeah. He also said he wasn't interested in genealogy."

"Probably just said that to throw suspicion from himself. Anyway, whether he or Alastair found it first doesn't really matter. Alastair's murder matters, and I think he was killed because he *did* find the jewel and Simon wanted it."

"Simon was strapped for cash," Mark said, nodding his head. "He could've thought the sale of the jewel was heaven's answer to his financial problem."

"Anyway, the vicar stated that he saw Simon arrive early Saturday morning at Alastair's. He'd gone inside and minutes later he got a pair of shoes from his car and returned to the house. I think that pair of shoes was his Irish jig shoes. Remember Alastair was wearing them and we found out the sword dancers don't wear that style of shoe?"

"Right. I didn't think much of it."

"I believe Simon got Alastair to wear those shoes on purpose."

"How the hell would he have done that if those were the wrong shoes to wear?"

"By giving Alastair's sword dancing shoes to his Springer spaniel puppy." I let Mark mentally play through the scenario.

He set the mug down on the table but gripped it as he talked. "Sure. Makes sense, Bren. The breed is famous for its chewing habits. Puppies, probably more so. Simon gives the puppy one of Alastair's shoes and the dog chews it so it's unwearable."

"Then he acts innocent and contrite and says he just happens to have his Irish jig shoes in the car. Alastair can wear them for the performances Saturday and Simon will get Alastair a new pair. The Irish shoes were the older style, left over from Simon's Irish step dancing days."

"And the toes and heels covered in those lovely iron nails. Electricity loves metal."

"Add to that the fact that Simon got water on the ground at the light box by cooling himself off. Alastair was sweaty and when Simon contrived to bump into him and spill his beer..." I paused to let Mark come to the conclusion.

"As I said, Brenna, electricity loves liquid. Alastair was covered from chest to toe with liquid."

"That act he put on about wanting to open the light box because the newspaper blokes were there very nearly fooled me."

Mark ran his fingers up and down the glass and stared at the tabletop. "Yeah. Me, too. Throw in the crocodile tears and sprained ankle and remorse and I swallowed the whole thing. Bloody hell."

"Neat little trick, all right. He controlled it all."

We sat without speaking, Mark staring at the table, I staring out of the window. The sun balanced on the crest of the western hill that Mark and I had wandered through last night, throwing its light into the hollow where the village sat. Every rooftop glistened with gold, yet still baked beneath the broiling heat.

"Graham wants to run a test on the jig shoes to see if Alastair's and Simon's DNA are present. It'd help prove the shoes are Simon's."

Mark waved the menu at me. "I think it's obvious he set it up, Brenna. That trail you described clinches it."

"Would he have been able to rig up the wires in the light box, though? That part has me worried."

"Simon could've had help."

"Like, Goodfellow?"

"Yeah. Wouldn't be too hard to learn. Especially in the nick. He was in for burglary, remember?"

"And he was an alarm installer."

"Which comes in handy for those tiresome electric wires in the light box."

# Twenty-Two

My mobile rang, cutting into our talk. Glancing at the caller ID and seeing it was Adam, I excused myself by turning in my chair toward the window. Mark busied himself with perusing the menu, though I know he listened to my phone conversation.

"Adam." I tried to keep my voice low but it was difficult. I felt like laughing at Mark's feigned disinterest. "Your project or whatever is over?"

"Uh, Yeah. You could say that. I'm sorry I couldn't ring you yesterday, but I hope you know that's no reflection on my love, Bren."

"I know. It's the job, Adam. I've had to plow ahead with a case or two and put you second. But that didn't mean I don't love you. I think that's part of what makes a strong relationship: being able to survive the separations and having faith that the other person will be back with you as soon as humanly possible." I wondered if I sounded inane, as if I were trying to convince myself that everything would be fine between us. Not that I had doubts about Adam's love, but Mark's suspicion crept into my mind and I found myself conjecturing about Adam's silence. His job didn't demand stakeouts or undercover work or overnight trips. There could always be a first time, but all Adam had to do was tell me he would be in Exeter, or wherever, on a case. A simple explanation did more for cementing tiny cracks in a relationship than a bouquet of flowers did after the crack had appeared.

"Maybe that's one reason we're so well suited to each other,

Bren. We're both in the job, so we both know what it entails and what the other person has to do. Uh, is this a good time to talk?"

Mark was still looking at the menu, though by now he must've had it memorized. Still, it offered him a cover for eavesdropping.

"Sure. I guess so. Is it anything particularly personal?"

"Is someone there with you?"

"Yes, that's right."

"Well, we can talk about this in depth later, but I just wanted to tell you that I put down the first month's rent on a house for us."

My silence must've conveyed more than I thought. He said, rather quickly, "You'll love it, Brenna. The owners are leaving the country next month. They'll be gone for a year. He's teaching in America. His contract could be extended after the year, and if it is and if they like it there, we'll have the option of buying the house. If they come back, we go elsewhere." His tone lightened up now that he had sailed through the preliminary explanation. "It's in a nice neighborhood; I checked it out. Low crime—just about non-existent, actually. Everyone keeps their gardens up well. Every house well lit at night. It's got—"

"Where is it?" I could barely keep my voice steady.

"Where?"

"Is that so hard to understand? In what city, town or village would I find this great prize?"

"You don't have to put it like that."

"How else should I put it? Why did you do this without asking me first?"

"I didn't have a lot of time. It was one of those now or never situations. A mate at work told me about these people. They had to find someone suitable to commit to renting their house."

"They couldn't have left it with an estate agent to find someone?"

"They wanted to do it themselves, save some money, I guess."

"That's not the point, Adam. You should have asked me first."

"I had to move quickly, Brenna. I would've lost the deal if I'd hesitated."

"You haven't told me where this gem is."

"Ripley."

"You're not serious." I tried to keep my voice low, but Mark looked at me, more concern than humor in his eyes.

"What's wrong with Ripley? It's where I work."

"I know the station you work out of, Adam. I live and work in Buxton, or has that escaped your notice?"

"And your point is…what?"

I took a deep breath but that didn't seem to cool my flushed face. "Now I've got a nice, long drive to get to work, thanks to your dream house. Probably forty-five miles or so round trip."

"Actually, it's nearly sixty."

"A nice little hop, especially in winter and at night, thanks."

"I didn't think it would be that bad. Anyway, I was hoping Graham would agree to transfer you here."

"What!" I dropped my hand to my lap and angled back my head, closing my eyes. This was beyond a joke. How he had the nerve to do this was outside my comprehension. When I glanced at Mark, he'd put down the menu and was standing up. He looked like he was about to sit beside me. I shook my head, picked up the phone again, and tried speaking calmly to Adam. "I don't want to work at Ripley. I like it at Buxton. I like working with Graham. And Mark and Margo and Scott. We're a good, close team. They're my friends besides being my colleagues. You have no right to even suggest I leave them for Ripley. And you had no right to rent it out before I've seen, approved or wanted it."

"You're angry."

"You're bloody hell right I'm angry! This is inexcusable, Adam. You've decided in the space of I don't know how many minutes to dictate where I live, with whom I work, and conveniently ignored the fact that I own the house I live in. Am I supposed to sell it, keep it for a weekend retreat, rent out, or turn it into a CID museum of Mistakes of Dire Consequences?"

"What's that supposed to mean?" Adam's tone took on an edge and his volume increased. "You're calling our wedding a dire consequence?"

"No. I'm just incredibly angry that you did this without

consulting me, as if you've plotted this whole thing behind my back. Which you have." I pressed my lips together and exhaled sharply as I tried to sort through this bombshell. Was I making too much of it? Would I be glad to work in a different police Division and make new friends? After all, I could always see Mark, Margo and Scott socially. And Adam had meant all this for our good as a couple. That he'd been overzealous didn't mean he didn't love me. But as soon as I'd about settled on that explanation a voice shouted in my mind. The whole thing was still inexcusable. What did this foretell about us as a married couple, about the decisions among us? Enthusiasm aside, Adam could've given me a ring and discussed it with me. He could've spared five minutes in his deal with the homeowners.

Adam's voice came over the phone. "Are you there, Brenna?"

"Yes."

"You're still angry, though."

"Yes."

"Would it help if I said I was sorry? I didn't do it to be dictatorial. I did it because I thought you'd love the house. It's got so many nice, modern features. The kitchen is smashing; wait till you see it! And the garden's big enough—"

"Adam."

"Yes, dear?"

"I need to think about this."

"What are you saying?"

"I'm saying just what it sounds like. I need to think about all this."

"You don't hate me because—"

"I have to ring off now, Adam. I don't want to talk anymore right now."

"You'll let me know tomorrow, right?"

"Good night, Adam." I slowly closed the phone and dropped it into my shoulder bag.

Mark leaned across the table and grabbed my hand. He squeezed it gently and handed me his handkerchief. "You're erupting," he said, guiding the linen and my hand to my wet cheeks. "What happened?"

"If I say the usual, that's not accurate. This is beyond that."

"He did something that's upset you, obviously. And emotionally hurt you. Want to tell me about it? I care."

Withdrawing my hand from Mark's grip, I stood up. He started to get to his feet, but I laid my hand on his shoulder and gently pushed him into his chair. "Thanks, Mark, but I need to be alone for a bit, sort this out. No reflection on you or our friendship. Just that there are instances when a person needs time to think. You understand, I hope."

"Sure, Brenna. No offense taken. Uh, you haven't had anything to eat. You want me to bring you something up to your room?"

"Maybe I'll get something later, Mark. I'll talk to you when I get back." I grabbed my shoulder bag but Mark wasn't about to let me leave yet. He stepped in front of me and placed his hands on my shoulders.

"Where are you going? You shouldn't drive; you're too emotional. Yes, you are." He traced a finger down my cheek and showed me the moisture on his fingertip. "You'll either do yourself a harm or injure some motorist. At least you can brood safely in your room."

"I'm going for a walk. Around the village. So there's no car involved. The worst I can do is stumble into the side of a building." I slung my bag over my shoulder and turned. "I'll see you later, Mark."

I strode out of the pub, not hearing anything but Adam's voice reverberating in my ear.

I can't recall when I've ever been so angry with anyone, or so disappointed. Granted, we weren't married yet, but I thought even in the fiancé stage we would discuss things and make joint decisions. For him to pick out a house, even if it was just a rental property, and then suggest I transfer to another police Division, was really the limit.

After a bit of wandering haphazardly around the village I

decided to burn off my excess energy and frustration by looking for Goodfellow. Not a formal search, but walk through the wood. It was slightly earlier than when he'd run from Mark and me, so perhaps I'd be able to see more clearly in the undergrowth. Anyway, I had nothing to lose other than my anger.

Evening was well advanced; the hill rose before me in shades of dark gray and deep blue. The houses around its base on the eastern side appeared as individual shapes, distant from each other in the twilight, not yet huddled together as only the blanket of night provides. Stopping at the foot of the hill, I drew my small torch from my shoulder bag, snapped it on, and played the beam along the path for several yards before I started the climb.

I hadn't gained too much height when the village noises faded away and I was enveloped in night sounds. Bird melodies, cricket chirps and rustles in the undergrowth crowded into the air and helped chase away the lingering ghosts of my childhood nightmares. Yet, some monster always seemed to be waiting around the next turn in the path, under the next dark clump of bushes. I focused my mind and torchlight on the path and went on.

It all happened where the path meanders closest to the cliff edge. I'd been walking for close to ten minutes when I thought I saw a boulder angled onto the path. I played the torch beam around the wood, looking for the rock face from which the boulder could have broken loose and fallen. Of course it was absurd—at this section of the forest the rock face presented itself to the west side of the village as a huge, hundred-feet-high slab of whitish gray stone. Yet, my surprise on seeing the boulder was so great that I looked for its source. When I came within a few feet of it I realized the boulder was a man's body.

# Twenty-Three

Light was slipping away fast in the wood. As I stood beside the body, with the sounds of night surrounding me, I knew I should ring up Graham, knew I should preserve the scene. But I needed to see if I could identify the person. I tiptoed up to the body, careful not to dislodge a leaf or twig. When I'd come close enough, I shone the torchlight onto the ashen-colored face. Delmar Goodfellow stared back at me, his lifeless eyes reflecting the light.

I lost track of time. The forest sounds faded under the whispers swirling in my mind: Delmar wanting to marry Megan; Delmar counting the church collection when some of it goes missing; Delmar proving himself trustworthy; Delmar a former member of King Roper's gang. Only he wasn't, I reasoned, ignoring the niggling voices. As we in the CID Team had learned this past May, no alumni existed for King Roper's gang. Like prison, you were in it for life; membership expired at your death—natural or arranged.

He lay on his left side, his arm beneath him, his right arm stretched out. The left leg was bent and propped the right leg off the ground. Like the arm, it too, reached forward, as though Delmar had been slain during his attempt to run from his killer.

I moved the torch beam over the front of the body. Nothing untoward presented itself other than Delmar's face, a lasting presentation of fear and horror. His back furnished part of the reason: he'd been stabbed.

Blood had seeped from the wound into his clothing, sopped

up like a sponge and staining the shirt red. The blood, still liquid, dripped off his hand. Delmar's death had been fairly recent, I reasoned, otherwise it would have coagulated and dried.

But the knife was not in the wound. Nor anywhere else near the body. I stopped after a cursory look. Even though I wanted to find the weapon, I knew better than to trample about in the darkness, possibly destroying evidence. So I gave up the search and opened my shoulder bag for my mobile. It was then that twigs crackled behind me and a tall, dark shape sprang at me from the gloom of the trees. As I jumped in fear, something flashed at the edge of my torchlight. Instinct or police training kicked in at that moment, and I ducked. It saved me from a probable stabbing but it threw me off balance. As I grabbed wildly for tree branches or bushes I dropped my torch. It fell to the path with a stomach-wrenching 'clunk.' The light instantly went out; the wood plunged into absolute blackness.

I fell backwards, screaming into the night and the wood. My sense of space and time froze as I plunged over the cliff face and into darkness. Branches grabbed at me but slid from my fingers as I plummeted toward the ground a hundred feet below. A thousand thoughts and images rushed through my mind and I felt I was about to die.

Fear or an injury must have knocked me unconscious because the next thing I knew was that I was lodged in the branches of a small tree. Up and down seemed the same to me, for I could see no moon, stars or village lights, and I wondered briefly if I had died and this was purgatory or hell. I lay where I was, afraid of the devil noticing me, afraid of notifying my killer of my position if I were still alive, afraid of falling from the tree and crashing to the earth.

Eventually I realized I was alive and that I'd landed on my back. A slight breeze rocked the tree and the leaves parted enough so that I could see the stars. The sky had never looked so beautiful or reassuring.

I had no concept of time, no idea how long I'd lain there. But my survival sixth sense urged me to keep quiet and not to move, so I remained how I had fallen, enduring the pain that coursed through every bone, muscle and nerve of my body, and listened.

Night birds continued with their song and the undergrowth screeched with unidentifiable sounds. The village lay somewhere below me, indistinguishable and quiet. Nothing above or below me moved, yet I listened for the crack of breaking twigs and the thwack of falling stones. I had no idea where my assailant was or what he was doing.

Minutes passed and the wind rose again. This time it was more violent, and the treetops curtseyed and circled under the buffeting. As I moved my head to see around me, I heard a sound at the base of the cliff face. A small light, perhaps from a match or cigarette lighter, flared in the blackness. It moved slowly, perhaps several dozen yards, in a zigzag line. Back and forth, back and forth it inched along the land. A muffled curse slipped from the searcher, for I could think of no other purpose for this nocturnal activity. My would-be killer was searching for my body.

Though I could see nothing but his light, I could hear the snap of branches as he looked through bushes and bent small tree boughs out of his way. Dry, tall grass cracked beneath his feet or broke in half as he strode through the clumps. A sharp tapping sound staccatoed above the snapping and cracking, and for a moment I couldn't understand what was going on. Then I realized he'd picked up a tree branch and was prodding the rocks and ground for me, rather like a blind man uses a white cane to tap the pavement in front of him. But my assailant's walk had a deadly purpose.

I held my breath. I needn't have, for I was probably still fifty or seventy feet above the light and the searcher. But my life depended on escaping his notice. So I remained still, taking the shallowest of breaths, and watched the light's journey until it went out and I heard the soft tread of footsteps on the village road.

I had no concept of how long I lay still, but I'd slowly counted to five hundred before my mobile phone rang.

Even now, years later, it's hard to convey the surreal quality of that night and scene. I lay suspended between life and death, earth and heaven, having escaped my killer, and the most common sound in the world announced my whereabouts and presence among the living.

I fought the panic surging within me, the desperate urge to get to my mobile and scream for help. And to silence the sound before my attacker returned. My shoulder bag's strap remained angled over my body but the bag itself had positioned itself behind my hips, probably dangling in the air. I arched my hips and tugged as quickly as I could to bring the bag to where I could get my mobile phone. Fear of dropping the bag, of me falling from the tree, and the caller hanging up welled within me. As soon as I had the bag in my hands, I shook it, praying with all my strength that the contents would settle into the bag's bottom and the phone wouldn't spill out and topple onto the ground. Another ring from the phone. I grappled at the zipper and yanked it open. The phone rang again. I plunged my hand into the opening and palmed over the items. My fingers closed around the phone and, clutching it for dear life, I flipped it open.

"Brenna?" Mark's voice sailed into my ear. Strong as an anchor, warm as a fire on a wintry night, healing as balm, his voice wrapped around me and protected me from the evil in the darkness below.

"Mark! Ye-yes. Can you come?"

"Brenna. My God, I've been waiting for you at the pub. Then I walked around the village, thinking I'd spot you. Where the hell are you?"

"What time is it?"

"Just gone midnight. Where are you?"

"Mark, please come quickly. I-I fell down the cliff."

An oath like no other I'd ever heard from him tumbled from his lips. "Are you all right? Do you need medical attention, an ambulance? Where are you?"

"I-I'm fine. I don't think anything's broken, but I can't really tell. I know I've got cuts and scrapes and every damned muscle in my body is screaming for a hot shower and ice compresses."

"Where are you? At the bottom of the cliff? I'll get the team out and we'll be there in a few minutes."

"Mark. Listen. I'm not at the base of the cliff. I fell and I-I think I'm in a tree. You can probably get to me by abseiling off the cliff top."

"Right."

"I lost my torch on the path, so I'm probably directly opposite that, but I'll keep my mobile active and wave it around so you'll see the light."

"Super. We'll find you. Don't worry."

"Mark?"

"I'm here."

"You'll have no trouble knowing where I am."

"Yeah. You said to look for the torch on the path."

"You'll also find Delmar Goodfellow's body. He's dead."

Mark let out a string of four-letter words. "I'll get Graham and the crime scene investigation blokes. If the village has no abseiling ropes and pitons and stuff, I'll get it somewhere, even if I have to burgle a mountaineering shop for it. Don't worry, Bren."

"I won't, now that you're coming."

"Oh, and Bren?"

"Yes?"

"Stay right there."

## Twenty-Four

That was the last many village residents had of a quiet night.
Mark was fast out of the gate and placed his phone calls. In minutes police officers and equipment arrived at the base of the hill.
Lights from the vehicles streamed across the road and onto the
grass. I waved my mobile phone in their direction, hoping to pinpoint my position. I needn't have done it for, as I'd told Mark,
Goodfellow's body was the best and biggest marker I'd ever used.
Still, put it down to my fright. I didn't want my attacker to come
back and finish his job.

I could see the light from the large police work lamps spilling over the cliff face. Next to Mark's voice, it was the second
most comforting thing that night. I didn't have to be present to
know what they were doing: the work tent would be erected, the
work lamps set up and the crime scene perimeter decided upon
and roped off; a constable would stay at the spot all night and
protect the scene; Graham would have a preliminary look at the
scene but be back in the morning with another team to start the
investigation; come daylight, the wood would be searched for the
murder weapon. All as familiar as worn out shoes.

Graham's voice floated down to me, asking if I were all right.
I yelled back that I was but didn't know how they'd get to me.
"Leave it to the experts, Brenna. We won't leave without you."

"That's reassuring, sir. Does this count as time on the job?"

"Pardon?"

"I've been clocking hours ever since I came upon Goodfellow's body. Standing guard, as it were."

Graham let out a blast of laughter and said Mark would be arriving soon with the rescue team. "Just hang around until he shows up," he said, and returned to directing the crime scene work.

I marked the time waiting to be rescued by the comings and goings of police vehicles, the movement of light from the work lamps, and the bits of conversation that drifted down to me. Snatches of jokes, Graham requesting a particular photographic shot, the arrival of the Home Office pathologist—it took my mind off my predicament and the possibility of further injury during my rescue.

Mark finally arrived, shouting to me what would happen with the ropes and litter and the men from the Edale Mountain Rescue team. Although their job looks exciting in the movies, I didn't envy any of them that night. Powerful lights lit up the hill face from the top of the cliff to the hill's base, catching me in the middle. Trees angling away from the rock face seemed to reach out and grab at the litter and the men. But somehow they got to me, maneuvered me out of the tree and onto the litter, and eased me down to the base of the hill. Mark was there and grasped my hands.

"God, Brenna, you scared the shit out of me. Do you know where you were?"

I shook my head, afraid to trust my voice now that I was on solid ground and Mark was there. "Don't show me. Maybe in the morning, but not now. I'll have nightmares enough without knowing how close I came..." I couldn't talk anymore. I started to cry.

"You're going to hospital to get checked over."

"Don't be absurd. I'm fine. Just a torn shirt, a few scrapes and bruises." I don't know why it was important, but I began pulling the forest debris from my hair. I asked the mountain rescue to unstrap me. "I can't thank you enough for getting me down. But I'm really fine. I just need to get to my room and put some antiseptic on my scrapes. Thanks." I sat up as one of the men loosened the straps. "If you'll just lend me an arm, Mark, until I get my sea legs once again…"

He knew better than to argue. Helping me stand up, he said, "You are the most stubborn woman I've ever known."

"Fine. Tell me about it later. If you can help me to my room, I'd be appreciative."

I fell asleep quite soon after he treated my scrapes and put me to bed. I didn't know until I woke up hours later that he'd stood guard outside my door all night.

~

Wednesday dawned entirely too early to suit my stiff, bruised body. After a mid morning breakfast fortified with paracetamol and caffeine, I wandered up to the incident room. The large number of police officers and police cars, many from West Yorkshire Constabulary, surprised me. Teams armed with firearms were making their way systematically through the village, entering homes and businesses. I wondered what was happening, but didn't get a chance to inquire, for Graham asked me to open the briefing by relating last night's episode. I did, leaving out my fight with Adam. Mark was pure gentleman and never divulged the true reason for my hilly ramble. Graham, I'm fairly certain, took my story as read, never doubting that nature lover Brenna Taylor had taken another late night stroll, and ended up with something other than a poison ivy rash.

"I've got a team searching the wood for the knife." Graham sat on the table, looking at me like a protective parent. "I'm not too concerned with the postmortem report. All that blood and the position of the knife wound…what else can it be but that the knife is the murder weapon? But I'll keep an open mind. Another team is searching Goodfellow's house, though if it's emptied of contents, as you said, Salt, I don't know what we'll find. But I'll make the show of optimism. Are you sure you're all right, Brenna? You ought to be recuperating, you know. In hospital, if you want my opinion."

"A few scrapes and cuts, and I'm moving a little slow, but I'm fine. I guess I took a false step on the trail." I tried to laugh it off, but no one else smiled.

"I realize it was night time, but did you get a sense of who attacked you? Height, build, something that you saw in the light of your torch?"

"I'm going to sound like most witnesses, but no, sir. I heard a noise behind me, saw a flash in my torchlight, and he was lunging for me."

"Did you have the sense that he was after *you*? What I mean by that," he said, not giving me time to ask, "is if you felt he knew it was police detective Brenna Taylor and he wanted you, personally, out of the way, instead of just someone who'd come upon the body?"

"It was dark, as we know. Even though I had my torch on, the light wasn't in my face. I don't know how he would figure out it was me, if he was targeting me."

"Unless," Mark said, "he saw you leave the pub. Besides the light outside over the doorway, light spills outside from all those windows. If he was across the road, even, he could easily see that it was you and follow you."

Margo groaned. "Thanks for that cheerful scenario, Mark."

I said I hadn't been aware of anyone watching me but I hadn't been concentrating on that.

"I doubt if you've ruffled any feathers during the investigation," Graham added. "Getting back to you on the path...was that flash something shiny catching the light, or was it a flash like a match?"

"The former. I got the impression that it was a metal object."

"Any idea why he was there? Other than most likely being Goodfellow's killer, of course. Since the blood was still liquid, he had to have just murdered Goodfellow."

"Speaking of killers, sir. I believe Simon killed Alastair."

"Really? Care to explain now?"

I went through the same explanation I'd given Mark. "So,

you see, it really comes down to Simon controlling every element. No one else could have done it."

"What about the knowledge needed to fix the electrical wires? Has Simon a hobby that's made him, if not an expert, skillful?"

"I've not discovered any, if he has. But Goodfellow might've fixed up the wires. He was an alarm installer before going to prison."

"Goodfellow seems too squeaky clean for that, sir," Margo said, looking at the board.

"In what aspect?"

"Well, the vicar trusts him to count the collection on Sundays. He works around the church. He also has a job at This Green Isle nursery. Everything seems to be going his way. He's not been in trouble since his release from prison. So why should he risk all that to fix the wires in the electrical box? Doesn't make sense."

"It does," I said, "if the reward for doing so outweighed any potential risks."

"Like what?"

"Share in a treasure. For an ex-con who's trying to get back on his feet and so far has been given low wage jobs, the sudden wealth was like an offering from the gods. Goodfellow wanted to marry Megan Powell. I doubt if he thought he seriously stood a chance with the wages he brought home as a van driver and church worker. Maybe he sees Simon wandering about Haddon Hall's grounds when he made a delivery. Maybe Simon asked for his help, figuring an ex-con would be ready for anything to bring him some money. I don't know if that's important right now. But staff at the Hall were used to seeing Goodfellow there. He even dressed the part to dig up the jewel, if that was needed."

"Gardening clothes," Graham said.

"Yes, sir. They wouldn't think it odd if Goodfellow had to do a bit of digging. They'd assume he was going to put in plants, since he was an employee of This Green Isle. Simon and Goodfellow knew each other; they both worked at the church. Maybe the vicar told Simon that Goodfellow'd just been released from prison.

I don't know. But Simon could've found out from Goodfellow himself. He could've approached Goodfellow for help with digging up the treasure."

Mark held up his hand like a traffic cop. "Hold on a minute, Brenna. Seems to make more sense if Simon asked Nicholas for help."

"Why?"

"Think back to Fiona Doherty."

"Okay. What of her?"

"Someone, can't recall who, mentioned how well she dressed, especially for a child day care helper."

"Yes, I remember that. What's your point?"

Mark leaned forward, his elbows resting on the end of the table. "Just that Nicholas is one of the three people who counts the church collection. The vicar told us he suspected theft periodically. What if goodly, saintly Nicholas is diverting some of the church offering to his own pocket, thus giving him the cash to buy all those lovely things for Fiona?"

Graham wrote the info on the whiteboard and drew a box around it. "But if Nicholas is stealing from the church collection, doesn't that eliminate him as Simon's heavy muscles for the treasure hunt? Nicholas wouldn't necessarily need any money. He has a non-ending gravy train, as far as he's concerned. Easy money without much risk of being caught."

"Plus," I said, "remember the way Nicholas dressed and the appearance of his desk?"

"You're right." Mark sagged back into his chair. "Neat as a pin. He'd not soil his hands if he could help it."

"Would he for a percentage of the jewel's sale?" Graham said. "Even if he is stealing from the collection plates, I don't know many thieves who would pass up an opportunity to increase their wealth."

"Especially if it's thousands of pounds."

I said, "It has to be either Simon or Nicholas who killed Goodfellow."

"Why?"

"Well, as with Alastair's killer, it comes down to control." I ticked off the names on my fingers. "Johnny Smith wants to land a job as a television show host. Killing Goodfellow won't land him the role. Robert Connoly wants a girl friend. Unless he was going to buy one from Goodfellow, I don't see how killing Goodfellow produces a woman. Mary Johnson has her eye on Connoly; she wants to be his girl friend but she's afraid she isn't considered good enough, having no family prestige. No matter how clever Goodfellow might be as an alarm installer, I doubt he can install an ancestor who'd do the trick. Declan Morris seems a non-starter. I can't come up with any link between him and Goodfellow."

"It does seem rather thin," Mark agreed.

"Brian Fireman made no secret that he eventually wants the head gardener position. While that's a motive for killing Simon, he has no connection with Goodfellow."

"I could see it if Simon had died instead of Alastair. Are you sure Brian didn't set up that light box with the intent of killing Simon?"

"He couldn't have done, Mark. Simon is the only person who controlled all the facts of Alastair's death: wearing the nail-studded shoes, the liquid spilled on him, the stand in for Simon to turn on the lights."

"Yeah. You're right."

"James Charles," I continued, "wants to increase his prestige in the community by landing a huge landscaping project. Nothing wrong with that. Most people want to increase their standing or popularity or income. But Goodfellow had no sway with anyone at Haddon Hall, so how could he help James secure such a project? Jack Darkgate dreams of writing a book about the history of sword and rapper dancing."

"Again," Mark said, "there's no way Goodfellow could help with that. Not unless he owns an independent press."

Graham said, "Nicholas might get his newspaper to help with that, suggest a small press, but this isn't Goodfellow's forte."

"Michael Green wants to open another stereo shop. He has big plans for expanding his business. I can't see him employing Goodfellow to strong-arm estate agents or competitors for a shop opening. Plus, as stated before, Goodfellow has no tie to any of this. Megan Powell is a jewelry designer and wants her own shops, too. The same reasoning applies to her as to Michael. Nicholas's wife, Alison, knew about his affair with Fiona. I can't connect either woman with Goodfellow, and there is no motive for them to kill him. Jonah Ellwood wants to marry Fiona, which is fine with Alison Martin, I should think. He also wants to increase his pub business and relies on the dance troupe to bring in thirsty visitors. Goodfellow has nothing to do with this."

"Not unless it's prohibition in America," Margo said, "and Goodfellow has bootlegging connections."

"Last person is Wilton Burgess, the vicar. Clergy, just like coppers and anyone else, can kill." I felt suddenly uncomfortable talking about clergy. Graham, of course, had been a minister before becoming a police officer. And I knew he didn't feel anything personally to the subject. I rushed on. "Wilton knew Goodfellow's history. But I can't see a motive for Wilton killing Goodfellow."

"Which," Graham said, "brings us back to Simon. And, to bring you up to date, the lab test of the paper found at Alastair's house…the paper on which that poem was written…showed Alastair's fingerprints and no indentations of other writing. An expert confirms Alastair wrote it. So, that's as far as we get with that." He paused, tightened his jaw, and took a long breath before adding, "Now I'm going to throw a spanner into the works."

Margo, Mark and I glanced at each other. Whatever Graham was about to tell us must be serious—his eyes had turned lifeless and dark, and his jaw muscle pulsated as it did whenever he was upset or holding back strong emotions. I slipped my hand into Mark's, ready for the worst. Last time Graham had addressed us in this manner was when he'd told us Scott had been severely wounded in a knife fight and was in hospital.

"I've kept some news from you. Bad news, I'm afraid. I'm

not proud that I did, but you do know me well enough to know that I don't make a habit of this unless it's absolutely necessary."

Though I wanted to whisper something to Mark, I kept my gaze on Graham's face. Was this another MI-5 situation?

"This is Wednesday. Late Monday night King Roper escaped from custody." He let the words and the implications sink in before he added, "I knew Saturday night that he was going to be transported Monday to Leeds General Hospital for surgery. I knew there was a likelihood that members of his gang might try to spring him. I did not know how, when or where they might try, nor even *if* they were planning such a stunt. But, knowing Roper and his gang, we assumed this was a strong possibility. By 'we' I mean Wakefield prison authorities, Detective-Superintendent Simcock and the West Yorkshire Constabulary. Yet, despite precautions, Roper escaped. I needn't have to tell you how dangerous this situation is."

I glanced at Mark. So this was why Graham had been distracted since Saturday night and why he'd had that confidential talk with Scott Sunday morning. Both of them were certainly on Roper's hit list as officers instrumental in Roper's arrest and subsequent prison sentence.

"He's been at large for approximately thirty-six hours," Graham continued, his voice low but hinting at anger. "He escaped, with the help of his gang, late Monday night. Around ten o'clock. They wasted no time in getting away from the hospital. He could be anywhere, even out of the country, but I doubt it." He paused, drawing in a breath, and the realization hit me that Roper could be hunting down Graham and Scott. I gripped Mark's arm with my free hand, for the room started to whirl. "I'm telling you this because you're police officers and need to know that Roper's on the loose. I'm also telling you so that you'll be vigilant in everything you do from this moment until Roper is again caught. Simcock held a press conference last night and details of the escape are now public." He looked at us, perhaps assessing how involved we should become.

I swallowed, my gaze locked on his, and nodded. My brother

had been in the same prison as Roper but had been transferred when he'd received death threats.

Coming over to me, he said quite gently, "The prison personnel know the situation and have taken precautions. Don't worry about Sam, Brenna; he's in the safest place he can be."

Which implied that Graham and Scott were not. I thought back to this past March, when I'd first encountered King Roper. Besides being egotistical, coarse and pretentious he also was insolent, terrifying and vengeful. The personification of Evil and Hate. A threat to the public, police officers and those who angered him. Which were Sam, Scott and Graham at the moment. And... I said, none too steadily, "Do you believe Roper killed Goodfellow?"

Graham leaned against the edge of the tabletop and picked up the dry marker. "Personally, yes. It fits, doesn't it? We know how Roper deals with informers or gang members who want to leave his organization."

I found myself nodding, recalling May's horrendous case.

"Delmar Goodfellow was a former gang member. At least, he tried hard to be. Roper escaped from prison Monday quite late, as I said." He broke off, and tossed the marker onto the table. I wondered how many other things had occurred Tuesday night but didn't interrupt. "Anyway, Tuesday night was most likely the first opportunity he had to deal with Goodfellow. Don't forget, Roper has eyes and ears all over the country, so I don't find it odd that he knew of Goodfellow's whereabouts. He may have known while still in prison. However and whenever he knew, he bee-lined it here, rang up Goodfellow, and met up with him last night in the wood."

My sharp intake of breath drew Graham's attention to me.

"If you'd happened upon that spot a few minutes earlier... well, you didn't, so let's be thankful."

Mark squeezed my hand and smiled encouragingly, which was nice, but it didn't erase Graham's and Scott's danger. "Do you think Roper's still in the area, sir?"

"Definitely, unless he's an idiot, which we know he's not. He has a mission—that's what drives him and that's the reason, in part, he had to escape from prison. Having accomplished what many thought was impossible, he's not about to trot off to some sunny isle. He'll pop in and out of hiding, keeping an eye on me, for example, and make his attempt at my life when he can."

So that was the reason for all the police roaming the village. And why West Yorkshire was involved. After all, West Yorkshire carried the responsibility for Roper's escape and associated murders. They needed him caught.

As if sensing my thoughts, Graham added, "Roper might not be bunked down with a resident, but he's close by. Maybe hiding in the wood. Wherever he is, he's near enough to strike when our paths cross."

Graham'd said it so matter of fact, as though reading a bedtime story, that I nearly forgot he was Roper's target. A thousand prickles, ice cold and red hot, coursed over my skin as a hundred scenarios ran through my mind: Graham walking through the village at night, Graham opening the door to his room and Roper jumping him, Graham driven off the road by a fast-driven car, Graham run down as he did his shopping...

"And Scott knows about Roper," I said. Even the worst news was more bearable than not knowing.

"Yes, Brenna, Scott knows. He's taking precautions."

"Sure, he is," Mark said, forcing some optimism into the proceedings. "You know Scott, Bren. He's not going to let Roper get the best of him. He can take care of himself."

I refrained from mentioning that even though Scott taught defensive tactics, he'd been bested by Roper in May. "I'm sorry Roper got his hands on Goodfellow."

"Roper would've got to Goodfellow sooner or later," Graham said. "You know his creed. Former gang member disposed of."

I nodded, feeling sick. "It's a nasty affair, killing Goodfellow."

Mark patted my hand. "Makes sense, put like that. Can't think of anyone else who fits. It's Roper's M.O., unfortunately."

Graham picked up the marker again and rolled it between his palms, something he always did when he fidgeted. "Right, then. Anything else?"

"I don't like you being the sitting duck, sir," I said.

"Not much I can do about it, Brenna. Right." He put down the marker and stood up. "Thanks for your hard work on this. And, Brenna."

"Yes, sir?"

"I'm glad you're all right."

I smiled and left the incident room with Mark, holding on to him with my entire being.

## Twenty-Five

Mark and I spent the rest of the day talking to the principle people in the case and reviewing our notes. The case had to be water tight, as Detective-Superintendent Simcock never tired of telling us. We had but one chance to convict a killer and we had better get it right.

We'd returned to Haddon Hall to talk to Brian again about his gardening knife. He swore he'd given it to Simon to fix. Yes, another gardener had witnessed him giving the knife to Simon. No, Simon hadn't returned his knife yet. No, he didn't know when he'd get his tool back, but Simon had given him another one to use. No, he hadn't thought it would take this long to repair a loose handle and to grind out the nick in the blade. He would've fixed the knife himself if he'd known, but next time he'd know, wouldn't he?

"That's the only knife in this whole mess," Mark said as we sat in the Hall's restaurant. "It's gone missing. Brian doesn't have it. And who knows what Simon's done with it?"

I took a long sip of my fruit drink and gazed outside. "There are a million places to hide that knife, if that's the murder weapon. Probably a thousand here at the Hall."

"It's probably keeping the treasure company."

"No," I said, staring at Mark. "It can't be. Wouldn't Simon have to give Brian an accounting of the knife?"

"I don't get you."

"Look, Mark. As head gardener, Simon's job also entails the

upkeep of the gardening tools. That's why Brian gave his knife to Simon, to get it fixed."

"Brilliant. I know that."

"So, Brian's still waiting for his knife."

"Simon gave him another knife to use, Bren."

"Right. But aren't there logs or forms or something to fill out? Don't they keep track of their tools, either new ones bought or old ones repaired or tossed out?"

"What's to keep Simon from doctoring the forms? If he used the knife to kill Goodfellow—setting Roper aside for the moment—Simon'd bury it or drop it into a reservoir. He'd probably figure that Brian will forget about his knife; he's got a nice, new shiny one to play with now."

"Well," I said, "I guess we'll never know if that's the case. As I said, a thousand places to hide that knife."

"You said a million, but what's a few thousand places, more or less."

"Speaking of hiding places, I can't believe Alastair didn't find the feather jewel in the Eagle tower. He wouldn't have kept the poetry if he'd been beaten to it. He'd have been angry or disappointed and torn up that verse. He might've even told Simon that it wasn't there. Instead, he keeps the verse and walks around the estate, presumably counting eleven steps everywhere he could."

Mark snapped his fingers and grabbed my arm. "That's it, Bren!"

"Smashing. Just what is it?"

"Remember early in the investigation, someone said Simon had some bloke in tow one day? What if that was Goodfellow? As you said, he looked the part in his nurseryman outfit. What if Simon and Goodfellow found the gold feather? And what if Simon kept it? He'd tell Goodfellow that he wanted to show it to Alastair, since he was family. Something like that, anyway, to put Goodfellow off for a few days."

I took up the story, growing excited. "And Simon kept giving Goodfellow excuse after excuse, explaining why he couldn't sell the jewel yet. Probably the market was down or he had to make certain no one had seen them and was going to threaten them."

"So Goodfellow, understandably wanting his share of the profit for doing some of the hard work, gets more disgruntled as the delays go on. He walked into church when we were there, remember?"

"Right. He said," I shut my eyes, trying to recall the exact words. I looked at Mark, hardly daring to breathe, "Goodfellow said 'I need to talk to you. It's about Alastair. It's praying heavy—' He didn't finish his sentence because we came through the sanctuary door and scared him off."

Mark nodded. "We'll never know, but he could've wanted to say that it was weighing heavy on his conscious because he helped kill Alastair."

"Or that he had found the feather jewel and therefore Simon had beaten Alastair out of any money."

"Either way, it didn't bode well for Alastair."

I picked up my drink. The chilled glass felt good in my hot hands and kept my theory grounded. "Alastair could have found the jewel first, you know. In his excitement he told Simon."

"Or Simon might've seen Alastair find it. Simon was roaming around the grounds, too, remember."

"It makes more sense if Alastair found it, though. That's strong motive for Simon to fix the wires in the light box. Then he doesn't have to split the sale price of the jewel; he can keep the whole thing."

"Sounds like he wasn't too good at arithmetic," Mark snorted.

"So Simon burgles Alastair's house one night, then knocks off Alastair, and plays the grieving cousin."

Mark sank back in his chair. "Why burgle first? Wouldn't it have been safer to lift the jewel after Alastair died? Simon ran the risk of Alastair being home or hearing him break in."

I grinned. "Had to have stolen it *before* he killed Alastair. You're forgetting Alastair's house has police in it or stationed outside it. No one could get inside."

"Yeah." Mark smiled and folded his hands behind his head. "Pretty slick."

"Right. Simon's got the jewel. Maybe Goodfellow kept pressuring Simon to sell it, or at least to pay him off for his help. And the demand to sell the thing culminated last night in the wood where Simon stabbed Goodfellow in self defense."

Mark frowned. "Why'd Simon have Brian's knife with him? It was supposed to be fixed, remember?"

I took a sip of my drink. "Because, having put Goodfellow off for so long, Simon feared that Goodfellow would try to break into his house to steal the jewel. Or kill him. It's logical to me."

"Simon didn't have a knife of his own? Why'd he use Brian's? It's so easily—" He nodded and snapped his fingers.

"You just said it, Mark. Brian's knife is so easily traced to him."

# Twenty-Six

"Of all the damnable, filthy tricks." Mark crushed the paper napkin in his fist and threw it at the waste bin. It bounced off the exterior. I got up, retrieved it from beneath a nearby table, and dropped it into the bin.

"We can't prove it, of course," I said when I sat down again.

"No, but it sure as hell fits."

"So could a dozen other plots."

"Yeah?" Mark scrunched up his mouth and grabbed the sugar bowl. He rotated it slowly as he spoke. "Name one."

"Roper. Like Graham said." I sat there, sipping my drink and watching Mark build a crenellated tower with the sugar cubes. When he was on his fourth design, I said, "Should we tell Graham, do you think?"

"Give me a minute."

"You've built four towers already, Mark. Come on, it's getting late. Besides, they'll be closing soon." We were one of two couples in the room, the other being an older man and woman. I watched him take her left hand and kiss her ring. A wedding ring, I presumed, then thought about Adam and me. Our wedding was less than five months away, but after last night I wondered if Adam wanted to go through with it. Or if I did. I looked at Mark, concentrating on creating a sugar cube car, and thought he had the perfect life: no girlfriend problems, no family problems, came and went as he pleased, popular at work, a fine detective. Why did I make my life more difficult than it needed to be? What was I looking for that I couldn't find?

The roof of Mark's car collapsed and he dropped the sugar cubes back into the bowl. Putting the lid back, he said, "Who's a mate of Goodfellow's who might know something about his possible fraternization with Simon? Or a drinking buddy whom Goodfellow might have unloaded his soul to? Do we know anyone like that?"

"Why not talk to Declan Morris? They were mates."

"Do you think Declan might've spent time over at Goodfellow's place between Saturday night and the day he went missing?"

I stood up and slung my shoulder bag beneath my arm. "We can ask. He may have confided in him."

"Were they on soul-bearing terms, do you think?"

"I don't know, but I'll be happy with just a tête-à-tête over a cuppa. You want me to talk to him?"

"Yes. He might speak more freely with you than with me. You know," he said when I made a face, "women evoke trust and the softer feelings. He may open his heart to you, whereas he'd clam up on me. But phone him from my car," he said as we walked outside.

"I can stop by his house, Mark. We know where Declan lives."

"Sure we do, but I don't want you out and about more than necessary."

"Why, for heaven's sake?"

"Roper."

"He's after Graham and Scott, Mark."

"He's after *everyone* involved in sending him down. And that includes your brother and you. Now…" He opened his car door for me, opened his mobile phone and handed it to me. "We'll sit right here. You ring up Declan and ask if you can visit him."

Which I did, and felt incredibly smug that we had given Roper the slip. At least for now.

⌒ ·¹

We checked in at the incident room, ready to tell Graham our latest theory, but he wasn't there. The answer to the knife wound was, however. A knife blade that was nicked and splayed along part of its length was the murder weapon. That it was probably unique was a plus for our side; it'd be easy to identify.

"Kind of confirms it's Brian's knife," I said as we got out of Mark's car. He'd parked in the car park behind the pub and now walked close beside me up to the front door.

"Now we just have to find it."

"Which reminds me. What do you think became of the gold feather jewel?"

"Assuming it was there for Alastair to find."

"It had to have been, Mark. We reasoned that Alastair had found it and that Simon stole it. You think it's in Simon's house? I can't see him hiding it somewhere." I gazed up at the hill as Mark stood there with the door open. It'd be a Herculean task to find it, maybe impossible.

"If it's hidden, he'd put it someplace where he could get at it quick and easy. He's not going to drive to a bank vault in Manchester to retrieve it. No, it'll be at hand. Maybe even in his house."

I unlocked the door to my bedroom and threw my shoulder bag onto the second bed as Mark came in and closed the door behind him. Without asking, I filled the electric kettle with water, switched it on, and put teabags in two mugs. "I hope it's not somewhere on the hill. I hope he didn't bring it with him when he met Goodfellow."

"What makes you think he met Goodfellow up there?"

"Or else they walked up there, but I think it was a rendez-vous. Simon's not going to kill Goodfellow somewhere else and then carry him into the wood. Doesn't make sense."

"There's the possibility that Goodfellow was up there on his own and that's when Simon found him and knifed him."

"Either way, Goodfellow walked up there under his own steam." Opening a packet of milk, I said, "I've got it. I'll bet you most anything you like that I know where the jewel is."

"I should take the bet, but I won't. Where? We weren't in any other room of Simon's house than the front room."

"It's not there. At least, I doubt it. That's too obvious. The police would search there first."

"Sure. I would've done."

"I'm betting it's back in its hidey hole of Peverel Tower at Haddon Hall." I smiled hopefully, watching Mark's skepticism grow.

"You're daft. We just checked that spot yesterday. The jewel was gone. Simon had barely enough time to replace it, if he did. Besides, why would he put it back when he'd just found it?"

"For the reason that no one would think of looking in the jewel's original hiding place. He figures we'll be running around the country, looking for safe deposit boxes and an X marked on a tree trunk or disturbed earth in his back garden. What better spot than to replace it once we've left the village?"

Mark nodded slowly. "I have to admit it makes sense when you put it like that. He just waits us out and then picks up the jewel much later, when the interest has died down. His opposition's been eliminated, so he doesn't have to worry about Alastair or Goodfellow watching his movements."

"It's brilliant, actually. It's the least obvious spot for the jewel."

"We'll have a peek in the morning, Bren. Will that make you feel better?"

"If it's there, yes. But if it isn't, I won't be fit to live with."

"Let me worry about living with you."

Plopping two cubes of sugar into my cup, I sighed. "I'm not trying to be difficult, Mark. I'd just like to recover the jewel. It'd seal up the case for me."

"You're a romantic, Brenna. That's your trouble." He walked over to the dresser and picked up the small, framed photo of Adam. Staring at it, he said, "What are you going to do?"

"Go back home, think about it and wait a few days before I make a decision. Here." I handed him his cup of tea and then sat on the window seat.

"You think time will change the situation?"

"I don't know. Adam is Adam, I'm finding out. He means well, but he charges ahead without talking things over. Maybe it'll be better after we're married; maybe he's just overzealous and he'll calm down."

"You're willing to take that chance, then."

I took a sip of tea and watched Mark replace the photo. He angled Adam's face away from me. "That's why I need to think about it when I get home. I can't think straight now. We've got the two murders and the lost jewel to get through."

"You know I wish you nothing but happiness, Bren, but are you sure this is the right avenue for you? I—there are a lot of chaps out there. Maybe one will present himself if you give yourself a little more time. Nothing against Adam, but he might not be for you."

"Yeah, well, I'll call you if some guy shows up on my doorstep. You can help me sift through all the offers if you're not doing anything for ten seconds."

Mark sat in his chair and stirred his tea, letting the silence grow between us.

I downed half my tea before I said, "What about the idea that Simon killed Goodfellow, and Roper, who'd been trailing Goodfellow to extract revenge, just happened to arrive on the hill too late? Roper gets there, finds Goodfellow dead or dying. While he's standing there cursing his bad luck, I come along. He watches me look at the body, realizes it's me, and decides that he's got the proverbial bird."

"So, he lunges at you with the knife that Simon dropped." Mark set his teacup down and angled his body toward me. "Smashing, but why did Simon drop the knife?"

"He heard Roper coming. It was getting dark, and neither Simon nor Roper would've risked using a torch for fear of someone spotting the light."

"And Simon gets scared, drops his knife and runs." Mark shook his head. "That's a lot of cobblers. You're making it too difficult. What's the matter with Simon or Roper killing Goodfellow? A simple, straightforward murder."

"I'm just thinking of the knife. Where's the one Brian gave Simon, and if Roper didn't have it when he attacked me, how'd he get a knife?"

"One of his mates gave it to him when they rescued him from the nasty coppers. I don't know; give it a rest for now. When are you meeting Declan?"

Glancing at my watch, I said he was going to let me know.

"Well, I hope it's soon. It's getting on to dusk. I don't want you roaming about alone. Though, of course, I could go with you."

"Nothing doing. You said yourself that Declan might be inhibited by your presence. I'll be all right, Mark. We'll meet somewhere, chat for a few minutes, and I'll scamper back here."

"Meanwhile, I'll sit here drinking tea with you. That is, unless you've got something else to do."

I was spared my retort when someone knocked on the door. I looked at Mark, momentarily nervous that it was Roper.

Mark got up quickly and pushed me down onto the window seat. "Sit. I'll see who it is." He strode quickly and lightly across the room, making no sound. Standing against the wall, he leaned forward and spoke toward the closed door. "Yes? Who is it?"

"Jonah Ellwood," the voice rang out. "I've a message for Detective Taylor."

"Who's it from?"

"Declan Morris."

I got up and walked toward the door. "It's okay, Mark," I said softly. "That's Jonah's voice. You recognize it, don't you?"

"I can imitate Cary Grant, but that doesn't make me him."

"And no one would open a door for you. Cary Grant's dead, Mark." I opened the door, thanked Jonah, who eyed Mark, and took the piece of paper.

Mark placed his hand on the edge of the door and said, "Just curious, Ellwood. Did Declan himself phone?"

"Sure. He rang up a few minutes ago. I wasn't sure that Detective Taylor was still awake, so I took down the message instead of letting Declan talk to her direct. That was okay, wasn't it?"

He peered at me, perhaps to discern if I were in my nightgown.

"You know for certain it was Declan who phoned?"

Jonah blinked rapidly, staring at me and then at Mark. "Yeah. Sure. He's grown up in this village. I've known him for years. Why?"

"Detective Salt is just curious," I said, and thanked Jonah again. He nodded and looked relieved to get back to his customers. As Mark closed the door, I read the message. "Declan says as long as he's talking to me, he needs to tell me something else, something pertaining to the case. He wants to meet at the church at ten o'clock." I looked at my watch. "Half hour, yet. Time for another cuppa." A roll of thunder rumbled overhead.

"Why the church? Isn't it locked? And why not come here? I don't like it."

"He'll get the key from the vicar, he says. And the church because it's quiet and no one's there."

"No one's there, is right. That should send up red flags, Bren."

"We won't be overheard. This is a delicate matter, if he's got information about the case. Plus, Declan won't want Goodfellow's involvement with the jewel known. If he is a true friend, he'll want to keep his reputation as clean as possible. Follow in your car, if you want. You can park somewhere close by, like at the incident room. No one'll give it a second thought if they see a car there; you're just another copper working late." I flipped on the electric kettle and put the teabag into my cup. "Will that do?"

"I don't have much choice other than hobbling you."

"I appreciate your concern and protection, Mark. Honest. But Roper's not behind this. He hasn't coerced Declan into setting up the meeting. I phoned him, remember?"

Mark nodded but still didn't look any happier when we left the room twenty-five minutes later.

# Twenty-Seven

Mark accompanied me into the church after all. As he explained it, he'd rather walk a ten-hour beat in Antarctica than let me go alone at ten o'clock to meet a possible informer in such clandestine conditions as the church. So I gave in. Anything to keep him happy.

The walk wasn't long from the incident room, yet I had time enough to think. It had been coming, this predicament that now hovered in my mind and threatened to destroy any normality I had. Delmar Goodfellow had loved Megan Powell, had wanted to marry her, yet he had died before it could happen. Perhaps the same applied to Alastair and someone he had loved. It could certainly apply to me.

It had in May, when I had accepted Adam's marriage proposal. I'd been all too aware of the life's shortness when you loved someone, the cruel stab of grief when that ardor was snatched from you by death. The ache I'd felt on imagining Adam gone from my life, my zombie-like existence devoid of real feeling and love, had been unbearable. My love welled within me—I had so much to give, I needed to give. And I needed love in return. I could not live the remainder of my days without someone to care for, to share life's accomplishments and disappointments with, to love without reservation. A person who knew the depths and secrets of my soul, yet built on our intimacy to create a trust and love so strong we could weather any storm.

I thought I'd found that person in Adam. But the subsequent

quarrels about the ceremony, reception and honeymoon waved red flags, as Mark might say. The house rental and job transfer were but the most recent alarms sounding in my head and heart. Did I believe what I'd told Mark not an hour ago? Was Adam too anxious to make the start of our married life perfect? Was he caught tragically in the middle, between his parents and me? I thought of the men I knew: Graham let no one, other than his superiors in the job, dictate to him; Mark had been strong enough to follow his heart to police work, forsaking his family business and enduring the derision of his father; Scott had an iron-tough exterior and marshmallow-soft heart, unyielding to criminals, yet limitless in concern and help to friends. How did Adam compare to them? Was that a fair question, I quickly countered. We're all individuals; we all mature and cope differently.

But the prickle in the back of my mind wouldn't cease. This wasn't about coping or maturity. It was about personalities and if I felt I could live with Adam.

We slowed our pace, staring at the church and the night sky. A bolt of lightning lit up the west side of the building, throwing its shadow into the trees crowded against it. For an instant it seemed that God spoke to me: 'Grab happiness while you can, Brenna. The future is uncertain. You can be certain only about this moment.' His voice died as the flash died. The black clouds hung lower, nearly grazing the church steeple. The wind increased and hurled the debris of cast off leaves, twigs and dust against our ankles and legs. We hurried to the church.

The porch door was unlocked, as Declan had said it would be. As I walked across the flagstone floor another jolt of lightning brightened the sky. Shadows of trees and the leading in the diamond-lozenge windows twitched on the floor before evaporating into the blanketing blackness. Mark opened the door to the nave and we entered the church proper.

A single candle burned, breaking up the dark. It sat on the small table near the door and cast a pool of yellowish light on the tabletop and floor around the table. I shut the door, aware of the soft whoosh of air and the scent of rain, and called Declan's name. There was no answer.

"Let me look around." Mark headed for the altar. "He may not be here yet."

I nodded and walked to the center aisle, shining my torch-light on the floor and nearby furniture. Pews that I'd seen in the daylight took on the appearance and threat of monsters as the light from my torch swept over the pieces. Stopping behind the last pew I again called for Declan.

Thunder crashed and a cloud opened up. Rain drummed against the roof and western windows. The copper gutters glugged and rattled in the onslaught. Somewhere beyond my torchlight a tree branch clawed at a window.

I crossed to the bell tower, for the opened door suggested Declan might be in there. Why, I had no idea. My footsteps sounded sharp in the empty nave. If Declan were hiding, making certain it was I, he'd hear me.

Standing outside the door, I flashed my torch beam into the tower area and called. The air was still, the place empty. The only sounds were the rain's tattoo and the sweep of the tree branch on the windows.

It seemed peaceful enough, ordinary enough. But something raised the hairs on the back of my neck. I'd had the same feeling in March when King Roper had come into the incident room and pulled every coppers' attention from their work to Roper.

I slowly turned around. The torchlight slid over the stone floor of the nave and came to rest on a pair of sodden shoes. I held the light there, afraid to see more, afraid to confirm my fear. But in the white light of the lightning strike the figure jumped into terrifying reality. A tall, dark shape stood silent in front of me, his stare burning into my eyes, his teeth vividly white as he grinned, his wet hair glistening. Thunder rumbled eastward. A second bolt of lightning threw his shadow behind him; it danced as the lightning flickered in the dark. In that moment the figure moved and reached for me in lightning-fast speed. His face lit up as I angled the torchlight upward. It was King Roper.

I screamed Mark's name and bolted down the center aisle. I don't know how I had presence of mind to turn off my torch, but I did. I crashed into the sides of the pews as I dashed toward the altar. Where was Mark? He'd headed for the altar, hadn't he? Yet he didn't answer, didn't appear. I was seized with a dread that something had happened to him and I yelled his name again. In a split second of illumination from a lightning strike I crouched and shuffled into the nave chapel.

It was dark among the return pews. But I couldn't stay there. Roper had blown out the candle flame and already methodically swept the beam of his torch around the nave. Up and down, back and forth, side to side he walked, slowly to cover every inch. Like a hunter with a metal detector searching for treasure. His shoes tapped dully against the stone floor, identifying his location. He had no need to hurry or be silent; the lion didn't fear the trapped mouse.

Roper's torchlight disappeared periodically as he searched behind the font, nave altar, piers and church chest. When he was farthest from me, hunting in the box-pew, I eased through the northern-most opening of the parclose screen. I moved slowly, afraid my foot would strike the wooden structure and alert Roper. The wood was slick beneath my hands, making my grasp difficult and precarious. I turned onto my side as my waist came up to the sill of the arch. My belt buckle passed noiselessly over the slab of wood. On my stomach again, I bent at my waist and grasped two of the upright carved frames. I pulled my legs through the opening and hooked my feet around the frames. I rolled onto my back, tucking my knees to my chest and praying I wasn't about to hit a chest or lectern. As my back rolled onto the floor I inched my feet away from the frames and lowered the rest of my body.

I stayed curled up on my back, staring into the rafters and listening for Roper. The steady beat of his shoes on the floor told me he hadn't heard my movement through the screen's opening.

I slowly rolled onto my hands and knees, and crawled to my right to hide in the chantry chapel.

He'd already searched the small structure standing in the north aisle of the nave, so I had a minute or two before he came back. I was opposite the south door, though the whole width of the nave lay before me. I waited until Roper was well into the chancel area before I ran for the door.

I should've remembered Roper was smart, that he'd not allow me to escape so easily. I crouched beside the chapel for what seemed an eternity, but no lightning flash showed me the route. Turning on my torch would bring Roper after me quicker than I could make it out of the church. So I trusted to my recollection of the floor plan and ran. In the center of the nave I tripped over the foot-tall houseling benches that he had placed there as a sort of burglar alarm. The wooden bench legs screeched across the stone floor, reverberating into the rafters and against the walls. I tried to get up but pain shot through my knees. I hadn't time to feel for broken bones; Roper had yelped and the bobbing light of his torch showed he was running toward me.

Not caring about the noise, I shook my foot free of the bench leg and rolled onto my side. I tried to take a deep lungful of air but the pain crippled me. I bent over in agony. The next thing I felt were Roper's hands under my arms, pulling me to my feet.

I screamed for the second time that night. An ear-splitting scream. It had no effect on Roper other than the tightening of his grasp and a slap to my face that killed the next scream already in my throat. He pulled me against him, my back against his chest, and whispered in my ear.

"I'm over the moon to see you again, Brenna darling, but you've got to quit throwing yourself at me. What would my girl friend say?"

His breath was hot in my ear and I turned my head away from him.

He held the torch in his left hand and the light angled crazily against the windows in the far wall as he laid his left arm across my chest. His right hand clutched a knife, but he slammed his knuckles against my chin, pushing my head as far left as it would go. "Not the happy prelude I'd envisioned for the culmination of tonight's event. But you won't be around too much longer to worry about that. Now." He played the torchlight around the nave. Forcing me to walk, he said, "Where's a good place? Do you favor death by height, or watching me as I slit your throat? Suicide or murder?" He paused at the nave altar. The cloth emerged startlingly white from the darkness, seeming to hover ghostlike as Roper flicked the torchlight around. "I'm embarrassed to say, Brenna, but I don't know your religious outlook. Are you religious, by the way? Does it please you that you'll die in church?" He grinned and lowered his lips to my ear. "But all cops are bastards, remember? And though I don't know for sure, I'd assume a bastard wouldn't be allowed a church burial. Sins of the father, you know. Or mother."

"Where's Mark?" I whispered, my words sticking in my throat.

"Taking a nap. Not the trustworthy type, is he? What would Graham say if he knew Salt was sleeping on the job?" He laughed close to my ear, his breath washing over my face.

Thunder crashed and I jumped.

"Steady, darling. Not much longer to fear anything. Are you one of those God-believers who figures there's an afterlife? Or don't you care? Maybe you're an atheist." He half-walked, half-dragged me toward the bell tower and shone the light into the ground floor room. "You won't get a church burial if you commit suicide, either, but it can't be helped. What should I do?" He suddenly turned the torchlight onto my face. "I think I fancy the personal touch. Stabbing or strangulation. I can do that now, you know." He flexed his right arm slowly so that the bicep bulged. "So kind of you coppers to arrange for my surgery, give me my arm back. I know I should be resting it, but there are times…like this…that you just have to ignore doctor's orders. It still hurts like hell but I ignore the pain for you, darling." He rotated his arm so he could see it in the torchlight. "It'll be right as rain in a week or so and then I can take care of Graham. You still got the hots for him, by the way?" He laughed and the noise magnified against the stone walls. "So painful, isn't it, unrequited love? Hurts nearly as much as my arm did when that bastard Coral snapped my arm ligaments. He's on my list, too. I like to keep in touch with old…friends." I must have stiffened, for Roper said, "But they're farther down on my list. You're first. See what a gentleman I am, darling? Sparing you the ache of attending their funerals." He paused, as though thinking of something or listening to the rain hitting the windows. "But you've just got to worry about your own funeral. And how you'll get to it. So, toward that goal, I'd like to personally help you discover the truth about that afterlife. Which I would've done the other night in the forest, by the way, but you got away from me. Where'd you end up? I thought I looked everywhere."

So it had been Roper who'd lunged at me with the knife. For some reason, the information terrified me. Graham was right: he was hunting down each of us.

Roper's whisper cracked through the silence. "Wanna keep it a secret? Fine with me. Take it to your grave."

"You killed Goodfellow, then," I managed to squeak out.

"That's something you lot will never prove. But between you and me, yes. The nerk had it coming. Normally, I wouldn't have confessed to you, darling, but since you'll only be around for…" He angled his arm and glanced at his watch. "Another three minutes…hell, why not kill your curiosity? Now, let's go back to the altar. Nothing like a sacrifice as in days of old, eh?" His arm tightened around my chest and he started to drag me across the floor when a sound stopped him.

"Roper!" Mark's voice rang out against the thunder's boom. "Let her go, you bastard!"

Roper turned toward the north aisle. He angled the light onto Mark. When he saw Mark was unarmed, he laughed. Hatred and conceit and disdain came out in one loud blast. "Gallant knight rescuing fair lady. How touching. Too bad she won't live to see your attempt."

He shoved me away in one powerful push. I fell against a stone column and slumped onto the floor. Switching the knife around so that the blade was leveled at Mark, Roper sauntered to within several yards of Mark.

Mark appeared to be pinned against the south wall: the knife and the light from the torch pointed at him, daring him to move.

Roper laughed again. "What's the matter, Salt? Lose your nerve? Having second thoughts about risking your neck? Maybe she's not worth losing your life for, is that it? Just another tart who sleeps with every guy she meets. Only, maybe, even you weren't her type. Not that she was that choosy. The word around Wakefield is that she can't get enough. A real wild thing when she's turned on. You want to see?"

Mark roared like a man possessed. He ran at Roper as the man thrust his right arm out, ready to slash Mark if he came closer. Mark picked up the alms box positioned near the south door. Using it as a shield, Mark approached Roper. As Roper jabbed at Mark, Mark threw the box at Roper. Roper dropped the torch as he bent sideways. The torch clattered to the floor and rolled back several yards. I got up, ran across the floor and grabbed the torch. Angling it on Roper, I darted around to the side, keeping out of the way. Roper lunged at Mark but Mark brought his fist down on Roper's right forearm. He grabbed the arm and hand simultaneously and, using his own forearm as a fulcrum, forced Roper's arm backwards against Mark's shoulder.

Roper swung his left leg and hooked his foot around Mark's calf. In one bellow of rage, Roper yanked his leg back. Mark's leg shifted and he lost his balance. Roper shoved against Mark's chest and Mark fell backwards, narrowly avoiding hitting his head against the floor. Seeing Mark down, Roper pulled his arm back, getting ready to slash Mark with the knife. I yelled, half turned, and aimed my foot at Roper's hand. It made contact. The knife clattered to the floor and I scooted it out of his reach. Finding himself without a weapon, Roper kicked Mark's ribs. I'm certain he would've kicked Mark again but I grabbed the knife and yelled at Roper as I came at him. He swung around. The light winked on the knife blade as I moved toward him. Mark turned over on his side and bent his right knee. Roper glanced from me to Mark and hesitated, perhaps unsure if Mark would grab his legs or I would slash him with the knife. In that hesitation, his expression changed from hatred to fear. He gave one last, hurried kick at Mark. His foot missed Mark's ribs and slid off his shoulder. He stumbled sideways from the ill-placed contact but righted himself to keep from falling. Yelling that we'd meet again, he ran for the door. He jerked it open and was through the doorway and outside before the echo of the crashing door subsided.

I ran to Mark, shouting his name.

He sat up slowly, grimacing and cursing. He grabbed his side and looked up at me. "Bren," Mark said between gasps for breath. His chest heaved yet he managed to wink at me. "I-I'm okay. Smashing. Just need to…damn!" He winced as he got to his feet. "Are you okay, Brenna? My God, you could've been killed. That bastard Roper—" He broke off, overwhelmed by emotions.

"He kicked you," I said, the tears welling up in my eyes. "He kicked you without any hesitation, without any remorse. He kicked you as if you were a piece of rubbish in his way." I touched his face. "God, Mark, your ribs…are you okay?"

"I'll be all right. I'm too damned obstinate to let this get me. Bloody hell."

"Stay where you are. I'll phone for an ambulance."

"I do *not* need a ruddy ambulance. Damn." He bent his head as he took a step. "I'll be fine. Let me get my breath."

"You get your breath and I'll get Graham on the phone."

His hand closed around my mobile. "What good will that do? He'll have my guts for garters for letting Roper escape, he'll lecture both of us about night time assignations, and he'll use up precious time that I need."

I looked at him, wondering what he meant.

"I have to say something, Bren."

Fearing a lecture, I said, "So do I. I'm thankful you insisted on coming. No, thankful's hardly the word. What do you say to someone who's saved your life?"

"Fat lot of good it did. Roper was hiding near the altar, in the darkness, and hit me on the head. Unfortunately, I blacked out. If I'd been a bit more lucky I'd have nabbed him."

"Be happy with Simon, then. We're about to nab him. We'll get Roper. He can't stay loose for long."

"Yeah." Mark looked around the nave. The storm had spent itself and the moon shone through one of the upper windows. The cool breeze from the window hinted that the heat wave had broken.

"Brenna?"

I smiled and lifted my head. "Yes?"

He swallowed and exhaled heavily, puffing out his cheeks. Jamming his hands into his trousers pockets, he said, "Have you, uh, given any thought to what I said to you earlier when we were here?"

"What you said…"

"We talked about your marriage and the difficulties you were having. And I said not to worry, that something will present itself."

"Some solution," I added. "After Adam's and my dust-up, I don't know what would present itself to solve the mess."

Mark spread his arms out to his sides and stared at me. His eyes glistened and he shrugged. "I'm presenting myself."

I assumed he was joking, but he was serious. I stammered that I didn't know what he meant.

"I mean that I want to marry you. I think, deep within yourself, you want to marry me, if you're truthful with yourself. You've tried to get along with Adam—God knows you have and no one will fault you—but you're like two boxers circling each other in the ring. You're always fighting, don't agree on anything. Now, I may not be your ideal of good looking, but I'm easy going. You know how you can wrap me around your little finger. Plus, if it makes any difference, I love you." He stood in the dim light and waited for me to speak.

In the silence I heard the steady drip of the water from the eaves, the voice of a tower bell as its clapper swayed in the wind, the rush of my blood through my veins. Mark's gaze never wavered, his stance didn't change as a thousand thoughts, images and emotions coursed through my mind. The tree branch stirred again and tapped at the window. Its shadow bobbed in the moonlight, thrown onto a large, western window. It seemed to be nodding.

I bit my bottom lip, unsure how to respond. Would I regret grabbing onto Mark as I now regretted accepting Adam?

But Mark had always been there for me. He had supported me in whatever I chose to do. He had listened and suggested, not dictated. He had shown love and concern. It had been gradual over our months together, but it had grown from strained tolerance to deep emotion. Thinking back over these last few days, I saw how he had been subtly leading up to his marriage proposal, planting the idea in my mind.

The wind picked up. Other branches joined the first one and clawed vigorously at the window. A deeper-toned bell sighed in the tower, creating a celestial duet. Was God whispering to me, answering my unspoken question, placating my fear?

I took his hand, sandwiching it between both of mine. With my thudding heart rate in overdrive, I said, "I think I've always loved you, Mark. I think I've been waiting for you my whole life."

He bent forward, enveloped me in his arms, and kissed me. "We could get married this weekend if you don't mind a civil ceremony."

"At a register office?" I sounded disappointed.

"Doesn't have to be. There are licensed venues such as castles, stately and country homes. We just have to book a date and time, and contact the registrar so he can attend. We just need one clear day after giving notice so the certificate and license can be filled out. After that, our wedding can take place any time, provided it's not more than a year."

"I don't think we'll have to worry about that time restraint."

Mark used his handkerchief to pick up the knife and loosely wrapped the fabric around the weapon. He then grabbed my shoulder bag and handed it to me. Wrapping his arm over my shoulder, we walked outside. The air was cool and fresh and held the scent of rain, wet earth and blooming hesperus. He pulled me close to him as we limped to his car—two walking wounded too euphoric with love to feel our pains.

I looked up at his face. He bent down and kissed the top of my head. I removed my engagement ring and slid it into my pocket as he said, "Fancy an outdoor ceremony at Haddon Hall?"

The following morning saw the case wrapped up. DNA results on the Irish jig shoe weren't in yet, but we had no doubts it would prove both Simon and Alastair had worn them. The rental car had been leased to a man known to us as one of King Roper's gang, so that just about clinched Roper's involvement in Delmar Goodfellow's death. The knife I'd kicked from his hand had a nicked blade and was identified by Brian Fireman as his gardening knife. And the blade fit Goodfellow's lethal wound.

Graham arrested Simon for Alastair's murder. During the interview, Simon confessed he'd dropped the knife sometime Monday near Megan's home. Which was not that odd, since they lived across the road from each other. He hadn't realized it was missing until Tuesday and although he'd looked for it, he couldn't find it. Roper conveniently came along Tuesday, picked up the knife, and used it to kill Goodfellow since traces of Goodfellow's blood and Roper's fingerprints were on it. Just as with Simon controlling every segment of Alastair's murder, Roper's signature was on Goodfellow's death. If he'd left bits for gang members to do, we might not have known it was Roper. But that's what an ego gets you.

I was just glad we had the upcoming weekend free…

# Twenty-Eight

*From the desk of Scott Coral*

Police Constable Scott Coral perched on the edge of the sofa, his attention focused on the incredible events unfolding through the television newscast. His fingers gripped the armrest as though the tactile connection would assure him it was no movie he watched. He swallowed slowly, the reporter on the scene little more than a blur as Scott stared at the circle of crime scene tape flapping in the wind. A passerby in the car park at Leeds General Hospital had stumbled across the bodies of two Wakefield prison guards, apparently brutally slaughtered, their throats savagely ripped open and left to die.

Even at this early stage in the investigation, the deaths could be linked to the shocking escape of convicted murderer King Roper, which ensured lead story status. Like sharks smelling blood, two competitive news helicopters circled overhead, sending their studios live feeds. Numerous law enforcement personnel scurried about below them; official vehicles seemed to outnumber visitors' cars. The car park looked like an annex of police headquarters.

As his wife came into the room, Scott looked at her, pressed his finger to his lips, and pointed to the telly. He needn't have done. Her colorless face mutely stated why she, too, was there—how could something like this happen?

The news reporter tried to interview a senior police officer, pointing the microphone at his face. Scott snorted and leaned forward. "What's he gonna say other than 'We've nothing further to add at this moment.' Daft."

Alexa sank onto the sofa, next to Scott, too stunned to talk.

The reporter relinquished his attempt to talk to Authority and asked the helicopter pilot a question.

Scott opened his mouth to comment on the repetition of information when the sound of his mobile phone rang over the news reporter's voice. Scott jumped nervously, picked up the phone and glanced at the caller ID screen. A 'work' call. Urgent, to be ringing him up at home. He answered, staring at Alexa. Odd that his heart rate increased as he sat, silently listening to the voice in his ear. After a full two minutes, which Alexa would later say seemed a good hour, Scott nodded, said he understood, and closed the phone.

"I have to go."

"I understand." Alexa reached for his hand.

"There's…we've having a formal briefing."

Scott felt light-headed, felt the room tilt crazily, but for reasons she didn't know. The phone call frightened him in a way he'd never experienced. King Roper had indeed escaped with considerable help, and his whereabouts was unknown.

Scott ran his thumb over the top of Alexa's wedding ring, then he squeezed her hand before dropping it. He didn't dare tell her anything more than what she'd just seen on the newscast. How could he? He had just returned to duty, recovered from the knife wound that scum had given him. Alexa had healed along with Scott during that month, for she was just about emotionally over the incident. How could he tell her the man responsible for all this was on the loose yet again?

He stood up, handed her the television remote, and told her reruns of *Hetty Wainthropp Investigates* were probably on a different channel. Kissing the top of her head, he muttered that maybe he should stay and take pointers. He put up a brave front. Or so he hoped. Forcing optimism into his voice, he told her he'd be back as soon as possible, smiled and grabbed his car key. But as he waved, he noticed Alexa wasn't smiling back. Maybe she'd been a copper's wife too long to be fooled by a hardy jest and a swift kiss. Maybe she gleaned the tacit explanation from the news report and the phone call.

The car door slammed closed as he got into his vehicle. He didn't hear it. The news of Roper's escape drowned out every sound, invaded his thoughts. He felt the familiar anger swelling within him, felt the heat flood his face. Yet he controlled his rage and shoved the echoes of the newscaster's voice to the back of his mind. That final thing his superior had mentioned on the phone whispered through the morass of noise banging inside his head. "I'm sorry to tell you like this, Scott, but I've no choice. You must come in at once. Roper's still on the loose and we're afraid he might be gathering his gang to avenge himself on DCI Graham…"

# Twenty-Nine

We were married three days later, on Saturday evening.

I'd been concerned about the short notice. I needn't have been: people rallied 'round us, everything got done as if the entire Constabulary had pitched in to help, and the day slid by in a dream.

I'd broken off my engagement to Adam the night Mark proposed. Later, I wondered if I'd imagined the relief in his voice, though at the time he said I'd always hold a special place in his heart. Which sounded a bit like some corny romance novel, but at least he didn't make a scene.

Margo was my bride's maid; Mark's older brother Niles was his best man. Graham gave me away, a little too eagerly, I thought.

I still don't know how Graham cajoled Those In Charge for permission for the wedding. It could've been a combination of his chief-inspector rank and ministerial voice, or a sort of emotional blackmail: these two people nearly lost their lives solving this case and really love the Hall, blah blah blah... Whatever he did, said or implied worked. We stood in Haddon Hall's garden, surrounded by friends and the heady scent and color of roses, clematis and delphiniums. The sky fanned out behind Peverel Tower in streaks of ochre, rose and lilac. Sunlight tinted the western-facing stones a deep golden hue, which we thought fitting, since the gold feather jewel was nesting in the tower's hollow step.

I'd planned on wearing a flowery print suit, which appalled Margo. "A groom wants to see his bride in something feminine,

Bren," she had said Thursday evening. We were at my house and Margo pushed aside fashion suggestions and garments in my closet with equal disdain and enjoyment. "This is your big moment to wow Mark."

"Margo, I'm not the wowing type. I haven't the figure to wow."

"You've got a smallish waist and a great bust line. That's a wow feature. Don't turn all red and say something derogatory. You have. I'd kill for that. You need to use your assets to your advantage. You want to wear something he'll remember, not a dress you might wear to the office."

"I usually wear trousers and a blouse, but I'll let that pass."

I didn't struggle very much. Margo is very persuasive and usually right in the topics of fashion and matters of the heart. We went shopping that night and, as much as I detest both shopping and trying on clothes, I concede that Margo knew her subject. Saturday evening I stood beside Mark in my white, strapless dress, and he was wowed.

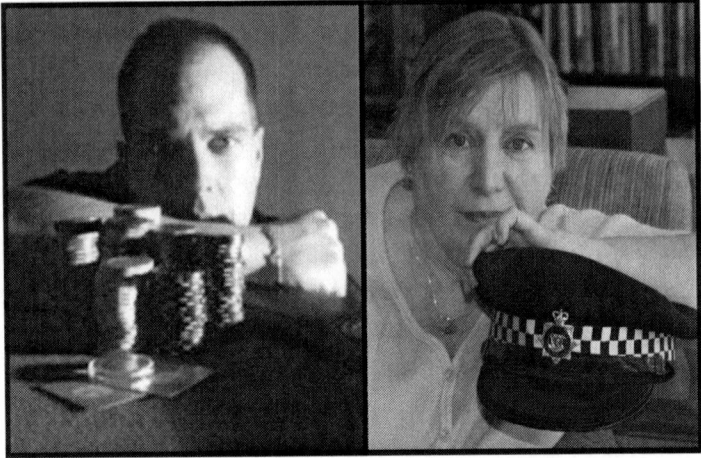

Paul Hornung                    Jo A. Hiestand

**Jo A. Hiestand** is the author of two Derbyshire-based mystery series. The Taylor & Graham series uses British customs as the backbone of each book's plot. The McLaren Case Mysteries feature ex-police detective Michael McLaren, who investigates cold cases on his own. Her cookbook, *Cider, Swords and Straw*, is a companion piece to the Taylor & Graham novels and features over three hundred recipes based on the customs highlighted in the plots.

Her short fiction work appears in three mystery anthologies, while several of her articles have been printed in publications such as *Mystery Scene Magazine*, community newsletters and newspapers. Her contest-winning play *Teething Pains* was produced on stage in 2010.

She has combined her love of writing, board games and music by co-inventing *P.I.R.A.T.E.S.*, the mystery-solving game that uses maps, graphics, song lyrics, and other clues to lead the players to the lost treasure.

In 2001 Jo graduated from Webster University with a BA degree in English and departmental honors.

Jo founded the Greater St. Louis Chapter of Sisters in Crime, serving as its first president. She is also a member of Mystery Writers of America.

Peter Lovesey, author of the Sergeant Cribb and Peter Diamond series, praises Jo's writing: "Immaculate research, attention to detail and an elegant style are the hallmarks of Jo Hiestand's writing. An atmospheric novel." For more information about Jo, please visit www.johiestand.com

**Paul Hornung** discovered his love of writing very early in life. With the help of a high school teacher and, later, a university professor, writing became a favorite pastime well beyond his school days.

A four year active duty stint as a military police officer for the US Army kindled the interest in Paul's eventual full time profession: law enforcement. During his career, Paul has served as a military police officer, military site security specialist, police patrol officer, field training officer, defensive tactics instructor, supervisor, and police detective.

A random encounter with Jo Hiestand during a police ride-along later grew into a lasting friendship—and writing partnership. Their first co-authored mystery, *Horns of a Dilemma*, was published in 2007, with Paul writing chapters as one of the book's characters. As a police officer, Paul adds a unique/realistic perspective to the Taylor & Graham mysteries, and they continue to co-author other novels in the series. In addition to creating part of the Taylor & Graham story lines, Paul also serves as consultant to the McLaren Case mysteries. His love of good dialogue and knowledge of police procedures blends well with Jo's strengths of exceptional scene detail and character development.

Paul's interests include playing a variety of sports, and he can often be found at professional sporting events in the St Louis area. An avid poker player, he continues to travel to poker rooms around the country. Paul graduated *summa cum laude* graduate from Lindenwood University, and plans to continue his education, with emphasis on writing. He and his family live in the St Louis, Missouri area.

A sneak peek at the next book in the
Taylor and Graham Series

## THE CORPSE ROAD
by Jo A. Hiestand and Paul Hornung

They hadn't expected to find a body among the fire's debris.

Mark and I stood several yards from the blackened section of the church and gazed at the still-smoldering rubble. Smoky tendrils drifted lazily skyward, their hazy ends curling into question marks that seemed oddly significant. Blue lights from the fire trucks flashed into the early morning light, bounced off nearby trees and sparkled in the puddles of water dotting the ground. The acrid stench of burnt wood crowded the air. I coughed and Mark grabbed my hand.

"You want to step away from this?" he asked. He nodded toward his right. "Might be a better place. It's upwind."

"I'll be fine, Mark," I said, giving a quick smile. "Just inhaled when I should've exhaled."

We watched a firefighter coil a hose and place it on the truck before we walked over to Graham. He looked up from the note he jotted in his notebook, the side of his face bathed in the blue light.

"I'm sorry to cut your honeymoon short. But it's going to need all of us to work on this one, I'm afraid." Graham turned to answer a police constable's question and his face slipped into the obscurity of shadow. When he looked again at us, I sensed he would've preferred the mask of darkness rather than the blue light that revealed his features. It was the first time I saw him look uncomfortable. And while he didn't blush, he came near it.

I mumbled it was all right and Mark said we hadn't been anywhere special. Which meant that our official get-away trip would take place in a few months. We'd married so quickly that we'd not had time to book a cruise or stay someplace.

Graham flashed a smile and his eyes held that look that accompanies unspoken gratefulness on getting out of sticky situations. I confess now that his uneasiness astonished me. As a former Methodist minister, Detective Chief Inspector Geoffrey Graham must have had his share of uncomfortable moments. I'd have thought he'd know how to handle any circumstance. Evidently he'd never pulled a week-wedded couple from their solitude before.

"So," Mark said, pushing us past the awkward moment, "what do you know about the fire?"

"Why don't we have Clark Tucker fill you in? Then, if you have questions, he can answer them better than I can."

"Clark Tucker. Is he the officer in charge?"

"Of the fire service unit from Bradwell, yes. He's just there, I believe." Graham nodded in the direction of a man walking up to us. He was dressed in the black protective clothing and yellow helmet regulation to all firefighters, but he wore no oxygen tank on his back. Graham shook hands with Tucker and introduced Mark and me. "I thought it best if you brought Salt and, uh, Taylor up to speed," he said, stumbling for a moment over my last name. Since I didn't correct him, he went on. "They've only just arrived. I had to call them in. We're thin on the ground, unfortunately, and I believe we'll need a good portion of the Derbyshire Constabulary on this one." He looked expectantly at Tucker, waiting to have his assumption corrected or affirmed.

"If my preliminary inspection is correct," Tucker said, "you're going to most likely put in some long hours, yes. Besides my suspicions that this is arson, you've got a dead body. And I suspect he didn't get that way by accident."

Join Jo's and Paul's literary community! Attend their talks and book signings; keep up to date with new book information on www.johiestand.com; become a fan of their books on Facebook (Jo Hiestand – Mystery Author page) and join her club **www.johiestandfans.org** Snail mail them at 330 W. Lockwood, St Louis, MO 63119. They will reply.

## REVIEWS FOR JO'S OTHER BOOKS

### Siren Song

"Siren Song is a mystery to sink your teeth into. Not only was the murder investigation top notch but also the peek into the life of the investigator added another layer to the mystery. This is my first Jo A. Hiestand book but it will not be my last."
—*Delane, Coffee Time Romance & More 4-Cups Review*

### Swan Song

"With SWAN SONG, Jo Hiestand once again moves closer to the front of the class in the British mystery field. Her Michael McLaren seems to occupy an area between the glens of M.C. Beaton's Hamish Macbeth and the labyrinth plots rippling through Louise Penny's Three Pines Village. McLaren's stubborn but relentless nature, coupled with the twisting and turning human landscape, create exactly what this genre calls for when mixed with a charming English setting. Then add multiple motivations to some well drawn suspects and wrap them around fun subjects—music, castles and fairs—to create the perfect anglophile confection."
—*Edward King, owner of Big Sleep Books*

### Torch Song

"With hints of the 1940s movie Laura, Michael McLaren is drawn with haunting music into the intricate path of attraction for a dead woman. It is easy to get caught up in the wonderful

descriptions written by author Jo Hiestand, and then suddenly
realize she just gave us a clue. Jo leads us along, following twists
and turns, making us guess who the murderer is. I was so sure
I knew who did it, and in the end, I was so wrong! Torch Song
is an excellent mystery and well worth reading."
—*Ann Collins, Librarian, Webster Groves Public Library*

### A Well Dressed Corpse
"The newest book in the Taylor-Graham mystery series by Jo
Hiestand is just fabulous! This is definitely a series worth the read,
from the first to the latest and Jo lives right here in St. Louis. Not
so unusual, perhaps, but these mysteries take place in England
and Jo has captured every nuance, both language and location,
perfectly! Each book begins with a "cast of characters," just so the
reader can keep everyone straight. A Well Dressed Corpse intro-
duces a local legend, a ghost story that comes back to life when
yet another body is discovered near the remains of a decades old
secret. Detective-sergeant Brenna Taylor and Detective-Chief
Inspector Geoffrey Graham discover murder, scheming, and
secrecy, all the while twisting and turning to the end. Very well
written, Jo's books will keep the reader entertained and amused
—and baffled, as the mysteries unfold into unexpected endings.
—*Robin Tidwell, All on the Same Page Books*

### A Terrible Enemy
"Hiestand raises awareness of global issues, layered in the unfolding of this grisly whodunit. And the mystery continues, for once
we know whodunit, we must follow through to the capture. This
intriguing mystery is well worth the reader's time."
—*Mystery Lovers Corner Review*

### The Coffin Watchers
"The CID team from the Derbyshire Constabulary are drawn
into the murders and burglaries in a small village which is home
to a rather odd custom—being a coffin watcher. Additionally,
a malevolent character from the previous Horns of a Dilemma

is a presence, one I hope is developed further in the next book. I won't give anything away by telling more. Suffice it to say, I found it incredibly interesting and a really enjoyable read. The only way Hiestand and Hornung can disappoint me is if they don't write another!!"
—*Amazon.com 5-star review*

***Horns of a Dilemma*** *(co-authored by Paul Hornung)*
"Immaculate research, attention to detail and an elegant style are the hallmarks of Jo Hiestand's writing. An atmospheric novel."
—*Peter Lovesey, author of the Sergeant Cribb and Peter Diamond series*

"*Horns [of a Dilemma]* is a realistic look into the emotions and personal lives of officers. Instead of looking at police as super-heroes, it looks at them as they are: real people with feelings and emotions who struggle with their own demons and lives while daily working cases."
—*Jon McIntosh, St. Louis-area police officer*

***Pearls Before Swine***
"The Derbyshire Peak District, campanology...and murder. Beautaiful scenery and a love-sick detective-sergeant add to the brew in this unusual crime novel. Jo Hiestand is an exciting writ-er, blending evocative description with the ability to intrigue. She kept me guessing to the end."
—*Geraldine Evans, author of the Rafferty & Llewellyn crime series*

"As a life-long resident of Derbyshire and a bell ringer for nearly 60 years, I felt completely at home immersed in this story. The book includes an excellent explanation of the mechanics of full-circle ringing and the principles of change ringing, complete with diagrams. But if you want to know who murdered whom, I'm not saying!"
—*David J. Marshall, Director, Taylor's Bell Foundry*

***On the Twelfth Night of Christmas***
"Jo Hiestand has made the Derbyshire Constabulary her own!
Brenna Taylor is compassionate, observant, and so believable
you feel with her as well as for her. It's a great setting and an in-
triguing concept."
—*Charles Todd, author of the Inspector Ian Rutledge mysteries*

***Sainted Murder***
"I don't usually read mysteries, but this woman's descriptive writing was so beautiful I just had to... Intriguing characters... clues
that will keep you guessing wrong. What more can you ask?"
—*Connie Anderson, Armchair Interviews*

"Atmospheric, intriguing and compelling. I wanted to savor every well-written passage, while racing toward the conclusion. A
gem of a story."
—*Karen Cahill, R.J. Julia Booksellers*

"A murder mystery in the classic vein set in England's snowy Peak
District. Laced with folklore and legend, and with a cast of sus-
picious villagers, this is a story to enjoy on a long winter's night.
Very atmospheric—the first scene was stunning!"
—*Ann Cleeves, author of the Shetland Island Thrillers series*

***Death of an Ordinary Guy***
"Set in a small English village, Jo A. Hiestand's Death of an
Ordinary Guy has all the smarts and intrigue you'd expect from
a good mystery. And something more: an authentic sense of wit
and a wonderful, moody feel for the English countryside."
—*John Dalton, author of Heaven Lake*

"A good and original story with good dialogue."
—*Anne Perry, author of the Pitt and Monk series*

CPSIA information can be obtained at www.ICGtesting.com
Printed in the USA
LVOW130356210912

299580LV00001B/63/P